Praise for

BOND OF FIRE

W9-CLN-104

"Audacious . . . Blends European and American history into a shockingly heady brew . . . Whiteside merrily rampages through history and vampire lore, building an impressively sturdy and compelling narrative from the wreckage." —*Publishers Weekly*

BOND OF BLOOD

"What do you get when you cross the Crusades, Texas, hot and steamy sex, and immortality? The first in a vampire romance trilogy by the master of erotic prose . . . [An] incredible, sensuous story." —*Booklist*

And the novels of Diane Whiteside

"Extremely titillating . . . an excellent and engrossing story. I know I couldn't put it down. I . . . eagerly look for more books by the amazing Diane Whiteside." —*The Best Reviews*

"A very interesting story related in prose so steamy that it fogs one's reading glasses." —*Booklist*

"Erotically thrilling and suspenseful story line keeps the reader riveted to the book. Diane Whiteside has created fascinating characters that turn an ordinary story into a work of sensual art . . . It's a scorcher." —*The Road to Romance*

"A devilishly erotic story . . . full of vivid imagery that sets your heart aflutter . . . A hero who will melt your heart and make your blood pressure rise all at the same time." —*Affaire de Coeur*

"Hot and gritty, seething with passion and the aura of the Wild West, Whiteside's debut presents readers with a solid Western as well as a highly erotic romance, and the combination is sizzling. Erotic romance fans have a tale to savor and an author to watch. SPICY." —*Romantic Times*

"A very sensual, romantic love story. It is very well written and leads you on a journey of sexual exploration sure to leave you tingling . . . Snatch this one off the shelf; it is a definite keeper." —*The Romance Readers Connection*

BOND
of DARKNESS

DIANE WHITESIDE

BERKLEY SENSATION, NEW YORK

THE BERKLEY PUBLISHING GROUP
Published by the Penguin Group
Penguin Group (USA) Inc.
375 Hudson Street, New York, New York 10014, USA
Penguin Group (Canada), 90 Eglinton Avenue East, Suite 700, Toronto, Ontario M4P 2Y3, Canada
(a division of Pearson Penguin Canada Inc.)
Penguin Books Ltd., 80 Strand, London WC2R 0RL, England
Penguin Group Ireland, 25 St. Stephen's Green, Dublin 2, Ireland (a division of Penguin Books Ltd.)
Penguin Group (Australia), 250 Camberwell Road, Camberwell, Victoria 3124, Australia
(a division of Pearson Australia Group Pty. Ltd.)
Penguin Books India Pvt. Ltd., 11 Community Centre, Panchsheel Park, New Delhi—110 017, India
Penguin Group (NZ), 67 Apollo Drive, Rosedale, North Shore 0632, New Zealand
(a division of Pearson New Zealand Ltd.)
Penguin Books (South Africa) (Pty.) Ltd., 24 Sturdee Avenue, Rosebank, Johannesburg 2196,
South Africa

Penguin Books Ltd., Registered Offices: 80 Strand, London WC2R 0RL, England

This book is an original publication of The Berkley Publishing Group.

This is a work of fiction. Names, characters, places, and incidents either are the product of the author's imagination or are used fictitiously, and any resemblance to actual persons, living or dead, business establishments, events, or locales is entirely coincidental. The publisher does not have any control over and does not assume any responsibility for author or third-party websites or their content.

PRINTING HISTORY
Berkley Sensation trade paperback edition / October 2008

Library of Congress Cataloging-in-Publication Data

Whiteside, Diane.
    Bond of darkness / Diane Whiteside. — Berkley Sensation trade pbk. ed.
      p. cm.
    ISBN 978-0-425-22354-3
    1. Vampires—Fiction. 2. Texas—Fiction.   I. Title.

PS3623.H5848B664 2008
813'.6—dc22   2008025602

PRINTED IN THE UNITED STATES OF AMERICA

10 9 8 7 6 5 4 3 2 1

The Texas vampires live in their own universe and it took a village to bring them to life.

This book is dedicated to Cindy, Leis, Leslie, the copy editors, the art department, the text designers, the folks in sales and marketing, and everyone else whose name or role in bringing the Texas vampires trilogy to life I may have forgotten.

Thank you.

The vocabulary for the Texas vampire universe is drawn from feudal Spain. That very special time and place, where Christians, Muslims, and Jews lived in a rich cultural synthesis, was also the origin of the *vaqueros'*—and later the cowboys'—cattle herding skills and specialized gear.

A detailed glossary explaining those words, plus any other non-English terms, is provided at the end of *Bond of Darkness*.

Brief prounciation guides to French and Spanish—with hints about Don Rafael's quirks—are available on my website, www.DianeWhiteside.com.

PROLOGUE

Steve brought her big Ford Expedition to a decorous stop before the impassive gates, gravel shifting under her tires like the butterflies flitting around her stomach. If she'd had any other choice, she wouldn't have come.

Posada would have her up on charges if he knew she was here. Especially if he even suspected she'd brought copies of the case files to a fortress which it would probably take every tank at Fort Hood to break down.

To be viewed by the A Number One suspect in a string of unsolved murders.

No, she was supposed to have sauntered up with another Ranger or, even better, a gorgeous, blessed-by-a-judge subpoena to haul her suspect's ass into town for questioning . . .

No way. Not him. Even if he was the only Texan she knew who could have put those bite marks on a woman's neck—a vampiro's M.O.

She slapped the button and sent the window skidding down.

"May I help you, ma'am?" A very smooth voice came from extremely high-quality speakers, not the usual distorted tones.

He'd cleaned up all the details, including putting money into stuff that didn't show, of course.

Or should she say *they*'d put money into? And just how many men did he surround himself with—and how well could he vouch for every one of them?

One Ranger, one riot. The riot's size didn't matter, since a Ranger could handle any number of bad guys. Every Texan knew that.

Even more, she had to believe Ethan's friends were all good guys—just the way she knew he was. The real killer had to come from someplace else. Somehow.

Would her stomach ever stop playing volleyball with that last slice of pizza?

"Ranger Steve Reynolds to see Ethan Templeton. Please."

She kept her face impassive and waited, without glancing at the four—no, five!—cameras watching her. Her hands stayed relaxed, easily visible, far away from her pistol. Her shoulders remained square, aligned forward, never twisting toward the back and all her tactical gear, including her assault rifle and shotgun. Guns wouldn't do her shit good against Ethan, anyway, given his speed.

She knew—God dammit, she knew every one of those girls' marks from personal experience, because she'd begged him to leave the same ones on her. Before she left today, if she left alive, he had to explain exactly what had happened to those victims.

Fifteen years of being his lover, off and on, said he couldn't have done it. She was betting her career and possibly her life on being right.

He had to tell her who'd actually killed those women.

Please, God . . .

Machinery whispered into life like ghosts gathering around a grave. The gate began to slide open.

"He'll see you now."

She gunned the engine into full, roaring life.

ONE

Three blocks away, the Mississippi swept toward the Gulf of Mexico, its brown waters running hard and fast. Fog tried to play games but couldn't hide the telltale regular slap of boats tied up to their piers. Nothing to worry about there.

A single big diesel purred like a kitten in the distance, ready to roar like a tiger if need be. Cut the rope, put her nose out into the current, and the fastest yacht in Texas would soon be far beyond the rich layers of decadence and greed called New Orleans. Out of sight and out of reach within seconds.

Ethan Templeton still wasn't entirely sure why he'd agreed to let Don Rafael Perez step off the *Matagorda Lady*. Probably because nobody said no to a vampiro mayor, a six-hundred-year-old vampiro capable of freezing you in your tracks or ripping your head off. Especially not when he was the patrón of the Texas esfera, the absolute ruler of every vampiro in Texas and Oklahoma, and the richest patrón in North America.

Ethan had been fool enough to let Don Rafael become a target tonight for any vampiro who wanted to grab that fat esfera by wiping out her ruler.

As if he could stop his creador—the vampiro who'd sired him—from doing any damn thing he wanted.

A growl rumbled through Ethan's throat. He snapped shut the tiny window with its view of a blank wall only six inches away, and spun around. A drab hallway lay ahead, the vines on its sour green wallpaper and threadbare carpet turned into flickering shadows by a single swinging light. Three men waited by the only door, just one of them his friend. Four strangers played poker in the office above the warehouse next door, their voices garbled by the thin plaster wall.

He started to walk back, counting every pace. Damn, how he hoped the ex-legionnaire had broken the rules and changed positions.

Greed was probably why Monsieur Armand, the New Orleans patrón, had invited them here. Hell, it would have been damn surprising if treachery wasn't on the bill of fare. The bastard had to have figured out some way to kill Don Rafael, even if it took an army sporting Greener shotguns and Thompson submachine guns. After all, he'd reduced Monsieur Lucien to ashes that way five years ago, right in the middle of Cathedral Square at midnight.

Or maybe some green cachorro would burst in, thinking he was something special, just because he'd managed to survive La Lujuria's madness long enough to think about something more than blood and emotion. The only fast way guaranteed to stop one of those fools was sunlight, dammit, which would kill everybody else in the room—except Don Rafael.

It didn't matter, though. Don Rafael was also the man who'd salvaged Ethan from hell and turned him into a man. Somebody who could hold his head up and be proud to look at himself in the mirror every morning. He'd spend the rest of his life repaying that debt.

As an invited guest, Don Rafael had the right to satisfactory protection and Ethan got to produce it. He'd woven a cordon of men, edged with steel and bullets, around this small warehouse south of the French Quarter, plus a path from here to the docks. He'd also guarded, equally thoroughly, the big stone mansion in the Garden District they'd rented. The big Spanish vampiro had a crazy habit of shrugging off danger and might just choose to stay ashore for a few days. After all, Gray Wolf was back home in Austin, courting the young oil geologist he'd just met. With his heir unlikely to go anywhere surprising, Don Rafael was even freer than usual to chase an adventure.

Three attacks had tested those perimeters before Don Rafael's arrival tonight. No way to tell how many vampiros had fallen, since they turned to ashes upon death. A good bribe had seen the prosaicos—the ordinary mortals—decently buried without any public outcry, especially since good jazz musicians had escorted their funeral processions.

A handful of rats played tag on the roof above him, the rapid patter of their feet as clearly audible as the jazz orchestra in the far larger warehouse next door. It was turned into a spectacular re-creation of a New Orleans square every year, lit to resemble daylight and filled with Mardi Gras parades. Half of North America's vampiros came here, just like the prosaicos did—or rather had done before Prohibition.

Not his problem, that. Texas wasn't nearly as dependent on tourists or booze as New Orleans was.

Seven paces.

Ethan was almost at the office door. Inside, Don Rafael and Jean-Marie St. Just—his heraldo or chief diplomat—were talking to Monsieur Armand.

The poker game next door was quieter, probably because the pot had gotten bigger.

Eight paces.

Outside, Angus Rough Bear—Ethan's number two or alferez menor—leaned against the wall, deceptively lazy as only a Kiowa brave could be. An ex–Foreign Legionnaire—a vampiro born in

Marseille and now Monsieur Armand's alferez—was standing across from Rough Bear with the other bodyguard, eyeing the silhouettes outlined on the door's glass panel. One half step sideways and they could put a bullet into Don Rafael's back, which was why they were supposed to have stayed still.

Nine paces. Damn fool was definitely out of position—and optimistic as hell if he thought two thirty-year-old New Orleans vampiros could take out Rough Bear.

The ex-soldier's right hand came up to the lapel of his very fashionable jacket. He started to slip his fingers inside.

Rough Bear tensed slightly. His bowie knife's handle dropped into his palm, its blade ready to gut the bodyguard opposite him.

Ethan released the safety on his Colt 1911 and aimed it precisely at the bastard's ear. Biggest advantages of being twenty-five years older than the competition were being faster and carrying less scent. Plus, he was carrying cocked and locked, bringing him the joy of a bullet already in the chamber ready to go.

The distinct click stopped the other alferez cold. His head swiveled, until he gazed straight down the gun's barrel. From that angle, all he could see was a little bit of blue steel and a hell of a large hole aching to deliver a .45 round into his face, with seven more rounds stacked up right behind it.

His black eyes narrowed, turning flat and hard. His fingers twitched briefly under his lapel, millimeters away from his own big Luger. He probably considered himself the best fellow around with a knife. But how much would he risk in a gunfight?

Ethan waited, his blood running just a little bit faster. First time he'd been in a fight was over sixty years ago. His only regret tonight was having to play the polite guest and wait for absolute proof of an attack. Otherwise, his so-called *host* would already be dead.

The other bodyguard was pasty white, his eyes flickering between Rough Bear's knife and Ethan's Colt. Smarter than his boss, though: He'd never moved from his post.

Ethan knew the instant the ex-soldier made his decision.

"Did you want something, Monsieur Templeton?" The New Orleans alferez cocked his head slightly, in a mockery of courtesy.

Ethan curled his lip. It wasn't a smile. "Just checking my gun," he remarked. "And you?"

"Cigarettes," the other answered a heartbeat later. "Care for one?"

"No, thanks. Not here." Ethan's voice conveyed his contempt for any fool who'd scatter hot ashes across this carpet.

The other's mouth tightened and his hand fell away from his jacket. He stepped back into his assigned spot, and was quickly rejoined by his still-silent fellow, leaving behind the faint, sharp aromas of anger and fear.

No signs of an attack from anywhere else, such as the roof or stairs. Don Rafael's Pierce-Arrow was still idling in the alley outside, peaceful as a grandma's rocking chair.

Ethan casually put the safety back on his Colt and holstered it, his pulse sliding back to a normal beat. He stretched, rubbing his back against the door's frame.

Rough Bear snickered softly across their mind-to-mind link. Only other Texans could hear them, thanks to being vampiros sired by Don Rafael. *Trying to spook the opposition?*

Not this time, no.

That alferez won't wear such a pretty coat next time.

Agreed. He'll make sure he has more men on his side, too.

Ethan tilted his fedora forward slightly, cutting down the damn lamp's reflection, while Rough Bear's knife vanished back into its sheath. He didn't allow himself to listen to the conversation in the office—nobody eavesdropped twice on Don Rafael.

A chair scraped back hard, followed by a second, and a third.

He came to full attention, standing away from the door.

Rough Bear promptly moved into the hall, blocking any shots from that damn little window, however unlikely they might be.

Both of them surveyed Monsieur Armand's men and were met with equally cold-eyed stares.

Two of Don Rafael's mesnaderos—Don Rafael's household guard and Ethan's most trusted men—came running up the stairs as backup. The Pierce-Arrow's big engine came to a stronger note, the town car's reliability and ruggedness more enjoyable than its luxury right now.

The door swung open, revealing Monsieur Armand, a hawk of a man with close-set dark eyes above a sharp nose, pencil-thin mustache, and narrow mouth. His pristine black tailcoat was a dandy's livery, tailored too tightly to permit most weapons.

He'd come to this continent forty years ago with de Lesseps, the creator of the Suez Canal, to dig the Panama Canal, only to be halted by malaria and rain. Tens of thousands of their fellows had died, while de Lesseps had been financially ruined and publicly humiliated. Armand had survived as a vampiro, but rumor said he'd never forgiven the Americans who'd succeeded where Frenchmen had failed.

Ethan would sooner have lain down with a rattlesnake than be alone with him.

There was a burst of French from within the room and Monsieur Armand's face changed, sliding into genuine excitement. *"Ah, oui, mon brave!"* he exclaimed, turning to face his countryman. He backed up, talking and gesturing.

The other Frenchman followed him, nodding and conversing equally enthusiastically. Jean-Marie St. Just, of course.

For a moment, he cast a long shadow across the hallway. It was sometimes all too easy, given Jean-Marie's polite manners and clean-cut profile, to forget how strong he was. Or that he was a damn good fighter and a better spy. He also had enough of a silver tongue that he just might be able to bundle this agreement into something which would hold together.

Then Jean-Marie was standing in the hallway, beside Monsieur Armand, and subtly blocking the two bodyguards.

A muscle twitched at the corner of Ethan's mouth. He could almost pity those two. If anyone tried to hurt Don Rafael, Jean-Marie would be able to grab the New Orleans patrón before that trigger-happy ex-soldier could block him. Bastard wouldn't stand a chance of getting past him, either—and Monsieur Armand would become the perfect hostage for Don Rafael's comfort.

The third man reached the door. The largest one, he filled the frame—and Ethan grinned. Thank God.

Don Rafael nodded to him, half smiling. He stood six feet four in his stockinged feet, with more than two hundred thirty pounds of bone and muscle. He had jet-black hair and olive skin, and looked like a straightforward young fellow working to build up his ranch. Until you looked into his eyes and saw six hundred years of pain and bitter living.

Ethan moved forward into position, ready to take his master home to find a little peace.

Chairs abruptly scraped back next door and four men sprang to their feet.

What the hell?

Don Rafael slammed into him, bowling him and Rough Bear halfway down the hall, moving with the blinding speed of a vampiro mayor.

Four shotguns snarled as their masters pumped shells into their chambers.

Trap! It was an assassination attempt, shielded against discovery by that blank wall.

Don Rafael was now in front of the damn fake poker game, thanks to having knocked him and Rough Bear out of the way. Breaking all the rules yet again by putting his own life at risk.

Monsieur Armand stared, wide-mouthed with shock. Jean-Marie yanked him, the obvious target, farther from the door.

The damn alferez started to smile and drop to the floor, ignoring his master's peril.

Kaboom! Four ten-gauge shotguns, firing triple-ought buck, blasted through the plaster wall as if it were newsprint. Ethan's ears rang from the concussion. Clouds of dust laced with lethal splinters burst down the hallway.

Don Rafael barreled into the gap, heading for his enemies.

Ethan fought to his feet, ignoring his broken ribs. *Texans, with me—but stay low!*

Kaboom! came the bastards' second round. Monsieur Armand's office was fast becoming a shattered wreck with crystal shards, wooden splinters, and scraps of velvet shooting through the air like malignant demons.

Monsieur Armand flinched, blood blinding him from a cut across his forehead. But without the dust caking the cut's edges, it'd heal within minutes, thanks to his vampiro metabolism.

Somebody screamed inside the assassins' den, only to be abruptly cut off.

Jean-Marie grabbed the treacherous alferez and cut his throat. Within a few instants, vampiro dust mingled with the wall's remains on the carpet.

A shotgun growled when a shell was chambered. But only one shell, not two. Nor was it fired.

Ethan raced down the hallway, trying not to breathe any of the choking dust, followed by Rough Bear and his two mesnaderos.

There was a loud thud from the room next door, then absolute silence. Light was filtering through the haze from the swinging lamp.

"It is safe to stand up now, amigos," Don Rafael called. "Our uninvited guests have departed for a better place, where they may answer for their—lack of manners."

Ethan stopped, silently cursing. Dammit, he was supposed to have prevented that—or at least clean up the mess. A quick ges-

ture brought the other mesnaderos to his side, ready to rebuild
Don Rafael's protection.

His master stepped back into the hallway, casually brushing
dust off his white linen suit.

"*Merci bien,* Don Rafael," exclaimed Monsieur Armand,
hastening forward to embrace the other patrón. "Do we know
who they were?"

"Vampiros, of course. They were difficult to smell and they
have all turned to dust."

"An infinity of thanks to you, Jean-Marie, for destroying
that worm." Monsieur Armand ground his heel into the carpet,
stamping out his alferez's few remnants.

"You would have done the same for me." Jean-Marie waved
the subject off. "Is there anything else we need to discuss tonight, *mon cher* Armand? Before the Texans leave us to the good
wine?"

Don Rafael chuckled quietly across their mental link at this
dismissal of his wine cellar.

"No, no, not at all." Monsieur Armand shrugged, taking
his lead from Jean-Marie's attitude. Although Ethan suspected
there'd be hell to pay later when Monsieur Armand questioned
his alferez's friends. "I will trade fine wines and liquors for Don
Rafael's black gold, as we just agreed."

"While you and I, *mon brave,* will negotiate the subtler
points." Jean-Marie's eyes danced. "How many bottles of Veuve
Clicquot per gallon of gasoline, for example."

"Trifles which can be readily settled by two Frenchmen,"
Monsieur Armand agreed.

Can you leave for Texas now, sir? Ethan asked quickly.

*No, I have to stay in case any sudden problems come up and
to approve the final deal. It should be very profitable for all concerned.* Don Rafael's mental voice was resigned. *Have you heard
any news from the local ghosts?*

Nothing dangerous to us—no, sir. Revenants had chatted

with him for as long as he could remember. They couldn't tell him much about what a patrón was planning, but they could usually say a lot about other threats.

"I'd first like your opinion on some Château Mouton Rothschild," the shorter Frenchman said, turning amicably toward Jean-Marie.

"Armand!" A woman's voice sliced through the hallway. "Who caused that disturbance?"

A Frenchwoman?

The New Orleans patrón stiffened and glanced toward the stairs.

"Monsieur Armand, would you please tell these bores to let me come up? I bring a message from your friends at the ball, which you're delaying."

"Merde," Monsieur Armand muttered under his breath. He cleared his throat. "Don Rafael, Celeste de Sainte-Pazanne is a New Orleans resident. I give you my word she's no, ah, physical threat."

Physical *threat*? Why the slight emphasis on the last word?

"I would be delighted to meet any beautiful lady from New Orleans," Don Rafael said gallantly, one eyebrow raised. "Mis hijos, let the lady come up."

The Texan mesnaderos stepped back, their sawn-off shotguns slipping back under their coats. A slender but very curvaceous female emerged like an actress taking her place onstage. Good Lord, but she was beautiful—dark-haired, ivory skinned, long-legged, like a she-cat made to prowl through a man's dreams. The only weapons carried under her silk chiffon dress were those conferred by nature, more than enough to blow away most men. Her black eyes were glittering pools of carnal knowledge, backed by an icy intelligence.

Most dangerous of all, she was hurling her will at them, insisting they hunger for her.

Every vampiro could inspire lust by aiming their mind-to-mind channel on their desired prey. Hell, it was sometimes the only way to feed. Usually a vampiro sent vague thoughts, an elastic yearning that would catch at least one of a dozen people in a room.

But this? This was like being lassoed with a steel cable, where a man couldn't cut the bond once it formed. Shit, a man might just do anything she asked—anything at all!—to get between those white thighs. No wonder she was the true power in New Orleans.

Ethan's breath was rasping his throat. If his cock could have burst his fly to reach her, it would have. He'd gone to full readiness without once hearing his pulse skip a beat.

Texans, stay alert, Don Rafael ordered quietly.

A curtain slammed down in Ethan's mind, bringing merciful clarity. It was the shield Don Rafael had forced upon each of his men before they left Texas: Nobody could force them to lust for somebody else, anymore than they could be compelled to break an oath to Texas. It had seemed silly back in the cedar-scented hills, but acceptable for visiting Mardi Gras.

He shuddered briefly, like a dog shaking off a brief rainstorm, and felt cleaner. Jean-Marie and Rough Bear echoed the motion, followed by the mesnaderos at the stairs.

Monsieur Armand's two bodyguards whimpered softly.

She sashayed down the worn carpet, hips undulating, her eyes measuring every man but always returning to Don Rafael.

"Celeste, *ma chère,*" Monsieur Armand began, almost pleading. Lust's knife-edge must be slicing deep into him.

"Your guests at the ball are wondering when you'll join them." She didn't even bother to glance at him. "Someone else can clean up this mess, since you're alive."

She owed her patrón an apology for that, even though she was far older.

Damn but Ethan would like to teach her a lesson in manners. Spank her until she couldn't sit down for a week, then fuck her until she couldn't walk for a month. That body was definitely made to be well ridden.

He kept his face impassive.

Stand aside and let her approach me, Don Rafael ordered quietly. *I learned centuries ago how to shield myself from far worse than her.*

Ethan grumbled silently but obeyed, giving her one last suspicious survey.

"*Bonsoir, monsieur.* Or should I say, Don Rafael?" She planted herself in front of the big Texan, visibly approving of his masculine assets. "I am Celeste de Sainte-Pazanne."

"*Estoy encantado, señorita.*" Don Rafael smiled down at her, amused.

Monsieur Armand muttered something under his breath. Jean-Marie answered him soothingly and began to ease them toward the stairs, followed by the two New Orleans bodyguards. Smart man. Of course, Jean-Marie'd avoided being under her sway by never, ever being around her physically on every previous trip to New Orleans.

"Will you be in town long?" She pursed her lips, almost sighing over the studs marching down the front of Don Rafael's shirt. The very expensive *pearl* studs.

Maybe she should be spanked until she couldn't sit down for a *month* before being fucked.

"For Mardi Gras, señorita."

"You'll need a guide. Someone who knows the city." Her eyes slid over his trousers approvingly. "And its most *intimate* pleasures."

"*Verdaderamente,*" he agreed.

What? Ethan yelped, echoed a second later by Jean-Marie and Rough Bear's even louder objections crowding the mind link.

¡Señores! Don Rafael barked, silencing them. *She cannot be*

allowed to influence Monsieur Armand against us. Can any of you keep her away from him and out of Jean-Marie's hair? No?

Ethan curled his lip but couldn't disagree.

Besides, I'll need physical companionship. Given this town's dangers, it's better if I find it with only one partner, rather than seeking multiple partners, sí?

Ethan remained silent, seething at his inability to disagree. They'd previously planned to have the mesnaderos provide Don Rafael with physical companionship on the rare occasions he'd need to feed as a vampiro mayor. God knows they'd compete for the privilege—and pleasures—of sharing his bed. But the New Orleans alferez's attack meant every man would be needed for guard duty, lest their enemies try again. As for Don Rafael sampling the varied delights—and unpredictable risks!—of New Orleans's vampiros, never on this earth would Ethan willingly agree to that insanity.

She's a vampira who's more than a century old and she should be strong enough to cope with me, Don Rafael continued. *She doesn't have a bad reputation, except for her enjoyment of parties and orgies. I'm five hundred years older than she is. She can't manipulate me with that desire trick, nor is she physically stronger. Any other objections?*

No, Ethan agreed grudgingly.

We'll stay at the house, so Jean-Marie can find me easily.

Ethan opened his mouth to object, received an arched eyebrow, and glared back but didn't speak. They'd all be safer on the yacht, surrounded by the Mississippi. But Jean-Marie had to stay ashore, coaxing the rest of the deal out of Monsieur Armand, which meant the rest of them would live in the best fortress Ethan could provide.

The Texas patrón's mouth quirked in the slightest of movements. His eyes swept over Celeste, who'd been ogling his body during the brief pause.

"Shall we go, *querida*?"

He offered Celeste his arm and she accepted it, nestling against his body with a voluptuous flutter of her eyelashes.

Ethan told himself the chill running down his spine came strictly from envy, not from wondering whether Celeste de Sainte-Pazanne's middle name resembled *T* for *Trouble*.

Two

The Pierce-Arrow town car had barely come to a stop before Don Rafael's mesnaderos closed around it, forming a solid barrier against attackers.

A shiver of delight ran through Celeste. Even Napoleon's beloved *Chasseurs à Cheval*—his bodyguards while on campaign—couldn't have done it any smoother or faster. It was even better than seeing cars scatter before Don Rafael's speeding motorcade, like pigeons fleeing a pair of hawks.

Stepping out of the shadows into the limelight, as she'd been born to do, was more exhilarating than a dozen new wardrobes.

Ethan Templeton, Don Rafael's handsome alferez, yanked open the door.

Rumor had said Don Rafael required his men to obey him in all things, whether in the boudoir or on the battlefield. Templeton was a superb soldier and had already proven to be as skillful in the bedroom under his patrón's eye. He'd clearly had the best of teachers.

Nom de dieu, no woman could ask for a better lover than Don Rafael. Her derrière had taken almost an hour to heal from last night's spanking and fucking before she could sit comfortably. Every movement had made her moan, reminding her of the exact pleasures which had given her those bruises.

Even the orgies with other French exiles hadn't left her so delightfully sated, and those companions had disappeared in the Civil War's chaos, taking their diversions with them. Oh, she'd gotten anything she wanted from the fumbling patrones who followed. But, *merde*, it was magnificent seeing the world fall into place before a strong hand.

Don Rafael rose from the car, drawing Celeste with him.

An instant later, they passed through the warehouse's double doors into a world of etched glass, gilded tracings, thick carpets, and sparkling lights.

They'd arrived late for this party, and the room was empty of guests. The Texas patrón never allowed anyone to guess his schedule, either where he was going or when he'd show up—no matter how much Celeste argued or wept for a chance to prepare the best possible attire.

He stripped off his cape and handed their wraps to a uniformed attendant, his midnight gaze sweeping the gaudy antechamber. The maid was a prosaica, of course, and under compulsion by Monsieur Armand never to speak of tonight's activities. God forbid prosaicos learned of vampiros, even here in New Orleans with its wide tolerance for other peoples.

Celeste preened in front of the mirrors, making sure her velvet kimono hadn't mussed her fancy dress, especially the few layers of embroidered silk chiffon which formed her skirt. Her bandeau top à la Cleopatra barely managed to support her breasts, making it hardly worth thinking about—except for how easily her lover could take it off.

Don Rafael's mesnaderos fanned out around them, blocking him from any hidden dangers or enemies with their bodies, as they always did whenever he entered a room.

She watched them from the corner of her eye, gauging their

attentiveness, while she tweaked the fragile chiffon into perfect symmetry.

The men were eager—indeed, hungry—to serve him with their lives. And their blood and sex, of course, as befitted his hijos.

In the past, she'd only gained such a strong reaction by forcing it out of men—first focusing her gift of seduction on them, then telling them their lust would only be assuaged after they carried out her orders. But his warriors behaved like this all the time, simply because he was their patrón. What would it be like to have so much power at one's command, without ever needing to demand it?

Oh, she'd manipulated patrones before. But they'd all died so damn fast, within a few dozen years, as patrones always seemed to do. Something about the role seemed to inspire as much greed in its holder as it did envy in all onlookers. Don Rafael was the first patrón she'd met who seemed worth latching onto. Why, he was even powerful enough to keep his men obedient to him, rather than falling at her feet.

And how very splendid her life had become, since the richest patrón in North America had chosen to pay attention only to her. Having the best dressmakers in town hurling other clients aside in order to work on her orders, getting the best seat at every nightclub, the rare vampiras hissing jealously when she danced with him. Wonderful, simply wonderful.

After a century's exile from Paris, she'd finally started enjoying life's true richness again.

"Are you ready, sir?" Templeton asked, poised beside one of the great double doors into the ballroom. "The second parade should begin in another five minutes."

She concealed her grin with an effort. The great carnival parades, with their immense floats, costumed revelers, trinkets, and wild carousing, were the year's most spectacular events.

Celeste threw back her shoulders a little bit more, making sure her breasts were displayed to their finest advantage. Damned if she'd let anyone else catch Don Rafael's eye.

He offered her his arm without looking at her, an excellent sign of how much he relied on her presence. She accepted it and tilted her chin high, as haughtily as her mother would have done at Versailles.

"We're still in the private box, correct?" Don Rafael asked.

"Yes, on the square and only a few feet away from the dance floor."

"We'll be able to be seen by everyone," Celeste cooed, delighted. "*Merci bien* for obtaining exactly the seats I wanted!"

"*De nada,*" Don Rafael disclaimed politely.

Templeton's mouth tightened and he turned, leading the way inside.

Too delighted to worry about a servant's megrims, Celeste strutted proudly on Don Rafael's arm. The guards closed around them before they'd taken two steps.

Despite everything he'd heard of Monsieur Armand's grand balls, Rafael hadn't been prepared to see a New Orleans city square resting cozily inside a great warehouse. Every building had been precisely re-created, from the tin roofs and stone and stucco walls, to black wrought iron signs and balconies. Cobblestones lurked underfoot to trip the unwary. Commonplace business signs, like hotels and drugstores, offered normality to the prosaicos present yet implied boundless opportunities to the vampiros crowding the sidewalks and square.

Most startling of all, great lamps hung overhead, bathing the entire space in light until it seemed to be a spring midday. Hollywood trickery made it possible, aided by huge fans and vents which could be glimpsed beyond the roofs. It was an incredible sight for vampiros, who rarely attained the two centuries after El Abrazo to see the sun again.

Music came from every corner, in a wild mélange of styles that burst together in a single glorious mix. A jazz band's instruments were starting to build a strong marching beat. Monsieur Armand was half dancing, half strutting in front of them, highly conspicuous in his golden excuse for a Roman toga. Other vampiros were dancing with him, ready to escort the musicians. Their equally gaudy costumes could be easily discarded for fucking or shapeshifting, should there be any disturbances.

Vendors offered wines and cocktails from pushcarts. A few enterprising men pitched pennies at plates, probably hoping to earn fancifully dressed dolls for their paramours.

The partygoers included both vampiros and prosaicos. Most of the women were prosaicas, of course, given the extreme difficulty of creating a vampira. Lust scented the air, but no fear from any side. Clearly, both vampiros and prosaicos were familiar with each other. Vampiros were always wary of dropping their guard around strange prosaicos, especially since it was wisest not to let prosaicos know exactly how old vampiros truly were. A frightened prosaico was a dangerous being who could create a mob, the only thing every vampiro feared.

Dancers, brilliant in orange and gold and black with exotic embroideries, were pounding out the latest steps on a great raised dance floor, high above the square's center. Other guests were laughing and chatting, spilling from the sidewalks onto the streets. Many corners held couples, although few did more than explore each other. Nobody seemed to have fed yet, a nicety that wasn't likely to last.

Rafael's nose told him the wines were the finest French and German vintages, while the cocktails were mixed with the best Cuban rum. He sniffed again, testing for every possible scent. Perfumes, synthetic silk and real silk for clothing, even fresh-made beignets and pralines for the prosaicos. What else was here? Something wasn't in the right place.

He followed Ethan through the crowd, allowing his men to make a path for them and keeping Celeste close. Rowdy as she was, this should make her very hot indeed tonight.

He smiled slightly, a fang touching the inside of his lip. She was a surprising diversion, although nobody he'd ever turn his back on. In this dangerous town, it was a pleasure to have an *amante* who was at least somewhat predictable.

Jean-Marie lifted his hand in a two-finger salute, from a narrow balcony half hidden above the crowd.

Bien. All was well and it was safe to use the assigned box. At least matters with Monsieur Armand were relaxed for now, the overly aggressive bodyguards having been reined in by calls to French brotherhood with Jean-Marie.

He'd still like to know what his nose disliked about this party.

Ethan led them up a few stairs to a pretense of a sidewalk café, barely two tables wide. A wrought iron railing separated them from the crowd, while more ironwork hung from the roof above. Even the tables and chairs were made of fanciful iron.

Jean-Marie slid over to the far side, allowing space for Celeste between himself and Rafael. Celeste stiffened and made very sure nothing of herself touched the Frenchman.

Ethan edged in next to Rafael, while his men flanked them in front. Most of them were in a loose-knit defense, of course, pressed in even tighter by the throng. Others, not obviously identified as his mesnaderos, were hidden throughout the partygoers, scanning for men with revolvers or perhaps a shapeshifter.

The crowd wouldn't stop him—or Ethan or Jean-Marie—from shapeshifting, of course.

"Thank you for arranging this. It's an excellent spot to watch the parade and bring a date," Rafael commented to Jean-Marie, automatically making small talk.

"Yes, indeed. In fact, I believe Gray Wolf might want to invite his beloved Caleb here next year, if the young man agrees, of course," Jean-Marie responded, his eyes sliding over the crowd.

"Indeed, spending Mardi Gras with only one man could be seen as a pledge by such an independent fellow."

Celeste yawned, bored with the conversation. A quick wave persuaded a street vendor to bring his selection of pearls to them.

"Our friend would have to work very hard to persuade him. It takes feats of strength and daring to impress Caleb."

The vendor jumped up and down and Celeste leaned forward, pushing past the mesnaderos. *Madre de Dios*, did she need a bribe to keep her quiet?

"Quite the courtship," he corrected Jean-Marie. "But a man in love will do much for his heart's delight as you and I both know, Jean-Marie."

He wrapped his arm around her, pulling her back from any potential danger. A C-note filled his hands with pearls, which he politely offered to her. Her eyes lit up and she bounced up to kiss him, then quickly draped the jewels around her neck.

His mouth quirked. Apparently detailed thanks would have to wait until later, in the bedroom.

Snipers? Rafael asked Ethan, automatically checking the other threats.

We negotiated a deal with the other patrones to put guards up on the rooftops, as backup to the more public protections. Didn't mention it to Monsieur Armand, though.

Of course not.

There's never been an assassination attempt during Mardi Gras, Jean-Marie commented, his eyes coldly assessing the street exits. As one of the finest vampiro assassins in the world, he would probably work from one of those openings.

Of course not. It would be bad for business, Ethan remarked cynically.

Celeste bounced up onto her toes and waved at a passing vampiro, all the while clinging to Rafael's arm.

He gritted his teeth but smiled as she obviously required.

The vampiro did a double take, becoming noticeably friendlier to Celeste.

One of the many things Rafael had adored about his late wife was that she'd never used him to advance her position at court.

Trumpets flared in an attractive, irregular pattern. The crowd roared happily, even the couples paying attention to it.

Celeste pointed. "Look! Here comes the parade."

Rafael's nose twitched again. What was he smelling? This had to be something not usually found at street level.

Somebody had been taking photographs here. But surely not of the ball. No vampiro ever permitted that to happen, since it could become irrefutable proof of his age.

His skin prickled.

Don Rafael? Jean-Marie asked.

Of course his oldest hijo would notice his preoccupation first.

Tell Ethan to call in the outlying guards. Now.

Jean-Marie asked no questions, simply slipped off the more intimate channel and spoke privately to his fellow Texan. *Gracias a Dios.*

Rafael sniffed again, hard, hunting for every faint aroma. Maybe it had happened so long ago he was the only one who could scent the residue. After all, he was the sole vampiro mayor here, guarded by the sharp senses that had kept him alive for so damn long.

He turned his head and a flash flared briefly into his eyes before dropping away.

His heart slammed hard against his ribs. *¡Ay, mierda!*

He looked up sharply and off to one side. Not toward the ceiling and the huge lamps, or the roofs with his guards.

But to the attics, where someone could see his face and record it with a camera. A photographer up there would be high enough he'd probably be beyond even a vampiro's keen nose— except for a vampiro mayor.

His fangs pricked his lip. Surely there'd been a reflection from a camera, where no polished metal should be.

Madre de Dios, maybe two.

Ethan. He didn't waste time looking at his alferez. *Tighten the cordon around us.*

His mesnaderos stamped their feet, their bootheels thudding on the cobblestones in unison, and started to close ranks. *Would they be in time?*

The drum was pounding. Lights sparkled and glass beads twisted, falling out of the sky. Celeste squealed and jumped for them, then cursed when her hand bounced off a man's shoulder.

"Photographer!" a vampiro shouted, and pointed.

The entire crowd fell silent and stared, following the long black exclamation mark of his arm. High above, a man leaned out of a window, a camera's damning black box clasped in his hands.

A man growled, and another, and another. A great rumble ran through the throng like an avalanche's beginning. *"Sacré mille diables!"*

Rafael yanked Celeste next to his chest.

A great hawk lifted from the throng and flew at the interloper, leaving a golden toga behind on the cobblestones. Monsieur Armand had shapeshifted to go on the hunt.

The spy ducked back inside, slamming the window shut. The horde roared and began to run toward him, wolves outpacing the others. Vampiros and prosaicos stormed down the sidewalk, howling for blood, trampling the vendors' pushcarts. They slammed into the mesnaderos—and the Texans swayed but managed to hold.

The mob surged past them and raced across the street. Doors and shutters were ripped off the buildings there with inhuman strength to allow for faster access. From inside, somebody screamed but the crowd kept breaking in.

There'd be no holding the rabble until they killed the bastard, raising bloodlust in every vampiro who tasted him. And bloodlust was an instinctive, demanding fire, long-lived and treacherous beyond belief. It was very unlikely only the photographer would die.

"Come on, let's get out of here," Rafael ordered sharply. "We're heading for the *Matagorda Lady*."

"Yes, sir," Ethan agreed, and started issuing orders over the mind link. There was too much noise to do so verbally.

They stepped down from the small dais and began edging toward the doors to the warehouse's antechamber, dodging wild-eyed vampiros. Rafael locked his arm around Celeste. Anyone trying to harm a priceless vampira would have to go through him.

Are we breaking off negotiations? Jean-Marie asked, his Colt graceful and deadly in his hand.

Rafael didn't have to think twice. *No, the deal's almost done.*

Do you think the photographer was the start of an assassination plot by Monsieur Armand? Ethan asked, his voice almost casual.

Damn town's a sieve for gossip, snarled Jean-Marie, who'd first encountered conspiracies in the womb. *It would be impossible to keep such a large ball secret. Plus, he's been giving twice-weekly balls every Mardi Gras for years.*

And his trigger-happy mesnaderos hate your guts, Ethan, Rafael warned. *They'd do damn near anything to make you look the fool.*

Including murder Don Rafael, added Jean-Marie, and shot an onrushing rioter, dropping him in his tracks. *As they tried the night you arrived.*

Ethan cursed under his breath but didn't disagree.

Celeste kicked Rafael, twisting and clawing to break free.

"Be careful, Celeste! They'll kill you, too."

"Let me watch!"

He choked, bile rising in his throat. Surely she didn't know what she was asking for. He shuddered, remembering the screams echoing down the streets of a vampiro court's mountain capital, hour after hour during that endless winter night. Cries which still lingered in his dreams, underlain by the snick of knives slicing through flesh and the crunch of boots shattering bone.

He started to touch her mind but withdrew. He had no right to force her into a changed opinion unless she threatened his life. Assuming he had the time—which he did not.

Fighting every protective instinct, he carefully eased his grip on her.

She promptly turned her head to look back over his shoulder and sighed. Rapturously.

His hand clenched on the Mauser in his pocket.

"Oh, *mon amour*, look! They've hung him out the window for everyone to take a bite!"

Why the hell had he chosen this bloodthirsty bitch to sleep with? Unfortunately, he owed her his protection until the city settled down.

If he was lucky, there was only one photographer.

He snorted in disbelief and raised his pistol, ready to start fighting.

THREE

Celeste fondled the satin-smooth teak paneling framing the stained glass image of a river maiden and reconsidered her cabin's potential.

No danger here of catching a splinter, if she entertained Don Rafael while standing up.

She smiled at her reflection and tried a pose, one hand on her hip.

And the lighting was certainly very flattering.

The wall sconces and overhead chandelier were made from mother-of-pearl, their many petals curving like water lilies. The carpet underfoot was a soft, silken ribbon of color flowing through her cabin, carved with rippling lines like waves. A matching silk coverlet swept over the enormous bed, while its twin was quilted into the headboard.

He could take her on the floor, or the bed, and she'd still look beautiful.

She twisted slightly, letting the light's soft glow reflect off the wood and highlight her own skin. Much, much prettier than naked bulbs.

The entire room was a delicious jewel box which begged to be used as the setting for a long, frenzied round of sex with Don Rafael. There were no secret cubby holes or hiding places full of his secrets. So he was obviously keeping her close at hand for some more delectable pleasures.

Which she hadn't enjoyed yet, dammit. Unfortunately, it had taken them forever to work their way out of the grand ball and the warehouse—and through the uproar on the streets. *Mon dieu*, they'd had to walk for blocks, dodging running vampiros and searching policemen, before his limousine could pick them up. She'd thought Monsieur Armand had bribed the police well enough to stay away from his parties no matter what happened.

She snorted in disgust, remembering how her feet had ached when she was finally able to sit down. If she were the patrona here, she'd make sure the police never came near her parties, whether it took money or terror.

Don Rafael had remained infinitely patient, while the night got later and later. She'd matched his calmness more easily once they'd left that exciting riot but hunger and keeping her temper had exhausted her. When he'd shown her to this cabin and left her alone, she'd lain down, expecting him to join her in a few minutes.

Instead, she'd woken up early the next evening. Alone, dammit.

He must have come in, found her asleep, and decided to let her recover, rather than wake her for his own greedy needs. She knew he'd been here, thanks to the faint whiff of his scent—and a very elegant new evening gown. Last night's contretemps had badly damaged her dress.

She purred, throwing her head back and caressing her breasts through the fragile silk. How marvelous to finally have a paramour who was focused on satisfying her needs first.

She obviously needed to tell her stallion she was fully recovered. He must be hovering outside, eager for admittance.

Humming softly, she waved good-bye to the room and put her hand on the doorknob.

"Bring the agreement into my cabin, where I can sign it," Don Rafael said from the corridor just outside her door.

Celeste went completely still. She'd known he'd come to negotiate something with Monsieur Armand but she'd thought he'd forgotten that nonsense, in favor of enjoying her attractions.

"Are you satisfied with it, Jean-Marie?" His deep voice was crisp and calm, appallingly businesslike.

"Completely, sir. Monsieur Armand would probably have bargained longer but he wants us gone so he can concentrate on quieting his city."

Gone?

She was certain he adored her. He'd proven that a thousand times over during his visit, especially with his talk at the ball about all the feats a man in love would do. When he'd hugged her afterward, she immediately knew he meant her.

But passion, even slavish worship, was not the same as a life together.

If he left, what would she do? Go with him—to Texas? The land of cows and dirt and Indians? Never, even if she could leave New Orleans.

Maybe she was wrong and he planned to stay. He was certainly strong enough to take over New Orleans, if he wanted to.

"And we can silence those drunken riots in the West Texas oilfields."

"The mesnaderos will shut them down within a few days, once we're back," the Frenchman agreed, and their steps faded down the hallway.

Celeste sagged against the door. Oilfield riots meant less oil and less money. Don Rafael couldn't remain here—and she'd hate living in Texas.

She flung herself across the bed and tried to think.

No, the only answer was to persuade him to move here,

which meant binding him into a permanent alliance with the New Orleans patrón.

Monsieur Armand, who couldn't even manage to throw a Mardi Gras ball? Bah!

Plus, the idiot barely controlled New Orleans and its suburbs, not even as far as Baton Rouge, only eighty miles away. All of Texas and Oklahoma bowed down before Don Rafael, more than three hundred thousand square miles.

A New Orleans patrón would probably have to hold everything from Louisiana east and south of the Ohio River, in order to have an esfera Don Rafael would consider impressive. And worthy of forming a lifetime bond with.

She rolled over onto her back and flung an arm over her eyes. But if she had such an esfera, she'd have a damn good chance—if not a certainty—of claiming Don Rafael for herself, for always. And ending this cycle of loneliness forever.

Her jaw set hard. She could do it. After all, she'd seen it done often enough in New Orleans that she'd memorized the techniques by now.

But every successful candidate for patrón always started with an absolutely deadly alferez. A killing machine to make everybody else fall back in fear . . .

Georges Devol blinked, forcing a little water out of his eyes, and tried to kick. The sun had long since set, making this a good time for traveling.

His right leg was no damn good with two bullets in it—but nobody's legs were worth much against the Mississippi, even when they were healthy. It was more important to travel far and keep the damn warden guessing as long as possible, no matter what.

He'd escaped Angola by turning the tables on a guard during an affair. The fool had thought he controlled Devol but had wound up serving him. Now he'd certainly keep his mouth shut as long as possible about Georges' methods and route, just to save himself.

Georges had to be close to the Mouth of Passes, where he could catch an oceangoing ship.

He was cold, so very cold. Probably because it was spring and the river was in flood. Hopefully not because the guards had gotten lucky and done more than nick him in the side.

He turned his head sideways, trying for a little pocket of air inside the waterlogged tree branches. But he overbalanced the fragile wood and it dipped, sending his mouth into the muddy river.

He spat and choked, gasping for air, and his stomach spasmed again. Water lit a trail of flame inside his nose.

Stars spun behind his eyes, fading into blackness, while his chest's objections eased into slow flutters, then stilled. The bayou had never seemed farther away.

"Man overboard!"

What? Police wouldn't be that polite.

He blinked, barely aware of the greedy river spilling over his head and shoulders. A light danced over the water and caught the tree, casting a net around him.

He'd be warm again, back in the pen. Back on Death Row.

Yeah, and they'd ask him again to be sorry for killing all those *respectable* women. Like hell. His only regret was he hadn't done it sooner. Or meaner.

Now, scarlet women—those beautiful bitches were something different and far, far better. He especially loved how the top-drawer bitches could have those high-powered SOBs pleading for a moment of their time. Hell, they were even immune from being sent to Death Row if they caused trouble.

He tried to push the tree away but it bobbed, catching his arms, dragging him down.

Water swept over him and he began to fight, thrashing, clawing, kicking, heedless of any injuries.

Suddenly, somebody caught him by the scruff of his neck and lifted him bodily from the Mississippi, as if he'd been a child. Something shifted nastily in his side and he passed out, a curse slipping from his lips.

Georges came to, stretched out on a fancy sofa in a very grand saloon. Polished brass everywhere, and teak glowing as if it wanted to be a mirror. Ducks were carved into the furniture and woven into the upholstery, yet everything was sturdy enough for a man's frame, not flimsy and stupid.

It was a rich man's palace, probably somebody who knew the governor and would start yelling as soon as they recognized him.

But how much did it really matter? His head ached; his throat was sour and sore as if he'd poured acid down it. His leg had no more feeling in it than a dead snapper. His body was icy cold, his clothes stiff against his clammy skin.

"Who is he?" a woman asked.

A woman? A *genuine* Frenchwoman? He tried to turn his head toward her voice.

"We just finished cleaning his face and don't know yet. He hasn't said anything, mademoiselle."

He managed to open his eyes just as she arrived beside him. She was a small woman, with ivory skin, raven hair, and the most superb breasts he'd ever seen, unashamedly displayed by a green silk dress which clung to her curves. She was beautiful, definitely not a respectable woman, and absolutely perfect.

"*Bonsoir, ma cher madame,*" he greeted her, offering her the highest accolade he could award, something he'd never willingly given another woman—the honorific of *lady*.

She smiled, red lips curving over sharp white teeth.

Lovely, truly lovely.

"*Bonsoir, mon brave,*" she cooed, her long black lashes magnificently framing her eyes.

She called *him* brave? Why was she being polite, let alone complimentary? Who the hell cared, when he felt like he could tap-dance across the Mississippi?

A long shadow fell over them. A tall, blond man was watching him, his good looks insufficient to mask his deadly calculations. Two more men stood beside him, one an impassive dandy with the lightly balanced stance of an experienced knife fighter.

The third was the most dangerous. He was massively built, and his hooded gaze, crooked nose, and scarred face bore witness to the deadly fights he'd already won.

"Georges Devol," the blond announced flatly.

"The Bayou Butcher?" the lady squealed.

Damn. Now she'd run. He kept his eyes fixed on the men but couldn't stop stealing quick glances at her.

"Are you sure?" the big man asked.

"Look at him. Average features, average coloring, but very strong. The perfect camouflage for murdering thirteen women, the officers and board of St. Mary's Orphanage."

All of those bitches had been liars and worse, pretending they knew nothing of the goings-on there. The boys and girls used for slave labor, or worse, raped night after night in their beds. And every month, those respectable vouduns had visited the orphanage for their fine luncheon, smiled at the children—while ignoring their bruises!—and left.

Georges kept his mouth shut. Talking had never helped, not from the day he'd been born at St. Mary's. But killing those female hypocrites had made him feel a damn sight better.

He concentrated on breathing slowly and pushing back the pain. The longer he lived, the better chance he had of escaping.

A woman's slender fingers curved over his wrist. His eyes shot up to her face, startled.

She smiled down at him, her small red tongue teasing her lips. "You'd fight that hard for me, too, wouldn't you?"

"I'd do anything for you, *cher*," he assured her fervently. Unlike most Cajun men who used the phrase freely, he'd never called a woman *sweet* before. But she was finer than whisky or honey. Perhaps there truly was a God, to have allowed him to meet her.

"You wonderful man." She sank down onto the sofa beside him, still holding his hand.

"Get away from him, mademoiselle," the blond ordered.

"No." Her retort was machine-gun sharp. "He'll be my first hijo."

"The Bayou Butcher? The man who tied up thirteen women, one by one, and raped half of them?"

She'd shocked the knife fighter out of his stillness.

"Before poisoning them all with strychnine, one after the other—and drinking champagne while he watched them die? Ten to twenty minutes each of agonizing pain, while the woman's every muscle separately locked into rigor mortis. *¡Chingado!*" The scarred brute looked angry enough to take revenge for their deaths here and now.

The scarred brute grabbed for Georges's throat, moving faster than a swinging scythe.

Despite himself, Georges flinched, as he never had in Angola.

"Don't touch him!" the lady snapped, holding up her hand. "You can't have him, since I've already taken hold of him."

"He should be executed for murder, Celeste!" The big man's fingers tensed again. "You cannot be so reckless as to claim somebody like him."

"A most creative and sadistic killer, *oui*?" the lady purred, and scraped her teeth over Georges's hand. A thin line of crimson sprang up in response, as if begging for her.

She began to lick him delicately, her tongue digging at him, delving into his sweat and his flesh, making him want to give more. Anything, everything.

He moaned softly, warmth building wherever she touched. Joy flickered over his skin and danced through his blood.

Her fingers fondled his hip, despite the reeking river-bottom mud which enveloped him. None of the partners he'd sought oblivion with had ever cherished him like that.

He didn't know everything involved but if it included her and not Angola's Death Row, he'd agree in a heartbeat.

"Celeste!" the big man snapped.

She stopped slowly, even reluctantly, and looked up.

"Celeste, he's a murderer," the big man warned.

She shrugged. "But he'll be *my* murderer."

Horror swept over the other's face and Georges hid his grin, enjoying his strengthening heartbeat, and watched his lady trample society's conventions.

"The perfect weapon, since he has no morals to stop him from doing exactly what I want." Celeste glanced back at him. "Isn't that right, *mon brave?*"

Do anything she wanted, in exchange for being her idea of perfection? His cock swelled, flaunting his masculine triumph. "Oh yes," he whispered.

Her tongue started sweeping over his wrist again, melding her saliva with his blood, driving Georges slowly insane. He made a rude gesture at the big blond, who had to live around a moralizing bastard.

The other flushed and took a step forward, reaching for his weapon. An abrupt gesture from his master halted him.

"I can't take him away from you, Celeste, since you've already sealed your claim by drinking his blood," the senior man warned, his deep voice rumbling through the saloon and making the guards even more alert. "But I ask you to think again before you give him El Abrazo."

"Oh, I know exactly what will happen, Don Rafael." She

smiled blissfully, kissed her fingertips, and brushed them against the bruise on Georges's temple.

His eyes turned to slits in pleasure at her open claim.

The blond all but hissed.

"He'll be the best alferez mayor in North America."

Whatever that meant, he'd do it for her, better than any other man in the world.

FOUR

Steve Reynolds pulled her Expedition to a stop, flicked her turn
signal on, and waited patiently for a count of three. She was well
aware nobody could see the black beast at this time of night,
even under a nearly full moon. She might not be able to bake a
cake or clean candle wax from a tablecloth, but she could drive
a cop car damn well. When no other vehicles passed by, she
decorously turned left onto Avenida dos Lagartos and headed
back to Gilbert's Crossing.

The state road led through nameless mountains, following an
ancient riverbed filled with scattered boulders and sand. Limestone bluffs towered overhead, with century plants' tall spikes
protruding like sentries. Almost two centuries ago, her ancestors
had served in the Rangers along this border.

She'd first met Ethan Templeton on a night like this, when
she'd pulled his black pickup over for speeding. He'd been handsome as a dream of sin, too, and just as irresistible.

Humming between her teeth, Steve automatically lined up
for another tight turn. Half an hour ago, she might have tried
to cut the corner a bit or push the speed limit in hopes of mak-

ing one of her rare dinner invitations. But fifteen years as a cop,
including all those as a state trooper, had taught her the benefits
of driving well—and the penalties of driving recklessly.

She still hated to have missed it. She'd have enjoyed drinking
margaritas and watching Fred drive off to a lifetime of guarding Chihuahuas for the bottle blonde he'd married. Yappy little
dogs, just like their mistress, that gave him no chance of ever
having his own child.

Served him right, the bastard. Steve had dreamed of being
a twenty-first-century Donna Reed, thought his big family and
steady job qualified him as a great husband. Shit, she'd even been
willing to talk to counselors about their endless arguments when
she wasn't around to do the things he demanded, like smile at
prospective clients. But she wasn't about to put up with a third
party in their marriage, least of all somebody like that bitch.

Her foot sank a little harder onto the accelerator.

An instant later, she emerged into a broad plain, its thousands of cacti shimmering in the moonlight like rifles at an assassins' convention. Another range of mountains offered their dark
canyons and promontories a few miles ahead.

A few well-established ranchers and large corporations like
the Santiago Trust still held sway here, those who'd long since
adapted their breeds and ranching techniques to the mix of barren rocks, hidden water, and harsh desert. Very hardy, ancient
breeds of cattle and goats made a good living here.

The radio scanner clicked into life.

"Two-eleven, would it be clear for a forty-three?"

Steve's mouth quirked at this sign of normalcy. Clark Duncan was going off duty for dinner in Gilbert's Crossing, probably
down at Uncle Junior's Diner. Thursday night was their fried pie
night.

Wonder if she'd make it in time to have any?

She was a Texas Ranger with a star in a wheel on her badge
and three counties to look after. Regulations said she should

obey all the traffic laws. But she could have toasted Fred's new leg-shackles with fried pies, almost as well as with margaritas.

Still, there was the speed limit.

The black truck growled its disdain, sending the speedometer creeping up.

"Yeah, you understand, don't you, big guy?" She laughed at herself but patted the wheel anyway. "Well, I spend more time with you than with anybody else."

She throttled back, easing down to the speed limit, automatically watching for any sweeping beams of light signaling other vehicles. Maybe a rancher, or somebody from town taking the old road down to the border. Or a couple of scientists, taking a break from studying the local fossils, those older lizards this road had been named for. Not that she'd seen any so far, or expected to.

"Two-eleven, stand by to copy."

Imelda was calling Duncan back from Uncle Junior's?

"Two-eleven, copy a signal sixty-three, five-nineteen Sunflower Street . . ."

Somebody wanted backup at Nikki Castillo's house? Odd, very odd. Nikki was a sweet lady whose biggest concerns seemed to be her two children, three cats, chocolate—and not talking about where she'd gotten that new Mustang from.

Scenes flickered behind Steve's eyes, the way they often did on a case: Nikki screaming, her kids running out the door in terror.

Cold whispered over Steve's skin, lighter than any breeze her state-procured vehicle could conjure up.

Her county, her town, her people. The speedometer's needle slid a little more to the right. She pushed a recalcitrant lock of hair off her forehead, clearing her vision.

"Shots fired, shots fired!" Clark Duncan's deep voice burst into the radio's silence. Oh damn, that must have been why the first cop had called for backup. The unmistakable staccato drumbeat of heavy weaponry reaffirmed the alarm call. "Officer down! Officer—"

A single, loud bang! cut off his words, followed by a muffled thud.

Steve's heart slammed into her chest.

Oh, hell, may neither of them have been hurt too badly. Two cops shot, one of them for trying to help a lady and the other for coming to their rescue. Damn the trigger-happy bastard, whoever he was.

She slammed the accelerator down, sliding her Expedition against the speed limit's edge. A quick grab shoved her blue flasher onto the dashboard and flipped it on, sending its eerie warning whirling through the night and her siren howling. She raced along the road's center line, watching for headlights, and praying she wouldn't meet a stray cow. Her hands were light on the wheel but adrenaline pulsed through her blood like a rock band's heavy bass guitar, hammering out the chase's fundamental chord.

"All personnel, signal thirty-seven at five-nineteen Sunflower Street. Both officers down. Actor has left the scene in a late model, light-colored Porsche . . ."

Her mouth stretched in a mirthless grin. Late model, light-colored Porsche, huh? Good luck with that city car on these excuses for roads. He was probably racing for shelter on the far side of the border. Only three roads out of Gilbert's Crossing for that: the river road, the main highway, and her route.

Goddamn murdering bastard, whoever he was. If those two cops died, the Texas courts would have a lovely party with the killer's worthless carcass—and she'd make very sure he showed up in time to be the guest of honor.

She picked up the mike, long practice making it easy to handle both it and the car. "Reynolds here. I'm inbound on Avenida dos Lagartos ten miles west of town."

"Copy that, Reynolds." Imelda's relief was painfully obvious.

Steve clicked off automatically, already calculating the road's potential for pure speed. It was charcoal gray, silvery where moonlight hit it and shadowed by ribbons of black, like a network of snakes. Once colorful mountains faded into pewter, their boundaries outlined by the moonlight, while their weather-beaten sides rolled onto the highway's edges. The highway's yellow line ran down the center, drawing everything else together—the asphalt, her eyes, every other vehicle.

What were the odds of Gilbert's Crossing finding enough cops to block all three routes? About as good as her finding a foolproof spot for a roadblock—plumb pitiful. For every narrow gap between a rocky turn, there was an arroyo spilling onto the plain which led down to the Rio Grande and Mexico and offered an escape route. Or a small ranch laden with hostages, or campfires encircled by campers, or scientists planning to ogle the ancient fossils, drat their naive hearts. There was next to no place where she could trap a fleeing suspect, without endangering civilians.

She'd just have to get creative.

The speedometer crept higher and she encouraged it to run. Her mouth was dry, her pulse humming in her veins.

The radio squawked and fumed like a committee of buzzards determined to get their share of a corpse, but not close enough to use their own beaks and talons.

The Feds were promising to close the main highway—toward San Antonio. Wonderful. As if anybody expected a shooter to hurl himself into an American jail.

But a truck's brakes had caught on fire, while waiting to cross at the big border crossing—a not-unexpected event on such a brutally hot day, given the long lines. The resulting upheaval had triggered a couple of accidents, shutting down the main highway just inside the border. Nobody would be crossing there much before dawn.

So the killer would have to choose between the two much smaller routes.

One city cop had managed to put his car on the river road. He hadn't seen that light-colored Porsche yet but he was still looking.

Which left Avenida dos Lagartos. The other city cop was racing down it, his voice as high-pitched as his siren. God willing, he'd drive more like an adult than like a choirboy.

A quick glance at the next corner showed a ranch's lights, half hidden by a rocky outcrop. One set of hostages behind her and out of danger. Their daughter would make it to the cheerleaders' camp next Saturday.

She grinned through her clenched teeth. Just had to protect the rest of them, right?

"Two-nine, signal thirty-nine, five miles west of town on Avenida dos Lagartos . . ."

The trigger-happy bastard was heading straight for her. Lovely. Would the aggressive idiot's testosterone be running so hot and fast he wouldn't hear or see her? Or care if he did?

After all, she had lights on the dash and a siren, plus some nasty surprises in her trunk. Even better advantages were her driving skills and her local knowledge. God willing, she could shove them down his throat before he found himself some hostages.

She began to sing a Shania Twain anthem at the top of her lungs, celebrating feminine strength.

The highway pivoted again, danced around a corner, and hung for an instant above a small valley. Lights flashed against the hillside below her—and were gone. Another pair of lights painted the rocks a minute later before disappearing.

Her hand seized the mike, faster than thought.

"Reynolds here. I'm less than two miles away, on the far side of Comanche Gap."

"Copy that, Reynolds." Two-nine garbled his words, almost swallowing his tongue in relief.

The road swooped down, allowing her an unobstructed view of the valley floor—and the large bonfire burning next to a dirt road and surrounded by four tents. Home base for that scientific expedition in the narrowest corner.

Shit. Her heart went into overtime and tried to shove its way out of her chest.

Try to stop the murdering bastard here—or farther west, back by the ranch? Both options stank.

Two-nine's siren hummed in the distance, too far away to be helpful anytime soon.

A half dozen figures were silhouetted against the fire. One was pointing at the road. Oh God, she couldn't reach her bullhorn to tell them to run.

She slammed her foot down, ignoring every rule about obeying the traffic laws. If she didn't head off that brute before he reached those innocents, what wouldn't he do to them?

The dusty Porsche reached the horseshoe bend at the valley's base. Steve charged down the mountain toward it, desperate to box it in. She could almost hear the sports car's engine snarl, as its driver fought to shift gears and master the narrow, steep turn under the sheer cliff.

Its wheels spun.

The city police car emerged on the valley's other side and raced forward, its siren abruptly magnified by the rock walls into a banshee's wail.

More campers emerged from their tents to watch. Did they have a death wish, ignoring the risk that a car would spin out into the valley? But innocents like them were why she'd become a cop.

The Porsche gained traction—but Steve's far bigger Expedition stood between it and the border.

It veered—and headed off the paved road and onto the dirt

road, toward the bonfire. Damn! Her heart forgot to power her lungs.

She swung the wheel over and went after the Porsche, shifting down hard and fast, encouraging her SUV to master the unforgiving terrain. It growled and leapt onto the sand, creosote bushes whipping against its undercarriage.

The Porsche broke through the desert's thin, hard crust. One wheel sank into dust, wallowing in it like a cat trapped by liquid tar. It came to a halt, the other wheels spinning frantically. An instant later, first one then another broke through and were sucked down, whirring and hissing.

The sports car's door burst open and a man leapt out, brandishing a Glock. Looked like he knew exactly how to use it, too. Great, just great.

The campers stood perfectly still and stared at him, clearly expecting him to explain himself. Goats would have had more sense than to stay there. If he took one of them as a hostage or they were hit by bullets . . .

Her throat tightened.

Steve slammed her truck to a stop and jumped out, her beloved Sig Sauer coming into her hand like a lover. Her Kevlar vest shifted slightly before settling back into position. "Stop! This is the Texas Rangers! Drop your weapon!"

He glared at her, still standing far too close to those campers. He was more impressive than she'd expected, average height and very fit. He seemed familiar, somehow. A wanted poster, maybe?

"Yield to a woman?" He shook his head and made a very rude gesture. He edged toward the closest camper, who eyed him warily.

Dammit, anybody who'd shoot two cops just for walking up to the door could hardly be trusted around a group of civilians.

Her brilliantly revolving lights splashed briefly over the bystanders, who squinted or threw up an arm—but still didn't run.

And her backup was still on the far side of those creosote bushes. It was up to her to protect them.

"Sir, drop your weapon! You're under arrest!" She repeated it in Spanish.

He cursed her and broke into a run.

Her bullet sent grains of sand flying into his face. He whirled to face her, his gun swinging up with the smooth familiarity of long practice.

"Drop your weapon!"

His finger tightened on the trigger—but she got off the first shot of a bitter fusillade.

The spectators finally screamed and scattered like turkeys.

By the time Emanuel Villalobos—or Gilbert's Crossing's two-nine—arrived, Steve was standing over a dead body. Several people were retching loudly in the background. Her empty stomach badly wanted to join them and she knew damn well she'd be pouring a lot of peppermint tea into it over the next few days.

Villalobos came up beside her, silent until he blocked her view of the corpse. "I called it in. Backup will get here within five minutes."

"Thanks." An empty paper bag had more potential than she did at the moment. The only colorful item in the world right now was that corpse's name, highlighted in red on a million wanted posters. She'd recognized the matching face the instant her flashlight's beam had hit it.

She turned to face Villalobos, accepting the need to follow protocol.

"Are you hurt?"

"Not that I know of." She could have used Ethan Templeton, though. He was the only man who'd ever understood when she needed to be cuddled or really well laid.

"Paramedics will want to look you over, of course."

"Thanks." She went back to pondering the dead man's identity. "At least we know why he was so trigger-happy."

"We do?" Villalobos cocked his head.

"He's Manuel Ramirez, El Gallinazo's top executioner."

"El Gallinazo? Shit."

"Yeah." Or worse, since the nickname "The Buzzard" came from the corpses that brutal drug lord liked to leave behind for scavengers.

And unless she could talk her captain out of following the rule book—hah!—she'd be unable to help protect her people.

COMPOSTELA RANCH

The night was oddly quiet, with only the fountains' babble to fill it. The horses' usual reassuring mutters and occasional thuds were gone, lost with the animals' departure to a safer stable. Even the dogs and cats had been evacuated, together with the unarmed prosaicos. If there was to be an attack tonight, nobody wanted the innocent beasts injured. The plants and trees barely whispered in the slight breeze.

Long limestone buildings, crowned with steep metal roofs, flowed over the hilltop, its elegant trees and rose gardens concealing the protective rifle pits and storm shelters. Jean-Marie and Gray Wolf, Don Rafael's two eldest hijos, patrolled the gardens, wary and dangerous as prowling mountain lions.

A single fountain flung itself toward the moon on a nearby hill. It was the only waterworks never silenced, even in drought or when a vampiro awoke for the first time, shaken and uncertain. A few white tombstones slept nearby, in between ancient oak trees.

A helicopter's blades beat through the night, fast and desperate. Nunez was the steadiest of their pilots; otherwise, he'd never have been chosen to convey their hell-born visitors here. But after Don Rafael threw out the uninvited third guest, Nunez had also been needed to take the sleek blond bastard back to the airport.

Only a few minutes spent with those bastards but it had left him spooked enough to fly like a rookie the next time he took off? Damn.

Well, if it had been the legendary Russian assassin, disguised as a boy toy, they'd kicked him out before he could cause any trouble or see anything important.

A whisper ran over Ethan's skin, despite the hot night, but he forced his expression to stay relaxed.

Devol, their unwanted second guest, strolled beside him around the helipad. He stank of blood and worse, until Ethan could hardly stand to draw breath nearby. It was probably a tactic to drive Ethan off, besides the mark of having fed far too well. Disgustingly so, on the emotions he and Madame Celeste preferred. He wore funereal black which would have done credit to the most stylish rock star. His pace was steady, his features calm. But his fingers twitched and his eyes never strayed far from the guesthouse.

Ethan glanced up briefly, scanning for the returning helicopter. If there was to be trouble, it would come soon, especially with Don Rafael and Madame Celeste closeted inside the guesthouse— thus removing Texas's greatest warrior.

Tendrils of scent slipped reassuringly down the hillside toward him. Something solid flashed briefly beside a chimney and was gone. One of his men.

The massed compañías—the great warrior companies of vampiros, compañeros, and prosaicos—guarded Compostela like great horned owls, those legendary tigers of the forest. Snipers lurked on the rooftops and sentries prowled every path, ready to take action at the first sign of trouble. A vampiro who'd shapeshifted into a wolf couldn't have slipped through their cordon without notice.

But Madame Celeste, the New Orleans patrona, had captured Memphis twenty years ago by treachery. She and Devol had slaughtered its large garrison with a bloody ruthlessness, which had shocked even vampiros mayores. How many had she killed that first night—and how many had she saved to destroy the second?

"Think you have enough men to protect you from a single unarmed man and woman?" Devol's mocking drawl cut through Ethan's tally.

"Think you have enough to steal another esfera?" Ethan shot back, wishing he could use his guns.

"We won't need to. We're going to be invited in."

"Like hell!"

"Oh yes. Up there—in that ugly little building—Don Rafael and Madame Celeste are *negotiating* an alliance." Were Devol's features taut with certainty—or anguish?

"Alliance?" Did he mean more than a simple treaty to ward off the reckless young Mexican vampiros?

"Consorts."

That slut? Ethan glared at him. "Not on your life. Don Rafael would never form an alliance with her."

"Don Rafael's just another man, as he proved back in New Orleans. You and I are about to become hermanos." Bitterness threaded through Devol's voice.

Brothers? Like hell. "I'll destroy you."

"If you can." Devol's expression regained its familiar angry mockery. "You aren't much, hiding behind a big estate and all these guards."

"If you weren't protected by the laws of hospitality, you'd already be dead. I'm fifty years older than you are and faster."

"Think you're such a big man? And just how well have you fed all your life—or did your fancy patrona make you beg for your prey, eh?"

"Beg? I *pleasure* my partners, in exchange for blood."

"My patrona made sure every meal was the best—rich and satisfying, as much as I could drink." He drew out the syllables, curling his lip at Ethan's far too blatant restraint.

Ethan clenched his teeth, wishing he could flash his fangs and challenge the bastard to a duel instead of playing the dissembling diplomat. Devol and Madame Celeste's orgies were legendarily long and vicious, making them incredibly good meals if you were a vampiro who fed on pain or worse. Vampiros matured faster the more they ate, so the son of a bitch could be more deadly than his years would normally permit.

The former Bayou Butcher chuckled, liquid evil rippling through the innocent night.

"You're a fool, Devol, if you think Don Rafael will ask Madame Celeste to be his consort." Ethan's patience slipped a notch.

"Are you insulting my creador?" The Cajun whirled on him, a knife handle appearing out of his cuff.

Ethan's fingers stretched for his gun. Just how the hell had Devol drawn first?

FIVE

A door slammed open up above and Madame Celeste stormed out of the guesthouse, Don Rafael a step behind her. The air almost crackled around them, seething with an interrupted fight. They came down the stairs to the helipad fast, lethal and supple as cobras.

Their conversation had gone foul already? Shit.

Ethan's eyes met Devol's, each of them snarling at the other, before they assumed expressionless masks. The fight would be continued another day—and would be far more vicious for the delay.

"I will dance on your grave, Don Rafael," Madame Celeste vowed, glancing over her shoulder, her voice all the more deadly for its utter quiet. "If I can't have you, then nobody will have you."

"If you try, you'll fail." His voice had deepened, gained a chain saw's harsh eagerness.

A young man's irrepressible joy flashed over Devol's face, an expression so utterly at odds with his callous, dissolute history that Ethan could hardly believe he'd seen it. Then it was gone, leaving the harsh, vicious strength of New Orleans's alferez mayor behind.

Two vampiros scrambled to open the backup helicopter's door before Celeste reached it. Devol smoothly handed her into the bird, careful to protect her dress.

She looked down her nose at Don Rafael, haughty as an Egyptian pharaoh. "Just watch me—and weep while you crumble into dust."

"It is you who will dig your grave here," he retorted sharply, finishing with an all-too-polite, "madame."

Devol slammed the door shut and ran around to the other side, an unusual lightness in his step.

An instant later, the helo raced off, carrying the two unwelcome guests back to the airport and thence out of Texas.

Jean-Marie and Gray Wolf came up to stand behind Ethan and Don Rafael.

Ethan flexed his fingers, double-checking their speed and suppleness. He'd have to start practicing even more, now he'd finally have the chance to blow Devol's head off. He wanted to have his choice of shots.

Rough Bear shifted slightly, sending his linen trouser legs whispering against each other. He was as much of a dandy in his own way as Jean-Marie, yet he retained all of the superb tracking skills which had won him Gray Wolf's respect more than a century ago.

The quiet warning of danger immediately made Ethan's head snap up and he warily scanned the perimeter.

Oh hell. The nighttime stars were just starting to dim in the east, letting the sky fade from black to indigo.

He lifted his hand and silently signaled his men. He'd better get his vampiros under cover now and his compañeros out in the open.

They obeyed him smoothly, his vampiros filing into the buildings and the stairs leading deep into the earth. The compañeros leapt up onto the roofs and took up their posts in the gardens and around the drives. Within minutes, every gun port, every rifle pit, every sentry post was occupied by a hard-eyed man ready to kill or be killed in defense of his family and his home.

It wasn't enough. He hated leaving Don Rafael pacing the garden when he was agitated.

Ethan hesitated for a moment, his heart beating uncomfortably fast. He brusquely ordered a handful of his oldest vampiros—Rough Bear, Hennessy of Dallas, Peter of Houston—to stand watch with him in the deepest shadows of the main house's great wraparound porch.

Gray Wolf and Jean-Marie joined them, their faces impassive. Given Gray Wolf's finely tuned sense of balance—or any lack thereof—and Jean-Marie's intuition, Ethan was hardly eased by their presence.

Don Rafael gave him a frosty glare, clearly disapproving of these dispositions. Ethan stared straight back, his face expressionless, certain his patrón wouldn't openly challenge his choices in front of the men. He could stand a lecture, or punishment, later, once the sun came up and there was no chance Madame Celeste and Devol would be back.

The radio crackled to life. "Don Rafael?" Caleb's voice asked politely. "May I speak to you, please?"

Ethan's throat tightened. Caleb Jones was their second-eldest compañero and Gray Wolf's cónyuge, his life mate. Despite having a redhead's temper, he was very unlikely to start a fight under any conditions. What had happened to make him call for help from where he stood watch?

Don Rafael flipped the two-way radio open, the casual gesture at odds with his intent expression. "Certainly, amigo. What is it?"

"We have a limousine here, at the ranch road east, out of San Leandro. The driver has an invitation in your name for Miss Shelby Durant, the Oscar-winning actress. He keeps apologizing for being late, saying he became lost on the ranch roads."

What the hell? She wasn't supposed to come here until tomorrow, to talk about the Special Olympics.

"And?" Don Rafael prompted Caleb.

"I haven't seen Miss Durant but her scent is, ah, unlike anything I've smelled before, sir. It's not prosaica. But it's not vampira or compañera, either."

What did that mean?

Don Rafael growled, baring his fangs completely.

Ethan's gun was in his hand before thought reached his mind. If his master was in a killing mood, then he'd be there as backup.

"Who else is with her?" Don Rafael snarled, his voice deeper and harsher than Ethan had heard in years.

Quietly, using the mind-to-mind link, Ethan told his men not to show any mercy if there was fighting.

"Lucien Saint-Gerard is the driver, sir."

The worst kind of New Orleans street trash. How much worse could matters get?

Don Rafael met the long, black limousine in front of the main house, where the drive made a great circular sweep before a spectacular view of the eastern valleys. The sky was still dark, with only Venus to give any illumination, although the sun would soon change that.

The grassy sweep between the house and the drive was in full shadow, as were the house and the porch, shielded from the rising sun by the eastern hills. The sun's rays would only shine down on Compostela when it rose high enough to be seen over those hills.

The sleek limousine slid to a stop on the macadam drive's east side, with Caleb's armored Suburban pulling in to block him from behind. The limo driver stepped out promptly and turned to face the house: Lucien Saint-Gerard, still just as much of a pimp as he always was. His fancy Italian silk suit was disheveled and bloodstained.

Luis Alvarez, Don Rafael's oldest compañero and siniscal,

moved to flank Don Rafael, while Caleb blocked Saint-Gerard from returning to the limo. The two oldest compañeros were a deadly force in their own right, especially since they could act in daylight, unlike a vampiro such as Lucien.

Only fifty more years until Ethan could be on guard during the day, as well.

"Don Rafael?" Saint-Gerard gave a very formal bow—one leg forward and flourishing his arm.

Don Rafael must have been furious. He only gave the minimum response—a perfunctory nod.

Saint-Gerard glanced hopefully at the stairs into the house. Don Rafael made no response but Luis took a single step sideways, completely closing off the steps. The visiting vampiro was now trapped in the open, hemmed in by Texans.

Saint-Gerard cast his eyes down, more like a snake than a courtier studying how to mend fences. They flickered sideways, hunting for escape routes from the rising sun. "Forgive me for being late but I was overwhelmed by the magnificence of your mountain scenery."

The longtime city dweller had probably been thoroughly lost. Ethan repressed a snicker.

Don Rafael twitched a finger, indicating the newcomer should continue.

"I have brought your gift as Madame Celeste ordered." Saint-Gerard turned and pulled the limo's door open with a flourish. A stench rolled out, worse than the foulest of sewers.

Ethan sniffed—and almost gagged. It had been decades since he'd had anything solid in his stomach, but now? It was a giant knot, writhing and twisted like a rattlesnake's den, fighting to hurl itself into his throat. More than blood, more than death, more than . . . The only time he'd smelled its like was on that trip to Chicago during the thirties.

Jean-Marie said something liquid and deadly in French under his breath.

Then Saint-Gerard yanked Shelby Durant, the hottest actress in Hollywood for the past year, out of the black conveyance. Today, a sewer rat would have been more attractive.

She was covered in blood, vomit, and excrement. Her dress had been clawed to shreds, as had her underthings. A few drops of blood welled sullenly, slowly, from long scratch marks on her breasts and belly. Two great, purple bite marks gleamed at the base of her neck. Other than those, she was ashen white, as if she could fade into a mist. Her eyes were squeezed shut, her face was contorted into a grimace, while her tongue darted out over her lips. One hand plucked at her nipple, while the other rubbed continuously at her crotch.

Time slowed. Even Ethan's breathing came to a halt, wrenched from his throat by pure horror.

Shelby Durant was a newly risen cachorra, who'd received El Abrazo only a few hours ago. Holy shit, women almost never survived it.

What the hell was Saint-Gerard thinking? Everyone knew a newly risen cachorro couldn't tolerate any strong sensations, not even the slightest of noises. Yet he'd driven her around the countryside in a limousine, full of machine sounds, unexpected jolts, and bizarre swerves.

When Ethan had awoken—not that he'd remembered much—he'd done so in a clean bed, on smooth linen sheets, in a darkened room, safe in the arms of his trusted lover.

Crap, there could be no trust between Saint-Gerard and Shelby Durant! Still, she was strong enough to have survived this long, even though she'd needed to claw at herself for blood and sex.

Ethan shuddered. How was she going to survive? La Lujuria was upon her now, the terrifying months when all a cachorro wanted—or needed—was blood and emotion. Where would she get it?

His chest tightened around his heart.

"What the fuck—" Caleb muttered.

Her once-golden head of hair came up in a terrible echo of her famous beauty. "Fuck? Yes. Now. All of you. We fuck." She stumbled across the grass toward the men, fumbling at the remains of her clothing.

Maybe—maybe Don Rafael would make an exception, just this once. Maybe? He'd sworn never to create a vampira and he was a stubborn son of a bitch. But perhaps he'd take pity on her now.

Lucien sauntered after Shelby, beaming like a proud father while she staggered forward. "You see, Don Rafael, the perfect fuck and the perfect meal, to seal the bargain with Madame Celeste. Durant will do anything and everything, just to get a little blood and sex from you, even when you kill her. Nothing like feeding on a dying vampira, while you're fucking her. We'll finish her off in the main house, then share a bottle of champagne."

Ethan closed his eyes for a moment. He'd have done whatever it took to obtain blood and sex during La Lujuria—and he'd been damn lucky to have Don Rafael as his creador. Don Rafael, the only patrón in North America who'd never lost an hijo.

Mother Mary, please soften Don Rafael's heart just this once—just enough to save this woman's life. Please. He's the only vampiro who can do it. I don't pray often but I beg you . . .

Don Rafael started toward the young woman, speaking very gently. "*Dulce* Shelby—"

This might work . . .

Suddenly the first bright shaft of daylight lanced across the hilltop. It caught her in the back, the shock arching her slender body like a flare from a welder's torch. *Oh shit.*

Shelby blazed—incandescent as a nuclear bomb, brighter than the sun itself. Within two seconds, she became a pillar of ash that quickly crumpled upon itself.

A pain too sharp and too deep to be named sliced Ethan's heart. Gray Wolf chanted something very, very quietly.

Maybe it was better this way. At least she'd had a fast, clean death, rather than the uncertainty of whether Don Rafael could tolerate rearing her.

"*Merde,*" the murderer muttered.

Don Rafael crossed himself.

"Don Rafael, she was only a female, nobody to fuss over," cooed Lucien, fingers twitching nervously below his blood-stained cuffs.

Time to clean up the trash. Ethan growled an order.

Behind Don Rafael, soft clicks told of safeties being set on sniper rifles, soft thuds as boot heels snapped into place. Another order and the compañeros began to march. They took up places as an honor guard, their weapons at rest before them, lining up around the drive until they encircled Don Rafael and Saint-Gerard.

"What is the first law of La Esfera de Texas?" Don Rafael asked, his deep voice carrying effortlessly across the hushed space.

"Only El Patrón de Texas may create a vampiro in Texas," the assembly growled behind him.

The oldest law. Sometimes the most logical—and sometimes the most bitter.

Saint-Gerard muttered something profane under his breath.

"What is the penalty for breaking this law?" Rafael continued, his voice as implacable as water breaking through a dam.

"Death."

How many friends had he seen welcome that ending, when their lover lay gibbering from La Lujuria? Knowing Don Rafael had the strength they lacked, even when it meant a quick execution?

Ethan closed his ears against the ghosts' voices. He barely saw the dawn's fire rip through Saint-Gerard, or the few ashes drifting away afterward.

His final thought, while he sent his vampiros deep inside to complete safety from the sun, was alarmingly self-centered: At least it had been Shelby Durant who'd died and not his Stephanie Amanda. He could handle knowing his Steve was married to another man, if it meant she was alive.

TEXAS STATE PARK EAST OF THE TEXAS HILL COUNTRY RAPTOR CENTER, JUNE 1, MIDNIGHT

Ethan seethed, more or less silently, and told himself again to just do his job—protect Don Rafael, no matter what the cost.

Even if it meant guarding a procession of vampiros and one prosaica through a Texas state park, while another prosaica trailed them.

The lady veterinarian—Grania O'Malley by name, although that made no difference to anything except her tombstone—had seen Don Rafael feed on a woman. So why the hell was she still alive? Worse, why had Don Rafael so changed his usual pattern as to display Brynda's delight in being his paramour? He had unnecessarily extended the woodland encounter, time which his watcher could have used to call in her friends for another assassination attempt.

After that evening's damn-near-successful sniper attack, Ethan was in no mood to take any chances with his master's life, no matter how lovely the lady was.

Crap, Don Rafael had almost behaved like some sort of lovesick suitor. As if he'd scented the lady's sexual arousal at the sight of his dalliance, then turned exhibitionist to increase her excitement and build her link to him. Incredibly unusual, especially when Don Rafael publicly had an orgasm. The most obvious trigger was the lady vet's climax but nobody influenced El Patrón that strongly.

No, Don Rafael had to be playing some wild, risk-seeking game, just to blow off steam after the sniper attack. A piece of folly which would have earned any mesnadero a week's stay in a punishment cell.

Not that a punishment cell was an option for the ruler of all Texas and Oklahoma.

They finally reached the lakeshore a mile from Calatrava Resort, a plush all-seasons resort and Don Rafael's latest investment. The road here was lined with great palm trees, tall but fat and round at their bases, providing good cover for surveillance. Beyond the public park's mesquite thickets lay a series of tiered gardens and, finally, the marina and resort itself.

The marina's bright lights flickered across the water, showing docks full of small sailboats and powerboats. Above it rose the resort's main buildings in an *Arabian Nights* fantasy. The nightclub was still open, sending country-western anthems pulsing through the night.

I'll say good-bye to Brynda here, Don Rafael said calmly. *Have a mesnadero shadow her steps to make sure she's safe and healthy.*

Of course, sir.

Thank God this was almost over. Don Rafael was well fed and they could get back to safety. God only knew who else was watching.

I'll go wipe Dr. O'Malley's memories now, Ethan announced, a pro forma statement if there ever was one. *Rough Bear and the other mesnaderos can escort you home.*

Hell no, Don Rafael barked. *I will talk to Doctora O'Malley.*

Ethan stared at his master, his free hand gesturing a man into motion after the departing female.

The vet has been spying on you! What if she's in league with others who want to kill you?

You will protect me, as always. Don Rafael's lips thinned to an unyielding line.

Ethan cut himself off before he argued with El Patrón on an

open channel. Don Rafael might be strong-willed and inclined to push boundaries, but he'd never openly gone against all safety precepts before. Why the hell wouldn't he leave interrogating a suspect to his alferez, whose job it was?

Ethan nodded curtly. *Of course, sir.*

An instant later, a great horned owl, all golden wings and black talons grabbing to take command, burst into the sky from where Ethan's master had stood. Don Rafael's shirt and jeans crumpled onto the dirt followed an instant later by his boots. No vampiro's clothing went with him when he shapeshifted.

Shit. Well, the Old Man would arrive at her location without a so-called logical explanation, which should spook her and make her more easily controlled. Not a tactic which would have worked with Steve, though.

On the other hand, it made protecting him a hell of a lot harder. If Ethan, too, shapeshifted, he couldn't take his weapons.

Rough Bear, grab El Patrón's clothes. I'm on point.

His friend dashed across the open expanse at full speed and snatched them up without breaking stride. Even a high-speed camera would have had a hard time glimpsing him, let alone a prosaica with a distant, blocked view. The lumps of clothing and leather vanished in an instant.

Ethan faded into the nearby shrubbery, knowing Don Rafael wouldn't land until his men were ready. He hid himself close to Doctor O'Malley, knowing her prosaica senses couldn't smell him, and waited, keeping his rifle close.

The lady vet poked her head out from behind the palm tree, her eyes wide and staring.

Hold her while we talk, Ethan. I won't use mind control.

But—

It didn't work earlier, when I couldn't make her stop watching, Don Rafael said on their private channel. *Forcing her would destroy her and I won't do that. Do you understand?*

Yes, sir. He'd never been able to make himself use mind tricks on Steve. But he wouldn't let anybody, even a woman, hurt Don Rafael.

She stepped all the way out into the open, her hand to her heart, and looked around. Who did she remind him of, with her long neck and coronet of red braids? His eldest sister? Surely not. His failures had left his family dead.

Don Rafael landed in the gardens next to the road and donned his clothes quickly, although he didn't take the time to pull his boots back on.

Come on, hurry it up. We need to get out of here.

Now, Ethan.

Thank God.

Ethan pounced. He grabbed her from behind in that most basic of holds, slamming his arm around her neck in a choke hold and dragging her back against him.

Startled and angry, she fought him damn hard, using every dirty trick she'd ever learned, but to no avail. She kicked; she jabbed him with her elbows; she tried to throw him. She'd been taught well in some very vicious schools. If he'd been a prosaico, he wouldn't have wanted to fight her.

But, dammit, they needed to finish this. He started to twist so he could throw her.

Don't hurt her! Don Rafael ordered.

Of course not, sir! Ethan froze immediately. After that, he simply used his strength against her and held her, letting her exhaust herself. Finally, she relaxed, although she was probably only waiting for an opportunity to escape.

Then Don Rafael walked onto the road, clad only in his shirt and jeans, and faced her.

"*Buenas noches, doctora.*"

"*Buenas noches, señor,*" she choked out. Good, they'd managed to catch her off guard.

"Did you enjoy your observations, *doctora?*"

She deliberately forced herself to relax a little more, matching Don Rafael's tone.

Despite himself, Ethan started to admire her but he couldn't afford to release her.

"They were somewhat—unusual, señor." She shrugged, striving for a light atmosphere.

Even though he'd promised not to use vampiro mind tricks, Don Rafael's eyes were searching her face as if he'd never seen anyone like her, the way a prosaico would, as if he wanted to read her every thought. His fingers curled and his hands lifted, almost reaching for the curve of her cheek. Trying to probe her more deeply? Caress a long-lost lover? Surely not, especially when his conversation was unexceptionable.

"Do you intend to share them with others?"

"What's to share? A man and woman did some necking in the woods. Would anyone in authority believe the man bit the woman for a nefarious reason, especially when he's such an important member of the community?"

He studied her, then nodded. *She won't harm us, Ethan.*

Very well, sir. Ethan reluctantly released the choke hold but didn't step away.

"May I remove this impertinent twig from your jacket, *doctora?*"

He wanted to seduce her? Just how many harebrained chances did the Old Man plan to take tonight?

Ethan! Let her choose freely.

Ethan gritted his teeth but eased off until he was barely touching her. If she started any trouble, he could wring her neck in an instant, given how close they were standing.

Still, the lady vet was one damn smart cookie. She eyed Don Rafael very suspiciously before nodding. "Certainly."

"You may depart, Ethan."

Ethan hesitated. If anything, his grip tightened on her. After

all, what if she was working with Devol? "She could be the bait
for another assassination attempt, Don Rafael."

"There is no threat to me here and now." Rafael's voice was
deadly calm—and it sliced the night air like the *doctora's* best
scalpel.

"As you wish, sir." Ethan reluctantly released her and left—
without a sound, of course.

What the hell was different about Grania O'Malley? It'd be a
pleasure to know why Don Rafael was behaving so damn oddly
for a woman he'd just met. She was either his salvation or his
biggest threat.

Ethan was still pondering that question when he arrived at
Calatrava Resort a few hours later. Having drunk twice from
Brynda, Don Rafael wanted to know if she was showing any
signs of distress.

Ethan stopped his big black pickup just below where the hotel
slept, careful to avoid the more revealing surveillance cameras.
Rough Bear silently emerged from the gardens, which were quiet
now without their jewel-like fountains, and stepped inside the
truck, inconspicuous in jeans and an ancient Willie Nelson T-shirt.

"How is she?" Ethan decorously turned the truck around,
trying to look like an early-morning landscape service.

"Fine. She said hello to her friends on the boat, then went
below and slept. She hasn't been seen since but her friends are
pleased she's already started to relax."

Ethan's gaze flickered sideways. For Rough Bear, that number of words at one time almost amounted to nervous chatter.

"Good," he said noncommittally, shards of ice playing hop-
scotch on his neck.

The verdant putting greens had faded into fairways, then
ranch lands, before Rough Bear spoke again.

"Steve checked in to the resort yesterday."

Steve? He knew a number of Steves. But surely not Stephanie Amanda.

"Which one?"

"The cop." Rough Bear's tone allowed no ambiguity.

Ethan's breath stopped in his throat at the chance of seeing her again. How soon could he get back to the resort? Shit, not before dawn.

But did it matter?

He shrugged. "So what? She's probably here on a second honeymoon."

"She checked in solo—under the name of Reynolds."

Ethan almost swerved off the road at hearing her maiden name.

CALATRAVA RESORT, THE NEXT NIGHT

Ethan stepped into the bar, reminding himself yet again he was only here for one quick look and then he'd be gone. Just to reassure himself she was fine after three years of no contact and her promotion into the Texas Rangers. After all, that kind of duty down along the border could jangle anybody's nerves.

Yeah, right—and to look for a flash of gold on her left hand. He'd played the gentleman once before and let her walk away, to find a husband for the home and children she wanted so badly, that he couldn't possibly give her. He couldn't even hope to offer her a permanent relationship, lest it cost them both their lives.

But he'd never been good at that sort of polite behavior, as his mother and sisters would have been the first to attest. He'd only managed it by not allowing himself to hear anything of what Steve was doing.

But if she was free, what would he do? What wouldn't he do?

He snickered at his fantasies and slipped past the heavy planters, whose massive palm fronds screened the bar from the resort's lobby. This was the most private and adult bar of the resort's many retreats, with leather and wrought iron furniture, tile floor, and discreet bartenders ready to pour very upscale drinks. One wall was glass, displaying a balcony offering a view of the alluring gardens and swimming pool beyond.

A handful of tables were occupied on this Saturday after Memorial Day. He assessed and dismissed them rapidly, as being of no consequence. Far faster than if he'd been guarding Don Rafael, where everyone was a potential threat. Tonight only one caught his attention, tugging at his pulse.

Steve was sitting at the bar, facing two would-be cowboys and lightly drumming on the counter. The soft lighting, designed to spotlight expensive liqueurs, instead highlighted her profile's purity and her skin's rich gold. Her sensual mouth was firmly compressed now and her winged brows were drawn together. If he could see them clearly, he'd wager that her whisky brown eyes had turned flat and cold as a gunstock.

He almost pitied the fools—but he couldn't blame them for trying to make time with her.

She was wearing a simple white wrap dress which delightfully flattered her trim figure. Its skirt hinted at her long legs' potential for wrapping around a lucky man's waist. The deep V-neckline offered glimpses of her beautiful breasts, although they were best enjoyed from a closer vantage point. The short sleeves displayed her arms' golden tan, all the way down to her beautiful hands, as easily capable of using a knife or gun as fondling his balls.

His pulse stirred, driven by memories of past delights.

And God help him, she was wearing her long black hair loose tonight. It fell down to her waist, rippling like a waterfall of darkness that a man could dive into for the rest of his life. When she brushed it over his hips or thighs . . .

She tossed it back to rub her neck. One of the two bastards promptly moved a little closer.

Ethan's blood immediately boiled with more than lust.

He circled around her, careful not to be seen, and sat down on her far side. A raised hand, two fingers, and a fifty on the counter brought the bartender's eager attention and two examples of Ethan's favorite *mojito*.

"Here you go, darling," he drawled, sliding one forward to replace her horrific diet soda. "Sorry I was a little late."

She whipped around to stare at him, one hand automatically reaching for her missing gun.

He raised an eyebrow. She'd grown considerably faster on the draw during her time on the border.

Shock, followed by incredulous joy, bloomed in her dark eyes.

"Hello, darling." She looked him over slowly, allowing her eyes to linger on strategic portions of his anatomy. "Well now, don't you just clean up fine when you finally bother to make the effort."

"Promised you something special, didn't I?" He toasted her, not bothering to hide his reaction to her survey, although his brain tossed a few crumbs toward caution.

Why the hell was she so eager to get laid? She'd only acted like this before when she'd come straight off a dangerous op, which surely wasn't the case here. "Care to make a thorough inspection?"

"Guess I'd better, since you worked so hard." She rose leisurely, forcing the two spluttering fools to move away. "You'll excuse us, gentlemen?"

He cupped her elbow, not allowing himself closer contact in public. There'd be time enough for everything they both wanted, once they reached his room.

Steve fought not to heave a sigh of relief, wondering how Ethan had known she needed him. The best lay in Austin, probably in all of Texas—and the one with the fewest strings. Thank God.

Damn, but she needed to be held. She'd come here to borrow Cousin Mac's time-share. He was her sole relative and very popular with Uncle Sam. Only God knew where the Army was working him to the bone right now, since they'd abruptly interrupted her visit with him at Fort Bragg.

She didn't want to think about her diminishing chances of ever getting two point three kids and a house with a white picket fence. She sure as hell didn't want to second-guess anything connected with Ramirez's death. But sitting alone in a strange bar, in a strange town, being ogled by strangers, was no way to shut down her brain or feel warm again.

Sleeping with Ethan had its own set of risks, of course. He was a vampiro and he knew far too much about the worst guys in Texas. But he'd never hurt her and she'd never *seen* him commit a crime. Besides, a little blood was a small price to pay for the kind of sex he could provide.

She almost bounced on her toes at the prospect. She had Ethan and life was going to be much, much better for at least a little while. Starting with the visuals, of course.

He was a beautiful man, but she'd always found him most dangerous to her equilibrium when he was paying the least attention to his own attractions. Blond hair, a Greek god's irresistible beauty, hazel eyes backed by the cool, calculating intelligence of a gunfighter, and a panther's lethal grace and power.

Not kind or gentle—but skillful, which was all she wanted now, thank God.

"Damn, I'm glad to see you," she breathed.

He glanced at her, both of them moving swiftly along the pathways between the villas. Exotic flowers scented the soft night, many still lightly bespangled from the earlier rainstorm.

"What about the husband?" His voice was definitely edged.

Jealous? Surely not. But he'd always been careful to observe legal formalities around her.

"Divorce." She made a moue of distaste. With Ethan's arm

around her, she could start erasing Fred's bedroom memories. "It's been final for a few months."

"That sounds—very complete and very fast," Ethan commented, turning into the truly exclusive part of the resort.

She blinked, startled they weren't heading for his truck. He wasn't somebody to stick around public places. Possible destinations started to dance through her head, all strongly approved by her libido.

"He got caught with his pants down." She shrugged, more than eager to forget the bastard. "At the church picnic by the oldest Sunday School teacher."

"Shit." Ethan's voice was a lethal hiss.

"Not exactly, but you've got the idea." She leaned closer to her longtime lover. His heat seeped into her from his shoulders to the roughness of his denim-clad leg rasping her thigh. "Must we talk about him?"

"Not if you don't want to." He unlocked an isolated villa and stood back, the porch light striking sparks from his golden hair.

She sauntered in, trying to breathe through a throat grown suddenly tight.

The villa was a modernistic vision of what an Easterner thought Texas style should be, with lots of overstuffed leather furniture, woven rugs, and tile floors. It looked comfortable, though, and there was a door which promised a bedroom.

He kicked the front door shut and kissed her neck, lightly scraping his teeth over her skin. Steve rose up on her toes with a little moan, steam sizzling through her veins.

"How long will you be here?"

"What does that matter?" she snapped, and tried to turn around.

He stopped her with an arm around her waist. "Tell me, Steve. Are we talking about a night, a week, or longer?"

Oh shit, now he was stroking his hands up and down her

arms, his calloused fingers somehow striking sparks from her satiny-smooth skin.

He locked his fingers in hers and hauled her closer to him. She squirmed against him and over him, driving herself frantic, heat rising through her bones and rippling across her skin.

All she wanted was to forget about everything and just take comfort from him. Why did they have to talk?

"Steve?" he prompted.

She wriggled again, but he wouldn't slip his leg between hers. Her heart was pounding, blocking thought from her brain.

"At least a week. Maybe a month." For the first time, her exile to Austin sounded enjoyable.

"Very good," he approved, and kissed her cheek, close but not close enough to her mouth.

Ethan's voice sounded a little tight but she ignored that, pleased his mouth had moved lower to explore her jaw and throat. She immediately tilted her head, moaning encouragement, her skin growing taut and flushed.

He turned her to face him, never lifting his head. She stroked his head, savoring how his hair's thick silk rippled through her fingers.

His strong fingers slipped inside her dress, fondling and kneading her breast. She groaned and arched, pressing herself shamelessly into their expert enticement, shuddering under every heated spike of her blood.

He stroked her thighs, teasing her under her skirt. She moaned, her legs squeezing his hand, her hips twisting and writhing in encouragement. Passion pulsed and heated through her veins, sizzling like steam on an overheated skillet.

She snarled in frustration, cream spilling to follow his lead. "Damn you, Ethan!"

"Tut-tut! Such language from a lady," he mocked lightly.

"I want to be fucked, Ethan, not seduced. It's been nine

months since I've had a man!" She and Fred had been seeing a marriage counselor months before the final breakup—although Fred had started his first affair days after their wedding. It'd be a long time before she forgot that discovery.

But Ethan wasn't a marriage candidate, since he was a vampiro. He'd never offer a gold ring or a family. She could relax with him and simply enjoy herself.

He stilled for a moment, his hands falling silent on her.

"Ethan, dammit!" She pushed against him, demanding his full attention again.

He chuckled, long and low, silky and dangerous. She shivered, recognizing the promise of eventual fulfillment—but not necessarily in the gentlest fashion.

He flipped up her skirt, half tearing her panties to bare her. Hot cream from her core gushed to follow, sliding down her thighs, scenting the air.

"Feeling eager? Feeling ready?" he queried, his voice harsh and demanding.

"Yes, dammit!" How often did she have to tell him?

A single, callused finger slipped between her legs and played with her. Rough, blunt, dragging through her slick folds, playing with her clit, teasing her, circling, probing and withdrawing until she was nearly insane. She rode it, adapted, fought to keep it. Her breath caught in her lungs, her legs rose and sank down to match its rise and fall, her heartbeat drummed in her ears. She clutched at his shoulders, keening his name.

So long, so very long since she'd had a man. Since she'd had anything more than her hand or a vibrator.

Wonderful. Best of all, it was Ethan.

He pressed down on her clit, in that expert stroke of his—and she climaxed, every bone and sinew vibrating with pleasure, cascades of joy tumbling through her.

Long moments passed while she fought to recover, shuddering

with the need for air. Then she slowly began to breathe again, frustrated she still hadn't had his cock inside her. "Damn you, Ethan!"

"What's the matter, Stephanie Amanda?"

"Ethan!" Only he dared to call her that.

His face was harsh with leashed hunger but he managed a hoarse laugh. "Still haven't had enough—Stephanie?"

She snarled but managed a civil response. There'd be no satisfaction until she accepted the name. "You know I want more of you, Ethan." She swallowed, her eyes drifting down over his chest. "Please," she whispered.

He picked her up and she tucked her head against his shoulder, her bones slowly regaining their stability in the shadow of his strength. It had been so long since anybody had simply offered her sexual release, without her job making them awestruck or turning them into sycophants.

He kissed her hair, murmuring something unintelligible, and deposited her on the enormous, silk-covered bed.

She bounced upright, staring at her lover. The bedroom was as modernistic as the living room. It, too, had probably come from an expensive designer—and a very hedonistic one, judging by the luxurious bed.

"What on earth?" she spluttered. When was Ethan going to do something about that enormous erection he was sporting?

"Perfect, isn't it?"

"For what?" she asked suspiciously, staring at him. If she wasn't so irritated at him for putting her down, she'd say something to him about how he'd opened up her dress so she was basically lying on top of it. Hell of a way to undress a girl without taking off any of her clothes.

"For this." He knelt down and lifted her legs over his shoulders, sliding her hips to the edge of the bed.

"Huh?"

He took a long, assessing lick along her thigh, then another. "Very nice."

She shivered, fireflies dancing through her skin and into her bones to shimmer into her blood. "Very *nice?*"

"But I think I'd prefer a taste of this." He buried his face in her cunt and nuzzled her.

She gasped, tension winding like a fire-edged watch spring along her spine.

He chuckled, the sound vibrating through her skin and deep into her bones, sending shockwaves from her womb to her heart.

She moaned on exactly the same frequency.

He settled down to eat her with the skill and wicked finesse of a master, clearly willing to take any amount of time at it. He slid first one finger, then another into her, stroking her, probing her. She heaved herself against them, tightened herself around them, howled her fury at his delay. She needed him inside and around her—him!

Orgasm after orgasm rattled her objections, especially when he began to slowly finger fuck her.

"Ethan, ohmygawd, Ethan! Please, Ethan, I want, oh, I want . . . Ethan!"

She lay panting from yet another orgasm, three of his fingers buried inside her, one broad fingertip lightly drumming on her most sensitive spot. Her eyes met his through a cloud of tangled hair. "Ethan, please. I just want you. Please?"

His features were edged in pure granite—or sexual desperation. "Are you begging?"

Beg? She tried to think but only instinct answered. "Yes, I'll beg. Please, Ethan?"

His eyes gleamed brilliantly green and his mouth curved in triumph. She smiled faintly, recognizing the signals.

An instant later, he'd shucked his jeans and was kneeling over her. "Steve," he said fiercely, and lifted her hips.

A single lunge brought him into her—and she was almost virgin tight around his big cock. Fire, which she'd thought banked down to a comfortable flame, reignited into blazing fury. Desire's eager quest flared back into full, throbbing demand.

He froze, gritting his teeth. "Steve." His voice was barely recognizable.

"Please, Ethan, now!" She clawed his shoulders, instinctively drawing blood.

He snarled, baring his fangs, sending joy and lust swirling through her veins.

His control snapped completely. He took her fast and deep, slamming into her with the implacable fury of a summer thunderstorm.

He bit her, his fangs tapping deep into her jugular. Blood flowed, fiery, rich, intoxicating, kicking her passion into overdrive. And orgasm slammed into her, knocking her into a world of spinning stars and black worlds where Ethan was the only shred of reality. Familiar and priceless, yet not completely hers.

He poured his come into her, filling her core with its heat. Higher she went, still higher, consciousness spilling into and over Ethan until there was nothing left of either of them except pleasure shared.

A cell phone's all-too-realistic impersonation of The Who jolted Steve from her doze. She groped blindly, coming up with a handful of sheet falling away from Ethan's strong hip.

"Templeton."

She rolled to listen in on the conversation. He was rapidly pulling on his clothes, silhouetted against the light from the living room.

He froze, his belt halfway through his jeans' loops. "How long ago? Do we know if there was anybody with him?"

Her skin prickled at his tone and she sat up, pushing her hair off her face. Her gun was in the other room, dammit. But why would she want to go into battle beside him? He might be a reliable confidential informant but that didn't make him one of the good guys.

"Yes, start searching immediately. I'll be there right away."

He hung up, holstering the fragment of plastic and electronics with the absentminded efficiency of someone completely at home with multiple weapons strung from a belt. His eyes met hers, remote and shadowed from more than the room's darkness. "I'm sorry but work calls. I have to go."

Steve nodded and came to her feet, wondering yet again about his world. She knew he wouldn't harm her. But he'd also helped her more than once in a criminal investigation, displaying an appalling familiarity with the completely illegal. He always brushed off any questions about his friends, his business dealings, or how he'd gained such expertise.

How many vampiros like him were there, anyway? And how trustworthy were they?

"If there's anything a Ranger understands, it's duty. I'll just head back to my room and get some sleep." She wrapped a polite mask over her face, the same one she used when she didn't want to answer questions from the public, and smiled. Drat it, she'd fallen into his grasp far too easily, yet again. "It's been great seeing you again."

He caught her chin in his hand, his eyes narrowing. "Don't say good-bye too fast, Steve. You'll be the one calling me for a date."

She bristled. She might be newly divorced and alone in town, without even a relative handy to make introductions. But she sure as hell wasn't desperate enough to crawl. "Like hell!"

His eyes narrowed. "Because I'm the best sex you've ever had, Steve—and the best partner on the job."

An instant later, his mouth came down on hers, all hard, assured persuasion.

Why was he doing this? Why was he acting almost as if he wanted to stake a claim on her? He'd always been the love-'em-and-leave-'em type before.

Worse, why was she just standing here, even though her body

was rejoicing in every contact with him, even the rub over his jeans' rough denim? She shouldn't do this, not if she wanted to have a future with anybody else.

Her hands came up to his shoulders to push him away.

He slanted his head, catching her mouth at just the right angle. His hand slipped over her shoulders, stroking the small of her back.

Dammit, she'd never been able to resist his kiss.

Helplessly, she sighed and yielded, enjoying the heated dance of their tongues, of shared breath, of exploring the tastes and textures of each other's mouths.

And the arrogant prediction that they'd meet again. The first time he'd ever offered that affirmation.

She was still lightly patting her bruised lips like a dazed high school girl when she wandered back to her room, his business card in her other hand.

Six

Lightning sparked halfheartedly in the east, hurling a few shards of light against the black clouds. Green lurked near the edges, as if anyone who looked long enough would see a doorway into hell—or a tornado, which was often the same thing. As it had been this evening for too many people in the surrounding counties.

The small town had been scoured clean by torrential rains, as though Mother Nature had decided to blast every grain of dirt away in a single hour. The World War II soldier glistened high atop his granite plinth in the middle of courthouse square, his bayonet poised to charge. Every business was freshly washed, their creamy limestone walls glowing as if alive under the street-lights. The twenty-four-hour drugstore's neon lights blazed, flashing a multitude of cures for the world's ills.

But not for everything. Not for what lay behind endless strands of yellow and black tape beside the ice cream parlor, under spats of harsh white camera flashes.

The ice cream parlor had always been one of the most popu-lar gathering places in town. Now its small tables and tiny chairs carefully separated anxious townsfolk, while they waited to give their statements to the cops in the corner booth. Right under all the photos celebrating San Leandro High's football victories and the flavors named for San Leandro's most popular beauties.

Roger Bresnahan's car's siren whined irritably but no cars moved. A few people glanced at him but only shuffled their feet.

"When was the last time you had an unexpected death here?" Steve asked Roger softly.

"About fifty years ago." The local sheriff—her former partner—slammed his car into park, grinding the gears slightly. He still smelled of crawfish, onions, and spices, the rich scents of his wife's famous jambalaya which they'd been eating when the call had come in. They were good friends, who'd even tried to teach her how to dance once so she'd look graceful in a bridesmaid's dress. "But don't worry; we'll figure out what happened here."

He jumped out without looking at her, slamming his baton into his belt. "You're welcome to look around, of course."

An instant later, he'd shoved his way into the crowd, heading for the vortex of activity in the center.

She shook her head slightly, not envying him. San Leandro was famous for its First Saturday concerts, when half of Texas sometimes seemed to descend on it. The rest of the month, it was a very sleepy little town. Having a crowd gather for something like this must seem like hell incarnate.

Steve settled her white hat onto her head and followed him. She stopped at the alley's entrance, unwilling to taint a potential crime scene. Still, she could see everything from here, not that there was much to observe.

Rookie cops had gone whistling past this spot for decades during daylight, certain the numerous trash cans hid only empty milk cartons. But tonight somebody had borrowed spotlights, normally used for First Saturday concerts, and mounted them on the rooftops. Glaring white lights taunted the narrow slot between buildings, chasing out every once-friendly corner. The ancient asphalt was cracked and dry under their remorseless beams, although a few corners and deeper crevices still gleamed darkly with the heavy rain's last traces.

A detective methodically worked over the ground, looking for any traces of a crime. Only her shoulders' slight relaxation revealed that she acted more from routine than outrage. A handful of cops echoed her movements more clumsily, occasionally silhouetted against the spotlights like gargoyles. San Leandro was so small and peaceful, it usually sent all its evidence to Austin for processing rather than having criminalists on hand as specialists to search crime scenes. A photographer methodically quartered the area, his closeness to the square suggesting either a long time since he'd started or a lack of items to be recorded.

Steve didn't envy those who'd have to search the trash cans. But the ice cream parlor itself used a locked, modern Dumpster, which meant there was nothing close by accessible to strangers.

Damn, this felt like the worst of bad dreams.

Still more cops, their colorful uniforms telling of other jurisdictions come to help, stood watch over the onlookers in the square, their voices crooning reassurance about what a terrible shame this was.

In the middle, like an ancient sacrifice, lay the shrouded center of their attention. She was still in the same posture and location in which she'd been found, sprawled beside the ice cream parlor.

Maribeth Rogers, age twenty-two, her family's darling. The star of the state synchronized-swimming team and poised to succeed in the national, even the international arenas, according to the dispatcher.

There had to be a simple explanation.

"But I don't understand!" wailed a woman. "She'd just had her physical, by the Olympic team doctors, and they said she was perfect!"

Steve frowned. Doctors had been wrong before—but Olympic-quality physicians?

She straightened up and started pacing back and forth along the alley's entrance, watching the shadows cross the shroud. Even for a corpse, it was remarkably ungainly.

Roger stopped beside her, looking years older than he had at dinner. He looked a question at her.

She shrugged. "Could be natural."

"Drugs maybe."

Was he hoping for a comfortable explanation? If so, they'd been partners for too long to let her give him the easy out.

"Maybe." She kept her voice deliberately noncommittal.

He grunted, unhappiness settling deeper into his face.

A deputy came up, talking fast and soft. "Sheriff? We're finished here. Can we move Miss Rogers now? The crowd's growing and her mother would like some privacy."

"Are you certain?" Steve asked sharply. This was damn soon to move a corpse.

"You know tonight's storm was a gully washer, Steve." Roger spun to face her, his tone sharp. "How much evidence do you think is likely to still be here, even if there was a crime?"

She made a sharp gesture, unable to disagree. But her nerves jangled every time she saw the light spill over that silent body.

Don't worry, Maribeth. I'll keep an eye on your autopsy and the investigation for you, she promised silently.

She studied every instant of the corpse's transfer and journey. By the time the slight figure had almost reached her, her previous doubts had crystallized into something more solid. "May I take a quick look, when she goes past?"

"Of course, Steve." Roger stiffened. A moment passed before he spoke again, painfully casual. "Looking for anything specific?"

She didn't answer him directly. Texas Rangers had jurisdiction over any crime committed in the State of Texas. Usually that

meant crimes occurring across multiple jurisdictions, like racketeering conspiracies. But it often meant helping out small towns
with nastiness they didn't see very often—such as murder.

She gently lifted the cloth up just high enough to see the girl's
head and neck. Her torso and legs were stretched out smooth
and straight, as befitted someone who'd soon be going into a
coffin. But her neck was canted awkwardly to one side, the
tendons achingly taut and her T-shirt's shoulder was so badly
wrinkled it looked pleated.

"Odd position for her head and neck, since she was found
lying on her back," Roger commented. "Well, maybe she'd been
using her cell phone, even though there was a storm coming.
After all, she was just a kid."

"Hmm." Unfortunately for that theory, Steve had seen the
crime scene tech pick up the girl's cell phone from a few feet
away. Plus, none of the wrinkles showed any impressions of a
phone.

*More important, what the hell had put that look of sheer
horror on the girl's face?*

Steve carefully covered Maribeth Rogers's face again. She
was willing to bet a month's pay natural death hadn't contrib-
uted to her expression.

COMPOSTELA RANCH, JUNE 9

Ethan prowled in front of the bookshelves, the two revolvers
in his shoulder holsters thin comfort. He'd expected bad news
when he was summoned during full daylight. But this?

Don Rafael was leaning on the stone fireplace behind his
desk, next to his centuries-old knightly sword. He could instantly snatch up the still-deadly blade and behead any intruder
in an instant, from that pose.

Luis was pacing like a lost soul in front of the heavy steel shutters on the window. Jean-Marie was at the big conference table, searching out more information on his stealthy little PC.

Caleb sat on the leather sofa, with Gray Wolf only inches away. They didn't often openly indulge in physical displays of affection, relying instead on their conyugal bond to link them together. Born of complete trust and confidence in each other, the rare bond allowed them to share each other's thoughts and sensations, a union that would last for the rest of their lives.

Ethan cast another fulminating glance at them and spun on his heel, heading toward the desk and the fireplace. Contentment in a relationship—especially security that the loved one was safe!—wasn't something he wanted to see right now.

"How many such rapes have been reported?" Don Rafael snapped out.

"Two so far, both in Waco," Luis gritted out, as he strode restlessly, his white shirt brilliant against the steel shutters that protected them from daylight.

Thank God Steve was in Austin, a hundred miles away. With her safe, he could start thinking about other women, the nameless ones he was sworn to protect.

"But there's been a half-dozen attempted suicides by healthy young women for no apparent cause. Or at least, no prior signs a mental health professional noticed," Jean-Marie amended, double-checking the messages on his PC. "And one successful suicide."

"*Coño,*" Don Rafael cursed.

"The rapes fit Devol's pattern: respectable women, badly beaten," Ethan commented. It was so damn easy to recognize the brute's handiwork. "But the suicides?"

"Beau's doing," Don Rafael said flatly, looking up from Jean-Marie's computer.

Ethan snarled, his fingers twitching. Beau was Madame Celeste's blond escort—and a legendary assassin? The fellow they'd thrown out of Compostela but hadn't been able to kill because he'd arrived protected by the hospitality laws.

Crap, he should be wiped off this earth. Killing him would be ten times harder now that he was a vampiro mayor, the hardest kind of vampiro to find.

"He feeds on fear, then wipes the memory, but he's never been the best at controlling minds." Don Rafael's mouth worked for a moment as if trying not to spit. "Many times, the women remember something, even if it drives them insane."

Christ, they'd better keep this quiet. If prosaicos heard about these attacks, they'd come hunting for the rapist, no matter who he was.

"Jean-Marie, have your men watch all the mental health databases very closely. We must be alerted immediately when young women commit suicide or suffer unexplained depressions."

Jean-Marie nodded, his fingers flying over the keys. "*Certainement, mon père.* We should also probably scale back San Leandro's Fourth of July picnic. It's a First Saturday, so there'll be large crowds coming in for the music. We don't want our prosaicos wandering about when Beau and Devol are nearby."

"Agreed," Ethan seconded immediately. "It's the only public event at which you, Don Rafael, are scheduled to appear next month. All Madame Celeste's rabid wolves will certainly be lying in wait."

"Then you will simply have to chase them off," Don Rafael retorted. "I will not break my promise to appear, especially since I am an American and this is my national holiday."

What the fuck? Ethan slammed his fist into the fireplace. If Don Rafael died, everything would be lost.

"You cannot risk yourself so foolishly!" Gray Wolf erupted. Jean-Marie and Caleb, both normally relaxed, came to their feet yelling. Luis cursed Don Rafael in a steady stream of *Galego*, their mother tongue.

Their master allowed them to vent for a minute before putting his foot down. *"¡Silencio!"* he roared at the top of his lungs.

The sound shook Ethan to the bone, taking him back to when he'd been a slave, prostrating himself in justifiable terror before the big Spaniard's wrath. Being forced to learn discipline and respect. He flinched—and reminded himself he was fighting for Don Rafael's safety.

Ethan's shoulders hunched. But he growled softly and bared his teeth—slightly—like a man, when his master looked him in the eyes.

"You will obey me in this," Don Rafael ordered, spitting out every word. "I gave my word to the mayor that I would light the fireworks and so I will."

Jean-Marie snarled deep in his throat. Don Rafael's eyes flashed to him but his heraldo spoke nothing in words.

"Your duty is to secure the area—by whatever means necessary. Do you understand?"

Don Rafael's will slammed into Ethan and bowled him over, as overwhelming as a tornado. He could no longer argue but he didn't approve.

"*Sí*, Don Rafael." Was he agreeing to help his master commit suicide? "We can pull vampiros and compañeros from the commanderies to form a perimeter around San Leandro that weekend."

But, dear God, how that would leave gaps in their defenses.

"Which will leave the borders very thinly protected, if bandolerismo try to sneak into Texas," Gray Wolf pointed out, his fangs showing in a rare display.

Don Rafael nodded emphatically. "We'll take the risk. What else?"

Ethan closed his eyes for an instant, then began planning how to redeploy his men. Thank God they had Peter and his compañía in Houston, guarding the eastern frontier against Madame

Celeste's forces. Even her most subtle moves couldn't easily dodge the former buffalo soldier with a grizzly's lightning reflexes.

Gray Wolf inclined his head in acknowledgment and began to tick off points on his fingers. "Roving patrols of all likely vampiro hunting grounds. Parks, nightclubs, hotels . . ."

"And honeypots, of course. Using entrapment to pull 'em in, not just guns," Caleb added.

Don Rafael shot him a quick glance, listening hard.

"And thin out the nightclubs in Austin and San Antonio along the River Walk, to make it harder for vampiros to feed close by," Luis put in. "We can yank their ABC licenses and get half of them closed down within a week or two."

"Before the Fourth, kill every foreign vampiro who's entered Texas without a passport," Jean-Marie suggested.

Now *that* would head off a lot of problems. But they could do more. And the faster the better, to protect Steve and other Texas ladies.

"I want to eliminate the criminal element, too, especially the prosaicos who'd help Devol for money. Those bastards have enough guns to be dangerous, even if they're not vampiros." Kill every prosaico who might be a threat—and forget about waiting for Steve's idolized judicial system to take action, if it ever did.

There was a murmur of agreement.

Ethan smiled, fangs pricking his lip in anticipation.

TEXAS STATE CAPITOL, AUSTIN, JUNE 10

Steve jerked her arms out from behind her back, refusing to assume parade rest, even though her lieutenant was pacing across the tiny room, made even smaller by ancient metal desks and filing cabinets. He'd told her to relax and she'd tried to obey.

Yeah, right.

She tapped her toe inside her boot, stopped that, and stretched her shoulders.

She'd have been happier if Posada had called her back to company headquarters in San Antonio—two hours south—for a chat, rather than the state capitol building. Dodging bureaucrats was more nerve-racking than facing armed robbers, especially when she didn't know what was coming. Surely even the worst message could have been delivered on home turf.

But heck, almost anything was better than hanging around, pretending to relax. If she spent any more time at the range or in a gym, her duffel bags might wear out. Her grandfather and father had first taught her how to relax that way, before Grandpa died of the heart attack. Hell, so much practice had even let Dad take out the three bank robbers who'd mortally wounded him.

Posada turned and tossed a cell phone at her, which she caught automatically.

"Your replacement. You've had so many death threats you need a new one."

"Thank you, sir." She could hardly argue with his reasoning. She'd be very happy not to hear any more of those sibilant whispers or, worse, a dying animal's howls. "Does this mean the investigation is over?"

"You did right when you killed Ramirez. IA has completely cleared you, of course."

Something inside her slipped free of its chain at his bluntness. She'd killed before in the line of duty, gone through counseling, and worked through the formal process to go back on duty. But somehow acceptance meant more coming from this soft-spoken Ranger with the missing little finger, lost when he'd stopped an extortionist's pipe bomb.

"If you hadn't, he'd probably have killed at least one of those campers. Even if he'd only taken hostages, we know he's killed them before."

She nodded, remembering the photos posted on the Internet as warnings. Hideous tortures, mutilations, and finally what must have seemed like merciful decapitations to their victims. Christ, she'd been sick when she'd seen them and she'd vowed El Gallinazo's bloody Mafia would one day see justice.

"Castelnuevo is transferring to Gilbert's Crossing to take over."

"It's my district!" Steve sprang to her feet. Castelnuevo couldn't do a good job there, not right away. He didn't know the people, or the problems, or the land. It would take him months to catch up. And in the meantime, El Gallinazo would play merry hell with people's lives. Plus what the other drug smugglers would do!

"Your people will be safer without you drawing El Gallinazo's fire. He's pissed as hell you wiped out his favorite enforcer." Posada's eyes were sympathetic but his features were unyielding.

"I should lead the investigation into Ramirez's presence," she argued, barely stopping herself from slamming her fist into a desk.

"You can't—and you know it. Stand down, Ranger," he said softly, his voice edged in steel.

She eased into a parade rest posture, simmering, her skin taut enough to throw sparks into her veins.

Dammit, Posada's tone was final, as if she'd never go back. Never sleep in her little house again, or dine with her few friends.

Even worse, for a century and a half, her family had been in law enforcement, all the while fighting to get back into the Rangers, a job originally granted to them because of their tracking skills but denied to later generations because they were Cherokee Indians. She'd been the one to finally be selected for the Rangers—and serve once again at the same post along the border, too! But now she'd lost it because she'd done her job? Crap.

El Gallinazo hadn't just threatened her life—he'd torn her world away from her, the bastard. The loss left her feeling even more isolated than the damn divorce had.

She forced those memories aside and focused on El Gallinazo, he of the bloody feuds and the insidious drug smuggling. He was the one who should suffer, not her.

Posada studied her, his steady gaze penetrating her surface courtesy. "Have you ever considered working in Austin?"

"At the *capitol*?" She bit her tongue before she could fully express her loathing. "Can't say I have, sir." *And please don't ask me to volunteer.*

"Dr. Parmenter's given you a clean bill of health, mental and physical, so no worries there."

She studied him warily. She'd thought any kind of work would be better than sitting around with nothing to do—but picking up after bureaucrats?

Posada didn't quite grin. "You're able to come off light duty now. The lieutenant governor has asked about you several times, Reynolds, since he saw the video of you during that convenience store shooting."

"Any state trooper would have done the same, sir," she answered stiffly.

"In a bridesmaid's dress with your hair gussied up? My wife still talks about seeing your photo."

She gritted her teeth. "Thank you, sir. I'll do my best to be a credit to the Texas Rangers."

His eyes danced. "There may be some different opportunities, though, around here."

Her heart began to beat faster, more hopefully.

"You spent a lot of time at FLETC on firearms instructor training, after you first left Gilbert's Crossing."

She shrugged, conceding the obvious. Federal Law Enforcement Training Center. Great school—but damn, its location sure deserved the nickname of Nowheresville, Georgia.

"The DPS Academy wants you to look over their firearms curriculum and make sure it's up to date with what you picked up there. Since it's summer, you may also be asked to fill in for some other firearms instructors on vacation."

"I'd be glad to, sir." Sure as hell be more interesting than being polite to politicians.

"CIS may also ask your opinion from time to time about a drug-smuggling case linked to El Gallinazo. Interested?"

"Of course, sir." She smiled, suspecting the curve was more edged than feminine.

And Ethan was a nice bit of relaxation on the side.

SEVEN

A SMALL FARM TOWN NORTHEAST OF AUSTIN, TWO NIGHTS LATER

Steve rode her Harley Sportster up to Hot Pepper Motorcycles and slowed, warily eyeing her surroundings.

The ranch road leading here had been long and blessed with only a few gentle curves. A few oak trees offered darker shadows against the early night and small houses shone like lighthouses. Fences unrolled ceaselessly at the tarmac's edge, enlivened by an occasional mile marker, popping up like a ghost. The soft, warm scents of cows and corn had blanketed the June night out there but seemed to creep only cautiously through the fence's narrow slats. Here, oil, rubber, and steel ruled.

The legendary custom bike shop had originally been a road-house, during the 1920s and 1930s. It became a truck stop during the 1950s, gaining an impressive set of facilities and fencing, only to dissolve into this backwater when the interstate highway cut through fifteen miles farther east. But it still boasted a flash-ing neon light overhead, lobbing fireworks into the sky like ar-rogant artillery shells.

The shop was an advertisement for Serrano Sam's genius. The lights were all on, shining into the night from the few win-

dows and the big open bays. All the welding equipment, boxes
of tools, rolling crates of tools, bins of parts—everything stacked
and labeled and gleaming with the joy only methodical men can
bring to their temple—all was in perfect order. Even the rubber mats on the bays' floors were smooth and straight. A half
dozen bikes, in various stages of completion from black steel to
luminous art, stood proudly on their stands. One loomed inside
the paint booth like a gold and black praying mantis from outer
space.

Outside, a pair of small, dusty Honda CRVs sat in front of
the old roadhouse's porch, across from a brand-new Cadillac.
A big pickup was parked in the shadows, rarely glimpsed under
the neon light's eternal announcement of "Hot Pepper's."

A black truck, perhaps?

There wasn't a living being in sight, not even a dog. Just as
surprisingly, she had the only working motorcycle—and a Harley Sportster had never been labeled *quiet*.

Steve frowned faintly, a whisper of air slipping over her skin.
Did she have the day of the week wrong?

But the building's lights were all on and the doors were
open.

She'd planned to come that afternoon to order a new bike,
symbol of her freedom from Fred and any plans for similarity
to Donna Reed. But she'd been delayed by having to fill in for
another instructor, suddenly called away for a sick child. She
wasn't about to wait any longer, since Hot Pepper Motorcycles
only took new orders in person once a week.

She wheeled her Harley around to the corner and parked it
pointing toward the exit, kicking the centerstand into place with
a bit too much vehemence. With luck, her instincts were only
practicing going on alert.

A tall, blond man stepped into the open bay just before she
reached it, his black leather jacket framing broad shoulders and
narrow hips.

Her heart skipped a beat. Ethan? Given his money, surely a top mechanic would come to him, not the other way around.

Her booted feet shuffled to a halt just before the shop's concrete rim.

" 'Bout time you got here, darling," he drawled.

She gaped at him, trying to form a coherent sentence. How the hell had he known she was coming? She hadn't told anyone.

He cupped the back of her head with one big hand, his other hand catching the front of her jacket, and pulled her up to him, lifting her up onto her toes.

She started to object and his mouth came down on hers—hard, fast, sinfully exciting, and bruising.

Steve choked, wished to God she could resist him, and yielded. She wrapped her arms around his waist and kissed him back just as fiercely, doing her best to ignore the pair of guns in his shoulder holster. And how quickly her skin became a shimmering conduit, carrying the heated electricity of his caresses into every hidden portion of her body.

She blinked up at him when he finally lifted his head. It would be far too embarrassing to rub her lips to see if they were swollen. She was entirely sure cream was drifting down her thighs.

"Problem?" somebody called from inside the office.

Ethan tensed but his response sounded casual. "Not at all, amigos. My bitch arrived much earlier than I expected."

"Bitch?" Steve hissed.

He frowned at her.

"Do you need help?" another asked greedily. Chairs scraped back.

Help? Her blood ran faster.

"No, I know exactly how to deal with her. Continue your poker game, *por favor.*"

"You are a lucky dog, Jerez!"

Jerez?

"But only because you won the last two hands." Furniture

rattled again. "*Bueno*, we will content ourselves with the cards while you enjoy the woman."

"What the—"

He clapped a hand across her mouth and towed her across the shop, between the immaculately arranged, thousands of dollars' worth of tools. Past the motorcycles in all their varying stages of birth. A quick glimpse of her own Harley, impossible to grab without being seen from the office, dammit.

She bit her lip and composed a list of questions, forcing them into numerical order, just as she had at the police academy.

And tried not to make each question's number match the count of her heartbeats, rising every time he rubbed his thumb over the pulse in her wrist.

They stepped into the narrow hallway and stopped in front of the women's restroom. A gaping hole marked where the doorknob had once been.

Ethan growled very softly.

Steve swallowed hard, automatically assessing the building's layout. If she guessed right, there were only three rooms where one could be assured of privacy—the office, the women's restroom, and the men's restroom. The office had once been the roadhouse's core and opened onto the front porch, facing the road. As befitted management's inner sanctum, it also connected to this hallway with the two restrooms.

But the women's restroom backed to the bike shop, while the men's room was next to the office.

Ethan spun on his heel and dragged her into the men's room, the only one with a solid seal.

Steve closed her mouth on a useless protest.

The men's room contained only a brutal minimum of equipment—sink, toilet, mirror, and trash can. It was square, though, giving it more space than expected, and the walls were dazzlingly white, behind photos of Texas landmarks.

He slammed the door shut, backed her against it, and kissed

her lips until she was dazed with lust, her fingers threaded into his hair, and her nipples rasping against her jacket's modern fibers. His hands spanned her waist, kneading her hips, heating her blood, reminding her of past delights and future potential.

He teased her earlobe with his teeth, nipping and rousing her blood.

She moaned, locking her knees against the urge to rub herself over his thigh. "Who are they?" she gasped.

"Two of Garcia Herrera's best men," Ethan answered, equally softly.

The top drug smuggler in Central Texas?

Steve's mouth fell open and Ethan promptly teased her tongue with his.

How many federal and state warrants were *currently* outstanding against Garcia Herrera? How could she tell Austin he was coming here? But if their audience even suspected a Texas Ranger was on the other side of that thin piece of particleboard, they'd kill her and Ethan, too, for helping her.

"Who do they think you are?" she whispered, rubbing her cheek against his beard stubble.

"A potential recruit." Ethan pushed her T-shirt up and fondled her breast, ignoring her shoulder holster.

"Ahh . . . Won't they be surprised you brought a woman?"

He chuckled. "No, they know me well enough to be more surprised I didn't bring a man to play with."

Didn't bring a *man* to play with?

He rubbed his thumb over her nipple, quickly finding all her hidden turn-ons.

She moaned, involuntarily losing a grip on her logic. Damn, but he knew exactly how to turn her on.

"Louder," he whispered, and squeezed her ass.

She groaned in ecstasy and her head fell back. Oh, how she loved that move of his. "Oh yeah, darling."

He pressed her up against the wall and made love to her. He

kissed her breasts, licking and nibbling, kneading and fondling. He opened her jeans, shamelessly encouraging her to writhe and fuck herself on his hand. She caught his head to her when he bit her neck, desperate for how the taste of blood would intensify both their pleasure and leave no lasting marks behind.

Hunger ran dark and aching through her veins, lancing deeper into her bones than she'd ever known before. Her clit swelled into a fuse for her lust, marking the door to her fiery, wet core. She yielded herself to the inferno building inside her, knowing it was her only camouflage—and his gift.

"Bend over the sink, darling," he ordered hoarsely. "I want to ride you hard until I hear you scream."

She obeyed immediately, too needy to do anything but agree. The cool air on the backs of her knees when he yanked her jeans down made her hesitate for a moment. But his eyes were green as emeralds, his face taut with lust looming over her shoulder in the mirror.

Oh yeah.

His hot tongue dived into her from behind and she slammed into her first climax, gripping the jutting porcelain like a life preserver, pleasure washing over and through her. She shrieked something wordless.

Before sanity could return, he spread her hips wider, his hands oddly gentle.

She moaned, aftershocks still vibrating through her.

His cock slid into her, the broad head lifting her up onto her toes. She tightened herself around him, embracing him. She was wonderfully tight this way, making it easy to savor every distinctive shape and twist of his perfect cock.

She moaned again and braced herself against the sink, using all the shoulder and arm muscles she'd built in the gym to steady herself, planting her booted feet firmly.

He started to fuck her, long and hard, just the way she liked it. Shattering curtains of agonizing joy ripped through her again and again. And still Ethan rode her, delaying his own fulfillment and promising her more, until finally the tip of his thumb slipped inside her ass.

Caught by that most intimate caress, Steve bucked hard, squeezing his cock and driving herself down on him. She came screaming, delight pummeling her body like a leap over Niagara Falls.

Ethan growled in triumph and climaxed, filling her cunt with his seed and heat.

She collapsed smiling, unconsciousness blurring her mind.

Ethan settled Steve on the floor, hoping she'd stay asleep. Christ, his heart had nearly stopped when he'd seen her ride up. What the hell had happened to the Rangers' informants, if they didn't know Hot Peppers was one of the favorite meeting places for drug Mafiosi? At least Devol shouldn't be anywhere around, God willing.

He began to dress as quietly as possible.

"D'you think they're finished in there?" a man next door asked, his zipper's closing sounding like a machine gun.

"Must be. Good show." Bastards must have jacked off while they listened.

They chuckled companionably and he could hear liquor being poured.

Ethan bared his fangs, fighting back the urge to simply grab his guns and slaughter the brutes now. God knows he'd occasionally fucked to gain an advantage before. But they'd heard *Steve*'s pleasure and for that, they would die before they could tell anyone else.

"Boss will be here soon. Can we use the warehouse outside San Leandro for the drop?" one of them asked, the sounds of shuffling cards coming loud and clear to Ethan's vampiro hearing.

"The refrigerated one? No. We've already loaned it to El Gallinazo for some of his friends."

Ethan cocked his head, considering. His fingers caressed his knife. Could El Gallinazo be working with Beau and Devol, Madame Celeste's two favorite killers? El Gallinazo represented a Mexican patrón, so those heathens could approach him openly. Plus, El Gallinazo had extensive smuggling connections in Texas. A refrigerated warehouse would be perfect for a vampiro to hide in, given its tight seals to hold scents in.

Yes, the warehouse and drug lord were both definitely worth checking out.

Ethan smiled, fangs pricking his jaw, and double-checked his Colts. Plenty of ammunition, too, to dispatch Garcia Herrera before he could discover Steve.

Good Lord, she was beautiful after lovemaking, when her eyes turned gentle and her neck had a swan's grace instead of being purely a support for that stubborn chin.

He'd kill Fred, too, of course, once he had a chance to find the jerk. Bastard deserved a slow, painful death for having destroyed her bright faith in the future.

As if summoned, she mumbled something and stretched, blinking. She studied him, proud and strong as always. Of course, he loved her like this, too—clever and sturdy enough to outwit a hurricane.

But damn, how the hell could he make her stay here where she'd be safe? Even vampiro mind control tricks took time to break through her stubbornness, and he wasn't about to destroy their relationship by forcing her to stay here. Maybe if they moved fast enough, he could get her to his truck before anybody noticed she was gone.

His men were out there, keeping watch from a distance. But they wouldn't move without a signal from him, something he'd be damn wary of doing now, lest he endanger Steve.

"Come on, let's try to get you out of here," he whispered.

She nodded silently, her thoughts blaring like a police radio. Call in the law right away and arrest Garcia Herrera whenever he showed up. Oh yeah, like that had worked well before.

She was dressed within a minute and he guided her out of the restroom and down the hallway, moving as smoothly as if they were a trained SWAT team. Cónyuges flowed more gracefully together, not that he and Steve had any chance of achieving union. It took decades for two people to gain enough trust that they'd instinctively drop every barrier between themselves.

A mechanical rumble shook the night and gravel splattered the fence posts. An enormous Mercedes G55 drove out of the darkness and pulled to a halt in the middle of the compound, gleaming like a silver cobra. Matching crystal and silver beads swung gently from the rearview mirror, casting shards of light into the uncaring black distance. Garcia Herrera's signature vehicle, an enormously expensive SUV.

Its headlights settled on Ethan and Steve, the neon sign's gold and red pulsing over the darkness.

Shit. Ice washed through Ethan's bones and retreated, ready to spur him into action. His heart settled into a heavy, steady beat, even as his body stilled, looking for an opening.

Garcia Herrera stepped out, escorted by two deadly-looking bodyguards in black. He was as short and squat as a Gila monster—and as gaudy and poisonous. The office door opened, and Ethan's two acquaintances tumbled out. They instantly and enthusiastically greeted their master.

He silenced his underlings with a single raised finger, his eyes on Steve, and sauntered forward.

A growl rose in Ethan's throat but he silenced it, rapidly summing up potential targets.

"*Hola*, amigo!" Garcia Herrera purred. "Welcome to my family and thank you for the woman. You did not have to bribe me, of course—but I thank you for the Texas Ranger. I liked her better in the satin dress with flowers in her hair but that can be changed."

He reached for Steve, rings glittering on his fingers.

"Garcia Herrera, you're under arrest!" Steve snapped. If

Ethan hadn't been so pissed at her for moving too soon, he'd have admired her quick draw. She'd actually caught two of Garcia Herrera's bodyguards off guard—but there were still two more, the ones going for their submachine guns.

Ethan's guns came into his hands before he thought, as they'd always answered his instincts. Fire and death blazed across the compound in a staccato roar, jerking the bodyguards into death, felling one beside the Mercedes and the other next to Garcia Herrera. Steve killed her two, sending them tumbling into the rosebushes by the front porch. Blood splattered the asphalt and the flowers, smearing the old porch and the famous criminal.

Garcia Herrera had the cold-blooded nerve to laugh, a small pistol clutched efficiently in his hand. "Do you mean to kill me, too, Ranger?"

Steve's finger tightened on the trigger before easing off. "I'm taking you in. You're going to answer to the law."

Ethan rolled his eyes and mentally counted the number of rounds he still had available for a fight. Why did cops always invoke "the law" as the answer to everything?

"Three times I've faced your courts and walked out free." Garcia Herrera snapped his fingers.

"Not this time." She glared back at him.

"No court has ever held me. You're a fool to think one can. Worse than that, you're disturbing my business—which can be very bad for your health, Ranger."

Ethan's stomach dived out of the sky. His eyes narrowed, centering his world on a single man. The neon sign threw off a fresh array of sparks.

"You won't have a chance." Her voice didn't waver.

"If I go to jail, you had best say your prayers."

Ethan killed him, dropping him with a single bullet to the head. He didn't know how good a shot the fellow was and he didn't care. Nobody who threatened Stephanie could be allowed to live an extra minute.

Otherwise, he'd have accomplished his mission later, after he'd escorted her to someplace safe.

Steve jolted and spun to stare at him incredulously. "How could you murder him, Ethan? You didn't have to shoot him."

"He was going to have you assassinated."

"He was going to try." She shrugged impatiently. "Even so, what does that matter compared to putting him behind bars?"

"You'd never have gotten a conviction, Steve. You know that, if you'd just think about it."

Her jaw set stubbornly. "We'd have done it."

"He'd have the best lawyers and the best bribes. He'd have gotten out on bail, made witnesses disappear—you name it, he'd have done it. He's been hauled up in court three times before—and walked away." Christ, she was pissed. But he had to do it. It was the only way to protect Texas from a murdering, thieving thug like Garcia Herrera—and to save Steve's life. He hunted for a gentler phrase. "Three strikes and you're out, Steve. Time to let somebody else step up to the plate."

"But that doesn't give you the right to shoot him!"

"He was a demon who tormented Texas. How many people had he ordered killed or kidnapped? How much drugs had he brought in?"

"You murdered him." She started to aim her Sig at him and he held up his hand, reinforcing his will with an emphatic mental command. *Stop.*

"Don't shoot me, Steve." *Crap, I hope this works quickly for once. I don't want to hurt her.*

"I'm bringing you in for murder." Her pistol wavered, her stubborn mind fighting him, before her arm slowly sank to her side.

Thank you, Lord.

Her chin set mulishly.

Dammit, she was an officer of the law, too. Why didn't she understand?

"Don't be a damn fool. You're not arresting me ever, even if I executed him—and saved your life." *Please, God, let her at least bow to superior force.*

"I don't believe we have anything further to say to each other." Her face was filled with great dark eyes, ice and shadows in their depths.

He bowed formally, gritting his teeth. Dammit, if she walked out on him now, would she ever speak to him again?

She made a violent gesture and turned away.

Steve yanked hard on the last half hitch, making the brown suede bundle bulge far beyond the narrow ropes binding it. A quick whack of her knife sliced through the twisted nylon, ending any objections to its hard usage.

Pity she couldn't castrate Ethan the same way.

She remembered how she'd shoved her hips back against him, begged so hard for him that her throat burned, ached to feel his cock until her cunt clamped down on him like he was the meaning of life itself!

Yet a few moments later, he'd coolly killed a man she'd arrested and had the nerve to call it an execution. What did he think he was, the representative of an older, more feral code of law?

Like hell!

No sense of honor, nor of justice.

She tossed the leather onto her shoulder and shoved her way out the door, barely pausing to pick up her purse and keys.

The jacket, chaps, and boots, which Ethan said marked her as his woman, were going to hell. She'd found a commercial waste incinerator, which would reduce them to flakes of ash.

And she'd forget all about how she'd thought he was the only man she could trust outside the office.

Even the lowest worm didn't deserve a death like the one Ethan had just dealt.

ACAPULCO, THE SAME NIGHT

Georges Devol folded his fingers around his brandy snifter, keeping his expression politely attentive. Much as he hated to admit it, even tequila would have tasted better than this overpriced Californian nonsense.

And a dying prosaica would undoubtedly sound more interesting than this greedy fool's demands for more money. Her blood and fear would definitely taste better than the brandy or the tequila.

A warm tropical breeze crept through the palm fronds and bougainvillea, rich with salt air. The heavy chandelier overhead swayed gently, its flickering light and heat bringing to life their leather furniture's soft scents.

Georges smiled slowly and swirled the golden liqueur, allowing himself to anticipate his future reward. Soon, he could claim one of the foolish American tourists and teach her the true meaning of terror.

Just as soon as he finished closing this deal for *cher madame*.

El Gallinazo eyed him wearily and steepled his fingers. Where did he buy his wardrobe—Hollywood? "Two million dollars," he pronounced.

Georges raised an eyebrow at him. Who the hell did he think he was dealing with, a cachorro? That opening demand was so absurdly high as to be hardly worth responding to.

"Per man," the greedy pig added.

A split second later, Georges's fist was wrapped in the fool's collar and the idiot's face was turning an unbecoming shade of red.

A bodyguard took a hasty step forward from the patio's other end and found himself facing the business end of Georges's Beretta. He held up his empty hands and retreated, eyes constantly reevaluating the situation. A very smart man and one worth recruiting.

"One million—total," Georges corrected El Gallinazo very gently.

His captive made a series of noises which didn't amount to words.

Georges shook him. Hard. Mexico had obviously gone far too long without any competent patrones, if prosaicos had been allowed to grow this stupid.

El Gallinazo's head snapped back and forth, his eyes crossing like a child's doll, before his eyelids veiled them.

Georges waited patiently for the prosaico to speak. If he didn't, his corpse would become an excellent incentive for his successor's cooperation.

Black eyes opened, filled with hate.

"Agree?" Georges asked, totally unmoved by the other's opinion.

"Yes," the fool rasped and was dropped back into his seat.

Georges emptied his snifter into the shrubbery and sauntered over to the bar, ignoring the hoarse gasps and chokes behind him. As expected, the tequila collection was excellent, if small, and he returned with a splendid example.

"One million *total* for transporting an unlimited number of my men into Texas," Georges mused, sniffing the new golden liquid. *Eh bien*, he should have chosen his own drink all along.

"The Texans will find and kill you." El Gallinazo coughed.

Georges was too pleased with his easy victory to take offense. "I have my own route through Texas. All you have to do is take me across the Rio Grande."

Black eyes narrowed into a quick reassessment and Georges concealed his smile.

But if you try to follow my path, fool, watch out for snakes and scorpions.

EIGHT

Steve grabbed for her fraying temper and tugged it back under control. She'd had to run to catch Posada in the training academy's parking lot, after spotting him from her office window, and the noontime heat wasn't helping her mood.

She set her duffel bag down on the scorching asphalt with exaggerated caution, determined to at least keep her beloved M4 carbine safe. She held on to the sealed pouch with the computer tapes, of course. She'd promised accounting she'd drop them off at a high-security off-site data-storage facility. Some of the vaults there were larger than she was.

"What do you mean, you're closing the investigation? I told you I saw a murder committed." Her drawl was getting thicker, dammit. But who cared about those trifles now?

"Reynolds." Posada turned to face her, propping one foot on his truck's running board. He spread his hands, his eyes hidden behind his sunglasses. "You saw a half dozen criminals fight. Afterward, only one man was still alive."

"Sir, you're skipping several important events."

"How much do you really expect me to do, Reynolds?" He blew out a breath. "Garcia Herrera was pure filth, who'd sold more children into more hell than I care to imagine. When his blood and brains were ID'd, do you know what the DA did?"

She stiffened. "No, sir."

"He went to church and thanked God. Then he started making phone calls to victims so they could do the same. There are many candles being lit tonight across Texas and Oklahoma."

She fought against surging toward him. A dusty black pickup truck reminded her of the real killer's getaway vehicle.

"It doesn't matter who was murdered, only that murder was done." Her stomach clenched, as if it had its own ability to raise objections.

Posada yanked off his sunglasses and stared at her, the crow's-feet at his eyes deepening into bitter grooves. "Yeah, that's right, Reynolds—and pigs fly every Halloween. You tell me you haven't fantasized about shooting brutes like him who needed killing, but somehow walked away laughing from the courtroom."

Honesty wouldn't let her say no.

"He was executed in cold blood." And she'd never forget the man who'd done it. The man she'd opened her bedroom door to for fifteen years, off and on.

"So what? It worked. Frankly, I don't have the resources to chase down this unknown criminal, especially when you can't give me a name or an address." He raised an eyebrow at her, challenging her to complete her statement.

She opened her mouth—and an unseen hand closed around her throat, throttling her. Damn Ethan!

She forced the thought away, together with any possibility of answering Posada's question. Not this time, not ever. Sweat trickled down her spine, settling into her skin along with the cold awareness she stood alone.

She coughed, choked, and wheezed until she recovered, waving off Posada's offer of help. She knew perfectly well what the problem was: If she tried to talk about Ethan, she'd die, the bastard. She could only talk about their liaison once—and she'd wasted that on a bachelorette party. Everyone there had been so drunk, they'd written off her tale as a wild fantasy.

"Are you sure you're okay now?" Posada asked again, his voice very gentle.

"Perfectly." She slipped her own sunglasses on, hiding her expression, and kept her voice in the same polite register she used with judges.

"Good. The bike shop staff have been cleared."

She spun around to stare at him. She'd never suggested they were involved.

"They were at a *quinceañera* for the chief welder's daughter. Given the number of people at that party, they've all got solid alibis."

Thank God. If they'd been considered suspects because she couldn't name Ethan, she'd have dragged his worthless ass in personally—once she found him.

"Maybe we can do lunch the next time I'm up here"—now that was a polite fiction, given the typically brutal Texas Ranger schedule—"but I've got to get back to San Antonio."

"Anything nastier than usual?" she asked, to cover her true thoughts—how the heck could one bring a *vampiro* to justice?

"Not particularly. We've been stretched a little thin the last couple of days, since we've had to work a few crime scenes longer than usual." He tossed his briefcase onto his truck's seat, obviously ready to close the conversation.

She'd need to find Ethan's address. Maybe that old business card of his would help, the one with his phone number.

"Long hours at crime scenes?" She could sympathize. She'd done that before—and she'd probably be spending some serious quality time with computers to track down Ethan. She retrieved her duffel, easily compensating for the guns' and ammo's weight.

"The MEs have been busy, digging deep for some women's death certificates. We had a couple of suicides but they had to track down the pollen-caused respiratory problems."

She blinked. Pollen? This early in the year in San Antonio?

Since they didn't have many fancy flowering trees like Northern-
ers, they normally didn't have any allergy problems until late
summer.

"We've been having a lot of wet weather, y'know, making it
worse than usual for ragweed. The ladies had their necks arched
and mouths hanging open from trying to breathe."

Yeah, that sounded like a wicked hay fever attack. But
bad enough to kill healthy young people? Well, if the doctors
said so.

Posada swung himself into his truck and held out his hand.

She shook it, recognizing dismissal—and the opportunity to
bring a murderer to justice on her own.

"Keep in touch, Reynolds."

She lifted a hand in farewell, wiggling her fingers. She had a
lot of work to get done before she could sleep that night.

Ethan stood at attention with Jean-Marie, Luis, Gray Wolf, and
Caleb in Don Rafael's office, fists clenched and cursing himself
over how close the afternoon's attack had come. All the days
he'd spent worrying about how to regain Steve, what weapons he could wield against Devol, where he could find allies—
everything had led to this.

Four bodies had been placed in ambulances, covered in sweat
and vomit, their faces hidden by oxygen masks, guarded by
hard-edged medics who spoke to no one else. A woman and her
three young children just like his sister Camille and her family,
who'd been destroyed during the Civil War. Correction—they'd
met their deaths because of his failure, just like today.

His preoccupation had allowed Beau to slice through their
defenses and come within five miles of Compostela. How that
legendary assassin must have been laughing at them when he
chose to attack the Perez family instead! He'd proved his own

superiority by making Ethan and his mesnaderos look like incompetent fools.

Ethan's stomach roiled again, sour with bile and dust from old graves.

The heavy shutters' darkness made the spotlight on Don Rafael's knightly sword all the more significant and hard to live up to. A session under Don Rafael's steel-tipped whip would have been easier than the lash of his tongue.

"It does not matter what you thought, Ethan, or you, Gray Wolf," Don Rafael continued, his dark eyes stabbing into their souls. "The enemy penetrated into the heart of my lands, something you said was impossible. He injured my people—innocent people—solely because of their connection to me."

Ethan had failed his master, the man who knew all his sins and had still brought him into his house. Ethan hadn't failed Don Rafael this badly since before he'd entered El Patrón's service the first time, when he'd stolen Don Rafael's horses and killed one of them in the process.

Every bone in his body suddenly turned to pure ice, chilling him from the soul outward. Christ, what a memory to stir up now. He couldn't afford to lose his creador's good opinion, lest he lose the path to his own soul.

"My humblest apologies, patrón." He prostrated himself before his master, something he hadn't done in decades. "It will not happen again."

"*Bien,*" Don Rafael all but snarled, gesturing him up.

Ethan climbed back onto his feet. He'd have to pay a very personal price, of course, to obtain forgiveness. It would not be pleasant but it would be welcomed.

"And you, Jean-Marie, your networks should have done better than this."

"*Mille pardons, patrón.*"

Jean-Marie, of course, could always be counted on for a smooth apology, even under the worst tongue-lashing. There was something to be said for what had apparently been a damn cold childhood.

Their master's frigid gaze passed over Ethan again, and he remained still, not about to twitch even to straighten his clothes. With Don Rafael in this mood, he didn't want to offer something small for him to take offense at.

"Take the men away from guarding me and set them to hunting these devils."

What the hell was he thinking of? Didn't he realize what would happen to Texas if he died?

Everyone burst into objections.

"Throwing more men into hunting for Beau will only cloud the waters. Mesnaderos are warriors, not spies," Jean-Marie stormed, words tumbling over each other.

"We already have plenty of men hunting for them," Gray Wolf argued, his voice deepening in a rare sign of imminent rage. "To add more men means taking away from—"

"That's a trap! It's exactly what Madame Celeste wants us to do," Ethan yelled, discarding any hope of being a quiet, invisible servant.

"Risking yourself like that is foolish, Don Rafael," Luis snarled, directly disagreeing with Rafael for once. "It won't help the prosaicos or the esfera if they lose you."

Their language filled up with curses.

"*¡Sí!*" Rafael roared.

They snarled and growled but ultimately fell reluctantly silent under the weight of his glare.

Ethan seethed, unable to argue. His creador could—and would—read any of his thoughts when he was this angry. Even so, Ethan wouldn't lie and pretend to approve.

"We must stop them, no matter what," dictated their master, forcing them to meet his eyes one by one. "The penalty for failure is death, *mis* hijos. You do not like my punishments—but you will hate those doled out by the enemy more."

Despite himself, Ethan flinched before throwing his shoulders proudly back. Don Rafael's punishments were creative beyond belief—and hell on earth. But he'd rather endure years of them than see his master dead.

A boot heel struck wood floor, instead of carpet, in the great room just outside. The assembly fell into shocked silence at its closeness and lighter tread.

A woman?

Ethan sniffed again, sorting through a heavy layer of foul odors until he recognized her. He flung an astounded glance at his master, who'd never previously brought a lover of either gender to Compostela.

Don Rafael closed his eyes for a moment, his mouth softening slightly, before he turned to face the door.

"*Doctora* O'Malley?" He issued the summons in his most formal and gracious tone. "Please come in."

Ethan gritted his teeth, then moved to a better vantage point, the better to watch his fellows. They hadn't believed his description of the lady.

"*Doctora.*" Don Rafael started to take command as usual.

Still dusty and sweaty, reeking of horse and deathly ill dogs, a tall, red-haired woman tossed her Stetson onto the hat rack, strode past everyone else without a second glance, and wrapped her arms around him.

Don Rafael choked with laughter and hugged Grania close, his body promptly curving into a protective, loving embrace around his lover.

His inner council gawked like children but Ethan's lips curled in a smile's travesty. He'd won his bet with Caleb about how strong Don Rafael's obsession was, but life would have been simpler if he hadn't. Madame Celeste would enjoy knowing where her enemy's emotional levers were and Texas couldn't afford any weaknesses right now. A moment's inattention by Don Rafael could prove fatal to all of them, just like the price for Ethan's own daydreams.

He should give up Steve or at least stop thinking about her until the war was over. But if her marriage hadn't kept her out of his mind, then nothing this side of hell would.

He just had to be more efficient. Somehow. While always putting Don Rafael and Texas first, of course.

"Glad you could have lunch with me, Dan. The food here is even better than you promised." Steve studied her old friend over her marinated chicken, still hot and crispy from the tandoori oven.

The midday glare picked out all his old wrinkles, plus a dozen new ones. At least the restaurant patio's sunny corner offered them the privacy to chat, if he chose to, especially this late in the lunch hour. The hauntingly sweet and complex smell of chai tea hung in the air like an invitation to share secrets.

Dan Schilling grunted, his mouth full of highly spiced lamb. He'd had a long, largely unintelligible conversation with the Indian restaurant's manager before he'd ordered their meals. Food was his passion—or rather, restaurant food was. He knew every establishment in Austin—every chef on every shift, every dish on every menu. Given the hours he worked as a deputy medical examiner, he didn't get to eat at home very often, let alone shop or cook. So he collected other people's efforts the way some folks collected jewels.

And his friends—the other denizens of long shifts—turned to him for a respite from brutal reality. He could always be counted on for a recommendation on where to find the best food, plus good beer or wine if served in the same establishment. Most of his pals didn't even grouse about how his waistline stayed narrow, while theirs kept expanding.

Dan tore off a piece of garlic naan and used the flatbread to sop up some gravy, his eyes measuring the patio's dwindling population. A mother and daughter left, their T-shirts brilliant against the ancient pecan trees.

"You were present when the Rogers girl was found, right?"

Steve frowned. What the hell? "Up in San Leandro?"

"The Olympic swimmer." He tore off another piece of bread, watching her very closely.

Ice trailed over her skin. "I saw the scene being processed. But I didn't arrive until twenty or thirty minutes after she'd been found. Are you the medical examiner responsible?"

He nodded, lines deepening at the corners of his mouth. He was usually much better at laughing than frowning.

She sipped her iced tea. "You have my statement," she added, underlining the obvious.

He nodded again, his eyes searching her face. "Did you see anything you didn't put into it?"

Dan was very, very good, certainly the best in the county and probably in Central Texas. Travis County handled over fifteen hundred investigations a year for itself and surrounding counties. They were highly professional and had the track record to prove it.

So why on earth was he watching her as if her few minutes of eyeballing the alley outside an ice cream parlor could save him considerable aggravation?

"The only unusual thing I noticed was her frightened expression," Steve commented slowly, carefully selecting every word. "Judging by the body's position when I saw it, she'd had her back to the oncoming storm. Plus, she'd had ready access to shelter. I'm not aware of any good reason for such alarm."

"No, nor is anyone else."

Shit.

Dan pushed rice around his plate. Steve shifted, came up against her Sig Sauer's hard bulk in her purse, and thumped back down in her chair. At least it was daylight and Ethan couldn't possibly see her being clumsy. He'd have given her a hell of a lecture, followed by some damn creative punishments—the bastard.

"We don't have a cause of death for her," Dan muttered, his voice little more than a whisper. "Not since we basically ruled out arrhythmia."

Steve's eyebrows flew up. "Where her heartbeat would go wild and kill her?"

"Yup." A muscle throbbed in his jaw. "She'd just had a complete checkout by the Olympic team doctor, up in Colorado Springs. Worse, since she'd been targeted as a potential Olympian for more than three years—"

"They have lots of data."

"Tons. All the other obvious causes of natural death are no-gos. Suicide doesn't look likely. No signs of a struggle or injuries. No head trauma, sexual assault, suspicious drugs. At least not according to Olympic quality tests."

"They sent some of their people down, didn't they?"

"Who are you kidding? Of course they did." Dan snorted and knocked back the last of his iced tea before refilling it from the sweating glass carafe. "Hell, I don't blame them—their reputation's on the line, too. We've taken tissue samples of everything possible and sent out for a full toxicology scan."

"Who else was there?"

"*Nobody.*" The single word hung in the air.

"Nobody?" Steve tilted her head, something shimmering just out of reach behind her eyes.

"No trace evidence of anyone else's presence was found at the scene or on her body," Dan stated flatly, and smacked his hands together. "I've told myself a thousand times the rain must have washed any evidence away. Then I remember there are no injuries, no bruises—nothing!—on the body or nearby."

"Only a frightened girl." Cop's instinct stirred deep in her gut.

"Who collapsed during a thunderstorm. Real bad thunderstorm, so maybe she was just scared." Dan's lips compressed, as if he didn't want to express his own doubts.

"Maybe." She'd have to put in some more range time when she returned to the academy. Having a gun in her hand always made her feel more settled. "I'm sure toxicology will come up with something."

He nodded, shredding flatbread as if it were theories.

Silence fell between them and was allowed to linger.

"I'd better head back to the office now." Dan signaled the waiter. "The Old Man has called a department meeting to discuss vacation schedules. Rumor says nobody's getting any unless you've already scheduled it."

"That won't make him popular," Steve remarked, and pushed her chair back.

"Not much else he can do. We've been getting more cases than usual from other counties and the ME insists we solve them all."

More cases than usual? San Antonio had been having problems, too.

"Respiratory illnesses?" she asked, trying to sound casual.

"Who knows?" He shook his head, counting out bills from his wallet. "Some respiratory, some heart problems, some just plain unexplained. A few more suicides than usual, but—"

Part of her brain was acting automatically, sorting deaths into categories. Deaths, as in *multiple*. Every other gray cell was hoping Dan would say he'd been making a joke. She nodded and wet her lips, wishing her skin felt warm enough to need suntan lotion.

"Yeah. We've got to explain the other ones, especially since they're all young women."

She stared at him, hearing Posada's words again. Young women were dying in San Antonio, a hundred miles south, supposedly from pollen.

Maybe it was just coincidence.

A shadow flickered just beyond her eyes, where neither trees nor shadow stood. Her mouth tightened. An instant later, she began to consciously relax her muscles. She'd been a cop too long to go against her instincts—she'd have to start asking around. Best to start at the academy, where there were students from all over Texas. That should give her enough of the latest gossip to narrow down where the problems really were.

But for the first time in days, she almost wished she could talk something over with Ethan.

"At least we've got the new DNA profiling machinery now and the GC mass spectrometer. They're so fast, they've really freed up our investigators."

"Sounds expensive if they've helped your workload that much," Steve commented, slipping her purse onto her shoulder. She automatically wiggled slightly, settling her gun next to her ribs where she could find it easily through the leather.

"Five million dollars' worth of high tech for the lot." Dan smiled, looking almost happy for the first time.

"Five million? From *our* legislature?" She almost stumbled.

"Oh, hell no!" He looked around to make sure nobody else was near them. Even then, he leaned toward her before drawing a serpentine figure in the air, shielding it with his body from prying eyes.

Steve stared at him. Her mouth opened and shut before she managed to form two words—*Santiago Trust*?

He gave a short nod and moved away.

The hair on the back of Steve's neck stood up.

Dan's smile broadened and he began to whistle.

According to Ethan's business card, he was the vice president of security for the Santiago Trust. Why the hell would his employer donate high-quality equipment to the state crime lab, especially if they were half as arrogant and secretive as rumor said? Machinery that would make it very, very easy to catch them or their underlings?

To make themselves look virtuous? Impossible; it had to be genuinely fantastic stuff in order to impress Dan.

Not that the gift mattered. Ethan was a murderer; she'd get justice for that killing—someday, somehow.

She needed to forget about that and focus on something she could accomplish now. She'd start asking about those young women's deaths right away. She had to find out if there was a good explanation or anybody else investigating them as homicides before she could relax.

And she'd shop for some new porn, too. Celibacy was not helpful when it left room for wet dreams of an SOB like Ethan.

CANCUN, THAT NIGHT

"Yoshi." Georges cuffed the Japanese vampiro, splitting his lip and drawing blood. "Did you go shopping in Mexico City— against my orders?"

"Fuck you!" The smaller man's tongue darted out to taste a single crimson drop. The dying moon barely lit the beach outside this small Cancun resort hotel.

"Clothes or women?" Georges demanded, lifting his hand for another blow.

Fangs flashed in defiance and Georges lifted his hand for another blow.

"Clothes," Yoshi sneered an instant later, proving he wasn't a complete fool.

"*Oui?*" Georges considered the other's attire, testing his answer's truth. Yoshi the Fair was as well dressed—and as pretty— as his name. Also an incredibly creative killer, a good lay—and unfortunately, all too easily bored.

"And I killed a couple of women, too—practicing for when we really start fucking Texas."

Merde. Well, he had to admit the boy was blunt—and a true member of the bandolerismo. As lawless as they came and always out for himself. At least there truly was enough land in Texas to give each of them an esfera, just as Georges had promised.

"But I came back, didn't I? Just like you ordered." Yoshi flipped his knife end over end, steel briefly catching the light. He shot Georges a quick glance, not meeting his eyes. "How much longer am I supposed to stay here?"

His tongue tasted his lip again.

"You must convince me you can be completely trusted." Georges said sternly, studying the slow glide of that telltale tongue. "At least tonight."

"Of course! You know I'd do anything . . ." He stopped, biting his lip. Anger flashed across his face for a moment.

Georges concealed his smile. Ah, the many uses of vampiro blood! Especially when one vampiro was decades older than the other. Yoshi was probably remembering the last time he'd crawled for a taste of Georges's blood, his eyes hot with lust.

Georges pinched the younger man's earlobe, twisting and squeezing it.

Yoshi flushed but leaned into the rough caress.

Georges rewarded him by running his thumb over the younger man's mouth, teasing him with vampiro sweat's mild aphrodisiac.

Yoshi hissed softly.

"And tomorrow there will be more than enough excitement when you begin scouting the Texas commanderies," Georges crooned, his teeth scraping the little killer's ear. A couple of quick flicks with his fingers opened the young dandy's new trousers.

Madame Celeste needed to know where the Texas warriors were, their fortresses, their supplies, their strengths, and their weaknesses. She'd grown a great deal since he'd met her, from the girl who always moved in a man's shadow to the strong woman who took her own counsel. *Mon dieu*, the fools who'd thought money would turn him against her!

"Spy? That's impossible! Not in Texas." The other's Adam's apple bobbed frantically, probably once for every nasty rumor he'd heard of Templeton.

"But you'll enjoy doing it for me, won't you? Because I'll certainly enjoy killing you, if you won't," Georges purred—and brutally twisted his fingers around Yoshi's cock.

Yoshi's hips jolted forward. "You bastard!" he yelped.

Georges laughed and squeezed the hardening shaft. Tonight's meal would be delicious, flavored with both terror and sexual excitement.

NINE

The night was velvety black, as if even the moon didn't want to watch. A few stars glimmered above the mountains' crests but failed to gild the saguaros' spines. Water lapped against the sandy shores, muffled by a few plants and occasional small rocks.

A half dozen Toyota Land Cruisers stood poised on the Mexican side, surrounded by narrow-eyed men, their guns flagrantly on display. A single dirt road stretched before them, running clean and clear deep into Texas through the ancient notch between the mountains.

A scanner spewed out a continuous string of polite chatter, often causing involuntary flinches among its listeners but never catching their full attention.

Their master paced back and forth, continuously scanning the mountains, river, and sky. The guards watched him, never their vehicles.

Suddenly he threw back his head and laughed, pointing at the sky. A single small light was flying very low away from them and a chorus of relieved laughter echoed his sentiments.

He twirled his hand and pointed down the road. Seconds

later, only plumes of dust and engine exhaust marked where they'd been.

Silvery apparitions shimmered into being along the mountain's flank—an Apache, a pair of Comanches, and a white man with a star in a wheel on his chest. They turned to watch the invaders pass, narrowing their eyes in disgust at the stench.

Blood will be spilled to erase this invasion, the Apache said flatly.

Someone must be warned, muttered one of the Comanches. *But how?*

The white man grunted. *There may be somebody we can talk to.*

AUSTIN, THAT NIGHT

Ethan slammed his pickup into park and swung its door open. An instant later, he was watching Steve's darkened apartment, her door barely visible beyond the parked cars in the complex's central courtyard.

Just checking it out to make sure everything was safe, of course. Yeah, right—and how many times had he told himself that before?

No robberies in the middle-class neighborhood she'd chosen and not much excitement, either. Was she hoping to find another Fred to settle down with?

Crap.

He had to make her understand what drove him or at least stop fighting it. But how could he get her to talk? He'd lost count of how many times she'd hung up on him.

Instead, he was stuck trying to meet her face-to-face. The goddamn war made finding time for that a near impossibility—especially since she worked days and the slightest touch of sunlight could kill him.

He scanned the house one more time, hoping for a single lamp to be lit and remembering how she'd demanded his driver's license the first time they'd met, silhouetted against her patrol car's headlights. Lithe and still very much a woman, especially with the Colt hanging from her belt.

No sign of her tonight. He was still tied to her in the darkness, whether she knew it or not.

He kicked the pavement, slamming pebbles against the curb, and spat a vicious string of curses into the air.

His phone vibrated against his hip, demanding his attention. "Templeton."

"Doctor O'Malley must attend a meeting in Austin today and Don Rafael is unhappy with the proposed security," Rough Bear announced.

Ethan blew out a breath before answering. "On my way."

He cast a last glance at her bedroom window and turned away, his lips compressed.

He never saw the ghost watching him, slouch hat pulled down and a star in a wheel on his breast.

AUSTIN, THE NEXT EVENING

The door's latch scraped against the lock, bringing Ethan to full alert. Emilio Alvarez, Luis's godson, slipped all too smoothly out of the grimy conference room into the narrow hall. The ceiling lamp's harsh glare passed over him, unfiltered by any screen.

Ethan's eyes narrowed and he reassessed the young SEAL more carefully.

Emilio shared his godfather's dark eyes, olive skin, and strong, lithe body. But his eyes sparkled with life now, surprising in a man who'd guarded his master's beloved for the past fourteen hours. He moved gracefully, as though he'd slept the clock around and only just woken up.

And he smelled faintly of Don Rafael, as if he'd drunk El Patrón's blood and gained some of their master's greater strength and speed.

Ethan knew damn well Emilio was one of Don Rafael's compañeros. But he'd always been very lightly bound, just enough to help him heal from injuries during his naval career. He'd never been given enough blood to strongly affect his scent, since that would mean a stronger emotional tie, although it would have given him a compañero's full strength and speed.

To have that change now whispered that Emilio had gained the stability to hold such a link. Or that Texas's situation was so dire Don Rafael would take the risk of hurting someone he deeply cared about.

Ethan glanced down at the younger man. "Are they finally done talking?"

"Finally." Emilio gave an exaggerated shudder, then grinned. "But only because the chairman's daughter called to remind him it was his wedding anniversary."

Wedding. Not that he'd ever even experience an anniversary! Ethan ground his teeth into a smile and telepathically ordered the armored Mercedes's driver to bring the car around.

As if to answer his prayer, Grania O'Malley emerged from the meeting, followed by her other bodyguard. She stopped in her tracks when she saw Ethan, one eyebrow lifting to challenge him before she came forward. Her voice held a queen's chill perfection when she spoke. His sister Aurelia couldn't have put him in his place any better after a bit of mischief. "I thought Caleb was going to drive us back."

"He's hunting with Gray Wolf, Doctor O'Malley." Ethan bowed slightly, an homage his aristocratic Creole mother would have strongly approved of. "Don Rafael asked me to personally escort you."

"Of course." She relaxed subtly and he gave a twisted smile.

It had been decades since he'd needed Don Rafael's bona fides to gain a woman's acceptance.

He indicated the way with another bow and a wave of his hand. Her cell phone rang an instant later. "Rafael! Yes, of course, I'm fine. Ethan has come to fetch me home to you," she cooed, evoking a rumbling purr from the man at the other end.

Ethan shot a disbelieving glance sideways. He'd never heard such an adoring tone coming from his master's throat before, even distorted by a telephone.

Thankfully, O'Malley was aware enough of her surroundings to walk safely outside and down the stairs, and get into the back of the car. A mesnadero drove, shielded by bulletproof glass.

It was the first time in his life Ethan had been alone with a woman he wasn't sleeping with, or didn't hope to sleep with, other than a family member. Shit, he didn't know what to do, lest he offend her, and Don Rafael, by extension. Sit close or far? Watch her or stare straight ahead? Keep his hands folded or at his sides?

Oh hell, he'd better pretend it was a buggy ride with his mother watching.

Ethan watched their surroundings pass by, listened to the other guards' chatter from the chase car, and tried not to think about Steve. Supposedly, there was a big birthday party for one of the academy's instructors that night.

If she took one of those prosaico assholes home . . .

They were well along the road for home before Doctor O'Malley hung up. Time passed, measured in the road's sweeping curves, high vistas of deep valleys, and far ranches. Other cars faded and disappeared.

"Are you entirely happy, Ethan?"

He whipped around to stare at her. "Doctor O'Malley?"

"You heard me—and you didn't say I'm wrong." She looked straight back at him.

He swallowed a curse. "It's not important."

"It is, if it affects Rafael."

Ethan stiffened.

"I haven't mentioned anything to him—and I won't, unless I have to."

She waited, the silence as compelling as any leash. Aurelia had always said the same thing whenever he got into trouble and needed help.

"There's a girl." He provided the briefest possible explanation.

"Oh."

Now she sounded unsettled. Good. Maybe she'd drop the subject.

"Can I help? Perhaps talking things over with another woman might suggest some answers?" She was tentative, a little optimistic perhaps.

On the other hand, his heart felt like it was slowly being torn out of his chest without Steve. Maybe somebody else might have some better ideas for how he could win her back.

And the doctor was the one person who might get away with keeping a secret.

"Ethan?"

He closed his eyes. How could he resist a woman who sounded and looked like Aurelia?

"We had a fight. I'd like to talk to her but she won't return calls. All I'm asking is a little time to talk, but—" He spread his hands and abruptly put them down, remembering where he was.

"Hmm. Have you tried a gift? Flowers perhaps?"

"Flowers? She's not a very frilly kind of girl," Ethan objected.

"Every woman likes flowers," Doctor O'Malley pronounced with complete certainty. "Even if she says she doesn't, it's just a matter of finding the right ones. Or maybe another kind of gift."

Ethan half turned to study her, caught by her humming joy in the idea. She was a woman, after all, so she should know.

A gift might please Steve but it would have to be something useful, not frivolous. Not something very expensive, either, lest her damn morals about taking any sort of bribe kick in. It was worth trying, anyway.

After all, what the hell did he have to lose?

Steve parked her Expedition nose out, automatically ensuring she could make a fast departure, despite the billowing mounds of roses spilling onto the gravel and encroaching on parking places. Long stone walkways led across an old-fashioned lawn to a pioneer's bronze statue, forever looking to the horizon. The old bank building's solid bulk rose comfortingly behind him, offering protection from the sun. Its narrow windows, heavy iron shutters, and chipped limestone blocks told of harsher trials it had successfully surmounted, including Indians, outlaws, and supposedly even bootleggers.

Machinery purred quietly in its rear. A lesser establishment's air-conditioning might hesitate or whine. But not here, not at one of the finest private collections of early Texas business and legal history, where not all of its oldest books were online. It also held a children's museum, famous for the working replicas which brought to life its extensive collection of antique children's books and toys.

She stepped out of her truck and edged down the path onto the lawn, trying not to collect too many thorns from the rosebushes.

Two small children raced past her from behind the oak trees, skirts fluttering in the breeze.

Steve's heart stopped in sheer surprise. She froze in her tracks, her fingers reflexively stretching for her gun.

One little girl squealed happily and ran faster.

Steve closed her eyes, her blood pounding in her ears. Her hand dropped onto her belt, hopefully casually, and gripped it until her fingers burned.

"Maryam! Kate! Time to go home now," called a woman, gathering her packages from the bench by the library's front door, her soft skirts rippling in the breeze.

"Daddy won't be there yet, Mom," one little girl paused to argue. Her counterpart promptly pounced on her and they tumbled across the lawn, in a giggling mass.

Steve tilted her hat forward, concealing her eyes and her lack of similar memories. Her mother had walked out on her father's career as a cop long before Steve had learned to walk, denying Steve any memories of playtime together. After that, her father and grandfather, a former patrol officer turned desk sergeant, had raised her.

She squared her shoulders, brought her hips into alignment, and marched indoors to find the reference desk. If her boots sounded a little loud on the wood floors, well, that only added to the place's historically accurate atmosphere. Right?

An immense arched entry led to what must have been the main meeting room, back when this had been a great bank, and was now the children's museum. Inside the room, a little boy was peering over a crouching man's shoulder, both of them intent on a very large rubber knife. Probably a precursor to a bowie knife.

Steve's mouth twisted. Grandpa had taught her how to use one of those as soon as she could safely hold it. The lady out front, in her silky dress, was more likely to understand the fancy décor here than the knife replicas.

An intricately carved molding surrounded the entry, so complicated it required a block containing an ornate *S* at each corner to transition between horizontal and vertical.

Steve broke stride and started to spin around. Could it be the Santiago Trust's brand, that very old Mexican brand she'd first seen on Ethan's business card? But linked to a children's museum? Surely not.

She might believe they'd donate to a police charity to draw attention away from their own nefarious deeds. Or the hospital wing—good Lord, that operating room must have been expensive! It could have been a hiding place for their own men.

But there was no conceivable reason for murderous vampiros like Ethan to be kind to children. None whatsoever. Ergo, this couldn't be their logo and had to be the carver's solution to a tricky design problem.

She shook off the fancy and moved faster for the sturdy desk and its reassuringly stolid guardian.

"Excuse me, ma'am, can you help me? I'm looking for information on the First Bank of L."

The older woman pulled over her mouse, her eyes alight with curiosity. "What else can you tell me?"

"It was around immediately after the War Between the States and apparently one of the more reputable establishments connected with the veterans' land grants."

Come on, talk to me, lady. Somebody's got to do so, sooner or later. It was harder to investigate these folks than a Columbian drug Mafia pulling off a black market peso exchange—and she hadn't even found any evidence of illegal activities. Let alone any idea of how many people were involved, other than Ethan.

"We do have a large amount of material on that period." The librarian raised an eyebrow. "Do you have a better idea of the name?"

"Maybe the First Bank of Lavaca." Steve gambled, seeing a fellow hunter. "They're related to the Santiago Trust."

The atmosphere chilled immediately.

"Lavaca?" The other woman leaned back in her seat, her expression suddenly much more formal. "Are you sure it's not Leon or maybe Lampasas, if it's named for a county? Or it could have been named for a town instead."

Steve kept her expression guileless, wondering what had gone wrong. Was it the bank's name or mentioning Santiago Trust?

"A reference downtown led me to believe the bank owned this building at one time. Also the Santiago Trust's board held their meetings here."

"Really? I'd be interested to see the precise reference. Memoirs really should be labeled as such and used with considerable caution." Soft clucking managed to express both sympathy and disapproval for another curator's carelessness. The mouse was pushed away slightly, indicating disinterest.

"Perhaps. But—" Steve tried again to talk about the bank, Santiago Trust, and where she stood.

"We don't have any memoirs here, except for Mr. Humphreys's accounts of his speculations on railroad stocks, starting in the late 1890s. Are those interesting to you? No? Well, then—"

Should she flash her badge? No, she wasn't on official business.

The older woman somehow managed to look down her nose at Steve, despite the foot difference in their height. "Young lady, we have no material here linking a bank and the Santiago Trust—whoever they may be—immediately after the War Between the States. As the senior librarian here, I would know. Unless you have a more precise name for the bank or are willing to look through our complete catalog . . ."

She swept her hand over the entire reading room and Steve ground her teeth, considering the reference books' towering stacks.

Shit. It had been a long shot but she truly hated to leave without an answer.

"I'll stay and look," she decided. "At least under Lavaca."

"Very well." The other shrugged. An hour later, Steve was glad she hadn't added, "You fool."

She'd found nothing under First Bank of Lavaca or First Bank of Leon linking either of those establishments to the Santiago Trust, let alone to this building. Maybe she wasn't looking in the right books but she'd tried. And, damn, how long could one keep looking before acknowledging there was nothing?

She nodded at the librarian and left, considering her few remaining options.

After a goddamn month of searching for the Santiago Trust during every spare minute, she'd exhausted all the online databases. She'd have found something, if there were anything to find. She'd searched the great historical collections but no luck there, either.

The only traces of Ethan's mysterious employer were their logo, that ornate antique brand, on charitable donations like the DNA profiling machinery. All things a monk would have been proud of. Crap.

But Ethan had cold-bloodedly murdered a man, somebody she would otherwise have been glad to see dead. Crap.

But how could she let any Tom, Dick, or Harry just up and kill somebody, even if he did deserve to die?

She unlocked the door and peeled open her Expedition, wanting nothing so much as a long, hot shower and a massage. Or a good lay, although that had always required Ethan and his unique notions. Sometimes leather, sometimes lace—but always damn excellent and impossible without him.

At least she had the long Fourth of July weekend to think about it, while she was vacationing in Galveston with the other cops.

And with any luck at all, she'd stop fantasizing about Ethan, whether he was fucking her—or a man. It was a hell of a way to have a good orgasm.

A single sheet of paper, very high-quality stationery and folded once, lay on her passenger's seat.

Her eyes narrowed and she reached for her gun.

How had that gotten here? She knew for a fact she'd locked all the doors.

She swung around, checking and rechecking her surroundings, keeping her Sig ready but not out in the open. Nothing, not even the faint whisper on her nape which said somebody was watching. This was the only vehicle in the visitors' parking lot, although three cars could be spotted in the staff lot, on the museum's other side.

She circled cautiously around her SUV and found no tracks. There wasn't even a crushed rose petal or a dog barking somewhere in the old residential neighborhood.

She eyed the paper again. One side was labeled with her name, clearly written in Ethan's bold, old-fashioned handwriting. Lines of closely spaced type covered the other side like wallpaper.

It probably wasn't a bomb, since it wasn't a sealed envelope. Besides, the thought of Ethan using explosives on her was laughable. Wring her neck, maybe. Kill her from a distance when he couldn't watch? Never.

Her fingers flexed, longing to touch that innocent-looking sheet.

She glanced around one last time to make sure nobody else was watching. Her heart was pounding a little too fast, probably because her SUV had been burglarized, certainly not because this was the first time she'd had any contact with Ethan.

Satisfied of that much at least, she very, very carefully picked up the paper.

Nothing at all happened. Her heart slowed into a more normal rhythm, warming her skin.

Clucking at her own idiocy, she stepped into the sun and unfolded the sheet. Her jaw dropped.

Good Lord. Ethan had just given her an extensive list of El Gallinazo's American bank accounts and at least some of his

Swiss accounts. They could put one hell of a dent in everything from his drug running to his money laundering.

Where had he gotten the information?

And why was he giving it to her? Did he hope to eliminate a possible rival?

GALVESTON, MONDAY, JULY 5, 2 A.M.

The fresh, slightly bitter tang of saltwater spray from the coming storm couldn't hide the heavy, pungent foulness of recent death. A string of lanterns hugged the hotel's façade but shrank from the alley's denizens, leaving those uncertainties to the irregular light from a handful of doors and windows, plus a single streetlight. Men and women muttered in a constantly increasing rising tide of unhappiness from the high sidewalks and inside the neighboring businesses. A reporter's nasal voice was pecking at a young patrolman, its owner eager to slice through the cordon to view the murder at its core.

Noway, nohow the press got to see this one—and they should count themselves damn lucky. Unlike the poor honeymooners who'd found the bodies.

Steve closed her eyes and yearned for a glass of ginger ale, her grandmother's sovereign remedy for an upset stomach. Even so, she knew damn well she'd have nightmares about being hemmed in by old brick Victorian buildings with dead people at her feet and palm trees lashing at the walls.

The place was crawling with cops but most of them were taking statements from the dozens of passersby, something they'd be lucky to finish before dawn. The photographers were still shooting pictures, their flashes briefly interrupting the alley's shadows in the erratic rhythm of men seeking something distinctive. Two hours of hunting and they hadn't found it yet, any more than Galveston's prized police dogs had brought back a gory-handed murderer.

A few cops still worked the grid pattern into the parking spaces between the hotel and the saloon on the other side of the alley. Others stood around in clumps, not quite blatantly wondering when the corpses would be released. Eyeing Steve but not talking to her, where she stood only a few feet from the shrouded corpses. A handsome German shepherd sat beside his handler in the hotel parking lot, both restlessly considering and reconsidering its exits.

Hell, she'd been having a great holiday before this happened. A long holiday weekend at Posada's condo with a couple of other Rangers, just lazing by the Gulf and calling it fishing. Then the phone rang late on Sunday night, bringing the Galveston police chief asking for help processing a crime scene. Of course, they'd agreed. They'd have done so, even if they'd known what they were getting into.

Two young coeds, dead for less than an hour, flimsy as crushed newspaper on the crimson-smeared pavement. Their cotton skirts were now gaudy road signs to their shredded thighs.

Jesus. Steve gritted her teeth. If it wasn't so damn hot, she could have blamed her shakes on the weather. Had any of the other killers' MOs involved draining women's femoral arteries?

Even so, this bloody alley had looked just a little too familiar after reading all those other case files. To say nothing of how few investigative techniques had shown any promise.

Although the girls' murderer—murderers?—hadn't sexually assaulted them, he'd taken the time to break every bone in each of their hands. Their mouths were contorted into gaping chasms of pain, their heads thrown back in agony, and their eyes staring in horror.

She'd seen that expression once before. She hadn't needed the witnesses' interviews to know nobody had heard these two scream, just like the girl in San Leandro. Unless they'd never made a sound . . .

Sirens whined in the distance, heading toward them. The irritating reporter slammed off to talk to eyewitnesses in an Internet café.

Posada separated himself from a trio of high-ranking cops, readily identifiable by the acolytes buzzing in and out with low-voiced questions. He strolled over to Steve, careful to stay outside the yellow-taped perimeter, the evidence kit dangling from his fingers as barren as hers. "How are you doing?"

"Fine." She flicked a glance at him, willing to make idle chit-chat. "Natives getting a bit restless?"

"Yup." His voice was as soft as hers. "Doesn't help that their crack K-9 ID'd the saloon's bouncer as the likely killer."

"Natural thing to do. He'd been the first guy on the scene, after the couple found the bodies." Hell, the dog was good enough to pick the trail up from an incredibly contaminated crime scene, then isolate its maker amid the huge crowds around here. It was more than almost anybody else's tracker had managed.

"Giving him the chance to pick up lots of blood, which he'd tried to wash off and didn't want to admit."

She could almost see her lieutenant roll his eyes. "Unfortunately, he also has the single best alibi in town, given the number of people in the saloon and passersby on the street who can ID him."

"Oh yeah, didn't take much time to establish *that* at all."

No, it hadn't been a good night for Galveston's finest so far. But maybe that would change.

A siren howled on a thinner note than that put out by a squad car. A small white pickup bounced toward the alley, its flasher whirling. Hopefully this would turn out to be the cavalry.

"Sure about this?" Posada murmured, even softer. "Police dog is a police dog. Are you sure you want to stay out on that limb by asking for another one?"

"Yes, because trailing or hard-surface tracking is harder. It takes a specialist." And if a vamp committed this crime, there wouldn't be any other evidence. Landscaping—grass or bushes and trees—to catch and trap bits of scent amid their myriad pockets and crevices would have made matters much easier. Instead, they'd have to rely on the pitifully few molecules still floating in the air or unlucky enough to be smacked firmly against the slick pavement or walls. But maybe this year's bumper crop of weeds would help.

"I've never seen a bloodhound work a crime scene better than a shepherd," Posada mused.

Damn, she really needed his support. Better give him more of the truth, no matter how nasty.

"Hays County had some success using similar tactics." By acting fast with a damn good team.

"*Hays* County? Had an attack like *this*?" His voice started to rise before he yanked it back under control.

"And others," she mouthed, shielding her features from everyone else. Yes, Hays was between Austin and San Antonio, dammit. Hours from here and only one of the many counties which had seen young women die.

"Oh, fuck." It was the first time she'd ever heard him use the *F*-word.

"Not really provable, though," she added. "Until maybe now."

Posada grimaced.

The high-pitched wail snapped to a halt, its accompanying light slashing the bricks as if it were trying to cut a portal. The truck's seal proclaimed Texas Department of Criminal Justice and a single big-dog crate occupied the back.

The driver was turning gray at the temples but was still trim around the waist. The creases in his uniform were knife-edged, despite the late hour and heavy humidity. A minute after he stopped, he had the truck's tailgate down and the crate open.

A big bloodhound emerged, gleaming red and gold under the few lights, with deep wrinkled jowls highlighting the long wet tongue, a runner's legs, and wagging tail.

The Galveston K-9 handler shot them a withering look and drummed his fingers against his leg. His big shepherd sat up a little straighter, furry tail stirring on the bricks.

Zimmerman, the chief investigator, pried himself away from the police chief and headed for the pickup. Steve and Posada joined him, moving in perfect unison, but stopped a few paces back.

"Evening, folks," the newcomer said. "I'm Sabathia and this here's Daisy, our best trailing dog. How can we help you?"

"Detective Ryan Zimmerman. Thanks for getting here so soon," Zimmerman replied, his burly shoulders straining his polo shirt. "We hope you can pick up the killer's trail for us."

"Glad to do our best, Zimmerman." Daisy had her head up, sniffing the night air curiously. "Do you have a sample for us to work from?"

"Yes, we found these a few feet away from the victims." Zimmerman's mouth curled before flattening into neutrality. They'd located it after their own dog had started hunting that bouncer and just before Steve had suggested bringing in a trailing dog.

She kept a straight face. *Careful, man; don't expect to triumph this easily over the bad guys. Nobody else has.*

Sabathia held the small bag so Daisy, now wearing a harness for easier head movement, could get a good whiff of its contents. She snuffled at it, concentrating deeply, almost like a sommelier tasting a new wine in a fancy restaurant. Finally she pulled away, long ears dangling, and he quickly loosened her leash, letting her test the air in all directions. She circled, head high, nose wrinkling with every sniff, moving farther away from him with every step.

Suddenly her entire body came alert, until even her toes and tail existed solely to drive her forward. She moved quickly down the alley and through the parking lot behind the hotel, gathering police in her wake like an empress.

"Ah-woooo!" she bayed, and lunged up on her hind feet, firmly planting both front paws on a cop's chest. A single swipe of her long wet tongue claimed him as hers.

"Drop your wallet in the street again, Smith?" Long experience rang through the Galveston K-9 handler's voice.

The man who'd been trying to protect his face abruptly slapped his hand over his hip pocket—and flushed angrily.

Steve sighed. How many times had she seen a cop swear nobody had gone inside the perimeter, only to have a dog prove them wrong?

Zimmerman cursed angrily. "Now we've got nothing."

"We've still got two corpses, who should have some of their killers' scent on them," Steve gently corrected him.

"The bodies probably reek to high heaven of everybody who've been near them or touched them in any way," he objected with lost hope's violent anger.

"But we have Daisy, who's a trailing dog. If anybody can find him—or them—she can," Roberts said flatly. "Even with all the hard surfaces around here."

A muscle throbbed in his jaw but he met the chief investigator's gaze steadily.

Strong man to tout another man's dog's superiority.

Zimmerman hesitated and finally shrugged. "What the hell do we have to lose? Let her try." He flipped up the yellow tape so Daisy could approach the two pitiful mounds under their white shrouds.

Steve watched silently, her stomach wrenching tighter and tighter, Posada and Roberts beside her.

If a human had killed them, there should still be enough scent on the corpses to give Daisy a good start. Otherwise—if a vampiro had done it—she'd have to take it from the air around them. And God help them all, in that case.

"What are the odds?" Posada quietly asked Roberts.

"Nighttime, with warm, moist air—that helps. But it was damn hot today. Asphalt traps heat—not good. Plus, all the tourists in the historic district seem to have tramped through here." He shook his head. "If I was a betting man, maybe one in five, just to pick up a scent, and only because she's a hound."

Zimmerman had delicately laid a sterile gauze pad on each victim, then placed each one in a clean evidence bag. Now he offered them to Daisy.

The dog's tail hung low, barely twitching, while she sniffed around the two bags. Suddenly she whined, deep in her throat, and pushed her muzzle into her handler's hand, edging away from the crime scene.

"What the hell? Good dog, Daisy, good dog." Sabathia stroked her head. "You can do it, Daisy. You've found worse crooks before. Come on, Daisy, come on."

Daisy leaned against her human's leg, shaking.

A cold vortex began to spin in Steve's stomach. Judging by Daisy's reaction, the killer hadn't been an ordinary human. But somebody like Ethan? Her veins filled with an icy slurry.

Daisy whined again but allowed herself to be eased down the alley away from the corpses. She worked toward the street, her tail rising with every step. Her head slowly came up, her nose wrinkling as she sniffed the air in all directions, swiveling back and forth.

Steve's pulse skittered.

Daisy reached the boardwalk and edged out onto the pavement, accompanied by her master. The once-thick crowd had thinned out, pushed back by insistent cops. A single reporter snapped a picture, the TV journalists having long since departed for their stations.

The great tracker circled at the end of her leash, twenty feet from her master, her red and gold coat blazing under the streetlights like Texas's star come to life. Her nose wrinkled, every fold working to hold and process the faintest bit of aroma. She sniffed a few cars and whined deep in her throat—but didn't linger.

Every cop was silent, even Roberts's big German shepherd.

She edged down the avenue away from the hotel—and stilled. "Ah-whoooo!" she bayed at the moon.

An instant later, she was trotting west down the street with Sabathia at her side. Away from Pelican Island and the harbor but toward what? The cruise ship terminal, the causeway, or the airport?

The other cops scrambled to follow, Steve and Posada walking, but some driving. Roberts trailed them slowly in his car, his shepherd watching every move from the passenger seat.

Once they knew the direction the bad guys had taken, Sabathia put Daisy back into the pickup. They formed a slow procession, following her like an empress whichever way her nose pointed.

Daisy grew more confident of the scent after they passed the big cruise ship terminal, somehow always able to retrieve the scent from a passing breeze.

Daisy turned away from the causeway, confirming their target hadn't driven the miles to the island.

Steve was damn sure he hadn't walked, either. Nobody with a lick of sense would subject himself to travel more than a dozen miles, by foot, through this kind of brutal humidity with only the hope of an occasional breeze from the Gulf through the shrouding buildings. The alternatives weren't pleasant.

She clenched her fists and fought not to think about the implications of a bloodthirsty murderer, striking as readily as the one she'd been studying. No woman in Texas would be safe. And, dear God, this little team was hardly prepared to catch a vampiro. She knew she didn't have enough weapons. Even if she did, could she pull the trigger on Ethan?

No. It might be sick, but she'd rather die believing Ethan was a good guy than live knowing he was a bad guy.

And if he hadn't done it, who had? Nobody in Texas had enough firepower to take down somebody like Ethan on his own. They'd need an ally—even Ethan himself, in order to have a chance.

Now they were heading straight for the airport but it was well past midnight. No way had this bastard taken a commercial flight.

"What do you think—charter flight or helicopter?" Posada asked Steve under his breath. "I can't believe he's still on the island."

"How about sending Daisy to the charter terminal, since she's got the best scent discrimination? But have the two local canines check out the helipads, since they work on most recent scent."

"Which will give us a fast answer. Sweet. I'll talk to Zimmerman."

She nodded, well aware he was saving his questions.

Minutes later, Roberts released his shepherd with a single guttural command after letting the dog sniff the same gauze square that had triggered Daisy's search. The big dog nosed the pavement and then leapt forward toward the helipad, ears laid back and teeth ready, desperate to redeem himself—and his human—with a successful search.

Steve and Posada raced after them, her heart pounding. Did she want to be wrong and have the bastard still be around?

They burst into the open, onto the circle of intricately marked concrete. A battered Jeep, top down, was parked only a few feet away—the getaway vehicle. It must have just enough ventilation to have allowed Daisy to pick up the killer's scent along the trail from the murder scene.

The police dog was lying next to it, rumbling happily deep in his throat, while Roberts examined something between the dog's great, furry paws. Gold flashed briefly in the flashlight's beam.

"What is it?" Steve asked, trying to see.

"A girl's earring. We've got its mate back in town with its dead mistress." He rubbed his dog's ears and pulled a big rubber ball out of his pocket. "Good boy, you found where the bad guys went poof!"

Steve's knees tried to dive for China and she stiffened them by sheer force of will. They'd found how the bad guys came and went. Unfortunately—or fortunately?—they hadn't encountered the sons of bitches.

"Do you want to start that chat now or later, Reynolds? Was asking for the bloodhound a lucky guess?" Posada asked very softly. "Or is there something you want to tell me?"

Steve's heart answered before her head.

"It reminded me of some other cases I've been investigating on my own time, sir," she said silkily—and mendaciously, avoiding the subject of who might have committed the crime.

There was a brief pause.

"Let's talk about that."

TEN

COMPOSTELA RANCH, JULY 6

Ethan took the last steps up the hill more slowly, the bouquet of yellow roses brilliant in his hand. He usually tried to bring red roses, with their hotter fragrance, but he hadn't been able to reach them tonight. Don Rafael had forbidden anyone to enter either that garden or his wing of the house, on pain of death.

Grania O'Malley had been forced—shit, forced!—into El Abrazo and would rise within the next hour. Even under the best circumstances, her chances of surviving La Lujuria, El Abrazo's first phase, would have been next to nothing. Now she might as well have been under a death sentence.

And if she died, Don Rafael would tear the world apart for revenge. As it was, he'd sent Jean-Marie to New Orleans, challenging her attacker to a duel *à l'outrance* which only one vampiro would survive. Ethan and the others would have their hands full getting Texas ready. But Ethan had come here first, to stand vigil while he waited to learn if Doña Grania survived those critical first hours.

He was still amazed Don Rafael had brought a woman to Compostela to rise as a vampira, no matter how obsessed he was with her. Given the oath Don Rafael had sworn never to create one, and the likelihood the lady would awaken so completely insane that death would be a blessing—there was every reason for Don Rafael to grant her a speedy, merciful death. But no.

Ethan shook his head and climbed faster, almost breaking into a run.

He rounded the last corner and the fountain's spray misted around him, welcoming him like an old friend. Low limestone walls terraced the hillside, interspersed with flowering plants and evergreens. Stone pathways meandered in between, their steps intertwined with tumbling watercourses. Junipers, roses, and jasmine scented the soft summer night, as welcoming as a friend's conversation. It was a simple garden, where deer could be found drinking from the crystal clear waters more often than men. Even Compostela's omnipresent guards were more concealed here.

Brass plaques were neatly embedded into the stones—sometimes next to a tree, or by a rosebush. Occasionally a half dozen were clustered together overlooking a small waterfall. Ethan could have named them all and their locations in his sleep, just as he could have recited the words engraved on every tombstone in the cemetery behind the tallest fountain.

He laid the flowers down on the great sundial embedded in the central plaza, and lifted his hand in salute. Every one of the men buried here had been his friend. The tombstones were for compañeros and the plaques for vampiros. If a vampiro's ashes could be found, they were buried here, too, whenever possible.

Now they could enjoy the sun, as he could not. At least not for another half century.

He pivoted and began to pace, always keeping an eye on Compostela. If anything happened to Doña Grania, surely there'd be an immediate uproar.

A breath of clean, dry, cold air washed over him.

"Evening, Mr. Templeton." The voice was thready and thin, with an odd flatness to it.

Ethan spun but didn't, quite, grab his Colts.

A slender man watched him, garbed in a long, fringed, leather coat and high leather moccasins. A silver star gleamed on his chest, the surrounding wheel fading in and out of the fountain behind him.

A ghost but not a vampiro, or at least not one he recognized.

"Good evening, sir." Ethan gave his most formal bow, as he'd been taught in a New Orleans drawing room before the War between the States. "Yes, I am Ethan Templeton. But it appears you have the advantage of me, sir."

The unexpected guest delivered a flourishing salute in the old Spanish style. "Erastus Smith, very much at your service, sir."

Ethan's jaw dropped. "Deaf Smith? Of the Battle of San Jacinto and the Grass Fight? The great Texas Ranger?"

"I hope I have been of some service to my adopted country." A faint color mounted to the other's cheeks. "That is not why I have come here, although I confess I'm glad you can see and hear me. It's very pleasant to converse again."

"I've always been able to hear, and usually see, ghosts." Ethan shrugged. "My best friend while growing up was a ghost."

"A most unusual talent that my own son never exhibited."

"I only mentioned it to my mother once," Ethan commented.

"You were brave to have mentioned it that often."

"Or foolish."

They chuckled together.

"How can I be of assistance to you, sir?" Ethan asked briskly.

"My friends and I have observed new invaders arriving from Mexico. While there have been others, these use the oldest road."

Ethan stiffened. El Gallinazo? Devol? The bandolerismo? "Can you describe them?"

"Large, smelly vehicles." Deaf Smith spread his hands, as if apologizing for the vague description.

Damn, did he mean SUVs or trucks? Or even semis? "How many wheels?"

The Ranger opened his mouth to answer but footfalls interrupted, speeding up the path from Compostela.

"Just a minute!" Ethan spun back. "Exactly where?"

But the ghost had vanished before he'd told Ethan which route the invaders were using.

Damn, damn, damn! Ethan threw a handful of pebbles across the pool. Now he'd have to do his own scouting.

Or he could call on Jean-Marie, whose spies had accumulated the list of banks Ethan had leaked to Steve. Well, why the hell not? Don Rafael wasn't going to attack El Gallinazo, a minor nuisance on his southern border.

"Ethan! The fountain in the rose garden has been turned back on."

Doña Grania lived? She'd made it through the first stage of La Lujuria, when almost every woman died? A woman would live at Compostela—possibly opening the door for other women to do so one day?

A grin cracked Ethan's face. Jean-Marie's eyes twinkled, a bit smugly.

Shit, could Jean-Marie have guessed he'd been seeing Steve far too often?

"Our creador will be much happier now, I think." Jean-Marie tried to look sober for an instant before his smile broke through, brilliant as the sun.

"Assuming he brings her all the way through," Ethan cautioned.

Jean-Marie drew back for a moment before waving that concern away. "He will succeed. After all, isn't he the only patrón who's successfully reared every cachorro? With a woman, especially one who holds his heart, he'll be certain."

Ethan nodded. Yeah, if he wanted to turn a woman into a

vampira, he'd bet his bottom dollar on the only patrón with the perfect track record.

AUSTIN, DPS HEADQUARTERS, JULY 7

The small room was noticeable for its efficiency, comfort, and lack of style. A conference table took up the center and was currently covered by stacks of large manila envelopes and several briefcases. Its more or less matching leather chairs had been shoved hard against the walls and the big bank of windows. A small corner table held a telephone, with a fiercely blinking row of lights and a pronounced tendency to erupt into peremptory trills, although it currently lurked under a pristine white Stetson.

A large map of Texas covered one wall, dozens of orange, chocolate, and black pins coiling across its center like a venomous copperhead snake. Its belly was thickest in Austin and San Antonio, but included Houston, Galveston, and Waco, although there were almost none in Dallas. Each pin was staked through a neatly lettered tag bearing a single name and a date.

The conference room contained twice as many people as originally planned, and half again as many as chairs. It reeked of conversations long since suspended.

Steve's mouth twisted slightly. She'd have been happier if they were chatting about tonight's baseball All-Star Game or comparing notes about the Galveston killings, rather than straining their necks to follow her every move. Thankfully, Posada still chaired the meeting by virtue of having convened it, so nobody else could interrupt her.

She tapped a final sequence of orange pins one last time, verifying their labels and positions. Dan was leaning against the corner beside her, his gourmet latte having long since turned cold and stale. Posada was pacing by the door, his thumbs in his belt and his gun very much on display. She doubted his irritation and abstraction were solely due to having so many gate-crashers at his meeting.

She forced her pulse to steady and turned to face them, satisfied with the record if nothing else. She would not, could not, let them learn of Ethan's possible involvement.

"That's it. Orange for highly unusual deaths of young women, categorized as initially unexplained. Chocolate are suicides for no solid reason, in the same age group. Black are the few that still don't have a death certificate."

"Jesus Christ," Dan muttered, and crossed himself. "We had no idea there were so many."

"That's why you didn't think the killer would be anywhere on the island, Steve," Posada noted, running his fingers lightly over the pins. "He'd have been a fool to stick around there."

"They've all been given death certificates," Dan protested. "Natural deaths, accidental, suicides—not homicides."

"But they also fit within the pattern Steve identified," Posada countered. "Eighteen- to thirty-year-old women, very healthy. Alone but not engaged in risky behavior—"

"In a heavily populated urban or suburban area late at night." Dan flung up his hands. "Who'd have thought picking up a prescription for your kid could be hazardous to *your* health, like the gal in Waco?"

A murmur of horrified disgust rustled through the room.

"Yeah. No signs of violence or a killer until the two in Galveston. The girls just—die." Steve drank her coffee, long since immured to lukewarm liquid, carefully not looking at the files on the table. Best to seem casual, lest anyone start thinking about them—and wonder if she had a set of copies stashed away elsewhere to do some private analysis. The results of which she wasn't sharing—in complete contradiction of every regulation in anybody's book.

"Has anybody been able to figure out how he gets the girls to walk away with him? Or stay quiet while he assaults them?" Posada's head swiveled between Dan and Steve, his black eyes drilling them into the wall.

"Nothing in the toxicology so far," Dan said flatly. "Not unless the Olympic labs come back with something."

"What about the two in Galveston?" Steve asked. "Those samples were taken sooner after death. Early enough to pick up roofies, for example."

Dan shrugged and started to scribble notes. "Maybe. But we haven't found any date rape drugs before, even when we were within the window."

"We'll ask the guys in Galveston to check, of course," added Moyer, the DPS criminalist.

"There are rumors El Gallinazo's pet chemist is cooking up a new brew, something to knock everybody else's date rape drug into the ground. Stronger, faster acting. Could that make a girl pliable and later kill her, Dan?" Posada's voice was far too relaxed.

"Yeah—but it should still show up in the toxicology!"

"Maybe it's also designed to pass even faster through the system, especially if it's mixed with a certain kind of drink?" Steve suggested.

"Like what?" Dan dropped his pen, his eyes widening. "Hell, if that happened, nobody would be safe."

Oh crap. A thousand tiny fingers plucked at Steve's skin and she closed her eyes. Texas wasn't safe.

"Is it possible?" Posada demanded, dropping his pretense of calm.

Dan reluctantly nodded. "Barely, mainly because El Gallinazo's chemist is a genius. He could make a fortune in the legitimate world if he wasn't so greedy and hot tempered."

"In that case, these deaths could be from a test run for such a drug, since they occurred along the interstate highways."

Steve frowned, the connection refusing to come into focus. Her gut said Posada was wrong but why?

"There's enough of a pattern here for me to take this upstairs. Do you mind if I ask Travis County to loan you to us, Schilling? You'd be working with Moyer."

"Of course not. I can show him how to do things right." Dan winked and Moyer snorted comfortably.

"That's it for now, guys. We want you to go back to your home offices and do some research. We'll need copies of the complete file for all these cases, plus any other deaths which might fit this pattern. After that, we'll go through them with a fine-tooth comb, looking for common threads."

Heads nodded, expressions betraying gratitude for having some standard police work to do.

"Any questions? No? Good. This is, of course, to be treated with the utmost sensitivity. God help Texas if the public got the slightest whiff of this."

More people than Steve shuddered at that possibility.

"There have been some rumors, sir, about single women disappearing from bars," a guy volunteered from the back row. "But they were tourists, down on the River Walk."

"Check into it."

"Of course, sir."

"Dismissed."

Cops began to file out of the room, mingling with others to talk more, their expressions both shaken and thoughtful.

"This might help, too, sir." Steve slid the single, precious sheet of paper out of its folder and handed it to Posada.

He lifted an eyebrow but said nothing, simply started reading. An instant later, his head snapped up and he stared at her. "Where the hell did you get this, Reynolds?"

"A CI gave it to me, sir. I've worked with that source for almost fifteen years and always found him completely reliable." Well, that was true enough, as far as it went. She kept her head up and her breathing calm, refusing to give in to nerves. "He gave me the tip which broke open the Llano Estacado Bank robberies."

"Wow." Posada shook his head. "Cordero!"

The only man in a business suit swung around and came back. Posada handed him the page. "What do you think?"

"Routing numbers look real. I'd have to double-check the account numbers. Inside—" He looked up. "I'm drooling, boss."

Posada slapped him on the back and the two grinned together.

Steve unwound just a little bit, marveling at how the room seemed a bit brighter now that Ethan's gift wasn't a trap. On the other hand, what would happen to her if Ethan ever became the only one who could help them?

SAN ANTONIO RIVER WALK, LATE THAT EVENING

The saloon's DJ cut the latest Keith Urban hit off short, apparently tired of hearing good lyrics. In its place, he installed a high-energy rock anthem from a new British band, cranking up the volume to stadium levels. How many patrons did he want to deafen with this ode to self-indulgence?

Ethan edged forward to count and bumped against the manager's wooden desk, sending a pile of liquor receipts sliding toward the floor. He slammed his elbow against them, hoping his MP5 would forgive the indignity of becoming a management prop. They settled back into place and he patted them down, stabilizing them against the music's insistent pulse. His beloved submachine gun nestled comfortably back into the crook of his arm, ready to be fired at the twitch of his finger.

He gritted his teeth and cooled his heartbeat, reminding himself yet again what he was here for. He was backup tonight, not primary, since he reeked far more than Jean-Marie did. At least to vampiro senses.

Jean-Marie was a superb spy, capable of learning any bit of information, and an astonishingly good assassin, judging by results rather than skill with guns. His two centuries as a vampiro gave him the ability to blend into crowds, with almost no identifiable scent. Only Don Rafael would have had a better chance to ambush any of Devol's bandolerismo. But he was back at Compostela, with Doña Grania.

Right now, Jean-Marie was concealed high overhead on the saloon's roof, upwind of any bandolero's likely approach. Ethan watched from inside, ready to move in any direction. Madame Celeste had hit San Antonio's tourists brutally hard, stretching the local compañía to its utmost. Hennessy, the Dallas adalid, had brought his compañía down to help, concealing them in the most scented shrubbery along the River Walk. Luis's men watched the police and commercial surveillance cameras, where they'd also ensure no vampiros' faces were permanently recorded.

All they needed now was for one of Madame Celeste's bandolerismo to walk past. For all the reports of prosaico deaths and rumors of vampiro sightings, there were no guarantees one would appear at the fattest nighttime tourist attraction in Texas—the Crystal Star Saloon on San Antonio's River Walk.

Ethan smiled faintly and subtly flexed his shoulders above his MP5. Should one of those bastards appear, they'd show him a deathly good time—after they got the prosaicos out of the way.

Steve would enjoy a party like this, plus her superb shooting skills and uncanny ability to sight opponents would be an incredible asset. But it was far too dangerous to involve a prosaica, even a trained cop.

"Two women are leaving," Rough Bear reported from the saloon's security station. "We're now down to seventeen prosaicos in the main room and two staff. Another woman is standing up."

Reckless female, Jean-Marie snorted.

Ethan grunted his assent. One a.m. was not when he'd advise a lady to stroll alone through a thickly landscaped park of cypress, palm trees, and other flowering plants and trees, scenically lit by ornamental lanterns. No matter how much the local bureaucrats touted their city's safety at all hours.

At least Rough Bear could see the saloon's classic décor clearly—its rough wooden paneling and brick walls, long bar with the large assortment of bottled temptations, scattered small round tables, bent-frame wooden chairs, leather- and denim-clad waiters and waitresses. And all of it under very modern lighting, sound, and security systems which could be discreetly hired at the blink of an eye. Such as the Santiago Trust had done tonight, to observe the other guests.

"Ethan." Rough Bear's voice sharpened, icily clear through their expensive headsets.

Even the hairs on his arms came to full alert. "Yo?"

"Roald Viterra—that big blond—is dancing with a prosaica. I didn't see him before because the DJ was blocking my view."

Shit. If that torturer got his hands on a girl . . . "Did you catch that, Jean-Marie?"

"Copy," the Frenchman said far too laconically. He must be evolving and rejecting plans faster than his tongue could tell them.

"Do you want to move now?" He had to ask.

"No, we have to wait until he comes out." Jean-Marie gave the expected answer.

I'm a good enough shot to take out Viterra from here, without harming the girl, Ethan countered, continuing the argument on a more private channel. *All I'd have to do is step into the entrance hall.*

How the hell would you explain shots fired inside a nightclub?

It's Texas. Somebody lost their head for a moment.

Nobody's that insane.

We're in Texas. We can fix the trial.

No. Women would be hurt. Jean-Marie slithered forward, the sound of steel grinding over a tile roof barely apparent.

Ethan snarled privately but deferred to his elder *hermano.*

"He just looked around but didn't seem to see anything," reported Rough Bear. "Now he's got the girl by the hand and is leading her outside, fast. The southern side door," he added.

South side? Crap. That was Jean-Marie's worst view.

"Positions, everyone," Ethan ordered, and bolted out of the office, racing for that side door. He had snipers atop several roofs farther downstream. Surely one of them could take out Viterra.

He shoved past a janitor, barely bothering to hide his gun under his denim jacket. *Prosaico* lives were his concern now, not their delicate sensibilities.

The door slammed before he could reach it and he wrenched it open. The night air was hot, moisture wrapping his throat like an unseen hand. Honeysuckle teased his nostrils, while a woman trilled with laughter over a man's compliment.

Why had he ever thought he wanted Steve to flirt like that with him? Thank God one woman at least had some sense.

"Who has Viterra?" he demanded of the men linked to him.

"I do. But I can't shoot him without hitting the girl," Jean-Marie reported far too calmly. Dammit, there was no time for Jean-Marie to come down from his roof.

Somebody else had to do better.

Would Steve accept the older, more feral *vampiro* code of justice under these circumstances, when a woman had been kidnapped by a known murderer?

Ethan sniffed, testing the layers of scent for the girl. Where were they? Ah, there!

"Too many trees," said Hennessy from the bridge, undoubtedly cursing the River Walk's curved layout which made it impossible to cover all lines of fire. "Plus, there's the—"

"Girl?"

"Aye, her, too, Ethan," Hennessy agreed, in his still-fluid brogue.

If Hennessy didn't have a shot . . . Shit. Ethan ran faster, dropping all pretense of being a tourist until he moved with vampiro speed. He was arriving from a different angle than the others and might have a better chance.

He slid through a clump of plants, saving valuable time and steps on the sidewalk, and ignored signs promoting the gaudy Mexican restaurant nearby. A carved stone bridge gleamed like moonlight ahead, shrouded in foliage but with a few gaudy umbrellas just visible at its base. Cars hummed on the streets overhead, faint reminders of other prosaicos nearby.

A woman was giggling softly a few steps ahead. "Oh, you're so sweet," she purred, clearly anticipating a delightful night.

Ethan bared his fangs. No, not in his Texas. And not where one of these bastards could hurt Steve.

A breeze whispered past, teasing his nose with honeysuckle and other flowers.

A boot scraped on the concrete and the woman's murmurs abruptly became a screech. Ethan glanced up at the bridge.

Viterra stared down at him, his face contorted in rage.

Ethan immediately fired a quick burst from his MP5. The bullets pinged off the stonework and the woman screamed, loud and long.

Viterra was already gone, and Ethan raced after him, tasting bitter betrayal in the honeysuckle's perfume. "Who has a shot?"

Empty silence.

The prosaica cursed him, words gentler than those he used for himself. A quick look over the parapet showed Viterra leaping off a boat and through a café's patio, shielded by the bridge's bulk from anyone's vision except Ethan's. He snatched a waiter away from making change and dragged him along, the man's denim-clad legs futilely scrabbling over the tiled floor.

Ethan snarled and leapt to follow, unable to shoot again.

Two steps later, the bastard had rushed into a hotel and was gone, dropping the waiter like a sack of flour.

Ethan ground his teeth and kept going, knowing damn well his chances of success were negligible. Shielded by their sense of smell, nobody could get close to Devol's followers except a prosaica.

ELEVEN

Steve balanced the heavy filing box on one hip and blocked the conference room's door with her booted foot, determined not to let the fast-moving steel nip her fingers yet again. They kept the room continuously locked now, hiding the towering piles of unanalyzed case files, like glaciers eager to break apart into icebergs. Once the task force had started asking around, far too many cases had come to light.

After that, files had poured into Austin, escorted by hard-faced cops with little to say and a desperate, uneasy hope in their eyes. It wasn't right to have one or two women die in a week from unexplained causes, when the same jurisdiction might see that many in a year. And when they were young and healthy? Hell, she, too, would run out of tests to call for and words to use in the "cause of death" box. Multiply that by four big cities and more than two hundred miles of interstate highway . . . She'd personally stopped counting at three dozen killings.

She slid the box onto the side table and picked up the log sheet, ready to start checking in its contents.

"How many do you have there?" Mike Morris eyed the innocuous brown and white cardboard suspiciously.

"Two, one of them a suicide. Suicide was a nurse so more toxicology work was done than usual."

"But nothing found." He double-checked his gun and shoved it into its holster.

"Not so far. Finished for the week?"

"Yeah. Put in my forty and the bosses have officially forbidden any overtime. Everybody else is already gone."

"Crap."

"You got it." He grinned, his teeth startling white against his normally somber face. "My wife's helping out at a camp for special-needs kids this weekend. Now I can go with her and enjoy the rug rats, too."

She smiled back at him, warmed by his simple joy. Once she'd hoped to be as comfortable around small children as he was. It probably would never happen. But if it didn't—"Show me your pictures on Monday, 'kay?"

"Sure thing. Don't let the cleaning crew walk you out again, hear?"

She laughed and waggled her fingers at him, silently promising not to be that stupid twice—especially after Posada's lecture on working late. Morris was gone a minute later, jauntily whistling the latest Tim McGraw hit.

She finished logging in the new cases and stretched, eyeing the possibilities for a late lunch. Cold cheese pizza, cold veggie pizza, and cold—she lifted a lid—mushroom and meatball pizza. Better options than anything in her kitchen certainly and she'd learned long ago not to turn down pizza if she didn't want to cook. Still, after years of eating little else, she wasn't in a hurry for more.

She tore off a piece of cheese pizza and settled down with her sweet tea to read one last case file before going home. And try not to think about spending another Friday night alone. Or more irritatingly, with Ethan.

This girl was a University of Texas coed, who'd died outside an Austin bookstore. Like all the other case files, hers was most notable for what it didn't contain. The X-rays were very brief, for example, with only the standard set and nothing highlighted. Toxicology had done a full screen and found nothing, including no illegal drugs. She had no known preexisting medical conditions and, thus, nothing requiring further explanations on that form, either. Nothing resembling a real cause of death was mentioned on any of the forms.

And yet there was far too much smoke, given all these deaths with similar modi operandi, not to have a fire.

Steve finished the slice and decided not to tackle the rest. She'd never worked out of headquarters before but Dan's list of suggested restaurants was posted on the back of the door.

Wiping off her hands, she turned the page and read the first observation about the girl from the forensic investigator who'd gone over the death scene. Most of this was as minimalist as everyone else's reports, except he described the deceased in a little more detail than usual.

The girl's head had been arched to one side and stretched back, like several of the others, thus exposing her jugular. A precise drawing was included, showing its exact angle.

Steve stirred, something flickering behind her eyes. But it was gone before she could catch it.

Given the hot weather, the young lady had been wearing a deep V-necked tee. The investigator's drawing also showed how she looked, with the fabric fallen open and two small acne papules just above the great vein. The investigator had even helpfully drawn the small sores with a red pen.

Outside, two secretaries were loudly wishing each other a very good weekend, as measured by success in hunting men. Cute men.

Steve turned the page, determinedly not listening to them. She propped her chin on her hand, curving her neck and shoulder against her arm. She'd rather be shacked up with a single, perfect lover. Tall, blond, beautiful as a god . . .

The autopsy report was just as neat and detailed, full of steps taken, tests run, observations made. It, too, included a series of excellent drawings, showing the deceased's exact condition.

Steve started to flip the page, looking for the full toxicology report—and stopped. There was something about that picture . . . The neck was wrong. Where on earth were the two papules?

Her pulse moving faster, she double-checked the autopsy report. Nothing about little red sores, whether in a drawing or the written report.

But the forensic investigator specifically described and showed red papules on the neck, above the jugular.

How could they have occurred? And why would they have disappeared?

Two papules. Just above the jugular.

She rubbed her neck—and remembered another time when a man's hands had done exactly the same thing, while his voice had purred enticements in her ear, and her body had trembled in anticipation. His mouth had closed over her throat and he'd bitten down hard, sucking her blood.

Her body jolted yet again, shuddering in an echo of that shattering orgasm.

She'd had two little marks on her throat afterward and nothing at all the next day. Just like this coed.

But she'd always put that down to healing. The coed had died. Could vampiro saliva so accelerate the process that all traces of contact vanished, even without assistance from a living body?

Ethan, Ethan the vampiro.

But he wouldn't murder women! Not Ethan.

She shoved her chair back so hard that it slammed into the boxes behind her. She flung herself out of it and began to stride around the room, barely noticing the boxes she dodged.

Next to this, his execution of Garcia Herrera faded into obscurity.

Ethan was the only vampiro she knew. He had the means to kill all these women, given his fangs and his strength, his ability to create the small bite marks which healed so very quickly. And no two women had been killed at exactly the same time. It was barely—barely!—possible one man could have done all the killings.

But not him! Oh, dear Lord, now she sounded like all the other women she'd ever interviewed who denied up until the last minute that their loved one would ever lift a hand in anger to anyone.

Except she was a trained investigator, a professional, a Texas Ranger. She should know.

Of course, there could be more vampiros but she'd never met any, nor seen any signs of them.

She pounded her fists against the uncaring boxes.

Dammit, not Ethan! Not her lover of fifteen years!

She swung around and leaned her back against the files, the silent witnesses to dozens of murders. She was a cop. Above all else, she had to have justice for these women. But how?

Risk everything to bring the truth into daylight, even if it meant talking to Ethan in person.

Steve brought her big Ford Expedition to a decorous stop before the impassive gates, gravel shifting under her tires like the butterflies flitting around in her stomach. If she'd had any other choice, she wouldn't have come, especially when she wasn't even sure she had the right place. After exhausting every other option, she'd finally checked out every large rural property which hadn't changed hands since Texas entered the Union. This was the only one big and secretive enough to hold Ethan, and its inhabitants had even agreed to let her in.

She gunned the engine into full roaring life and roared down the winding road, passing through miles of green pasture. Longhorn cattle lifted their heads to watch her, maneuvering their sharp horns with a society matron's grace. Great oak trees and heavy boulders leaned over the road, providing shade and cover for watchers.

Her mouth twisted briefly. Given how her skin was crawling, there were at least a half dozen men observing her every move. Some were probably using security cameras but at least one or two were physically present, undoubtedly somewhere close to the skyline.

Well, they could relax—she hadn't come to kill anyone, although she'd surely like to make an arrest.

The road opened out abruptly into a valley, centered on a surprisingly large complex. Steve's foot came off the accelerator for a moment before she drove on. Boy howdy, the place was big!

An immense ranch house, three stories tall under a deep mansard roof, was solidly built of limestone blocks. The front was covered with a two-story porch, while the other three sides had a multitude of chimneys. It could have withstood a siege, given its steel shutters, especially if the wooden porch was added after the Indian Wars were over.

Pergolas, covered in fruiting vines, framed the stone walkways connecting the dozen other buildings. She could make out a barn, a chapel, at least one dormitory, and more. Was that a pistol range—with an armory beside it—off there to the south? Had she heard automatic weapons firing?

All in all, it was an independent, self-sufficient world, not a small-time, arrogant bastard's little property.

Her fingers tightened on the wheel, cats' claws inside her skin urging her to turn around now.

She bit her lip. She'd have to apologize to Ethan somehow about her reaction to Garcia Herrera's death—or he'd never talk to her. She'd also have to not think about him as a lover—which would be a first when seeing him in the flesh.

Her hands, without any instructions from her brain, stopped

the big truck in front of the house and turned off its engine. The sudden silence ripped cold air through her lungs, shocking her back to the here and now.

She sucked in a long breath, reminding herself of who she was and whom she represented. Stephanie Amanda Reynolds, Texas Ranger. Almost two centuries of Texas law enforcement in her veins. Not just a woman who'd been wretched without her lover.

She wrapped her fingers around her father's battered leather briefcase, which held the cases' summaries, and unlatched the truck door. It opened sweetly for her, obedient as a bolt-action rifle.

She stepped down to face two men, both with the subtle reserve and smooth movements of those who've spent far too long practicing with weapons. They were dressed casually, wearing rock concert T-shirts and jeans above cowboy boots. If they meant to reassure her by not overtly displaying their guns, they failed, given the number of possible hiding places for one on their bodies.

"Reynolds? This way, please." They took her past the house and into the storm cellar, one walking in front of her and the other behind. They set a fast pace, too, giving her very little time to consider her surroundings, while they went down two, three, four flights of stairs.

Why had she forgotten how much Ethan loathed the sun? Had she truly been foolish enough to hope she'd see him the minute she arrived?

Steve's lips stretched across her teeth, while she called herself a thousand names for fool.

Except for the lighting, the underground hallways could have been found in any expensive office building or lawyer's office. Soft carpeting covered the floors, deadening any sound. They were superbly furnished, down to the high-quality maps and artwork which decorated the walls. Snatches of conversation drifted through like smoke from the few rooms before fading away.

Her party passed a pair of metal detectors without pausing, an oversight she decided not to mention. On the other hand, how much chance did she really have of pulling a gun on Ethan, given his superior speed?

Metal detectors were easy to identify. The number of intersections and doors, left and right turns, were not. She'd have bet a month's pay her escorts were trying to befuddle her.

The few men they encountered, all openly wearing pistols, silently made room for them. Their hard eyes swept over her but they said nothing, simply pressed against the wall or stepped into a doorway. Steve nodded politely to them but kept silent as well. Were they vampiros like Ethan?

They finally arrived at a pair of smoothly polished double doors, gleaming like satin under a single overhead spotlight. Her leader knocked once, paused, and knocked again.

"Enter," called Ethan.

Her throat was ridiculously tight. She straightened her shoulders, threw her head back, and marched inside without waiting for either of her far-too-careful escorts to show her the way.

The buildings above ground came from limestone blocks, as rugged as the men who strode below them. This room was smoothly polished, with satin-soft plaster rippling over the walls. Great wooden cabinets rose from floor to ceiling, intricate and subtle as a boatbuilder's art. Oversized leather chairs offered comfortable seating near an oval glass table. An oriental carpet warmed the hardwood floor, while skylights and French doors mimicked daylight.

Its sole occupant, even more masculine than the others, was definitely the king of this domain, standing arrogant and tall in his white starched shirt and crisply pressed jeans. His expression was impassive, his eyes green and gold chips of ice under those thick golden lashes. Lord, how she'd always envied him that gaze.

How the hell could she have forgotten how beautiful he was? But he'd changed in the past month. His eyes were deeper set, fine lines fanning from their corners. Deep grooves bracketed his once-curving mouth and his cheekbones were higher, more angular. His stubborn jaw was more blatantly carved from intransigent bone, not soft skin.

Now he resembled a medieval sword, lethally attractive, and not the invitation to sin she'd once thought him.

He nodded curtly and the door clicked shut behind her escorts. No one outside this room would give her any help.

"Good afternoon, Ethan." Her voice was deep, huskier than she remembered ever hearing it before. Surely she could not be finding this version of him more appealing.

"Ranger."

She winced slightly at the impersonal greeting.

His eyes swept over her again, impossible to read. "Would you care for some coffee?"

"Thank you." She couldn't bring herself to be completely formal, not when she could see his chest rising and falling under the pure white cotton.

He turned toward a small passageway, possibly the door to his private quarters. Her chest tightened. She needed to wipe the slate clean of old business.

"I, ah . . ." This was not the time to start stuttering!

"Yes?" He glanced back at her, raising an eyebrow.

She swallowed hard and blurted her prepared speech, rushing through the unpleasant phrases as quickly as possible. "Thank you for the list of El Gallinazo's accounts. It's been very helpful, Ethan," she added, determined to keep some connection with the man she'd thought she knew. "And I'm sorry I lost my temper when you shot Garcia Herrera."

Both of his eyebrows went up. Then his eyes narrowed. "Is that all you have to say?"

"Yes." She planted her feet more firmly. She wouldn't apologize for wanting to bring him in, no way. But she shouldn't have lost control of herself. People's lives could have been placed at risk.

"You're forgiven—and thank you for your honesty."

Steve flushed, heating to a more uncomfortable shade than any time since high school. Dammit, why the hell did he have to read her so easily?

"I won't apologize for shooting him," Ethan continued, his gaze softer now but still unreadable, "and I'll never let you put me in jail for it, Reynolds."

"Understood." She inclined her head, never taking her eyes away from him, the briefcase heavy in her hand. She could swallow hard and overlook that killing, if it would help solve the far longer string of deaths.

"Make yourself comfortable; I'll be back in a moment." He disappeared and she swung around to consider her surroundings. Any chance she could break into anything? Was there anything which offered her an opening, like a keyboard, a monitor, an open drawer or cupboard? No.

Just a few pieces of sleek modern furniture and equally impenetrable walls. Not that she'd ever expected him to yield secrets easily.

She set the briefcase down on the glass table, absently admiring its gracefully curving edge. It was hugely different from her grandfather's old oak table, scarred after decades of handloading ammunition atop it.

Ethan came back into the room silently, carrying two mugs. "Cream, two sugars?"

"Yes, thank you." They'd always teased each other how they never met at work so he'd never shared with her a cop's basic food group—coffee. She tried to drink anything and everything else away from her job. "What're you having?"

"Coffee, black." He handed her the far creamier brew. "Black as the Duke of Hell's waistcoat."

Darkness indeed. Her smile was a little twisted but she lifted her mug to him. "Thanks."

He sipped, watching her, and let the silence stretch out. She recognized the tactic all too well, having used it a few thousand times herself: He was going to let her take the risk of starting the true conversation. Dammit, he'd always been more of a gentleman before. But she hadn't insulted him before, either.

Bowing to the inevitable, she opened her briefcase and pulled out the case files' copies.

Ethan's eyes narrowed briefly but he said nothing.

"At least three dozen young women have died over the past month, in cities from San Antonio to Galveston. We've ruled out natural deaths, accidents, and suicides. Heavily trafficked urban areas, no signs of violence, no apparent reason for going off alone with their killer."

She watched him closely for any change in expression but a meditating Buddha would have been livelier. She dug her fingernails into her palms for a moment before continuing.

"Some of their expressions were alarmed, while others had very extended, even arched necks."

He raised an eyebrow and she paused hopefully. When he said nothing, she said one last prayer for inaccuracy.

"More than one had two small, red papules over the jugular at the death scene. Those papules were not found by the ME during the autopsy. Exactly the same as the ones you left on me time and again, which disappeared—as you promised, Ethan!—within a day."

His lips were compressed to a thin, white line.

"Why, Ethan? What the hell is going on here?"

He stared at her, green fury blazing out of his eyes, his hands opening and closing like frustrated clamps. "Why should I tell you? So you can try to haul me into one of your prison cells?"

"No! You didn't do this, couldn't have done these killings, Ethan."

"How can you be sure?" he shot back at her. "I'm a vampiro."

"You'd never murder a total stranger." She shrugged in frustration, looking for words to explain her certainty. "You'd gain nothing by it and you don't hate the world that much."

"You're not saying that my morals are pure."

"Are they? Would Garcia Herrera's executioner make those refined distinctions?"

He snorted. "Hardly."

"When you kill—which is probably far too often—you do so for a purpose, like Garcia Herrera. Since you lacked a reason—correct?" He nodded, watching her closely. "Then somebody else must have killed them."

"You are completely certain of this." His eyes were narrow, laser bright.

"Absolutely." There was much she didn't know about Ethan and more she wasn't sure of. But she had a clear picture on this subject and her gut concurred. No way he'd done these killings, even if she couldn't prove it.

He relaxed slowly, hiding his expression behind a long drink of coffee. Exasperating man!

"Am I right?" she demanded.

"Yes." He set down the mug.

"Are there other vampiros?" Her blood was pounding, from her ears through her legs. If she had someone to go after, that'd be a start, no matter how hard it would be to make an arrest.

"Hundreds."

"Hundreds?" The word faded away like her pulse. She grabbed for the table and held on desperately.

"Probably thousands, if you included the entire hemisphere and Europe."

Thousands. Great. She could still conduct an investigation, one vampiro at a time. Somehow.

"Texas doesn't permit foreign vampiros to enter without permission." He propped his hip against the table. "Given the current war, we've closed our borders so we're limited to the local vampiros. Plus a few, uh, terrorist vampiros who've infiltrated Texas."

"War? Terrorists?" The familiar word brought her head up and she set her mug down with a clang.

"Bandolerismo, to be precise. They're vampiros who owe allegiance to no patrón or esfera, which are the vampiro rulers and territories. Instead, they live to cause trouble and hope to gain their own territory in the resulting chaos."

"Terrorists." What a foul taste saying that left in her mouth.

"Exactly."

"Do you know who's responsible?" Her voice deepened, roughened. Her fingers flexed, longing for her guns.

His eyes narrowed and his face hardened into older, darker lines. Just before she would have yelled at him, he opened a concealed drawer in the wall and removed a remote control. "How much history do you remember from your criminal justice degree?"

College? She'd spent as little time as possible in classrooms. Continuing education was easier since it didn't last for months.

He was clicking a series of buttons. One of the cabinets opened and the lights dimmed. "Well?"

"Not much," she admitted. The computer screen hummed into life, revealing it was actually made of four smaller screens. How many toys could a man fit into one room?

He chuckled, his face brightening. "Lovely. The university would be devastated to hear that. Have a seat."

She sat, her eyes fixed on the immense monitor. An old mug shot appeared of a young man—average height, probably Caucasian, brown hair, brown eyes. Unremarkable features schooled into dutiful obedience, which was probably a mask.

"Recognize him?"

She started to answer and stopped. Ethan's voice had been too casual.

She studied the photograph again, considering the expression. He looked obedient but who really felt that way in an old-fashioned prison uniform? She'd have rated him more toward the very-angry-but-intelligent-enough-to-hide-it end of the scale.

"Louisiana?" she guessed, squinting at the old labels. "Uh, 1920s?"

"Very good. Care to try for a name or his crime?"

The fellow didn't look violent unless you studied the eyes. "Murder."

"Mass murder, to be precise."

"Mass?" She stared at Ethan, then swung back to the monitor. She frowned, her mind rapidly scrabbling for old class notes. "Is he Devol?"

"Bingo! Georges Devol, murderer of thirteen highly respectable women."

"He killed an orphanage's entire board of trustees during their quarterly meeting, very messily. Didn't it destroy the orphanage, hurting a lot of people?"

"It was the largest secular orphanage in Louisiana at the time," Ethan said neutrally. A series of clicks sent the monitor dissolving into grainy newsprint photos. "Of course, some also called it a workhouse and a brothel."

"An orphanage?" Her voice rose to a near shout before she dragged it back under control.

"Yeah." His voice was clipped and harsh, his throat working hard. "Taking in children from infancy through high school."

"The bastards. Dammit, if I'd caught those responsible—"

"Not many such laws on the books back then, Steve, and fewer prosecutors, especially when the suspects are from the finest families in Louisiana."

"Son of a bitch!"

"Actually, the bitches themselves."

She gaped at him, unable to fathom such treachery on the part of women toward children.

His lip curled. "Even so, Devol's methods of killing them were noticeably sadistic. Rape and strychnine."

Steve fought not to gag. There were some crime scenes she didn't mind missing. Then she remembered something from an old textbook.

"But he's dead, isn't he? Went to the electric chair at Angola for the killings."

Ethan raised an eyebrow. There were very few interpretations of that expression and she chose the most obvious.

"Did he escape? Over the hills? But they're nearly impassable."

"No, he went into the Mississippi during spring floods."

"That's insane!"

"No, he's one of the smartest criminals you'll ever meet. He gambled they wouldn't look for him there and he was right."

"Shit. And now he's a vampiro." A sadistic brute, with a proven track record as a mass murderer? She was cold, very, very cold. "Is he the one who's killing the girls?"

"He and the rest of his bandolerismo."

The pieces assembled themselves into a picture.

"But the bandolerismo are terrorists and those guys want to overthrow a government. You're in the middle of a war. Are they trying to kick you and your friends out of Texas?"

"Got it in one, Steve. Got it in one." He tossed his hair out of his eyes and came gracefully to his feet. "I'm the alferez mayor—the military commander—not the patrón."

"Vice president of security?" She joined him by the monitors.

"At your service."

She considered and rejected going to the top. "You're probably the guy who actually gets things done, not this patrón fellow. I'd rather talk to you."

Ethan's jaw dropped before he slowly closed it. Unholy glee began to replace the stunned shock on his expression. "We're trying to boot them out of Texas but it's damn hard for us to find them."

"Why? I thought vampiros had very keen senses."

"They're also vampiros," Ethan pointed out.

Steve opened her mouth, stopped, and reconsidered. "They can hear you, see you, smell you, as well as you could them."

"Yes, all of that. We know where they're likely to be and we can occasionally find one or two. But we've never been able to get the drop on one."

"Shit." She'd always thought of vampiros as so powerful but this sounded like a Mexican standoff. "And the girls?"

"They're either feeding very clumsily or greedily."

"Greedily?" She blinked. What did greed have to do with death?

"I can only take sustenance from pleasurable emotions, such as your orgasm. It's far more common for vampiros to feed on disgusting emotions, such as terror or death."

"They kill to survive?" The enemy would get stronger every time they destroyed somebody? Her stomach dived for her boots. How gross—and how damn difficult to stop.

Surely there had to be a way out. "Can't a vampiro change his, uh, dining preferences?"

"No, never. The first emotion you taste as a vampiro sets the pattern for the rest of your life. You have my word. I will never start feeding on death, nor will any vampiro sired in Texas." Sincerity was laced into his words.

She nodded slowly, remembering all the times they'd slept together. He could have destroyed her but he never had, even when she'd rejected him.

She rubbed her hands together and blew on them to warm them, carefully not looking at Ethan's beautiful, warm body. For midsummer, she was still surprisingly cold.

Standing around talking wouldn't do any good. It was time to take action. She swung around to study the rotating display of pictures and articles about Devol.

"We have to find Devol and his men."

"Not we," thundered Ethan.

Who did he think would help—Superman? "Of course *we*. If you can't get close to them, then you need my help. Obviously ordinary women like me can and do pull that off just fine. I'll be undercover, of course."

"No." This time his voice was all the more emphatic for being quiet.

"You got a better idea, big boy?" Anything would be better than cozying up to a murderous vampiro.

He was silent, disapproval roaring through the room.

"Ethan, please. You'll be my CI, telling me where and when to go to catch these bastards," she coaxed, emphasizing his role. "When I show up, you and your men can be there, too—thick as fleas on a coonhound. Has anything else worked for you?"

"No." A muscle throbbed in his jaw.

"Then we'll go with my plan until something better comes along." She moved closer, stopping only a few feet away. His body heat teased her, rich and inviting as the sun, miraculous in a man who lived in the darkness.

"Very well. But I'll pull you out of any situation that goes bad."

She snickered. "We've both worked undercover before, Ethan. You've got the right to call off an op against these bastards and so do I." She stuck out her hand. "Deal?"

He swallowed hard but he shook. "Deal."

TWELVE

HALFWAY BETWEEN NEW ORLEANS AND BATON ROUGE,
THE SAME NIGHT

Twan Eldridge rattled through the pine forest, torn between
watching the road ahead and his odometer. It was easier to be
amazed Big Sis's sunflower yellow Beetle could keep moving
along this swampy morass than think about the meeting ahead.
Let alone remember why he'd been crazy enough to buttonhole
Passard at the last police chiefs' conference.

Two red reflectors flashed at exactly the promised point and
he turned hard right, sliding on the mud and almost smashing
the Beetle against a pine tree.

No cop would pull over a black man driving this piece of shit,
no matter how desperate they were to make their ticket quota.
No, they'd just laugh and wave the poor darkie on, figuring
he had apron strings stretching all the way back to his mama's
knee. Which was why Big Sis had made all her sons learn how to
drive in it and why he'd borrowed it for this trip, instead of his
official Crown Vic. No way he was having his license checked
by some ticket-happy rural cop and letting anybody in NOPD
know he was out here.

But it would have felt damn fucking good to meet his peers

like a deputy chief, with a big car and a driver. Not like some teenage boy sneaking around in the woods hoping not to be caught by his old man.

He snarled a curse unused since his years in Vice and hit the gas a little harder. It was still a better way to observe Jamaal's seventh birthday than laying flowers on his grave.

One last turn at a Y-fork. This part of the bayou was blacker than an Algiers Point back alley so he couldn't tell how many had come before him. Or had left unable to wait for him, no matter how much work they knew Chief Broussard liked to dump on his deputy chiefs.

Twan shrugged and turned left. He was in too deep now to back out, no matter what it cost.

The track abruptly widened into a muddy trough, leading to a small cedar house, with a half dozen cars and pickups parked in front.

He closed his eyes for a moment and whispered a prayer of thanks, before stopping in front of the house and extracting himself from the so-called car.

"Yo, dude, whassup?"

A short, square man bounded down the steps to seize, hug, and buss the newcomer on both cheeks like a long-lost cousin. "'Allo, Antwaan! Tante Cecille sent jumbo jes' for you!"

Passard must have been spending more time outdoors lately. His skin was swarthier than usual, a dark gold next to Twan's matt brown.

"What, me miss your auntie's cooking?" Twan retorted and offered an enormous shopping bag. "Brought some coffee and chocolate."

Passard's grin deepened. Coffee meant Twan had the files, while chocolate indicated he hadn't been followed.

But to be reduced to using code words with another cop, especially an honest one, was like being fucked over, even if it meant they could relax a little.

"Why are we standing out here? Let's go inside and eat."
Passard clapped an arm around Twan's shoulders and led him
up the steps. The front door shut behind them, unleashing a
storm of friendly voices.

Passard's hunting cabin was filled to overflowing with men
and women. Every seat was taken in the single room, and a
couple of men sat on the stairs leading to the attic. At least everyone could see everybody else, even if the furniture looked
decades old, and it was unlikely those bare wooden walls could
be successfully bugged.

"That chair's yours, Eldridge," Passard announced, and held
up two beers.

Twan accepted the seat and one of the cold bottles, twisting
it open after a quick nod of thanks.

For the first time in days—weeks? months?—he allowed himself to relax and enjoy friendly company. Robuchon from Baton
Rouge, pallid and plump, deadly as a water moccasin. Jenkins
from Plaquemines, with the steady cunning of the very poor and
the very realistic. Montagné from La Fourche, with the huge collection of knock-knock jokes and shooting awards, and more.

The greetings, the hugs, the slaps on the back, the warm concern that he eat a good meal, the lack of any questions, whether
spoken or not . . .

Cops he could trust with his life, who'd sometimes helped
each other block one of Bacchus's Temple's smaller tentacles,
but who'd never come together in a group this large before. If
anything went wrong, they'd be lucky to escape with their lives.
Their careers would be dead meat for sure.

But everyone here, both men and women, were openly
armed, whether their physiques screamed desk pusher or SWAT.
Twan was pretty damn sure Robuchon, for example, hadn't
heard a shot fired in anger for at least twenty years. On the
other hand, that dude was the best and dirtiest political infighter
in Louisiana.

"Are we sure your home is clean?" Robuchon asked Passard, echoing Twan's half-formed question.

"Oh yeah. Feds swept it floor to ceiling yesterday, as part of a training exercise. My boys have watched it ever since."

"You sure it's still safe, this deep in the woods?" Twan asked, remembering his long trek.

Passard's eyes twinkled briefly. "We're only about a mile from the highway on the other side. We brought you in the long way to make sure you weren't followed."

"I wasn't." That was for damn sure. He hadn't forgotten that many of his old skills.

"No—but we'd have stopped them even if you were, since this is an oil company hunting lodge. They agreed to run a joint exercise with my boys to see if anybody can penetrate their perimeter."

Twan studied his host, his brain rapidly recalculating the odds. The oil company was changing sides? That could really start changing the balance of power.

"They don't know exactly who's here and they don't want to," Passard assured him.

Which made this piece of real estate the most private place in Louisiana.

Passard tossed him a two-finger salute. "Any other questions?"

"No way, dude." Twan bit the bullet and pulled the files out of his briefcase. Maybe taking action would quell his incipient ulcer. God knows the divorce hadn't made him sleep any better.

He dumped them onto the coffee table, letting the slim folders slide from one end to the other. His companions leaned forward, their earlier banter entirely gone.

"There've been a lot more murders in New Orleans lately. It started on July sixth and has gone on at the same pace ever since, if you include all of the neighboring parishes."

Startled looks flashed around the room.

He pushed the last few folders out of the bag and onto the others. The mound trembled, too large for the surface, and several folders started to dive off the edges. Hands, both black and white, shot out to rescue them.

"How many?" somebody whispered.

"At least ten a day, maybe more."

He could pity them their shock at the numbers. He'd been able to figure that out more slowly. But he continued the briefing.

"All killed by having their throats ripped out."

"Dear God," somebody muttered. "I'd heard that before but—"

"And every one linked to Bacchus's Temple, the big casino," Twan finished and sat back, brushing his hand through his rough, short-cut 'fro.

"Madame Celeste's? The bitch who owns the state? Jesus, maybe now we can get some changes."

"That's why people have started to mutter in my parish."

"Yeah, tourists are starting to comment online. Concierges are warning single women against going out alone," Twan agreed. "Getting bad for business."

"But nobody can speak openly." Passard stated the obvious.

"Against Madame Celeste? Not unless you want to die." In a really stupid way, that is, as opposed to accomplishing something. "I can't even investigate individual killings. Officially, they're all accidents."

"Accidents—with torn throats?" A man's voice turned soprano.

"Yeah." He finished his beer.

"What about something statewide? The governor has loathed Madame Celeste ever since she hosted the party that got her son killed."

"What can she do that Madame Celeste wouldn't find out about?"

"Ask Washington for help," said Robuchon.

Twan stared at him. Where the hell had that idea come from? Silence sliced the room.

"They're only one phone call away," Robuchon pointed out. "Any governor just has to ask for agents from Washington, not local, same as if they're investigating an ordinary corruption case."

Twan swung around to look at Passard. Could it be that simple? Other heads swiveled and voices surged like buzz saws.

Then they started to smile.

SAN ANTONIO RIVER WALK, EVENING OF JULY 14

"Are you absolutely sure I can't wear an ordinary T-shirt?" Steve demanded. "Got my Harley tee right there. Tonight's only a dry run, after all."

She waggled her thumb at the heap of black and white cotton beside the yard-wide display of fresh flowers.

"And have anyone believe you're staying at a top boutique hotel on the River Walk? Sorry." Ethan paced slowly around her, eyeing her critically. He was wearing all white, including a guayabera, the traditional Cuban embroidered shirt. Thanks to that, his now black hair, and some much more subtle changes courtesy of a makeup artist, he looked like a wealthy Latin tourist, not an arrogant Scandinavian bastard.

She fumed, trying to think of another approach to becoming comfortable.

"And before you ask, yes, we do have to stay here, since it has the best layout for tonight's exercise. Could you please lift up your hair?"

She cocked an eyebrow at him and obeyed. Paranoid, that's what he was. She'd buy him a drink when this was over. "All I have to do is order a drink in a restaurant, Ethan. And you've got how many men for this op?"

"Altogether? About a half dozen."

She supposed she didn't blame him for not telling her all about how he conducted his business, after she'd told him her opinion of it. But, damn.

"Thanks, Steve, the wire looks great."

She shook her hair out, letting it fall over her shoulders. His eyes flashed but he said nothing. Once he'd have followed up that look with a mind-numbing kiss. Crap.

She rushed into speech like a rookie.

"It'll go fine, Ethan. This silk tunic has enough flowers to hide my mike. It's also so loose nobody'll ever see my Colt."

He opened his mouth but shut it without saying anything. Maybe he thought the tunic was so roomy there'd be enough extra fabric nobody could see through it. God knows the designer jeans underneath weren't designed for comfort, even in what was supposed to be a relaxed fit.

"Plus, I'm wearing high heels so I can strut like all the other rich bitches here." She put her hands on her hips and waggled them at him. "See? I can do arrogant."

"Yes, you certainly can," he agreed drily.

Maybe even sexy? Risky thought.

"But we promise to keep you away from any bad guys, even if one stops by. Now come on, let's introduce you to the guys."

Steve threw back her shoulders and sauntered out of the bedroom beside him, into the sitting room. Only Ethan's men were there tonight, since she'd told Posada she'd gone to meet her CI. She could feed any information they found back to her task force.

A half-dozen men came to attention when they entered, all of whom had arrived since she'd checked in to the hotel. Although they were all dressed casually, none of them struck her as anyone to start a fight with, under any circumstances.

But Hollywood had it wrong: These vampiros were not pretty. Masculine, very tempting for a night of pleasure, but only Ethan could be described as pretty.

Unless she was more prejudiced in his favor than she cared to think about.

"Gentlemen, this is Ranger Stephanie Reynolds."

"Ranger," they chorused, nodding to her.

"Steve," she corrected them.

"Steve," they agreed after glancing at Ethan.

"Steve, this is Angus Rough Bear, my second in command. He's a vampiro, a few years younger than myself."

Angus? An unusual first name for an Indian, especially since he'd been born before there were many white men around.

A tall, broad-shouldered man with raven black hair, strong features, and dark eyes inclined his head, his expression very reserved. Steve's Cherokee grandfather had treated strangers the same way, with distant courtesy until he knew their intentions and capabilities.

She smiled warmly and acknowledged Rough Bear with a slightly deeper nod of her head, younger warrior to elder.

"Emilio Alvarez, a compañero who'll be nearby. He's as strong as most very young vampiros but can readily go out in daylight, should there be a very long chase."

"A pleasure, Ranger," Alvarez greeted her heartily. He had dark hair and eyes, olive skin, and hawklike features. Compared to the others, he was very young, almost like a puppy, yet there was a wealth of bitter experience in his eyes.

"McAllister is a vampiro, as are these two." She shook hands with the indicated men, automatically memorizing their appearances. Ruggedly masculine, not pure perfection, but definitely deadly, especially around the eyes.

"Plus, Hennessy will be our sniper. He's already in position so you can't meet him in advance. But you'll recognize his voice over the air by his Irish brogue."

Brogue? She blinked. Just how long had Ethan and the Santiago Trust been recruiting men? Where did they find them? And was Hennessy from the IRA? She shrugged off such trivialities;

there were more important issues to consider, like how to carry herself in this damn costume.

At least in a bridesmaid's dress, the skirt concealed any wobbles. Jeans gave her no such help.

"What about her Colt?" Rough Bear asked.

"That's why she's carrying an antique," Ethan drawled, packing a startling arsenal into a duffel bag. "It's her great-great's Colt 1911, which he was issued during World War I and carried throughout that war. He gave it to his son, who used it throughout the next world war."

"So what?" Steve demanded, and pivoted, relearning the art of wearing high heels while walking through the suite.

"It smells of all those events, not a modern gun's fragile scents. In character, you have it for sentimental reasons, because it's handy and you've heard rumors of unusual events."

"It's an antique, which implies I don't really know how to use it." She grinned, warm mischief glowing through her veins. "Won't they be surprised?"

"Careful, Steve," Ethan warned. "If things go wrong, you probably won't have much chance to use it. You'll have to rely on us."

She opened her mouth, ready to attack misogynistic, overprotective bastards, but caught his eye. He was watching her, those white lines cutting deeper around his mouth.

Good Lord, he'd meant every word. Lovely, just lovely.

Her stomach promptly devoted itself to creating flip-flops and Gordian knots. Undercover work was always dangerous, but there was usually some opportunity to protect oneself. She fought to breathe steadily, reminding herself she'd be heavily protected.

"Steve." He wrapped his hand around hers, squeezing it warmly. "You're part of our team now. We've worked together successfully for a long time and tonight should go well."

She stuck her chin out and parked her nerves in her pocket.

"Damn straight it will." She gripped his fingers, her skin still a little chilly.

"Listen up, boys." Ethan's voice strengthened after he released her. "Remember, Peter has loaned us one of his Houston vampiros for tonight's dry run, who's fairly unfamiliar with the Dallas and San Antonio compañías. He will walk through the hotel's café, checking to see if Steve has an escort. If he doesn't spot anyone, our setup works."

"How good are his senses?" Alvarez asked, his dark eyes calculating.

"He's approximately the same age as most of Devol's bandolerismo." Ethan shrugged.

"Any of Devol's vampiros around? The River Walk is still the biggest tourist draw in Texas," Rough Bear pointed out. "At least after dark."

"Unlikely, after last week's dustup. They know we're watching it."

Alvarez nodded slowly. Steve was grateful for the reassuringly awkward presence of her family's Colt, deep inside her jeans' waistband.

"Any other questions?"

Men shook their heads, their expressions blatantly confident.

Steve stepped in. "Do you believe in group huddles before an op?"

"Of course." Rough Bear and Alvarez came forward first, quickly joined by the others. Everyone linked hands, pressing close together until they were joined at shoulders and hips as well, their heads bowed.

She leaned against them, savoring their closeness and drawing strength from it.

Rough Bear began to chant in his own language. The others hummed, thumping the beat with their feet. Although she didn't understand the exact words, somehow she knew he asked for blessings upon all of them during the coming hunt. She could almost feel her own Indian ancestors humming in approval.

Strength and calm flowed into her, plus coolness and confidence in the men around her.

After all these decades, this would be the first time a member of her family would fight for Texas justice, beside other law enforcement officers—with all of them under the Great Spirit's protection. She'd needed to step into the vampiros' darkness to reunite with her roots.

She was still smiling quietly when the last man slipped out to take up his position.

She sauntered out, head high, every inch the rich bitch suffering from insomnia, and headed for the café on the River Walk. Time to go down, have a couple of nonalcoholic drinks, eye the local scenery, and come back. No big deal, right? This was only a dry run. Even if they did attract a bad guy, they'd succeed in taking him out.

Except for Ethan a few paces behind her and her abiding hunger to haul his ass into her bed.

By the time she took her seat in the café, she'd convinced herself high heels were the only footgear for showcasing a girl's legs and ass. Maybe she'd try it again sometime, when she had a hot date. The few men still around certainly thought so, ogling her as if they'd never seen a female walking alone.

The café was full of leather and wrought iron chairs, gathered around wrought iron tables set with homemade tiles. Palms sprouted in every available corner and screened the café from the River Walk's sidewalk, giving the patrons a private view of the river.

She settled into her chair and ordered a club soda and lime. An abrupt wave of her hand permitted the waiter to bring a menu and she pretended to study the list of hors d'oeuvres.

Alvarez was reading a playbill at the nightclub next door to the hotel. Ethan and Rough Bear were nowhere in sight, but instinct, more confident than her eyes, told her the pattern was complete with them there.

"Thanks." She signed for the overpriced example of fizzy water and fruit and pushed the menu aside. "Chicken quesadilla, please."

Thank God this was going on somebody else's expense account. She couldn't imagine explaining triple the usual cost to Posada.

Now if that Houston vampiro would just show up soon, they could call this a day.

A man sat down at the table next to hers. He was Caucasian, with regular features, probably five foot ten and a slender build, wearing a corporate polo shirt. She'd seen men just like him a thousand times before in Austin, Dallas, and San Antonio. His head was bent, his eyes intently focused on the café's long list of specialty margaritas.

She glanced over at him, wondering if he was too close and she needed to move. But tables were always packed tightly together in tourist traps.

She sniffed and started counting all those overgrown bits of garden, screened by palm fronds. The after-hours sweep for drunks must be time-consuming around here, if they had to comb all of the landscaping.

Time-consuming. Maybe she could check her smart phone to see if Ethan or any of his men had left her a message.

She stretched her hand toward her purse—but nothing happened. She couldn't even waggle her fingers.

She tried again, gritting her teeth.

Nothing, although her fingers ached until they burned. *Ethan?*

Her heart slammed against her chest, then lurched into a panicked gallop.

She needed her gun. Get her gun.

She pictured it, every detail, including the serial number and the long, never explained scratch on its butt from World War I. Bend her arm at the elbow and slide it around, then down her back . . .

Her fingertips touched her chair and stopped. No, she needed to go farther!

Weight slammed into her brain like a sonic boom. Her eyes widened.

Heat flashed across her chest and throat but a glacier imprisoned her muscles in a wall of ice. A vise began to slowly move up her throat.

For the first time in her life, she could do nothing at all.

"Steve?" The beloved voice was in her ears.

Oh dear God, Ethan. *Please come.*

She demanded her mouth to open—but her lips remained stubbornly closed. Knives stabbed every muscle, like the pins to a marionette's strings. Although she fought every inch, the knives forced her to look at the closest bit of garden.

Shit, it was just big enough for two people to lie down inside.

Something—someone?—silently spoke to her somehow. *Stand up.*

No! she retorted. *Never. Dear God, how was this conversation possible?*

The man sitting next to her chuckled very softly.

Was this what had happened to those poor girls?

She started to rise, sweat pouring down her face.

Something thudded into the man next to her and the weight disappeared from her mind and muscles.

Steve scrambled desperately away, knocking over her chair. When she had her back to the wall and her Colt in her hand, she dared to look back.

That corporate polo shirt was settling into the man's chair, a few pinches of dust atop its chest and shoulders. What the hell? Where had he gone?

Somebody was screaming but it didn't seem to be her. At least, she was very cold and her throat didn't hurt.

"He's dead, Steve. He's dead." Ethan wrapped his arm around her, completely disregarding her gun, and pulled her hard against him. Rough Bear and Alvarez raced in behind him to pour soothing words over the café's uproar.

"Are you okay?" Ethan gently brushed her hair back from her face.

"I couldn't move." She stared up at him, tremors starting somewhere deep inside and building until they shook every bone and muscle. "It felt as if he could read my mind—and was laughing!"

Ethan flinched, his face turning gray.

"Oh crap, he could." She shoved her Colt back into her waistband, her hand vibrating like a cement mixer. An instant later, she buried her face against him and clung like a Victorian maiden.

Ethan handed Steve another cup of sweet coffee before sitting back down on the sofa beside her. Her apartment contained only a few pieces of furniture, all of them cheap. But the big sofa was comfortable enough, if they sat close together.

God damn Devol and his bandolerismo! Hell, when he'd seen her terrified face and realized she couldn't speak, his own veins had run cold. If anything happened to her, he'd personally destroy Devol and the hell with waiting for orders from Don Rafael.

Mercifully, everything had turned out well enough—but only because he needed to see her face every few minutes, regardless of what his plan said. If she'd been his hija, he'd have known sooner what was going on. But he couldn't give her El Abrazo, even if nobody except Don Rafael had a chance of pulling her through La Lujuria.

The café's occupants had noticed nothing except a woman drawing a gun—and a pile of clothing's sudden arrival. That was quickly smoothed over by claiming Steve had thought she'd seen her worthless ex-husband walk past.

Apologies over, Ethan had quickly taken her away, murmuring agreement with her insistence that she could take care of herself. Of course, she could—after she recovered from her shock. Poor darling. She'd only nodded when Emilio had offered to ride her Harley back to Austin, a very forward request at any other time.

He'd left Luis's men to destroy all video surveillance, of course. The siniscal's men knew where all records were kept, as befitted good householders.

At least they knew the basic plan worked. Steve hadn't slept with Ethan for more than a month so she didn't have even the faintest trace of vampiro scent left. Pity; it might have kept those brutes away from her. They were obviously preying only upon women in a blatant challenge to Don Rafael's protectiveness toward the gentler sex. Normally, even bandolerismo would feed upon both men and women, reflecting vampiros' usual bisexuality.

"If I have any more of this, I'll stay up all night, spinning like a top." She sipped at the hot coffee, her eyelids slightly translucent.

His mouth tightened at her fragility. "Looking very lovely."

"Flatterer."

Not really.

"You had quite a shock. The coffee will help." Oh hell, that sounded like something his mother would have said.

She sniffed in disbelief and gently blew over the milky brew's surface. It stirred, shimmering under the light.

Once she'd have teased him that way. Intimately.

He shifted, looking for a more comfortable position.

She wiggled, snuggling her hips and the curve of her breasts closer to him.

He froze but gritted out a smile.

"I've never failed like that before, Ethan," she muttered.

"Failed?" He rapidly scanned through the night's events. "What are you talking about?"

"I couldn't stop him. He wasn't ten feet away from me. But I couldn't shoot, shove. I couldn't even scream like a high school girl," she finished on a whisper. "I was useless."

"Dammit, Steve!" He grabbed the cup out of her hand and slammed it down on the table, sloshing coffee across the cheap wood. The hell with that.

"Uh, Ethan, what—"

He snatched her onto his lap, forcing her to look him in the eye.

"Stop that. D'you hear me? Don't blame yourself. No prosaica can stop a vampiro from taking control of her mind. You had no choice."

He shook her by the shoulders.

"But surely I could have done more." Her eyes were enormous.

"Every sense is enhanced when we become vampiros, including the psychic ones. We're all telepaths, at least in comparison to prosaicas like yourself. It gives us the ability to dictate what you think or do."

She frowned, thoughts starting to run again behind those whisky eyes before they went dull again. "But he walked through my mind and I feel used. Dirty."

"You are not dirty. You are incredible. No other prosaica could have managed to move at all, let alone touch her chair, after a vampiro took control of her." His heart was pounding, his voice turning husky. "You're strong, very strong—and special."

"Strong? Do you really think so?" She ran her finger lightly down his cheek, her calluses catching on his stubble and sending lightning strikes deep into his heart and lungs.

"I know it, darling." He kissed the palm of her hand.

She gasped—and he captured her mouth, offering her his warmth, lips to lips, breath to breath. She sighed and opened, accepting him.

It was the gentlest of kisses, like feathers taking to the wind, their fingers twining together. He cupped her face, protecting her, giving her the most comfort and security possible in the embrace. Ignoring the aching beat of his blood, like molten lava under his skin wherever she touched.

"Ethan," she murmured, and moved closer, sliding her fingers into his hair.

He kissed her again, deepening the contact, allowing more of his passion, his absolute confidence in her to show.

She pressed herself against him, still trembling, but willing at least. Damn the bandolerismo!

He nuzzled her, feathering kisses over her face—the straight nose, the passionate mouth, stubborn jaw, high cheekbones, winged eyebrows, broad forehead. So perfect, so beautiful, so nearly gone forever.

He caressed her hair, threading his fingers through its fine silk and gently kneading her exquisitely sensitive scalp underneath.

She purred with pleasure, rubbing her head against his hands like a cat. His lady, his darling.

And so little time to enjoy her. Ever.

He licked her throat, lightly flicking his tongue against the hidden pulse points.

She chuckled and arched her head back, utterly relaxed.

He nuzzled and kissed his way up and over her jaw until he found her mouth again. This time, she kissed him back eagerly, warmly.

He rumbled approval, stroking the small of her back underneath her clothes. Lovely, lovely Stephanie Amanda.

She arched closer, rubbing her breasts against him. Sheets of fire rolled across his skin and spilled into his flesh. His pulse kicked hard and began to run faster through his veins. "Oh God, yes, Stephanie."

"Mrmph," she agreed, and gasped into his mouth when he ran his thumbs up her back, underneath her tunic. She arched even closer, blatantly willing.

His cock swelled against his trousers, straining the white linen. Denim would have allowed far more discretion, dammit.

He rose, sweeping her into his arms. A sofa, no matter how big, wasn't the place to continue this.

And damn, but she looked good a moment later stretched across her bed. It jutted into the room like a throne, covered in silky layers of yellow and gold cotton. A chair and a single dresser were the only furniture. A magnificent dream catcher hung protectively over her bed, its eagle feathers and netting glinting as it slowly turned in a slight draft. But everything he wanted was contained in Stephanie.

She blinked up at him and licked her lips, smiling with a bit of her old sassiness.

"Ah, Stephanie." He started to grin, his heart relaxing a bit. That was his girl.

"Steve," she corrected. She ran her eyes over him and blushed when she reached his crotch.

His smile darkened to something primal and masculine. His woman.

He dropped down beside her on the bed and kissed her again, sliding his leg between hers. She moaned, tossing against him.

He teased her tunic upward and unclasped her bra, catching his breath at her beauty. Her rosy nipples were already tightly furled with hunger, calling to him for fulfillment. They needed his mouth, teeth, lips. Or maybe he should explore her breasts first with his hands . . .

He went a little insane and tried to do everything, make up for all the lost days and weeks he'd lived without her. Relearn the taste of her velvet flesh, the salt of her skin, the arcs of her sweet areolas deep within his mouth . . . The driving pulse in his own veins when he lost himself in loving her.

She sobbed his name over and over, begging him for more, demanding completion.

His hands shook when he tugged those damn high heels off and threw them across the room. His hands were shaking when he unzipped her jeans, so badly it took him two tries to get them off.

But her scent was a wonderful perfume—rich and musky, uniquely hers. He shuddered, inhaling it, before he dropped to his knees and kissed the inside of her thigh. His cock was the definition of madness, the center of every driving, mindless, hungry pulse in his body.

He tasted her, swirling his tongue along the delicate trickles of cream. He found his way higher to the source, to her sweet folds, her plump clit now standing proudly erect. He nuzzled and sniffed, his heart thudding like an artillery barrage in his chest.

"Ethan. Ohgawd, Ethan, please." Her hips lifted toward his hungry mouth.

He hummed approval and she jolted, her hands pulling him closer. "Oh, Ethan."

He rumbled his insistence on his own timing, his own choices. But his zipper was biting into his cock like iron rails and her legs were frantically clasped around him.

He pulled away, reluctant to leave her for even an instant, and yanked off his damn shirt and trousers. She gasped, just a little, but she was licking her lips at the sight of him.

"Stephanie." He took her into his arms and she flung herself at him, immediately wrapping her arms and legs around him. "Stephanie."

She was so hot for him and they were so accustomed to each other that they joined easily. He scissored their legs and rolled onto his side, making sure she felt every detail of both their bodies, their pleasure, their breathing.

He rocked against her slowly, using his hand on her back to control their pace. She orgasmed, her delight spiraling through both of them.

Yes, and yes, and yes.

He shifted her, rubbing her clit against his leg, gritting his teeth against his own desperation. Waves were pounding through his spine, building in his balls.

"Ethan!" she shrieked, climaxing again, and higher, before she'd fully come down from the first.

His smile was edged with a tight triumph. Surely he could wait a little longer.

He kissed her throat, her pulse vibrating against his tongue, and delicately teased her clit with his finger.

She rocked against him, moaning—and scratched his shoulder. The salty-sweet scent of blood filled the air.

Sanity snapped.

He rocked deeper into her, finding her sweet spot and sending her straight over the edge. She howled in ecstasy and threw her head back. He bit down, hard and fast, plunging his fangs into her jugular, and tasted the rich perfection of her passion. Fire bright, whirling through his blood like torches through the night.

Orgasm raced through him, shattering his links to the earth. He poured himself into her, filling her with his heat and his fire.

Stephanie, his love.

He cradled her afterward, watching her sleep. She needed her rest, after all, so she could live a long time. Regardless of how he'd cope with watching her die of old age, when he'd barely handled being without her for a month or nearly seeing her die tonight.

He kissed the top of her head, gathering in her scent, storing up the memory of her soft breathing.

They'd think about the war tomorrow.

Thirteen

The Gulfstream jet circled the Texas hills, its luxuries no comfort now for Celeste. Even her entourage remained strapped silently into their seats, too astonished—and cowed—to speak.

The football stadium below was all too easy to spot, its banks of lights blazing into the sky. Streams of people danced across the grass, forming and re-forming colorful knots under the great heraldic lion. Soon they'd be frolicking horizontally, the ecstatic bastards.

"Imbécile!" Madame Celeste threw another bottle of champagne into the galley, its door wisely left open by her steward. The bottle burst against the cabinet like a shotgun blast, wine and glass shards spewing over the floor. "We should be drinking this in that stadium, while they beg us for mercy. Another minute and Don Rafael would have been dead!"

"Beau is lucky he died so cleanly, *cher*," Georges agreed, rage running clean and cold through his belly. "Otherwise, you'd have made his last hours hell on earth for such an elementary mistake as to let Don Rafael slip away."

"Only to win, with the help of his cónyuge bitch! There is no other answer."

"No, only a cónyuge could have fed him strength when he'd been almost dead." Georges' fangs pricked his lip. If Templeton's mesnaderos hadn't been in the way, he'd have shot Don Rafael while he was on the ground—and that fool was indulging in an early celebration. But no, Don Rafael recovered and won. *Merde.*

The plane began to level out, heading east for the Mississippi and home.

"So Don Rafael still lives to attack us, while his heraldo will make more supercilious announcements of Texas virtues." She spat. "Until we kill them both."

"We have another weapon at our disposal, *cher madame*," Georges pointed out. "As you have mentioned before."

"Hmm?" She raised an eyebrow.

"We've been feeding on Texas women but discreetly, except in Galveston. If we were more blatant about our presence . . ." He paused suggestively.

"Those Texas cattle would stampede and destroy him." She chuckled, a wickedly mirthful sound.

He grinned back at her, anticipating his rewards for evoking that much glee.

"Excellent idea! And you did so well in Galveston, too. The broken hands, to increase pain."

"The femoral artery—a major blood vessel, yet unexpected, exquisitely sensitive, and linked with sexual violation." He sighed, remembering the excellent meal. "Ah, madame, you taught me so well!"

She patted his arm. "And you shall do even better when you return, *mon brave.*"

COMPOSTELA RANCH, JULY 22

Grania screamed, full-throated, the sound piercing Rafael's heart like a lance.

Grania, mi vida!

His men rushed to their feet, reaching for their weapons, but he utterly ignored them. He bolted for his bedroom, slamming his office door so hard it reverberated and shattered a hinge.

Grania, luz de mi corazón! He skidded on the hardwood floor, his feet hurling the soft rugs under the bed. Her face was buried in the pillows and she was sobbing as if her heart would break. *Grania, mi alma,* he crooned, and dropped to his knees beside her.

Loneliness battered him through the conyugal bond, heart-breaking and despairing. Her throat was raw, shredded with pain, as if she'd wept for hours instead of the few minutes since he'd left her.

"Grania, *querida*," he croaked, her agony instantly lacing deeper into his bones. He choked for breath but laid his arm over her shoulders. "I am here. Please wake up, my darling."

She shuddered. Did her sobs slow, just a trifle?

"Grania, *mi corazón*." He gathered her closer, coaxing her to shelter against his chest. "All is well, *querida*. Content yourself and relax. Shh."

Dios, he couldn't reach her emotions, the deepest levels where cónyuges always understood each other.

She whimpered, sobs shaking her slender body.

What now? He trusted his own instincts and bit his lip until blood flowed, scenting the air, calling to his beloved vampira. He eased himself onto the bed until they were lying down side by side, bringing his entire body to comfort her.

Gracias a Dios. She kissed him fiercely, clutching his shirt and tasting him. He gave her everything, his heartbeat thudding until he couldn't think. She shook her head—and he clutched her closer. But she buried her face against him, clinging as if the end of the world were near. Her sobs began to moderate and the daggers stopped tunneling into his heart.

Grania, mi alma y mi vida. He rocked her gently, tears trickling down his cheeks. If he lost her, his life and his soul, there would be no light in his heart and he would follow her to the grave. He could not bury her twice.

She finally gulped, the sobs long gone. He unceremoniously dumped a pillow out of its case, and handed her the fine linen. She sniffled and blew her nose hard, looked at her handkerchief, then glanced at him.

He shrugged off any concerns. This was his house and he'd do as he damn well pleased, especially to ensure his lady's comfort.

She smiled a trifle, her eyes very red. But at least she could feel laughter.

"*Querida,*" he breathed, and kissed her gently, his heart starting to beat at a more normal rhythm. "Would you like some wine or a bath or . . . ?"

"No!" Terror, searing as acid, flashed through their link and he flinched, before snatching her closer.

Her heart was pounding again. He cuddled her close, unable to speak.

"All I want," she said slowly, keeping to the spoken word, "is to hold you close."

"You have me," he assured her promptly, "always. Your creador is dead and no one else can come between us."

Her lips curved into a smile but there was little pleasure in it.

"I dreamed . . . No, I remembered," she corrected herself.

He came to full alertness. Grania was the reincarnation of Blanche, his long-dead wife, and could usually control when and how she accessed those memories. But sometimes she relived them fully, unable to control what events she saw or how deeply.

"*¿Sí, querida?*"

"After the Infante's army was destroyed by the Moors and you were captured, Toledo was besieged. For months."

Her voice was almost colorless. But so was fine steel, or a

knife twisting through darkness to rip through his own memories. "*Ay de mi*, no Moorish army had come that close to the capital in decades. There was no army, no knights of the blood royal to lead the small garrison, nobody. And your Princesse—"

He stopped short, careful even after all these centuries not to speak his true thoughts about that feminine monument to selfishness and stubbornness, lest he offend her most faithful servant.

"Was in hysterics, day and night, over her husband's death." Grania sighed, her eyes very dark with memories.

"Demanding all your strength." The bitch.

"I had your little ones to give me joy," she protested mildly.

But they were so very young . . .

"Fernando and Beatriz could walk just well enough to find diversions"—mischief—"everywhere, while Ana was a newborn babe." Her voice trailed off, old lines of worry and exhaustion scoring her face.

And you were alone, he whispered, mind to mind.

Yes, she agreed, a single tear trembling on an eyelash.

"*Dios mio,* I should have been there!"

"How? You were a captive and close to dying, as well. But I was so deadly afraid without you."

He caught her hand and kissed it, offering comfort and apologies in the only way he could.

"Relax, my love." Her blue eyes poured love's true light over him, brilliant as *Santísima Virgen*'s mantle. "Sobs will never tear me apart again, now I know in my bones you're alive."

He could give her earthly assurances, such as they were.

"I swear, *mi vida*, you will never have to face such trials by yourself again."

"Ah, darling, do not swear to do what circumstances may force you to change. You are the Patrón of Texas and your duty must come first, especially when there is war."

He winced but nodded, accepting her grasp of brutal necessities. Even so—*mierda*, how he'd fight not to see her suffer again!

RANGER TASK FORCE, AUSTIN

The door clicked rapidly, paused, and clicked again before swinging open. Posada quickly stepped inside and yanked it shut, carefully blocking the view of any passersby.

His unusual caution made Steve narrow her eyes. But she stood up from her computer, as casually as possible. "Hi, Lieutenant. Come to grab a doughnut before they go stale?"

"Thanks but no thanks. I've already hit the gym this morning." He set a stack of newspapers down on the center table.

She glanced at it thoughtfully, considering its unusual dimensions. "Coffee then? We've got some espresso, plus some new cases to look at. Just arrived from outside of Waco."

"Waco?" His head jerked up and he stopped smoothing out newsprint.

"Mmhmm. Technically, halfway between Waco and Galveston. The local sheriff heard of us and brought the two cases down."

"We're starting to get attention," Posada muttered.

She nodded. "At least by fellow cops. Nothing on the streets that we know of." Or that Ethan's men had heard.

Ethan. She shifted slightly, testing for tenderness after last night. Around them, men had gone back to work, providing a screen of phone calls and clattering keyboards.

Posada tapped the newspapers with a long, callused finger. "Brought this week's small-town and special-interest papers. This one's the *Corncobs and Cows Gazette*."

"Corncobs and cows?"

"Yes, it's a weekly, specializing in organic farming and energy issues."

"Ohkayy." She eyed it again, giving it the same enthusiasm she'd offer a rotting rattlesnake.

"It has an article on how the increasing health of Texas pastures is causing sinus infections, as evidenced by the higher death rates among young women this summer," Posada said very softly. "As further shown by their arched necks and terrified expressions."

Her head shot up and she stared at him.

"One commentator to their online edition suggested those symptoms sounded more like a date rape drug and murder. He was quickly shot down. Date rape drugs weren't used in farm towns."

Steve hooted in disbelief.

"Exactly. Even so, we're running out of time before other media carries the story." He paused significantly. "And the public really starts getting nervous."

Chills shimmied over her spine. "We know single women rarely frequent bars anymore."

"But that's not mass hysteria," Posada pointed out. "It's not high school girls being forbidden to go near an ice cream parlor or young mothers letting their babies scream because they're afraid to pick up a prescription after dark. If that happens, or worse—"

"Texas is toast," she said flatly. *And the real villain is a vampire, who you have no chance of defeating.*

Damn, damn, damn.

FOURTEEN

Steve strolled along the sidewalk with Ethan, contemplating the uneasy mix of tourists and nightclubs. At least this was Austin, where manners were generally civilized. Plus, it was summer so the university wasn't in session, cutting down on any football fan rowdiness. Even so, Austin's legendary live music scene had brought in enough out-of-town gawkers and drunks to fill the bars and fray the traffic laws. But it was a happy crowd, enjoying the songs which spilled out through open doors or were screeched into the steamy night air by electronics.

They slipped into a recessed entryway, its door blocked to encourage usage via a paid portal.

"Anyone *interesting* here tonight?" she asked.

"Nope." His gaze reassessed the Driskill Hotel's white and gold bulk, lingering over every spotlit arch. "No sign of any bandoleros or snipers," he added, lowering his voice.

"Nothing at the capitol, either." She jerked her head slightly toward its fairy-tale dome, barely visible between a covey of skyscrapers.

His head shot around and he stared at her. "Have they upped the guards on that, too?"

"Yeah, the governor's feeling nervous."

"Shit."

She couldn't agree with him more. "At least he's being close-mouthed about the threat."

Ethan glanced down at her, a smile playing around his mouth. "He's been encouraged to be discreet."

She blinked, sorting through the implications. "The way I can't talk about our affair?"

"Mmhmm."

She whistled softly. "Do your folks do that often to politicians?" she asked a few minutes later, after the traffic light had changed and a new set of tourists had ambled past.

"Only when necessary."

"That's not an answer."

"Best one you're going to get."

She sniffed. He might look like an old-fashioned cowboy in his Western shirt, jeans, and fancy boots. But he didn't have to be just as laconic.

He suddenly stepped onto the pavement and watched a gleaming black and chrome motorcycle stop for the light. Steve immediately joined him, caught by his intensity.

"That's a fine Road Star," she commented.

"Top of the line." Ethan's gaze never wavered from the bike. The man and woman aboard were hidden behind motorcycle leathers and full face masks, and golden hair could be glimpsed beneath the woman's mask. She pressed herself against her companion, graceful as a cat, while he gently caressed her leg.

"Do we need to worry?" Steve asked.

The woman ran her hand gently over the man's chest, anticipating and yet also somehow amazed.

Steve swallowed, fighting down jealousy.

Ethan lifted his hand and the male rider waggled two fingers in response.

"Your friend." Steve turned away. What would it be like, to find such joy with a lover?

"My oldest hermano," Ethan said flatly. He lowered his voice. "The first vampiro my creador sired, as you would say, and truly my brother."

The light changed again, bidding the Road Star and its lovers good-bye.

A woman who was confident with a vampiro? If Steve could quickly pull off similar unspoken communication with Ethan, like a well-trained team, they could try another ambush. Setting up sentries and marching around cities wasn't going to work. They might be having fewer attacks but the ferocity was growing far worse.

"What if—" She stopped, tripping over her tongue, but tried again. "What if we tried another ambush? Instead of guarding hunting grounds and searching out likely 'nesting' places?"

"What are you talking about?" He stared at her.

She firmed her jaw and took a deep breath, prepared to argue for as long as she needed to.

He glanced around, obviously concluding they needed privacy, and guided her into an alley, finding a jagged corner between buildings.

"Go on." His tone was barely civilized.

"Suppose you and I worked together as a team? You know, where we've trained together so long each of us knows what the other will do before they do it?"

"Steve, there's no time for that much practice." His voice was much gentler. "I'll work with you and nobody else. Hell, I'm the only vampiro who'll do that much. But—"

Good, she had the first crack in his armor.

"Can't your vampiro biology help us?"

"Huh?"

"Speed things up so our bodies communicate better? Like

something in the movies, maybe?" She waited hopefully. The alley was quiet, with the street far away like a distant curtain.

"Ah, Jesus." He pulled his hat off and slapped it against his leg, rubbing his hand over his mouth. "Movies—and books—lie, honey. Or at least they tell so little truth it might as well all be false."

"Explain it to me then." Something whimpered inside her heart. But she wasn't giving up, not that easily. "Well, skipping over the vampira option . . ."

For a moment, his eyes blazed with green fire and his fangs flashed. Her chest tightened, sending treacherous heat diving into her pussy. She gulped and hurried on. "Isn't there an option where I could remain a Ranger?"

His expression shifted into an icily polite mask and she found herself mourning the loss of her heated lover. "No, only becoming my hija or cónyuge—my life mate—would give me the access you're talking about."

"Hija?"

"If you became a vampira and I was your creador." He could have been discussing a library cataloging system, except for the muscle throbbing in his cheek.

Drink blood for the rest of her life? Live in darkness? Give up the Rangers? Uh, no. "What about the cónyuge option?"

"The conyugal bond is one of complete trust and can exist between a vampiro and anyone—a prosaico, a compañero, or another vampiro." He swallowed hard.

A prosaico? Somebody like her? That sounded promising. She trusted Ethan a lot. "How can we make this happen?"

"We can't." He laughed but it provided no mirth. "The conyugal bond can never be forced. It usually takes a long time to form."

"Months?" Maybe if they worked at it?

"Years or decades." He tipped his hat back onto his head.

"Shit."

He nodded, the lines in his face deeper than she remembered. "It's extremely rare, Steve. There are two pairs of cónyuges living in Texas, which is astonishing."

"But surely if you like somebody enough . . ." She struggled, trying to find a path for developing this all-important bond.

"You must trust them completely if they are to communicate with you body and soul, on a level below speech or even telepathy. For example, since I became a vampiro, I've only slept with one lover who I trusted enough to sleep through their rising."

"Well, that's promising!" she encouraged.

"I was lucky with my creador. Not every vampiro can trust theirs."

Shit. She shivered at the ugly images that conjured up, if a vampiro had to obey somebody they didn't have complete confidence in.

He rubbed his hands up and down her arms. "It's okay, Steve. He's always done the best for me."

He'd misread her misgivings. Had there been incidents where his creador mistreated him?

"Your scars. The son of a bitch!" She spat and spun on her heel. If she could track Ethan down, she could find his boss, too.

"Hey, Steve, calm down." He caught her by the shoulders.

"How can you defend him?" She stared at him, her heart in her throat. Good Lord, she'd seen many dysfunctional families and studied a lot more. But she'd never thought Ethan came from one.

"The whip scars are a constant reminder of the destructive fool I once was," he said flatly. "Like a tattoo, in some ways."

"Ethan!"

"He healed all my other wounds, Steve. Have you ever seen a gunshot scar on me? Or a knife scar?"

"Well, no, but still—"

"Nothing else would have reached me. Don't judge us and our world, Steve, until you've walked in it."

"A world of darkness."

"We keep you—and them"—he jerked his head toward the chattering tourists milling along the sidewalk—"safe, while we live in the night."

"Never to see the sun." She could barely force the words out.

"If a vampiro is lucky and survives two centuries, he can walk in twilight. Three centuries and he'll enjoy high noon again." He shrugged. "It's a pretty good deal."

Protecting people for centuries, at the risk of his own life? How much recreation did he ever get, especially when killers like Devol started running wild?

She shook her head, letting her hair conceal her blurry eyes before she was thought weak. Best to change the subject. This conversation was going nowhere and it was time to talk about something else. Surely their relief must have showed up by now, ready to keep Devol's men away from the Austin tourists.

"Hey, cowboy, care for a ride?" she crooned, and managed a flirtatious wiggle of her hips.

He blinked and started to grin. "Why, ma'am, I thought you'd never ask." He swept her up against him and headed out of the alley at a trot, snarling at a traffic light that dared to delay them.

Steve chuckled and stuck her tongue out at him when he shot her a mock glare.

A lifetime with him might be worthwhile, however long.

VALENCIA, THE NEXT NIGHT

Ethan jumped down out of Steve's Expedition, controlling the urge to shake himself like a dog. The big truck's interior had suddenly shrunk with a woman at the wheel, even though she was a damn good driver.

Steve closed the hatch and met him, now openly carrying a Remington 11-87 shotgun in its tactical sling.

His eyebrows flew up. "Do you think we'll need that? This is a ghost town being turned into a high-class golf resort."

"Pattern's wrong here. Can't you feel it?"

Too many ripples were pattering over his skin for him to argue.

"Yeah. Just testing you, honey."

She sniffed and turned slowly, considering their surroundings. He grabbed his Benelli M2 tactical shotgun from the backseat and joined her.

"And you call me paranoid," she muttered.

"At least mine doesn't sound like a car crash going off next to your head," he pointed out.

She gave him the finger and went back to studying the quiet landscape. He concealed a smile but slipped an extra speed-loader for his Benelli into his belt. At least she was wearing full tactical gear, including her Kevlar vest and a well-equipped weapons belt.

"If you need to shoot, go for head or heart. Anything else will only give you a short delay."

"Head or heart? Do you mean I've got to immediately stop the brain or the blood flow in order to have a chance?" She didn't bother to look at him, the concept clearly being so foreign to her training as to be not worth talking about.

"Exactly." It was that simple and that serious.

His answer's flatness brought her swiveling around to test its truth in his eyes.

"Gotcha," she agreed, her face a little white as the implications sank in. He didn't blame her for quickly stepping out to study the old town.

Late in the nineteenth century, Valencia had been the center of a prosperous granite quarrying industry, high in the Texas Hill Country northwest of Austin. But when the railroad chose to bypass it in favor of carrying both cattle and granite, Valencia's citizens had speedily departed, leaving behind few residual signs of their presence.

Ethan and Steve stood on a bluff overlooking the river, babbling softly while it curved around the hill and dived toward the rickety old bridge. A gentle rise on the opposite side held the few marble placards and iron fences, which marked Boot Hill. Beyond that were acres of rolling pasture and cornfields, dotted with cedar and live oaks.

A few square blocks—of scattered buildings, tire tracks, and old gardens—showed where the residents had once lived. The town fathers had built for the ages, even in their simplest shelters, and the results proved it over a century later.

The top of the hill was crowned by Valencia's remaining glory, its courthouse and surrounding park. The park was a beautiful swath of green, bordered by elegant walks and guarded by a Confederate veteran, proudly carrying his rifle with its bronze bayonet over his shoulder.

The town had once prided itself on being the county seat and built a magnificent stone edifice to showcase its power—two full stories of exquisitely faced granite blocks plus an intricate mansard roof and an immense clock tower. Similarly sturdy construction had laughed at Hitler's best bombers for months in Malta. All of which was crowned by a golden ball which could be seen, some had said, in Austin.

Carved owls, the symbol of wisdom, hovered over the four entrances, built at every point of the compass. Balconies jutted out above them, the perfect focal point for political speech making. The dedication ceremony had taken eight hours, one of the many times Ethan had been glad he could no longer go out in daylight.

"How did you find it?" he asked more quietly, listening hard with more than his ears. Something or someone was watching them.

She shot a quick glance at him and didn't answer immediately. He didn't push her.

"I put my finger on the map, which showed possible targets. This place insisted that we come," she said slowly.

"Then we had to be here," he agreed promptly.

"You don't think I'm insane?"

"For using more than your eyes? Hardly."

"Thank you."

Companionable silence fell.

"Is there a balcony around the edge of the roof, too?" Steve asked, eyeing the great building.

"Yup. Be careful, though—the railing is no more than a foot high."

"Until they restore that, too."

"They'll probably fix the windows first," Ethan pointed out. At least one pane was broken in every window, while some of them were completely missing. The fifteen-foot-tall windows on the second floor had been magnificent in their day, when all the chandeliers were lit. He'd be glad to see them brought back to their old glory. "Who bought this?"

"El Gallinazo's holding company did, two weeks ago. Our analysts have been working to track his assets, especially the more recent acquisitions."

Ethan frowned, remembering Luis's last report. "One of the president's cronies filed the paperwork to turn this into a golf resort. Isn't the courthouse supposed to become the clubhouse?"

"Correct. But that went through a year ago, when they cleaned out the unsafe buildings and designed a championship-quality course. Now they're in the first development phase."

"During which the courthouse is supposed to be readied for human occupancy." They started walking toward it.

"At least enough to permit entrance into it," she agreed, half turning to scan the horizon, her shotgun always at the ready.

"You probably wouldn't notice a change in ownership, given all the permits and other paperwork going through."

He grunted, unable to argue with her logic. Still— "But there's nothing here. We've already searched the quarries."

"Are you sure?" She frowned, considering the half-ruined buildings. "All of them? And the town?"

"Of course. Checked with the ghosts, too." Who had just gone back to sleep in Boot Hill.

"You're joking, right?" She gaped at him.

"Hardly." His mouth twisted. "When you become a vampiro, all your senses increase, including your psychic ones. For example, my best friend as a child was a ghost but he was the only one I could hear. Now I can speak to any ghost who wants to talk to me."

"That must be fun." Oddly enough, she didn't seem to completely disbelieve him.

"We've had some interesting conversations," he admitted. Which hadn't told him a damn thing about where Devol's bandolerismos were!

"I'll bet."

He stopped in front of the entrance. "Does the town still seem edgy to you?"

"Yes, but the threat isn't imminent." She blew out a breath and rotated slowly, then let her sling take her shotgun's weight. "Let's go upstairs and look around. Those balconies and that clock tower would make great dummy sniper hides."

"Always the professional." And his blood ran faster for it.

"Are you making eyes at me, mister?"

His voice must have changed, which wasn't surprising. Classic Western clothing on a figure like hers would be an enticement to any man. If he could persuade her into a striptease, where she'd carefully take off her guns one by one, then the belt. And slowly unbutton her shirt, teasing him with the knowledge of how little skin he'd see at first . . .

Hell, he'd be hotter than Hades to get her out of that Kevlar so she could reach her bra!

After that, would he want her to take off the boots first or unzip her pants? One would let him go down on her sooner but the other would let him kiss his way up her legs—and bring his cock into action sooner.

Decisions, decisions, decisions.

"Would I dare—when you're armed and dangerous?"

She blew him a kiss, from just inside the courthouse. "After we get back to my apartment, mister. After."

He followed her, whistling softly.

DPS HEADQUARTERS, THE NEXT DAY

Steve took the stairs two at a time and moderated her pace just enough not to burst out of the door. A quick survey of the room numbers gave her the necessary direction and she spun on her heel, checking her watch. Only a couple of doors to go, although it was hard to tell how far a room might stretch. Bosses needed extra room for hot air in their offices and conference rooms.

Yup, that was it: Chief, Texas Rangers.

A quick double-check of her uniform, thanks to reflections from the trophy case opposite, and she walked inside, glad her heart was no longer pounding double time. "Ranger Steve Reynolds, ma'am," she announced to one of the two women guarding the anteroom.

Laser-sharp blue eyes under faded gray hair drilled through her. Immaculate desktops with neat stacks of paper dared her to cause trouble.

Steve perfected her stance, having heard all the legends about the chief's secretary.

"Please make yourself comfortable." A knowing smile dawned. "He should be back from the governor's office any minute now."

Governor's office?

"Thank you, ma'am." She sat down next to Posada and pretended to watch CNN on the overhead monitor.

"How many new cases did we get this morning?" he asked, sotto voce.

"None, officially. But we had two calls—from Brownsville and Victoria."

He shot her an appalled glance. "That'll be Victoria's first."

"Mmhmm."

"Distribution network is spreading off the interstates."

"Or widening its grip by moving into smaller towns."

"Is that supposed to be comforting?" he demanded.

"No." How could she tell him Devol and his men weren't interested in drugs?

"Hmph."

They both watched the big monitor with all the enthusiasm of a hospital waiting room's crowd.

"Today, the New Orleans cathedral was full of worshipers praying for protection from vampires after the latest round of attacks. Supplies of silver crosses and even garlic are dwindling in the city." The dark-haired announcer leaned forward, his face serious above his extremely expensive suit.

A chill ran down Steve's spine.

"What the hell is he talking about?" Posada demanded.

"Two more women were discovered drained last night," the announcer intoned, "fang marks over their jugulars and their necks extended."

Oh shit.

"As you know, we've sent three reporters to New Orleans but we haven't heard from them since they left Atlanta."

Posada stared at her. "He's crazy, right?"

"Must be." Her throat wasn't working very well.

"We have this report from our New Orleans affiliate . . ."

The monitor spun into pictures of Dracula, Southern planta-
tions with fog-drenched gardens, and black-clad women, dripping blood from their necks, while they lay crumpled against
wrought iron balconies.

"After we return from break, we'll go to our Dallas affiliate
for a report . . ."

"He's not going to say what I think he's going to say?" Posada's horrified eyes met hers.

"God, I hope not."

"On this morning's attacks in Brownsville and Victoria . . ."
Her stomach twisted and heaved.

"Posada, Reynolds." The chief's quiet voice cut through the
journalistic hysteria.

"Sir." They sprang to their feet.

Chief Baker was a big African American with a pronounced
twinkle in his eyes and an amazing ability to sniff out criminals,
whether he personally brought them to justice or not.

But Steve's jaw dropped at the sight of his companion—
Captain Zachariah Howard. He was the Ranger who'd tracked
and found the two kidnapped fifteen-year-old daughters of a
senator, while accomplishing the equally unbelievable feat of
turning every Texas TV station into his ally. He was tall and very
weather-beaten, as if he'd been enjoying his favorite hobbies of
bass fishing and hunting white-tailed deer even more since he'd
retired.

"Howard, do you remember Posada and Reynolds?" Chief
Baker asked.

"Yes, we've met several times at the Ranger Museum's an-
nual picnic." They shook hands, Steve trying to appear coolly
professional. But she'd grown up on stories about Zach Howard's exploits, as told by her grandfather, one of his classmates
at the DPS academy.

"Let's talk in my office." Chief Baker held his door open and they trooped in after him to find seats at the table. This was a working office unlike the antechamber, full of papers and books, tumbled over tables and bookcases, leaving just enough room for visitors to sit down on the classic leather furniture. The curtains were wide-open, allowing sunlight to pour into the room and strike sparks off the gold eagle atop the Texas state flag.

Baker didn't waste any time giving them the bad news.

"The New Orleans folks are half-hysterical because they're having so many murders. The national and Louisiana media believe there are vampires."

Posada opened his mouth to object but the chief held up his hand. "I know, I know, they're probably only saying so to sell advertising. But, frankly, nobody's got a better idea."

Steve kept her mouth shut. If nothing else, it was a great way to avoid throwing up—or talking about Ethan.

"Furthermore, somebody has finally figured out we've got a lot of deaths in Texas which look like the same thing."

"Damn," Howard said very softly.

Posada flashed him a wry smile.

"I don't want to mention any Mexican drugs, because some fool will figure out how to buy and sell them even faster. Vampires aren't real."

Steve's skin tightened further around her polite expression.

"So nobody will take them too seriously, making them a great cover story, while we hunt down the real crooks."

She smiled wryly.

"How?" Posada asked bluntly.

"Louisiana and New Orleans cops, acting secretly, have formed an anticorruption task force to investigate the murders."

"Whooeee," Steve whistled.

"Exactly—and they got the governor to bring in the Feds."

Three stunned faces gaped at each other, then at Chief Baker.

"A federal anticorruption task force, with local and statewide support—in Louisiana?" Howard questioned, rather as if he'd just learned hogs could fly to China.

"Yup."

"They might be able to accomplish something," Posada said, rubbing his jaw.

"Very much so, if they solve the murders."

How? Devol's goal was in Texas and his support base was in New Orleans. Steve frowned, spinning options over and over.

"Our governor has decided to join forces with them."

"Of course," Howard and Posada promptly agreed. Steve shot them a sideways glance but said nothing.

"Zach, we'd like you to lead the task force, including the combined Texas, Louisiana—and federal task force."

He hesitated, then inclined his head. "I'll explain the situation to my wife. I'm sure she'll understand why I'm coming back for this."

"Thank you, Zach. I'll do my best to ensure you don't regret this too much." Baker grinned at him for an instant before continuing. "Posada, we need to turn the screws on the real problem—those drugs coming out of Mexico. You've been working those issues for a long time. Can you lead a DPS task force with the Feds?"

"My pleasure, boss." Posada nodded, his fingers flexing on his portfolio. "I've got some ideas which should help."

"Excellent. We've got some new grant money so funds won't be much of an issue this time."

A grin burst across Posada's face and Steve gave him a thumbs-up under the table, more than pleased for her old boss. She might not be able to go after El Gallinazo but she'd be very happy to see him hang, no matter who tied the noose.

"One more thing, Chief."

"Yes, Zach?" The chief was gathering his portfolio together.

"You're taking my best candidate for top lieutenant away from me and sending him down to the border," the gravelly voice complained mildly. "When I don't know much about the murders or their investigation or the team itself. I don't think that's quite right, do you?"

"What do you want, Zach?"

The two big men eyed each other across the table. Steve wasn't sure who held the better hand.

"Reynolds as my deputy."

On a multi-jurisdictional task force, including the Feds and another state? He could ask for, and get, somebody much more senior than her.

Baker drummed his fingers on the table. "She'd have to back you up on briefing the governor."

"Think you can handle that, Reynolds?"

"Of course, Captain." She'd never briefed a big-time politician before but she'd learn fast, especially since Ethan had ensured the governor would always be discreet.

"Then I've got my core team, Chief." He shot a steely eyed stare across the table and the chief met it blandly.

"Congratulations, Zach. I'm looking forward to seeing the two of you on TV this afternoon, with the rest of your task force."

"Television?" Did she squeak? Steve cleared her throat.

"Don't tell me, Chief: The governor wants a press conference?" Howard looked like he'd swallowed a rattler backward.

Press conference? At least Captain Howard would almost certainly have to answer all the questions there, not her. It made educating politicians in private look like a piece of cake.

"Yup, but in Baton Rouge, with the Louisiana governor, the U.S. Attorney, and our lieutenant governor."

"Well, now, aren't we going to be blessed." He shot Baker a gold-toothed snarl, which the chief blandly returned.

"Indeed you are. Now, if you'll excuse us, Posada and I have another meeting to attend."

Posada rose, still grinning like somebody who didn't quite know where his feet were.

Steve stood up a little more slowly, light-headed and cold like a hydrogen balloon heading for outer space, and reminded herself she was damn lucky.

Stupid, really; Posada wasn't blood kin. So why did she feel as if she were losing her last family member?

Fifteen

COMPOSTELA RANCH, THAT NIGHT

Ethan frowned, rubbing his hand over his chin, and leaned back in his big leather chair. Allocating men was becoming more and more difficult the longer the damn war went on, no matter who worked on it. Jean-Marie had gone off to stand watch in one of the local nightclubs, saying Ethan might come up with a better configuration on his own.

Ethan snorted softly. If he had a lady like Jean-Marie's Hélène—who'd traveled from London for a reunion and looked damn good riding on a motorcycle with him—he, too, would probably find a good excuse to meet her away from Compostela. Lucky bastard.

He moved a pair of vampiros from Houston to Waco, snarled at the resulting gap along the border—and whacked the joystick, erasing all traces of the proposed arrangement.

He gritted his teeth and began again.

A solid guard for Doña Grania at Compostela. Everything else could change, but not that. As Don Rafael's heart, she was also the esfera's soul.

Numbers sprang to life at the map's lower edge, reflecting the usage and availability of men. They were automatically adjusted every time he slid an icon from one location to another.

Next, Don Rafael's personal guard, the core of his mesnaderos.

A bare minimum at each commandery, watching over Texas and Oklahoma's key points—Dallas, San Antonio, Tulsa . . .

And damn those floods in Houston, which kept so many men busy. Move the rest of the vampiros, compañeros, and comitiva—at least those who could fight—to guard the innocent women at known attack points.

How many would remain to Jean-Marie, their master spy, to search for Devol or the thirty in his bandolerismo?

About enough to field a football team.

He snarled at the unyielding totals. Discussing this with Steve would clear his head—but that was impossible.

"Have you included rotating the searchers and mesnaderos—the top fighters—so both remain fresh?" Don Rafael asked from just behind him.

Ethan's heart jolted and he started to rise.

"No, no, remain sitting." Don Rafael lounged against the wall, only a few feet away. His posture sang of contentment, while he reeked of sated lust.

Ethan closed his eyes briefly in sheer jealousy but he managed to answer normally. "Yes, sir. There's a special line at the bottom, for rotation."

"*Excelente*. Perhaps if we move two from Midland to here." He grabbed the other joystick and drew up a chair.

Ethan tilted his head, seeing the new pattern. "And these go . . ." He clicked.

Companionable phrases spilled between them, highlighted by the electronics' gentle percussion. They'd often worked together like this, so much they spoke in code words more than sentences. Even mind to mind would have taken more effort.

His heart eased a little, given this first such session since Doña Grania's arrival.

The map finally settled into a new pattern, which both men rose to consider. No changes arose after five minutes and Ethan turned to fetch them drinks. According to watch center tradition, only strong coffee and tea were served here.

"Where do you plan to take the rapid reaction force, since our forces are so stretched?" Don Rafael's voice was very quiet.

"From Compostela." He shrugged and handed his master a cup. "It has the most mesnaderos, so it should be best able to spare them."

Don Rafael grunted unhappily and sipped his beloved, overpoweringly strong coffee. "Plus, it's close to my Gulfstream jet," he acknowledged, "which I saw them use in my vision."

Ethan nodded agreement, not about to tread harder on this delicate subject. He was damn lucky he hadn't been savaged for openly stating he was reducing Doña Grania's guard.

"Do we have any hope for help from our law enforcement friends, such as your Texas Ranger?"

Ethan stilled, cursing his guilty flush. Vampiros influenced cops, not the other way around. His gaze shot to his master.

Don Rafael frowned. "Are they concealing information from us? Do we need to start watching them, as well?"

"Hardly!" He could be open about that much, at least—and hope his creador wouldn't decide to walk through his thoughts. He resumed sprinkling cinnamon over his coffee with great deliberation. "She's done much for us, especially sharing intelligence."

"You've stopped her tongue about us, of course?"

"Years ago." He could be honest about that, too.

Don Rafael clapped him on the back. "Yet another link in a long chain of protecting Texas indirectly."

Ethan inclined his head, keeping his eyes veiled. Life would be much easier if Steve had ever fit in that category.

"Tell me about our latest Ranger *amiga*." Don Rafael leaned against the desk, his eyes just a little too intent. "The name is familiar. She provides intelligence, of course."

"Of course. There was Reynolds the Intrepid, of course," Ethan suggested.

"The great frontier lieutenant? Is she related to him?"

"By adoption, yes. Her family were Cherokee Indians who were forced to take a white man's name when they left the reservation. Their former commander honored them by accepting them as kin."

"Blood to be proud of. And she, too, proved that she could not be stampeded, as all Rangers must?"

Ethan choked and Don Rafael raised an eyebrow. "I'm not aware I made a joke, mi hijo."

"Do you remember a few years ago when the two murderers managed to break out of Death Row and kidnap two women who were driving to a singing competition?"

"Of course. They were rescued a few days later, as I recall."

"At a convenience store, late on a Saturday night. Reynolds had been a bridesmaid that day and stopped to restock her refrigerator." Since all of its contents resembled science projects more than food. Good Lord, would she ever learn to cook?

"She was a cop, sí? Then her attire must have made them disregard her as a threat."

Ethan choked again.

Don Rafael's eyebrows shot up.

"Was she wearing one of those hideous concoctions that American girls foist on their friends only at weddings?"

Ethan nodded, biting his lip.

Don Rafael's eyes narrowed. "Brilliant pink with a tight bodice and diagonal neckline? Plus immense sleeves one could hide a small arsenal in, as I recall, and an enormous skirt upheld by netting. Her long hair was ornately arranged, too, with flowers and ribbons."

"She had her Sig in the matching purse," Ethan pointed out.

"There wasn't any place else to carry it, as regulations required her to do."

"*Madre de Dios,*" Don Rafael murmured, his inscrutable gaze resting on Ethan. "No wonder those slime didn't think she was a threat."

"Exactly, although she was carrying an extra magazine as balance for the dress's—more memorable qualities."

Don Rafael's eyes danced briefly before he signaled Ethan to continue.

"The escapees allowed their captives to openly use the restroom. The women were afraid of the *male* store clerk"—Don Rafael growled—"but they jumped at Steve, begging her for help."

"Whereupon the convicts reacted poorly and shooting broke out."

"In the end, the store clerk and former hostages were fine, while one of the convicts died of his wounds."

"She did extremely well." Don Rafael steepled his fingers. "No wonder the store's surveillance tapes are so often shown on television."

"Entitled *The Bridesmaid's Revenge.*" Ethan grinned, as proud as if the shoot-out had occurred yesterday. Better not remember how his heart had stopped a hundred times while he'd listened to it over the scanner, though. Thank God she'd had the extra magazine for her gun.

"She is your *amor, sí?*"

His gaze flashed to his creador and was snared by the bittersweet chocolate eyes. He hesitated but nodded, committing himself to the darker question underlying the few words.

Yes, Steve was his love, not just his lover. He wasn't sleeping with her to obtain information but because he couldn't live without seeing her, whenever and wherever he could.

Don Rafael's jaw set hard under the golden skin, accentuating the strength which had kept this esfera at peace longer than any other.

There is no place for a vampira in Texas, mi hijo, Don Rafael warned.

I know that, not under Texas law. Ethan looked straight back at him, hiding nothing. The pain of future loss carved his bones but he'd adjusted to that. Or rather, he would learn to. Memories were better than complete emptiness.

I am a Texan. Texas is worth everything, even saying good-bye to her.

Don Rafael inclined his head, his eyes hooded.

Steve considered the ancient cellar, bereft of a barn with its jaunty red walls for a cover. She eyed the steep ramp, now pitted and over-grown with brambles. She studied the circular frame of an ancient well, still tall enough that it wasn't quite a complete hazard.

"It's been decades since this ranch was occupied." She stepped back, her boots soundless on the dirt road. "Maybe the Depression?"

"A little more recent." Ethan held up a small jet fighter.

"At least the cellar isn't deep enough to have sheltered any vampiros. Maybe the well, but not the cellar."

"High noon would send daylight down either," Ethan said flatly.

"Incinerating the enemy and saving us the problem. Pity." She kicked an inoffensive pebble. "I can't imagine where he's keeping all of them."

"He's probably rotating them. Letting some terrorize us, while others rest."

"Or hiding them in plain sight." She sighed, turning around once again, to look at the deserted hulk of a ranch. "My gut says there's nothing here."

"Same for me. Let's get back home so you can be ready for the Feds in the morning."

"Yeah, the *Suits*." She grinned. "They're kind of cute, though."

"Why?" he bit out.

She glanced sideways, a little surprised by his harshness. Was he jealous? Silly boy.

"They're sooo well dressed, y'know? Badge, gun, cuffs, ankle holster, extra pair of cuffs, extra magazine, radio. What am I missing?" She leaned against his pickup and tapped her cheek, pretending to consider.

"*Two* guns and *two* sets of handcuffs? Do they think mass murderers will stay put so they can be hog-tied?" His lip curled.

"Gotta be prepared, y'know." She tried to sound impressed.

"You only carry a badge, *one* gun, and *one* pair of cuffs," he pointed out.

"For everyday wear, not tactical gear." She gave up the effort and laughed. "Exactly, we're so different. The Louisiana guys are always teasing us both."

He laughed with her, his face softening, and settled comfortably against the hard metal. She leaned into his shoulder, cuddling as best as she could, given their respective quantities of armament and her Kevlar vest. He laid his arm over her shoulders companionably and they stayed like that for a few minutes, letting crickets and a distant owl do the talking.

"Ethan." She had to ask this. "What if Devol decides to make more vampiros?"

"Are you asking if we'd need to face more than thirty vampiros?" He glanced down at her. "There's no danger of that, honey."

"Why not?"

"It takes a minimum of two years, sometimes as much as nine, to give somebody El Abrazo and make them a vampiro."

"Oh." Well, the bad guys wouldn't overrun the countryside

right away. "But in all the movies, baby vampiros are dangerous right away."

"Cachorros," Ethan corrected, a muscle throbbing in his jaw. "Actually, most people die after being given El Abrazo without ever rising as a cachorro."

"You're joking!" She spun to stare at him.

"Not at all." He shook his head, his hazel eyes deadly serious. "Very few cachorros survive La Lujuria—The Rut—immediately after they first rise, when they're insane for blood and emotion. It's a time that lasts for months."

"You're crazy that long?" It sounded like a prescription for complete disaster.

"Yeah—and it's much, much worse for women. In fact, so few survive that it's almost impossible to predict which ones will make it to become vampiras."

"Oh," she said flatly, and swallowed. She spotted a hole in his argument and dived for it. "But you've got plenty of vampiros here in Texas."

"Don Rafael, El Patrón of Texas, is the creador of every vampiro here." The lines in his face deepened to a harsh mask. "He is the only North American patrón who has never lost a cachorro. But he refuses to give El Abrazo to a female."

"That's a stupid, old-fashioned, patriarchal attitude!"

"It's his law and it will be obeyed here." Ethan rested his hands on her shoulders very gently. "Stephanie Amanda, I have seen ladies' brains scalded and destroyed by El Abrazo. I won't argue with my creador—especially since his methods have *always* been successful."

She started to spit out another angry retort but stopped, caught by his emphasis on the single word.

"Is it *always* so difficult then?" she asked slowly, feeling her way through a bloodshot darkness.

"The San Francisco patrón has the next-best record at little more than ninety percent. That's for men, of course."

"What about women?"

"Nobody has ever done better than ten percent. Usually it's less than five." He gently tucked a loose strand of hair behind her ear and released her. "Come on, let's go home and have some fun together. Or do you want to keep talking statistics in a dirt patch?"

"Sure thing, cowboy." She smiled as he intended her to do and brushed her knuckles against his cheek.

She was silent while he expertly drove the pickup out of the old ranch, barely noticing the frequent gearshifts needed to get over the rough terrain and across the old riverbed.

Vampiras in the abstract were one thing. Becoming a vampira herself—could she do it? Her family wouldn't be pleased but the only one she really had left was Cousin Mac, the overprotective dude who spent all his time chasing bad guys for the Army.

Okay, the odds of survival were horrific. Worse, she'd have to live in a brutal world where law and justice often depended on one man's whims.

Her mouth worked, shoving away the foul taste.

But her brain kept dragging the idea back to her.

She'd keep Ethan forever if she became a vampira. Ethan, the only man who'd ever understood her. Ethan, who'd been her lover off and on for fifteen years. What more could a woman want?

To live in light, not darkness, where she'd still be a Texas Ranger.

NEW ORLEANS, AUGUST 6

Twan knocked twice, paused, and knocked once more, still surprised at the rendezvous choice. He'd walked in for the last half mile, of course, knowing there'd be no safe parking close by and with his nerves jangling worse than during any stakeout. But he was dressed like a gangsta, in an oversized Saints jersey and baggy jeans used to hide weapons. He carried himself like one, too, flaunting the cockiness he'd once envied. Nobody had bothered him or given him more than the usual wary looks, simply accepted him as belonging to these brutal streets.

He'd always known a Livingston Brothers warehouse lurked behind these boarded-up storefronts, sheltered by their famous layers of security. But they were an old family, who'd been making money here since before the Stars and Stripes first rose over the Crescent City. He'd never thought they'd risk everything by getting involved in something like this.

The tiny side door opened and a brief ray of light flashed over the ancient cars and motorcycles squeezed into the narrow street. Robuchon poked his head out, glanced around, then nodded and stepped back.

Twan followed, catching and closing the battered door. It swung easily and silently, betraying a steel core under its painted exterior. He eased his duffel higher onto his shoulder, finally able to carry it more blatantly. The strap snagged his jersey, displaying what he wore underneath.

"Good, you're dressed," Robuchon grunted, leading the way through a jumbled warehouse of dimly lit Mardi Gras props, where oversized papier mâché heads jostled for space with gilded spears and small tractors.

"You're not," the taller man pointed out. It had been years since he'd worn body armor for any reason other than to prove he could still fit into it. With luck, this set could still do the job, despite being out of warranty and ripe for collapsing at a bullet's approach. At least his night vision goggles were new, courtesy of a salesman so unfamiliar with New Orleans that he thought a deputy chief could authorize new equipment if he liked the item well enough.

He peeled the football jersey over his head and worked to replace it with an NOPD jacket from his duffel. He'd wear his own team's colors to meet whomever was waiting.

"Doc said he'd only okay it if I passed the treadmill test."
The bureaucrat squeezed between an immense green alligator's
jaws and a princess's purple skirt, his skin briefly gleaming like
a ghost's. "So I'm handling comms."

Ouch. "Good to know that'll work smoothly for once."

Robuchon spun around, his eyes blazing with rage above his
crisp shirt and tie. "Crush the bastards for me. After what they
did to my daughter—" His voice broke, his fists opening and
closing. The single lightbulb's harsh glare carved brutal lines
into his face.

"Your daughter? I didn't know you had one." Shit.

"Not many people still remember." He gave a joyless bark.
"She was dragged into Bacchus's Temple thirty years ago but the
scum denied ever seeing her."

"I'm sorry, man." The same stark light roughened Twan's matt
brown hand when he gently touched Robuchon's shoulder.

"Fished her body out of the Gulf a month later, looking
like an ME class poster on difficult victim identification." He
stopped, his Adam's apple bobbing.

How many stories had he heard like this over the decades?
Didn't make it any easier now and it sure hadn't helped improve
his nightmares about what happened to Jamaal.

"Tonight we're taking back our city, dude. I promise you
we're going to start seeing some justice around here."

Their eyes met in the single bulb's harsh glare, under a gigantic Roman centurion's sword. They clasped hands, one light,
one dark, locking their fists until they were linked forearm to
forearm. Icy fire leapt between them, the pledge stronger for
being wordless.

"You out there, Eldridge?" Passard called.

"Betcha!"

Twan separated from Robuchon, tapping their fists together
to seal the vow, and stepped into the next room. It was much

more brightly lit, filled with vehicles, from bicycles and scooters, to tractors and pickups. Three walls were covered with equipment racks and an occasional boarded-up door. But a massive, rolling steel door occupied the fourth—and a half dozen hulking, black trucks were parked in front of it with a glorious logo on their sides. Dozens of men and women were gathered around, all heavily armed.

For the first time in far too long, all traces of a migraine disappeared from Twan's life.

The FBI's Tactical Support Branch had come to help his town. *Thank you, Jesus.*

"Evening, Passard." He tried to make it sound as if working with the FBI was no big deal.

"Eldridge, this is Brian Roberts, who'll be leading the FBI tonight."

"Pleasure," Roberts said, a hawk-faced man with a five o'clock shadow and a piercing stare. "Thanks for that heads-up you sent us a few weeks back on those human traffickers. It really panned out."

Twan nodded and shook hands, keeping his expression noncommittal. He had a CI he'd only met once but whose information was always golden. For the past few years, he'd made a habit of sending the tips onto the Feds rather than watching them disappear forever down Chief Broussard's corrupt gullet.

Roberts beckoned another man forward, a tall blond with a horseman's easy stride. "Templeton, here, is a Texas deputy sheriff, who's dealt with Madame Celeste before."

Eldridge shook hands, paying more careful attention this time. Anybody who'd tangled with that voudun and survived deserved respect. Cold hazel eyes—well, that figured. No fool was going to escape her clutches. But his tactical vest? He was wearing that superexpensive, flexible body armor which cost as much as Twan's nephew's motorcycle had. If he was an everyday deputy sheriff, Twan would start drinking tea out of those sissy little decorated cups and saucers.

Templeton nodded to him, his mouth twitching. "And this here's Hennessy," he drawled, all sweet reasonableness, "who's a fair hand with a shotgun."

Fair hand? Probably meant better than expert.

Twan cast an assessing eye over the equally well-dressed dude beside Templeton. His black hair was a little longer than fashionable, enough that he'd put it into a tight clip at his nape. But his eyes were gray, like silver shards of light in a hawk's face. Not the type to relax too easily around, although the ladies probably swooned over him.

"Listen up, fellows," Roberts said from in front of his truck, his voice effortlessly carrying across the room. "We just got our search warrant from the judge. There are a lot of RICO charges, as we expected, but we also got the murder charges."

Hot damn, he'd never thought any judge in this state would go that far out on a limb against Madame Celeste. Racketeering— well, that was a criminal case. But murder? The evidence must be even better than he'd hoped.

"We figure we've got no more than an hour before Madame Celeste's crew learns the warrant's been issued. I'll do the knock-and-announce, as the team leader," Roberts went on.

Of course. His warrant, his team.

Twan waited politely for the rest of the speech, so they could board the fucking trucks and get on the road. Good thing he spent so much time working out to vent his frustrations and ward off the damn migraines. At least he wouldn't be bringing up the rear behind these buff young agents tonight.

"Eldridge, your folks will turn out the lights inside the casino at our signal."

"Yo." Big Sis was watching for their arrival and would signal their father, a master electrician who'd worked for the city for decades. The Old Man would throw the switch, cutting the power to the sub-grid containing Bacchus's Temple, something he'd been dying to do ever since it had hijacked that brand-new power plant planned for a hospital.

"And, Eldridge?"

He cocked an eyebrow.

"This is your town. Want to fire the breaching charges and blow the door open?"

Twan's heart stuttered against his ribs. A New Orleans cop was being given the chance to open the gates on the biggest corruption case during the past century—and a black cop at that?

"I can't think of a damn thing I'd rather be doing, sir."

"After that, Templeton and his men will be the first ones to enter."

Only a half dozen men in the lead to take the brunt? That'd be a bitch and everyone else would have to hustle to be effective backup.

"We're heading for the watch center in the rear of the building, on the fifth floor." Roberts' finger drew a circle.

Where the bitch ran the entire town, and the state, and the whole fucking Southeast, like a goddamn puppet master. Not caring who or what she killed, even if it was only a little boy who'd gotten in her way.

A muscle jerked in Twan's cheek.

"Once we get up there, Eldridge will take the horn and start soothing ruffled feathers, especially his fellow NOPD cops. We've got to keep him safe. Everybody got that?"

There was a murmur of agreement. Crap, now he'd have babysitters watching his ass.

Roberts tapped a big but remarkably simple diagram pinned to the wall.

"The watch center is in the old warehouse, separated from the casino proper by bank vault doors on every level. Two flights of stairs—one team for each flight. The sudden power failure should be automatically interpreted as a burglary of the casino, causing all the doors to close."

Twan's old man had been mulling his revenge over for years, even figured out how to sabotage the cutover switch which was supposed to automatically trigger the backup power generator in Bacchus's Temple whenever they lost city power. Just to make sure their UPS would provide enough power to close the doors and latch them shut, after the casino lost power and the backup generator failed.

He'd pulled that off a couple of days ago, calling it routine maintenance, same as he'd looked after them for years. Hell, he'd even gone into the fucking casino and bought beers for the electricians there!

He'd nearly scared the shit out of his two oldest kids. Twan still couldn't believe he and Big Sis had let their dad go through with it.

The result should keep one set of bad guys in the casino and another, smaller set of bad guys in their dormitory. Totally separate from each other.

Messing with them could be fun.

"However, the guards' dormitory is outside the casino in this area and we expect to encounter at least three dozen hostiles. We'll let those locked up in the casino stew until we have the time and leisure to take them out slowly."

Roberts was sounding happier and happier the longer this went on. Was that how a fellow got through the FBI's tactical training? Jesus.

"We have one advantage: There's been a big fire at Rose-meade Plantation, Madame Celeste's country estate. Given the house's great age and distance from a fire department—"

Arrogant witch probably terrorized every hamlet for miles around the place, stomping anything which might support a fire department.

"It's burning very rapidly and is expected to be a complete loss. We anticipate Bacchus's Temple won't receive many reinforcements from there."

Templeton was smiling. Not openly and not nicely. How much did he know? Maybe they'd have an easier time blasting their way into Bacchus's Temple than they'd hoped. God willing.

"We believe the main armory is in the casino itself, near the vault." Roberts drummed on the map.

Good location.

"However, another one is probably near the watch center. Try to move fast before they can resupply."

Yeah, like that'll be a cake walk. Twan exchanged disgusted glances with Passard.

"Since the casino is closed to the public between two a.m. and five a.m., we're not expecting any civilians to be present."

Most casinos stayed open twenty-four hours a day. Bacchus's Temple allowed the privileged few to remain that long, if they were already within a private suite. But nobody except its own staff was allowed to move around during that three-hour window. Word on the street said they needed the time to clean up the worst forms of debris, such as orgies and murders.

Twan had never had any reason to doubt that bit of gossip.

"Therefore, if you receive fire, you are free to return it. However, if fighting spills out onto the public streets, Marines will come ashore from that amphibious assault ship currently paying us a shore visit."

What the hell? Twan glared at the obnoxiously calm son of a bitch. Federal troops on his streets?

"They will form a cordon around the Treaty Museum, which is federal property." Roberts looked significantly at Twan. "Plus its approaches, including Bacchus's Temple."

Bringing in 'bout the only folks with enough firepower to save civilian lives and keep that voudun fenced in. But, crap, this stuck in his craw! He forced himself not to shout. "Governor agreed to this?"

"Yes, she did. The Marines can't come inside Bacchus's Temple but they will only allow law enforcement personnel to exit."

"Sounds okay." *Just pray it don't happen.*

"These instructions have been cleared all the way to the top. Questions?"

Place could become a bloodbath, if they got this wrong. Twan bit his full bottom lip and said nothing else.

"Very well, let's load up and move out. Eldridge, you'll ride with Templeton and me. Passard, you're with the other team."

"You get those sons of bitches." Robuchon's harsh whisper trailed Twan toward the trucks. "No matter what it takes."

Twan nodded shortly. Tonight he was going to start reclaiming his turf.

"Your gun, sir." A fresh-faced kid of about thirty handed him a Remington. "We'll give you a fresh one, with an autoloader already mounted, just as soon as you fire."

"Thanks." This one fitted into his hands sweetly, just like his old piece had. Perfect.

"Sweet scattergun." Templeton grinned at him, holding the truck's door.

"The best." He stepped inside and found a seat beside Hennessy. His pulse was steadier now than when he'd walked to his desk that morning.

The ride was short, his prayer inside the truck heartfelt and brief. He rubbed his gold detective's badge with his thumb, making sure the star and crescent would stand out. Those dawgs were going to know it was New Orleans police who hit them.

The truck turned onto Canal Street, immediately identifiable by the smoother pavement and faster pace. A few minutes later, it turned again, sweeping through a one-eighty, and stopped. A fist pounded from the cab and they tumbled out to form up. The other truck pulled up on the casino's other side, its team just visible by that entrance.

Bacchus's Temple loomed over them from above the cobblestones, four stories of purple and gold monstrosity, edged by streetlamps. The back showed the original bricks' outlines, especially where windows had been filled in. A narrow porch stood just above the street, sheltering heavy brass double doors used for bank deliveries, supposedly a re-creation of something from ancient Rome.

Twan tried not to think about the multitude of surveillance cameras rotating regularly back and forth. But why no outside guards? Had the fire at Rosemeade confused their leadership that much? Who gave a damn, if it meant an easier time serving the warrant?

Was Big Sis watching as they'd planned?

He scanned the high-rise overlooking the Temple and the Mississippi River beyond. She loved her view, especially in the summer, but if she was using her secretary's office tonight instead of her own . . . Nope, there was her flashlight, a little pinprick of light against the blinds.

"Now, Eldridge," Roberts hissed.

He saluted her with two fingers.

An instant later, every light vanished, collapsing the block into velvety blackness. Twan's old man and Jamaal's grandfather had taken the Eldridge family's first piece of revenge.

Twan's night vision goggles automatically compensated.

Roberts ran up the steps to the porch, with Templeton at his heels, ballistic shield at the ready. Twan matched strides with them, determined not to shame New Orleans's rep. The others pelted behind in a deadly chorus.

Arriving at the top, they leaned against the narrow columns for an instant, listening for any bullets singing an unfriendly welcome.

Nothing.

Roberts glanced at him, the movement marked by moonlight glinting on his NVGs until he seemed a creature from a Mardi Gras allegory.

Twan nodded fiercely. Dear God, how many years had he been stoked for this? He quietly flicked off his shotgun's safety and all but purred at its near-silent smoothness. Time to show those bastards who the man really was.

Templeton chuckled softly.

Roberts pounded on the brass doors. "FBI!" he bellowed, providing the knock-and-announce so they could legally enter. But as brief as possible, to give those murderous dawgs little time to form up.

Two cameras hissed and swiveled, pointing their silver eyes at him.

Crap. The insiders had taken manual control of the surveillance system. They were definitely on the alert.

Roberts sprang back and Eldridge lunged forward. He settled the shotgun against his shoulder, aimed it—and blew out the first hinge in an extremely satisfying whump!

An instant later, the second hinge also vanished in another whump!

Templeton sprang at the brass door, slamming it open as if it were plywood. It collapsed backward into the casino and he raced forward. Hennessy followed an instant later, his black hair lifting, and their men fanned out around them. Shots rang out, lacing the darkness in massive fireworks.

Payback had finally started.

The kid shoved another shotgun into Twan's hands and grabbed the first.

Twan grinned his thanks. Riot gun time, just like he'd learned on the streets so many years ago. He racked it happily and headed inside.

He had a rectangular tower to climb, built of old bricks and framed in wrought iron. The stairs were also iron but modern and harshly sturdy, with an equally efficient heavy metal door leading to the casino on each floor. If he craned his neck a bit, he could see the occasional chair or stool, maybe a battered wooden door cut into the wall at an odd angle. Just an antebellum warehouse, with plenty of space to cause trouble. All the windows had definitely been bricked up, becoming deeper splotches of shadow. Given the power failure, it would have been darker than a voodoo queen's tomb without his NVGs.

Five flights up to the watch center and his head wasn't even throbbing.

Twan grinned and started running, the white kid at his side.

A man jumped at him from behind a door and he blew him away, the fellow's lungs evaporating into a red mist.

Another popped up from behind a stair rail only to have the young agent beside Twan put two rounds into his skull. The dawg went down like a puppet, limbs slack and eyes staring.

Another bastard burst out of a hidden doorway, gun blazing, and Twan instinctively fired—tearing out a chunk of wall but no enemy. The agent spun, getting off a single shot. The bastard dropped, a fist-sized hole in his chest—but the kid was writhing on the floor, holding his leg.

Twan knelt next to him. Gunshots were firing so hard and fast around them that the stairwell itself was shaking. Cordite's acrid stench burned his lungs and feet drummed on the stairs.

"No, sir, you go on." The young man's face was ashen but his eyes were resolute. "You've got to make it to the watch center. Medics will pick me up."

Twan hesitated before nodding. He lunged to his feet and ran, reminding himself his body armor hadn't been out of warranty more than a few years. Surely it'd hold up to pistol rounds or a glancing hit.

He racked his shotgun again, fiercely thankful for his hours on the range. Man could never spend too much time practicing with a good piece.

Four more flights.

There was blood on the stairs and the walls, plus bits of flesh. He kept his gun at the ready, more than willing to pull the trigger. This was the payoff for all those hours in the gym and on the range, when he'd thought he was cursing his bosses.

Three more flights.

He'd run out of FBI dudes in front of him on the stairs. The ones he'd seen were either fighting to keep the casino doors closed, or wounded.

Firing was heavier now, an almost continuous blur of sound that jarred his bones and rolled his teeth together. It came from everywhere, above and below him, echoing through the stairs and the old warehouse's bricks.

How were Templeton and his boys doing?

There weren't quite enough bodies on the next landing, given the number of shots being fired. Good news, maybe.

Shooting was even louder after the next corner and Twan slowed down. He twisted cautiously around the landing, careful to keep his shotgun ready.

A great bank vault door stood at the top of the next flight, gleaming under recessed lights, its latch blatantly uncocked.

The dormitory's armory. What else could it be, given the damn big door, unlike that on any other floor?

Two men fought hand to hand in front of it. Full-contact karate was a sissy sport compared to how they went at each other, fast and bloodthirsty like angry wolves.

One of them was Hennessy—and he wasn't winning.

How the hell could Twan help?

The latch turned, lifted up—and the door swung abruptly open, shoving Hennessy against the wall. For a moment, he was separated from his opponent—and Twan put two solid loads of double-ought buckshot into the dawg. BOOM! BOOM!

The bastard dropped—and crumpled into dust, disappearing

within seconds into little more than a fist-high pile of chalky powder.

Twan's pulse lurched. *What the hell? Who the fuck had that been?*

The armory door opened farther and two more bastards edged through. Hennessy's silver eyes met Twan's, fierce enough to hurl knives. "Get on with you, boyo. I'll hold 'em here."

Twan nodded and ran. Not the time to deal with a man's injured pride—or find out too much about what had been going on. As long he had bullets, he was good to go.

Two more flights.

Another dawg popped up from behind a pile of bodies.

Twan pulled his shotgun's trigger—and it clicked on an empty chamber.

Shit. How the hell could he reach his backup piece?

His attacker grinned and jauntily flaunted his pistol.

Someone else's feet appeared on the stairs above, clad in superb cowboy boots. Templeton?

The bastard spun to face the newcomer and spat a string of feral curses.

"You idiot," Templeton remarked calmly. Why the hell was he distracting the guy? Never mind that; use it!

Twan grabbed his beloved Colt and fired.

The dawg collapsed onto the stairs, the top of his head blown off.

Templeton took a few more steps, careful not to get his boots dirty.

"Why the hell did you do that?" Twan demanded. "Asshole could have killed you."

"No, he wouldn't. You'd have fucked him over first," Templeton pointed out, calm as if they were talking football plays. "Come on up. We've secured the watch center, although the other staircase is still pretty lively."

"Why the hell didn't you say so?" Twan charged forward.

"Where's Hennessy?" Templeton turned to lead the way.

"One flight back."

Templeton gave him a long look, those hazel eyes seeing beyond the words.

"I helped him out some," Twan admitted and started to grin, remembering Hennessy's ungracious expression.

"You did what?" Templeton chuckled softly, his head swiveling as he scanned the top corridor. This place was modern and high-tech, with every edge polished to a glossy finish, unlike the rough brick and wrought iron below. Shots echoed from the staircase at the corridor's far end and a hole gaped beside the heavy bank vault doors, guarded by two hard-eyed men with shotguns.

Judging by the wall, Twan didn't think their pieces were loaded with double-ought buckshot. In fact, he might pity anybody who tried to take them out. Then again, he'd more likely enjoy watching such a stupid dude's funeral.

The watch center's steel door swung loosely on one hinge, its edges curled and blackened. He stepped inside to find a world of crimson-smeared electronics but no shattered glass. It was smaller than he'd expected, allowing no more than three men to work there at a time. Parallel streaks on the carpet showed where at least one corpse had been dragged out.

"Only one man standing watch when we got here," Templeton drawled. "We used knives, not guns. Didn't want to disturb anything if we didn't have to."

"Thanks."

Tinned voices bleated from the radios, bitching about gunshots and ignorance. Chief Broussard, in particular, was whining long and loud about disrespect. His mouth'd be filthier after he saw how many counts the indictment listed against him.

Twan's grin deepened, rising from somewhere he hadn't known could still set fruit. It broadened, flashing white teeth against dark skin, and was reflected back in a fancy computer monitor.

Other monitors above the watch desk showed New Orleans, image after image spilling into each other. His streets, about to start getting clean for the first time in how long?

Twan shoved the chair back and sat down. This deputy chief had a lot of work to do.

When things got a little quieter, he might ask Templeton to explain what the fuck had been a man one minute and dust the next. Didn't want any more like it on his streets—but how the hell was he going to keep them out?

Sixteen

Ethan propped his chin on his fist, considering the miserable specimen of humanity before him.

The fellow blubbered again, too terrified to form words, whether verbal or inside his head. Neither torture nor threats had been needed to achieve this result, just the reminder that Madame Celeste didn't appreciate losers. It didn't take a fool to realize he'd spoken the truth.

Finally, Ethan waved him away, letting Jean-Marie's man finish questioning him.

Time to call his oldest hermano and his cónyuge, a couple who looked forward to sharing eternity together. Ethan had known they were a matched pair from the moment he'd seen them riding Jean-Marie's motorcycle through Austin. Jean-Marie had been a loner for too long to let his guard down around just any woman, let alone allow her to seduce him in public. And his Hélène had been so visibly delighted every time she touched him—hell, it had made Ethan and half the men in Austin jealous to see them.

Covering her escape from Madame Celeste's clutches was

why they'd blown up Rosemeade Plantation, and he'd have been happy to do more. Although a pair of cónyuges was a priceless asset to any esfera, Jean-Marie's happiness was worth far more.

"Jean-Marie, do you read me? Jean-Marie, come back."

A long pause ensued.

Hell, if he was riding across country with Steve on their motorcycles, he wouldn't answer the radio, either.

Ethan's mouth thinned.

"What is it, Ethan?" At least Jean-Marie was more polite than Ethan would have been.

He cut to the chase.

"According to the rats here at Bacchus's Temple, Madame Celeste is flying to Hollingsworth's ranch to reclaim her arsenal."

"Oh, hell," Hélène muttered.

"Yeah, that's just what I said. Did you have a chance to look it over when you made Hollingsworth talk last month, Jean-Marie?"

"Yes, it'd be a good start to World War III. Didn't touch it, though, since we left him in place as a double agent."

"Not much of one, considering he's in Aspen with his girlfriend," Ethan grumbled, remembering that lost argument with Don Rafael. "Madame Celeste is in the air right now, and I can't get there before she does."

"Houston's got their hands full with the floods, and you've got Dallas with you," Jean-Marie said slowly, identifying where the two closest compañías were—and why Ethan hadn't called them.

Ethan kept his mouth shut, letting his elder hermano make his own decision about involving himself and his cónyuge. Much as he'd like to have them involved, he wouldn't ask Jean-Marie to do so—nor would he beg two recently reunited cónyuges to risk everything on a very dangerous venture, even if they were the only ones who had a chance of succeeding.

"Hélène and I will go." Jean-Marie's voice crackled through the night.

Ethan threw back his head, almost shouting with relief.

"We should be able to reach Hollingsworth's ranch just before midnight," Jean-Marie continued.

"You should have a few minutes before Madame Celeste arrives." Ethan gave what encouragement he could. "Don Rafael is flying in with the mesnaderos, but I don't have a precise arrival time for him."

"Also, Hélène stole the names and addresses of Madame Celeste's bandolerismo in Texas."

"Thank God! I'll start putting together a hunting party so we can bag them quickly."

"Keep me informed."

An emphatic click ended the call, probably signaling two cónyuges who needed to encourage each other. What couldn't they do if they stood together, secure in their love?

Ethan slammed his chair back and stood up. Stupid to dwell on possibilities he'd never know. It was more important to think about the here and now and the few decades he'd have with Steve afterward.

HOLLINGSWORTH'S RANCH, EAST OF HOUSTON, LATER THAT NIGHT

Devol brought the Cessna lower, cursing the arrogance which had set his hand to a jet instead of a prop airplane. Jets were far faster, *oui*, and *cher madame* undoubtedly needed help quickly. But props could land anywhere, unlike this clunky, noisy brute.

The runway was covered with grazing cattle, indistinct shadows in the waning moonlight. Even if he succeeded in moving them—hah!—someone would have to taxi Madame's jet out of the way before he could join her.

And if that motorcade of armored Mercedes sedans coming

down the main road didn't contain Don Rafael, he'd be polite to a priest for an hour.

Pine trees and cedars shivered, their needles lashing the breeze like a small hurricane.

Crap. He couldn't put down here, either.

He hauled back on the yoke and forced himself to fly higher. There had to be somewhere he could land and join the battle. Assuming there was still a fight by then.

Templeton was in New Orleans and Gray Wolf never willingly left Texas. It had to be the heraldo but they were only important for their treacherous tongues. Yes, he'd taken out two of Devol's mesnaderos but they were the least. Surely his best men could handle that rat, while Madame Celeste handled the vampira.

"Mathiot," he ordered. "Come in, Mathiot and Folse."

Silence.

"Mathiot," he snarled, mentally rehearsing the most painful disciplinary methods.

A single shot answered him, clear as crystal through his very good radio, followed an instant later by a blur of bullets.

Merde! His gut twisted, sucking his hopes into a monstrous vortex.

Now *cher madame* was alone down there but she was no duelist. He could not fight for her, could not kill for her.

She needed to be warned—but how? Why hadn't he insisted *cher madame* take one of the headsets, instead of sending all of them with the men?

He circled again, cursing the trees which made it impossible to even guess at the number of wires concealed among them.

Killing himself wouldn't help her. He was her only defender, now those four assholes had gotten themselves killed inside the house.

Ah, there was the heraldo's motorcycle, glinting in the moonlight between the road and some trees and looking entirely too innocent. Hell, there were a thousand different ways to blow one up and all of them were very fatal.

If *cher* tried to ride it . . . No!

He gulped and tried an experiment for only the second time. *Madame?*

Nothing. He could have been talking to a fog bank.

Of course, she never, ever liked to speak mind to mind with anyone.

He beat on the instrument panel with his fist and circled in the other direction. If he was to save his love, his darling, he had to get his feet on the ground.

This time, he brought the jet in very low, looking for someplace, anyplace to put down.

Instinct led him toward the motorcycle. *Cher* Celeste, the one person who gave life its savor, was running toward it as fast as she could.

What had they done to frighten her?

Cher madame!

Time slowed and his veins chilled.

Fire burst out of the pine forest in a torrent, shooting for the impassive stars and tossing his plane forward.

Noooo! Tears burned Georges's throat and eyes, too bitter to touch his skin. His goddess was dead, destroyed in a fire brighter than the sun. Everything that made life sweet was gone.

He automatically circled again to mourn her brilliant pyre, but his brain stirred slightly when the motorcade pulled up.

Don Rafael and his cónyuge embraced their heraldo and his slut. Celebrating their victory, no doubt, the bastards.

Georges started to snarl, his heart pounding for vengeance.

Blood for blood.

If Texas women thought they'd suffered before—hah! He'd destroy the greatest, most respectable woman in Texas as payback for their esfera's murder of Madame Celeste.

COMPOSTELA RANCH, AUGUST 7

Don Rafael's office was very crowded the next afternoon, with vampiros and compañeros squeezed onto every seat and standing against the wall. The heavy steel shutters were completely closed, protection against their enemies and the sun. Recessed lighting picked out every detail of weapons openly worn, glinting when men shifted slightly.

Today, Don Rafael displayed a cónyuge's full unity with his lady. She was seated at his desk, while he stood behind her at the fireplace, before his great sword. They moved with the same gestures, finished each other's sentences, echoed the same facial expressions.

Gray Wolf stood shoulder to shoulder with his cónyuge, Caleb, so close the same air could have passed through both pairs of lungs. Jean-Marie and Hélène, Texas's third pair of cónyuges, sat on the sofa with her head on his shoulder and their arms wrapped around each other. Last night's exhaustion no longer bruised her face, although she definitely clung to her lover.

Amazing that Don Rafael had accepted her, even though she was a fire starter and therefore a great weapon.

A muscle throbbed in Ethan's cheek and he turned his attention back to his master.

"We know now where Devol has been hiding his bandolerismo, *mis amigos*—in off-site storage vaults for computer data, which are similar to safety deposit boxes."

Just as Steve had said—the brutes had been hiding in plain sight. So simple, once you knew where to look.

"A thousand apologies for missing them, patrón," Luis growled.

"There are dozens of such facilities scattered across Texas and Oklahoma, to be found near every major city," Jean-Marie drawled. "Each one contains many locked vaults and is guarded day and night by a single guard."

"A vampiro only needs to wake up and command the guard to release him and then forget he ever did so. A similar process will handle the vampiro's return," Ethan added. Steve had explained the process that morning before leaving for Dallas, thanks to having previously dealt with a computer fraud case.

"At least some of them may have moved by now, since Madame Celeste died well before dawn and we haven't seen Devol since then," Gray Wolf pointed out quietly.

An unhappy silence swept through the room.

"We still have to check every address on the list." Doña Grania was pragmatic as always.

"Agreed." Don Rafael rubbed her shoulders as if drawing strength.

"Rough Bear, you have the lead, as alferez menor, with Hennessy's Dallas compañía as your shock troops. The attacks will begin immediately after sunset."

"We will be very—thorough, sir," Rough Bear purred. Rafael allowed his fangs to flash in acknowledgment, probably certain one of his eldest hijos would prepare suitably memorable departures to the afterlife for those bastards.

"Gray Wolf, I'd like you and Caleb to personally search Austin. The list is longer here."

Gray Wolf nodded silently.

"Jean-Marie, you and Hélène will go to San Antonio, to ensure it's thoroughly cleansed after so many attacks."

"Of course, *mon père*."

Just how far did Don Rafael intend to strip his defenses? Ethan kept his expression impassive.

"Luis, I want you to work with Jean-Marie on a list of every other similar place those brutes can move to."

"We have already started."

"*Excelente*—but be creative and thorough. I place my full reliance on you two."

Ouch. Luis would work himself and his entire staff into the ground after that.

Doña Grania wrapped her fingers over Don Rafael's without looking at him, a gesture of such love and compassion, it made Ethan's throat tighten.

He lifted his chin and stared at the great sword, that symbol of knightly honor and duty.

"Ethan."

"Sir?" He met his master's eyes calmly.

"You and I will stay here to coordinate the attacks."

"Of course, sir."

Crap. He'd have enjoyed bashing Devol's head in.

"You have much to do, everyone, in order to prepare for tonight's—frolics. Dismissed."

Rafael sat down on the desk and eyed his darling. "What do you think?"

"Of the plan?" She shrugged. "It's the best you could do."

"And my men's reactions?" He picked up her hand and started playing with her fingers. The left hand, of course. Thumb, forefinger . . . The square little box shifted in his pocket, as if eager to meet her.

"Gray Wolf is very pleased. Jean-Marie is glad to stay close to Compostela, so Hélène can continue to rest. Luis wants to redeem himself. You know that." He nibbled her fingertip and she raised an eyebrow.

"Ethan?"

"Wants to fight, of course."

"I won't let my best fighter go far from you."

"But you're here." She gulped, her pulse racing when he kissed her wrist.

"I'm the only vampiro in Texas who can walk in daylight, *querida*."

"But . . . Oh damn." She threaded her fingers through his and pulled him close. He readily slipped onto the floor at her feet, kneeling before his gracious lady.

"*Pequeña*, all will be well."

"I lost you once. Worse was living without you." Her voice was muffled against his hair.

"It was so for me, too. Even a small tumble felt like an abyss because you weren't there."

She sniffled, intertwined courage and terror flooding their link.

"*Mi corazón*, will you bind yourself to me in this life?"

"Whazzat?" She pulled back to stare at him, her blue eyes enormous.

"Will you marry me? We will have a proper marriage this time, not a rushed ceremony in a little chapel."

"Chosen so my Princesse couldn't change her mind about being able to spare my services?" Grania laughed and threw her arms around his neck. "Of course, I'll marry you, my darling— even if we have to go to Vegas!"

"Vegas!" His horrified objections were drowned in the most delicious fashion possible, by her kisses.

He came up for air finally, while sitting on the floor and cuddling her on his lap. He'd unceremoniously shoved his chair out of the way and they were facing his fireplace, with his great sword hanging above the empty hearth.

She nestled closer, her soft curls tickling his throat. Joy stirred in his heart, followed by caution, but Rafael pushed back the wariness. Surely now they had time.

He flipped open the lid and offered her the small box.

"Ah, you romantic!" Her dazzled eyes shot back to his. "A sapphire ring for me—and for you, too?"

"It's traditional, *la luz de mi vida*." Hers featured a single great sapphire, bracketed by perfect little diamonds, while the stones in his were set in a single, twisting band. "Our wedding bands will unite each betrothal ring into a single, triple ring—a puzzle ring, in a symbol of our love and our long lives."

"Perfect." Tears dripped down her cheeks but she held out her hand. He slipped the ring on her finger, his own hand shaking a little, to his great disgust. But he quickly disguised that with a tender kiss.

She caressed his cheek and retrieved the other ring. This one went on more smoothly and she kissed his hand quickly, cherishing his scars.

He lifted her chin. "Grania, *mi alma, amarte para siempre no sería suficiente.*"

"Even forever doesn't seem long enough," she agreed, and leaned forward to seal their pact.

A polite cough from the hall interrupted them just before he could start unbuttoning her shirt. Dammit, why hadn't he closed the door?

"Yes?" he snarled, wishing Luis at the bottom of the sea. Of course, if it had been any of his *prosaico* servants, he might have thrown something.

"Captain Howard and Lieutenant Posada are here from the Texas Rangers, sir."

Madre de Dios, what were they doing here? Rangers never came to Compostela because they weren't supposed to know there was anything interesting here.

His eyes met Grania's, both pairs equally stunned.

"Are they working with Ethan?" she whispered, and sat up.

"No, not that I've heard." He filled his eyes with her one last time, mourning his lost opportunity, but stood up. Duty was a very hard taskmistress sometimes. "Where are they now, Luis?"

"The library, sir."

"*Bien.*" He reached down and lifted his lady to her feet, stealing one last kiss before he left the room. As for his speedy pace? It was only polite to greet his visitors as rapidly as possible, *es verdad*? Hardly because he was a *novio* eager to return to his beloved *novia*. He grinned privately and moved a little faster.

Two men turned to face him, both tall, weather-beaten, and smelling of long familiarity with firearms. But one was older and warier, while the other held the barely leashed eagerness of a fine hunting dog who'd just scented wild boar.

"Welcome to Compostela Ranch, gentlemen. I'm Rafael Perez."

"Zach Howard, and this here's Jorge Posada."

Handshakes followed, and Rafael gestured them to the big leather chairs, silently dispatching Luis for drinks.

"What can I do for you, gentlemen?" He waited, well aware his insatiable curiosity was why he'd been summoned. Normally Luis or one of his men dealt with any visits from law enforcement.

"We understand you rent land outside Gilbert's Crossing," the older man started the conversation, his Texas drawl gentle but his eyes sharp as the edge on a good bowie knife.

Rafael's eyes flickered. Although he ferociously hid true ownership of his land in order to hide its full extent, he did occasionally rent it back to himself. When that happened, he wasn't as careful about hiding the traces.

He wouldn't make that mistake again.

"True. I have some goats and sheep grazing on it. Why?"

"Do you know an arroyo called Rio Oso?"

Ice ran through his veins. *Santa Madre de Dios*, what had gone wrong to make the Rangers ask about a road only two living men still knew how to follow?

Ethan!

What the hell? Coming, sir!

"Why?" he asked the Rangers bluntly, dropping all pretense of indifference.

"Are you aware Ramirez, El Gallinazo's executioner, was killed near there a few months ago?"

"Yes, of course." By Ethan's Ranger. "It was in all the newspapers."

"During our investigation, we learned El Gallinazo has recently been running massive convoys of illegal goods through the area." The younger man took up the story.

Massive? ¡*Maldita sea,* he must have started immediately after we thinned our border patrols to provide troops for the war! Is that how Devol brought his *bandolerismo* into Texas?

"Go on," Rafael gritted out.

"We understand his preferred route is through someplace called Rio Oso. The only map where we can find it is pre-Republic and not very accurate. But it does seem to indicate Rio Oso falls within your ranch."

Its southern entrance did—the only part anyone ever wanted to guard.

"Why are you talking to me and not my landlord?" Rafael asked warily, grabbing for one last chance to avoid the inevitable. "Surely they should know all about the land."

"They're a corporation and you're somebody we can speak to, face-to-face. Can you show us where the arroyo is on a map?"

Rafael hesitated. How much did he want to admit to *Rangers*? Especially during a face-to-face journey to the border? Only he and Luis knew how to find Rio Oso during the dry season.

Given El Gallinazo's treaty with the Mexican vampiros, he almost certainly wasn't crossing the border without at least one vampiro present to ensure the Feds were looking the other way. Sending the Rangers down without help would only get them killed. Nor could he send Luis there, whose compañero abilities would be of little use against multiple vampiros.

"We have reason to believe," Howard said quietly, his deep voice rasping through the room, "El Gallinazo traffics in both cocaine and slaves. Tonight's convoy is supposed to be especially large."

¡Coño! No way would he allow that filth to touch his land another day. *But* Santa Madre de Dios, *I do not want to make this journey.*

A sword twisted through his heart. He closed his eyes for a moment but reached for duty yet again.

"I can take you there," Rafael said softly. "I can't show you on a map, since it's an *arroyo seco*—an arroyo which disappears underground during the dry season, leaving no traces on the surface."

"But—" The younger man started to argue.

Howard stared at Rafael, who glared back implacably. Messages were passed between two old warhorses until the Ranger captain finally coughed. "Looks like we've got a civilian guide. We'll have a bunch of Feds with us, too. Do you think you'll be bringing anybody, too?"

Rafael nodded, his throat very tight. The compañeros from his fast reaction force were all he could spare from the hunt for Devol. He'd leave Ethan behind to guard Grania, of course, with Emilio and the few remaining mesnaderos.

If only his visions would let him reliably see threats to those closest to him . . . But no, he could see hurricanes, ice storms, even droughts. If he saw something endangering his loved ones, it was truth—and he could count those occasions on his fingers. He'd have to pray Rough Bear, Jean-Marie, and his other men would sweep the land free of Devol and all his filth, never letting a single iota slip through to endanger *dulce* Grania.

San Rafael Arcángel, protect me on this journey. Let it not be like the last time I rode out to protect the border from an enemy invasion and never returned to my beloved lady . . .

SEVENTEEN

COMPOSTELA RANCH, THAT NIGHT

Ethan headed out for the cemetery as soon as full darkness fell. As the senior vampiro present, it was his duty to walk the inner perimeter.

It also gave Doña Grania time to compose herself after Don Rafael's departure. She'd been very brave when she'd waved him good-bye, but she'd left for their rooms immediately afterward, her face far too desperately calm.

Jean-Marie, on the other hand, had gone off hand in hand with his cónyuge, both of them relaxed and eager for the fight. A little nervous as any good warriors should be but still stronger for each other's presence, with no hesitation because Hélène was a woman. Jean-Marie was damn lucky Don Rafael had accepted her and he knew it.

Ethan kicked an inoffensive pebble out of his way, hurling it over the hilltop, and jumped onto the last step. The fountain greeted him with a delicate mist, sparkling like diamonds under the waning moon. Moisture beaded on his forehead and shoulders, darkening his hair like a veil. A breeze caught the spray and tossed more at him, wrapping him in it until the world fell away.

"Templeton." Deaf Smith saluted him, still wearing his fringed leather coat and high leather moccasins. The silver star on his chest burned brighter than the moon, the surrounding wheel spinning through the mist.

"Ranger Smith." He returned the salutation, his blood running faster.

"There will be a fight at the border tonight," Smith commented. It wasn't a question but Ethan chose to treat it that way.

"Yes. Federal troops and the Rangers will be there, plus our men."

"And some of my friends. But that is not why I came. I had a wife and daughters who I loved more than life."

Ethan bowed slightly. "Texas cared for them in your stead, sir."

"For which I am deeply grateful." He paused, his hand gripping his bowie knife. "A brute and his followers have been killing Texas's women."

"Devol!"

"Correct. He plans to kill Texas's greatest lady, Doña Grania."

"We know where they sleep—"

"Do you expect your enemy to wait for you?" Sam Houston's greatest scout cast him a scornful look and Ethan winced.

"Devol and his best men will gather tonight at midnight, at Valencia. We watched some arrive last night."

"All of them?"

"A half dozen, with more to come."

"Do you know where the others are? The cities in their old hideouts or coming directly here or meeting someplace else?"

"We can't see their former resting places," Smith admitted reluctantly.

"Giving us no idea of how many are doing what or where. Shit, shit, shit."

Smith's silence provided eloquent agreement, even if it lacked profanity.

"Hell, I don't have enough men to send a party after Devol but he's the big threat."

"I can talk to you, as a fellow warrior and scout, but no one else. My friends and I will do what we can to help, but we are limited."

"Any aid in this crisis will be deeply appreciated," Ethan assured him. He took another turn around the fountain, barely noticing his now-soaked torso.

"I'll have to go there alone. I should be able to thin their numbers considerably." He scored his lip with his fangs, eagerly tasting the fresh blood. "Losing one vampiro from Compostela's defenses won't be pleasant but won't cripple her, either. I'll leave Emilio in charge."

"A compañero?"

"You know our ways, then?"

"Do you always try to teach your grandmother to suck eggs, young man?"

Ethan chuckled and bowed his head, accepting the reproof. "Emilio is a proven warrior in a hard trade, with the U.S. Navy. But he has doubted himself since the attack on Doña Grania, even though he figured out how to use an owl as a weapon. This should give him the chance to redeem himself."

"Very well. Until my friends meet yours in Valencia, Templeton." Deaf Smith raised his hand and was gone.

His friends? But he was going alone.

HIGHWAY FROM DALLAS TO AUSTIN, LATER THAT
EVENING

Steve drummed her fingers on the steering wheel and changed channels on the police scanner yet again. Nothing. Not that she'd expected to hear anything, given how far north she was from the action. But she would have liked to have known something—anything!—if only as a small payback for briefing the governor on their activities, while he was in Dallas on that fund-raising trip. After all, she'd kept him out of the team's hair while everybody else went off to the border in search of El Gallinazo and his drugs. Lucky them.

And she got to drive up to Dallas and back down to Austin. All in the name of executive oversight. Whoopee.

Nor did she get to see Ethan tonight, since he'd already called her, claiming all-night sentry duty. He'd mentioned Devol would be taken care of soon, but he hadn't said how. Damn him for being a close-mouthed son of a bitch.

Given that she was guaranteed to be alone tonight, she'd chosen to return on the older, more scenic highway, rather than the interstate. Maybe she'd have enough peace to think about that new bike she wanted instead of another date with a battery-operated boyfriend.

Yeah, right.

She eyed the silent scanner again, shot a glance at its frequency display, and said a few extremely impolite phrases about folks who observed radio discipline all too well.

Her headlights flashed on a sign for Valencia Estates, the golf resort developing Valencia. "Final stage sold?"

But they'd been still laying the basic water and sewer systems when she and Ethan were out there a week ago. How could they have sold all their lots by now, given all their acreage?

She jerked her truck over to the roadside and reversed it rapidly, barely watching for either oncoming traffic or the deep irrigation ditch edging the highway. An instant later, she halted it with a screech of brakes, hopped out, and stared at the real estate sign suspiciously, her big police flashlight blazing like a searchlight.

Yes, it truly did say Valencia Estates had their final stage sold. But the lettering was a trifle ornate, almost calligraphic. Odd, very odd—and something cold sank into her bones, like a swamp's putrid damp reaching out on a wintry night.

She needed to find out what was happening, no matter what it was. Because if Devol was there, not where Ethan expected, there'd be hell to pay.

But before she went, she'd change the sign a bit, especially the directions on how to find Valencia. The development's owners could fix it tomorrow, if they chose.

And she'd put on her tactical gear—quickly, very quickly. Because her twisting, tightening gut wasn't happy spending more than a minute without body armor.

VALENCIA, MIDNIGHT

The old town slept under the scudding clouds, its scattered buildings looking more like markers to a forgotten age than a current metropolis. A sturdy stone structure here, a leaning wood shack there, a curving oak tree in a corner, tombstones canted crazily, branches and leaves dancing in the wind, while all roads circled or led to the courthouse square. The old gray courthouse rose tall and strong in the waning moonlight there, its clock tower reaching for the light.

Green streaked the western sky, between banks of deep black and purple. The clouds were running fast before the wind, whipping each other in hissing fits of thunder and blinding light. The earth trembled when they ripped into each other, as if realizing its own turn was coming soon, when wind and water would lash it like saber blows and electricity would pummel it like a prizefighter.

The clock began to strike, its tone as rich and pure as it had been a century ago. One, two, three . . .

Ethan shifted forward another infinitesimal inch until he

could see out of the attic window. The courthouse was the tallest building in town, especially situated on the low rise which took up courthouse square. He'd bugged it so Emilio and everyone else at Compostela could listen in to happenings in the square. Not that any of the compañías would return in time to help him, given how fast the bridge was likely to wash out in this storm.

Steve . . . What a joy it would be to have her beside him in this fight. Mercifully, she was safe in Dallas.

He could see everything—and he could smell almost everything, too, since scent rose—without worrying about being detected. None of his enemies was his age so his senses were keener.

On the other hand, if he moved another inch, they'd know where he was and they could see all of his possible exits.

So what? Sometimes a good first strike was worth everything.

Five, six . . .

A man dressed in a black T-shirt and jeans stepped onto the courthouse lawn. Ethan's eyes narrowed and pure, liquid pleasure filled his veins. He started to purr, very softly. Devol.

And Ethan was finally free to take action against the bastard.

Eight, nine . . .

Other men were stepping out onto the courthouse lawn. But how many would appear? He couldn't act until he knew what Devol planned and how great the danger was. He'd ordered Emilio to stay back at Compostela, assuming Devol didn't use mind-to-mind speech.

He bit his lip and waited, a single grenade in his hand, ready for use, his fangs pricking his lip.

Six men faced Devol when the clock finally finished chiming. Seven vampiros ready to attack Compostela—Devol, Yoshi the Fair, Gerald Hunter, Roald Viterra . . . More than enough to cause a damn sight of trouble for the few men there. Damn, damn, damn.

"Is this everyone?" Devol demanded.

Yoshi the Fair shrugged. "Directions were difficult, man. You didn't give us much time, in case we got lost."

"Imbecile!" Devol spat and Yoshi flinched.

Ethan grinned wryly, pleased despite himself to see somebody discipline that smart-ass psychopath.

"How much time can we afford to spend waiting?" Viterra asked, a more pragmatic killer.

Devol shot him a look of sincere dislike. "None," he admitted. "We need to leave for Compostela immediately."

"Compostela *Ranch*?"

"Where else would I be talking about?" Devol shot back.

The astonished chorus grew until Devol shut it down with a shout. "You will obey me or die! Do you remember what led you to join me or do we need to repeat the lesson?"

He glared at each of them until they dropped their eyes and begged forgiveness.

Ethan snarled deep in his throat. He'd have been happier to see one or two leave.

"Forget about the others," Devol snapped. "There are enough of us to carry out my plan and gain the full glory for its success."

That earned some wary nods.

"We'll go in on Yamaha Grizzlies."

What the hell? Big all-terrain vehicles?

"Satellite photos showed me an old horseback trail which cuts across the service driveway, climbing onto the mountaintop. It's very steep"—No shit!—"but the Grizzlies will take us in fast enough to get past the guards before they can raise the alarm."

Crap, that really could work. The Grizzlies were sturdy

enough to carry the men and their armament up that god-awful trail. And Emilio didn't have enough men to completely block the entire mountainside against seven vampiros, even knowing they were coming.

"I've loaded my explosives in backpacks to cut down on the weight," Yoshi volunteered. "I'm only taking the minimum necessary, of course."

Shut up, kid.

"Good. After we're inside, we blow up the watch center and kidnap Don Rafael's bitch using mind control. She's very young, only a cachorra, so she can't resist any of us."

Doña Grania under Devol's control? You bastard!

"We get to enjoy her after that, right?" Viterra asked all too eagerly. Probably picturing her enduring some of his more legendary tortures, or inventing some new ones for her—and photographing their results.

Ethan's blood ran faster, curving his fingers into claws.

"After we steal Jeeps and break out of Compostela, back to Louisiana," Devol corrected Viterra. "Then you can have her *after* I'm done with her."

The hell you will in my town. A soundless growl vibrated in Ethan's lungs. He silently pulled the grenade's pin, curled his arm back, and tossed the now-live grenade into their midst. A quick roll back into the attic's protection, and he waited for the ensuing explosion to announce their departure to the seven circles of Hell.

"Incoming!" shouted Devol.

Damn his quick eyes!

Somebody yelped in astonishment down below and feet scrabbled in alarm across the dirt. An instant later, the grenade exploded, shattering the courthouse's few remaining windows.

A brief burst of cordite's acrid scent touched the air and was gone, ripped away by the storm.

Crap, he hadn't gotten everyone—and Devol was probably

one of the bastards who'd survived. But if the brute was here, he wasn't causing trouble at Compostela.

The front doors slammed against the wall.

Ethan came to his feet, his blood running cool and steady. He dropped into the old second-story courtroom through a gap in the attic's floorboards. It had been almost completely gutted in preparation for renovation, with the mantel, mirrors, statues, and chandeliers removed. Even the walls had been opened up to allow plumbers and electricians to work, including the heavy copper conductors for lightning protection. A few piles of debris stood near the corners. There was less trash on this floor than the lower ones.

Once, it had been the stage for great legal duels. Now it would serve very well as the backdrop for his duel with Devol. The bastard's followers could look after themselves. Like a snake, his attack wasn't dangerous without a head and fangs to deliver the venom.

ALONG THE RIO OSO BETWEEN GILBERT'S CROSSING AND THE MEXICAN BORDER

Rafael waited patiently, or at least impassively, in the appalling storm. If he was being buffeted by a thunderstorm like this, his enemies were, too—and El Gallinazo's pet vampiro would not be able to smell them.

His gut wrenched, twisting itself like a moor's turban, more unsettled than it had been at any time since his first battle. Grania had been fearless when she'd said good-bye to him, as gallantly as Blanche had kissed him for the last time at Toledo. Blue eyes or brown—always the same expression, loving, direct, fierce with courage.

Grania's sweet heart and mind touched him again, warm with love and faith—and faded, leaving him free to concentrate on the coming fight.

He shook himself like a dog, ridding himself of stupidity and rain at the same time. *Dios*, what an arrogant fool he'd been to have separated himself from her wisdom, in order to protect her. Yes, she was a cachorra, but she was also his cónyuge and a proven duelist, thanks to having helped kill Beau, the vampiro mayor assassin.

Rafael pulled out and fiercely kissed the gold cross fleury she'd given him, its ornate curlicues digging into his hand like her eager grip. Ignoring any sidelong glances, he slipped it back inside his T-shirt next to his skin, under his Kevlar vest. He'd make very sure to live and return to her this time, no matter what it cost anyone else.

When he lifted his head, he deliberately looked around with more than his eyes. It had been decades since he'd been here and the land had been soaked by blood even then. Although he suspected watchers, they didn't seem unfriendly to him or his men. No use wishing he had vampiros with him, whose psychic senses might be strong enough to see or hear deeper than he could. In some ways, he was as isolated as he'd been at Ecija—just himself and a few good fighting men to face down a ruthless enemy on unfriendly ground.

Rio Oso cut through the mountains inside Texas's border with Mexico, marked now by waterholes frequented by goats and sheep instead of Comanches. Its steep sides were too unstable to be popular with hikers and photographers, keeping it remote and largely unknown to foolish modern men. The ground itself was largely gravel, although heavy boulders were scattered along the mountains' feet. The remains of an ancient landslide, now reduced to a small cairn, stood at the top of the pass. Even in this condition, it was enough to divide rainwater into interlaced fingers, rather than a single massive sweep of mud and water.

Another sheet of green fire lashed the skies, exploding into sheets of gold when it struck another black cloud. For a moment, it briefly revealed the mountain peak, hidden in a black cloud of rain. None of the prosaico warriors flinched, even the FBI agents from Washington.

A light flashed, long and low along the canyon wall. Could it be? But surely even El Gallinazo would not be so arrogant as to use headlights less than a mile from an official U.S. border crossing.

The beam split into two, and was joined by another, and another. *Madre de Dios*, he was driving his Toyota Land Cruisers along Rio Oso as though he were delivering groceries!

Worse yet, Posada had been correct: This convoy contained an immense number of vehicles, too many for the small number of Texas Rangers and federal agents to stop, should its commander decide to argue. Or if some of its gunmen went into the rocks to fight. And The Buzzard had never been known for docility, especially when faced with U.S. lawmen.

Rafael sniffed again, fighting not to gag. At least there were no slaves in the vehicles—only enough illegal drugs to make a carnival fun house seem completely logical.

Still, they had to try peaceful means first. Even so, Rafael was personally glad all his men had excellent credentials as deputy sheriffs. Those bits of paper had smoothed the way for their guns' presence, especially their M-15 clones. His lip curled, flashing his fangs.

The lead vehicle reached the three flimsy wood barriers scattered across the arroyo.

"Halt!" snapped Posada, standing between the barricades and a large boulder, only a few paces away from Rafael. "This is the . . ."

A violent shove bounced off Rafael's mental shields. El Gallinazo's pet vampiro had gone into action.

"Texas Rangers," their leader finished in a gasp, all but doubled over in anguish.

Madre de Dios, he was strong to have spoken at all.

¡Silencio, chingado! Rafael shouted at the enemy *vampiro*, hurling the full weight of his mind at him. From this close, it could easily be a death blow—and he'd be damn glad if it was. That *hijo de su chingada madre* had undoubtedly caused more than one fine man's suicide while serving El Gallinazo.

A single scream split the night and faded, its echoes washed away by the clean rain. The pressure against Rafael's mind vanished.

The Ranger stood erect again and surreptitiously rubbed his temple. "Stop for inspection," he ordered in a clearer voice. The lead Toyota lumbered closer and Posada gallantly remained erect, shooting a quick glance at the nearest boulder.

Rafael clucked his tongue and silently signaled one of his men. He'd never willingly permitted good fighting men to die needlessly.

A window spun down, the sound startlingly clear in the brief pause between thunderclaps.

"Go to hell!" a deeply accented voice sneered. Other windows instantly opened and guns sprang into the night, gleaming like miniature lightning. They burst into action, hurling a hail of bullets at the barricade.

The flimsy wood exploded into splinters but the Texans and Feds were already firing back. Posada lunged for the nearest cover and Rafael's *compañero* swiftly dived on top of him, rolling him behind the rocks where other Rangers had taken shelter.

Cursing under his breath, Rafael began to carefully fire his M-4T, steadily picking off any of El Gallinazo's men who were foolhardy enough to try for the rocks. *Gracias a Dios* for his assault rifle's light trigger, which gave his vampiro eyesight and reflexes the speed to catch those devils.

Unfortunately, he'd never glimpsed enough of El Gallinazo to ensnare his brain.

So this fight was going to have to be done the old-fashioned

way—hand to hand, and very messy, especially if those beasts
were armored.

The enemy leapt up the stairs and burst onto the courthouse's
second floor, dressed like the foundling he'd once been, in grubby
jeans and flaunting a pistol. Not that prosaico weapons would
help him in this duel.

"Good evening, Devol." Ethan bowed mockingly to him,
never taking his eyes from him.

"You should have known better than to interrupt me, you
effete bastard, let alone destroy one of my best men." His gaze
swept the room, probably looking for Ethan's allies or escape
routes.

Lightning blazed once again, revealing the space's utter lack
of anything except wood and pipes, plus the narrow gaps in the
floors on either side.

Ethan's mouth twisted slightly. Little chance of any quick
retreat from this cockpit.

"Now I must kill you." Devol's eyes were brilliant, glazed
with a killing lust.

"Now you can *try*," Ethan corrected him, and bowed again,
using the move to scan his enemy for weaknesses.

"You were a fool to have come alone, Templeton." Devol spat
and began to circle. "But your doing so will save me time."

Ethan raised an eyebrow and started to pace, always facing
his enemy. Damn, how he'd like to see the bastard reduced to a
pile of ashes in that fireplace.

Suddenly a jet of mist burst out of Devol's clothes, instantly
transforming him into a great gray wolf. It sprang, jaws widening to rip out Ethan's throat.

Ethan's new black wolf shape met it in midair, twisting like a
snake for a good hold. Devol's teeth ripped into his shoulder but
he slammed against his opponent's hips and broke free.

Devol tumbled but landed upright, his clothes falling unnoticed to the ground, followed an instant later by Ethan's shirt, jeans, and boots. They backed away, spitting out blood and fur, and circled again.

Ethan's leg burned, a painful wound but not crippling. Better to call it a nuisance since he'd lose blood from it, which he'd prefer to use for shifting or fighting. And the smell would madden them both. Sanity fled quickly, faster than friendship between vampiro duelists.

What the hell had Madame Celeste fed the bastard all these years? Death and terror, yes—but how much? Christ, he was stronger than a vampiro twice his age!

Thank God for all those years when Don Rafael had drilled Ethan on tactics. Cunning might be a better weapon than his greater age. Best to shift as seldom as possible. A wolf could give out punishment and receive it for a very long time, longer than logic dictated. Which might just be the length of this bout.

Another thunderbolt rattled the windows' broken glass and Devol charged Ethan again.

Steve waited and watched, forcing herself to keep her breathing steady. Why had she ever thought that was easy, even during tournaments? Because it sure as hell wasn't in a darkened, ruined city when her lover was fighting for his life.

She pressed her belly deeper into the mud until she imitated an earthworm. She was downwind of town where no vampiro could smell her, where she'd arrived in time to see seven vampiros talking on the courthouse lawn. She couldn't hear what they'd discussed, but it didn't take a fool to realize their plans didn't involve Christmas presents—especially when two of them flourished bloodstains from their wrists to their elbows. Bastards. An electric chair would be too easy for them.

She'd glimpsed a familiar golden head watching from the

courthouse's second-floor window. Ethan, thank God—but alone? Was that why he wouldn't answer his phone? What the hell kind of idiot tried to take on seven brutes by himself? The sort who needed help—but good Lord, she wished there was more handy than just her.

The bastards' chat had been interrupted by a grenade tossed out of the courthouse, like a verdict. God bless Ethan, he had taken out one of the brutes but the rest had scattered like quail. The leader had raced inside after Ethan and was fighting him even now, in a cacophony of snarls and growls and thuds of bodies against walls and glass.

But she couldn't go there to help, dammit, because they'd smell her coming and make her do—oh, God, who knew what? Scream like a silly virgin and distract Ethan? Shoot him in the back?

Instead she had to crouch out here in the dark and pray they didn't turn her into a helpless puppet, as they had in San Antonio.

Her breath froze again in her throat despite the night's heat. She closed her eyes and tried to think.

Ethan. Remember Ethan. Ethan needed her.

Ethan of the blond hair, hazel eyes, and crooked smile. Ethan, her heart's only true delight.

Her lungs began to sigh in and out, once again. Thoughts began to lurch forward within her skull.

She could stop reinforcements from reaching him—or even better, kill the sons of bitches out here in the storm, where they couldn't find her.

She'd found herself a lovely hiding place—a future sewer ditch, almost five feet deep, which bordered one entire side of town. Nobody could easily see her in it, although a dog could smell her. If vampiros were as good as a police K-9—well, she was keeping her head down.

One vampiro down, six to go. Ethan had one more pinned, which left five for her. Plus, she had plenty of ammo.

She watched the lightning-sparked streets, her finger light and steady on her M4 carbine's trigger. Locked and loaded, a round in the chamber ready to go. Night vision goggles, her beloved NVGs, showed her anyone who might stroll through the old town.

Come on, boys, it's time to party with a big girl.

Eighteen

Yoshi squatted in the construction office and stared at all of his materials. The old bank made a lovely place for sorting this stuff, thanks to its heavy stone walls. Of course, it didn't have a good roof—but that's why he'd headed for the ground floor where everything was dry. He had plenty of explosives—he smirked—enough det cord, and barely enough detonators to do the job at Compostela. Man, people would be talking about him for decades after this job! To say nothing about the truly excellent meal Don Rafael's bitch was going to provide.

Awesome, man, just awesome—whether or not he managed to escape Devol.

But the newcomer who'd thrown the grenade had to be Templeton, Don Rafael's alferez mayor. He needed to be stopped but how?

Yoshi wasn't a gunman—he shuddered, remembering how heavy and clumsy rifles were. But he could work magic with bombs. Like make a little bundle of joy to drop into that courthouse and immediately blow up the bastard who was spoiling his plans.

Still, he needed explosives, det cord for fuses, and detonators.

He stared at the three piles in front of him. Explosives, yes, with plenty left for Compostela.

Det cord? Yes, but only if he made the bomb into a drop-and-run. The fuse would still be far shorter than he'd like, though.

Detonators? He grimaced. No, not if he wanted to have any of his good ones for the real target.

But Templeton needed to be killed here and now or they wouldn't get there.

Maybe if he used his cell phone for the detonator instead . . .

A man sauntered down the street from the old livery stable toward the bank, singing a scatological aria about dead enemies and casually spinning a scoped Barrett .50-caliber rifle over his head like a helicopter rotor.

Steve stared, goose bumps running down her neck away from the newcomer. He sure as hell wasn't anybody she wanted to let loose on a Texas street, if he planned to use a sniper rifle firing heavy machine-gun ammunition.

Her finger eased a little deeper onto the trigger. She slowed her heartbeat, matching it to her breathing.

Exhale, no pulse, utter stillness throughout her body—except her trigger finger. Just as she'd been taught.

Bam!

His head exploded into a cloud of dust.

Before his few powdery teaspoons of remains could reach the ground, Steve was bent over and running, her retreat camouflaged by the intensifying storm. This hideout had been lovely but, unfortunately, was the only one with a clear line of fire to that now-lonely sniper rifle and its two full box magazines.

Two down, four to go, with one for Ethan.

Viterra burst into the construction company's offices in the back room, his beloved Steyr AUG A3 cocked and ready. Futuristic looks matched with brutal efficiency, it had never failed him.

Nothing here.

He swept his assault rifle's muzzle slowly over the silent room, itching for a chance to eliminate whoever had run across this floor.

Dammit, this was the place closest to where Hunter had died. Why else would anyone be in here?

Maybe the killer had gone farther into the old bank building, to where it became two stories instead of only one.

But who wanted to assassinate a prosaico when they could smash him into the ground instead? Yoshi's explosives could make that happen faster than anybody.

Viterra rested his AUG on his hip and flipped his cell phone out of his chest pocket.

Over his head, Deaf Smith smiled at his old friends. Together, they faded into the walls.

Twenty feet away, in the construction office's lower floor, Yoshi finished the final touches on his drop-and-run delight.

He sat back on his haunches and beamed. Beautiful piece of work, especially given these conditions and his total lack of time.

Nice, half-pound chunk of C-4 to make sure the interfering bastard and everything around him for a hundred feet was destroyed, plus a very short bit of det cord, and his cell phone.

All he had to do was find one of the other guys and borrow a cell phone.

After that, once they got anywhere near the little twerp, just toss the package in his direction, dial Yoshi's number, and presto! That asshole would never cause trouble again.

Maybe Viterra would loan him his cell phone. He was the only one, other than Devol—Yoshi shuddered reflexively—who had any appreciation of explosives' beauty.

Yoshi's phone lit up, displaying Viterra's name as if the man had heard himself asked for.

Yoshi started to smile. An instant later, letters began to spill across its display and he scrambled onto his feet.

Kaboom!!!

Ping! A bullet splatted against the rock above Rafael's head, sending deadly shards flying in a dozen directions.

One of his compañeros grunted briefly, the small sound laden with pain.

Rafael's mouth thinned. He didn't need to be a vampiro mayor to smell all the blood in the air, or know how many of his men had been injured. More so than necessary, since his personal guard had to be present in order to protect him.

He cursed himself yet again for being an arrogant fool. What had he gained by being here, so far from Grania? If he died on an errand which a compañero could have done better—after being suitably warded against vampiro mind probes, of course—he would have failed his duty, because he'd denied his esfera the union of its finest duelist and his cónyuge in an unbeatable team.

Lightning hurtled through the sky, its green fire mocking him. It blazed for a moment against the mountaintops, showing the black buckets which poured water over their shoulders and any man daring enough to lean out when he fired.

Were there shapes standing amid the rocks, after the lightning faded, forms edged in fire?

He cursed the tattletale under his breath and shoved another magazine into his M-4T. At least they'd forced El Gallinazo's convoy to remain on the pass's far side, beyond the bluff which the arroyo swept around. There'd been enough rain to make Rio Oso's waters gleam in its old bed. The old river was running fast and sweet now, concealing its depth as always. Three inches or three feet—who knew without checking it in person? And who'd willingly try that, given Rio Oso's uneven footing?

Another lightning bolt struck the ground, hitting the riverbed.

Everything shook, even the armored Suburban Rafael had arrived in. He ducked, instinctively grabbing anything handy for stability and slicing his hands on the jagged rocks, just as his neighbors did.

Upriver, the ancient cairn melted into the river, frothing water marking its killer's jaws. Boulders flexed against the water but who could judge their true size or the water's depth at this distance or in this light?

But with the plug gone, how high would the water rise now?

For a moment, the shooting stopped. When it resumed, El Gallinazo's men were more vicious, as if desperate to prove their right to cross.

Rafael fired again and again, forcing his enemies to fight for every inch of ground. Guiding his men to their best advantage. Thinking about the ostentatious duty he'd foolishly chosen, not about where he should be.

Lightning sparked and swirled across the sky, while thunder pounded the clouds and the ground. The air sizzled with electricity, rain hissing angrily as it bounced off the ground.

Suddenly all of El Gallinazo's Toyotas began to roll forward together, charging at the barricade's remains.

A single massive lightning bolt burst from rock to sky, splitting the darkness in a single, glowing sigil which burned itself deep into Rafael's eyeballs. He instinctively flung his hand up to protect himself, muttering an ancient Arabic charm against the evil eye.

High above, between the walls of rock, came a wall of white, flecked with darkness. A flash flood was racing down Rio Oso, taller than a man and strong enough to roll over semis.

"Run for the mountains!" Rafael shouted. "Climb, everyone!"

"You heard the man!" Posada joined in. "Take cover!"

The Texans ran for their lives, trusting their native earth would protect them. They scrambled up the slope, diving into cracks between the boulders, eager to reach safety above the tumult to come.

El Gallinazo's fighters charged faster onto the riverbed, eager to take advantage of the gap in shooting. The bluff hid the oncoming flood from their eyes. They fired again and again, leaning out of their Land Cruisers' windows or running alongside. El Gallinazo led them himself, easily identifiable by his protective cordon of bodyguards

The Texans began to shout warnings. "Go back! Flood! ¡Inundación!" But laughter and bullets were their only answers.

The waters rose only slowly around the trucks' tires at first. Foam began to dance, tumbling pebbles and small rocks end over end like a dangerous children's game. Little could be heard of the true danger, given the steady hail of bullets—until lightning splintered the night again.

Somebody screamed in one of the trucks. El Gallinazo shouted a string of profane orders.

The trucks tried to speed up but couldn't, given the treacherous sand and gravel underfoot. They slipped sideways or became stuck, their tires spinning hopelessly as their doors sank lower and lower. El Gallinazo pistol-whipped his bodyguards, demanding they carry him out. They dropped him and turned to run, like so many others.

The flood crashed over them, whipping through them like a gigantic hand of fate. In less than a minute, there was nothing left but a boiling froth of muddy water with a few large boulders, which had once been called Land Cruisers. A handful of men spun helplessly in the torrent, facedown and arms limp. There'd be dozens of corpses washed up in the desert, fodder for El Gallinazo's namesakes.

El hombre propone y Dios dispone. Man proposes and God disposes.

Rafael crossed himself and bowed his head in prayer, giving thanks his companions were healthy. *Sabe Dios*, his other men were safe.

Steve withdrew a little deeper into the old building's shadows. From here, she could see all the way down Main Street to the courthouse and across that big intersection to the still-smoking hole. She could see anybody moving but they shouldn't be able to see her.

She didn't know why the construction office had blown up, killing its two vampiros in that long, complicated explosion. She was only thankful she hadn't needed to figure out how to destroy the little bastard inside with his explosives smorgasbord, without killing herself, too.

Four down, two to go, with one for Ethan.

Anybody walking into the courthouse would have to pass in front of her sights. Anybody trying to reach the ATVs in their trailer or the expensive sports cars sinking into the mud would probably go down the road on the right, to the parking lot. Given the sparks flying from tonight's electrical storm, she might be able to see their shadows.

It was a good hideout, too, made from hefty granite blocks as if its original architect had planned for a siege. They provided a dark interior, allowing her to look out but permitting almost nobody to look in. It was also reasonably unlikely anybody could smell her from outside, since she was still downwind of the courthouse.

She eased a little deeper into its depths, eyeing the courthouse square. Four entrances to that building but only one working staircase to the second floor, where Ethan fought that devil behind the big windows. If she stood sentry at the foot . . .

She flinched, terror's ice freezing her hand on the trigger. She could still be turned against him.

She closed her eyes and fought for breath, forcing her pulse to level out. She couldn't help Ethan if she had hysterics. Calm down, calm down.

She blew out a last, slow breath and rechecked her perimeter. Twelve o'clock, three o'clock, six o'clock . . .

Shit, a black shadow was working its way down the street toward the courthouse, dodging from side to side in an irregular pattern—probably to avoid the unknown sniper who'd left the Barrett lying in the road.

She grinned and gave her beloved M4 a congratulatory pat.

But this guy sported an even nastier silhouette, thanks to the LAW antitank missile he carried on his shoulder. That little bastard could take out the courthouse's entire second floor, assuming they were at a high enough altitude—which they probably were. Shit.

She sighted down the barrel, easing her pulse and breathing into steadiness. He should be crossing again—now!

She fired, crosshairs perfectly aligned on his heart.

But his free arm came up, pointing directly at her through the window—and he pulled the trigger on an MP5.

She dived sideways, her heart in her mouth. A bullet splatted into the wall behind her, followed by cascading rock shards. Fire burned her arm and she squirmed, coiling herself into a tighter fetal position, protecting her neck. Her skin flushed cold, then hot again.

A loud thud sounded outside.

Thunder boomed again, shaking the walls, and rain continued to pour.

Steve snatched up her rifle and ran for her alternate exit. A quick check showed no watchers and she dove for the next building, a glorified storage shed. No bullets touched her; no voice shouted at her—and slowly, infinitely slowly, her heartbeat began to slow. Her throat was tight enough to seal a bank vault.

An instant later, she ran again, winding up behind the former livery stable. From here, she could once again watch a stretch of Main Street. It was bare of anything except a LAW missile and an MP5.

Was he dead? Probably. Who'd give up an MP5? Count it five down, one to go—and one for Ethan.

She laid her head back against the wall and began to tally up her resources for the next strike. Her left arm was sore as hell, blood dripping into her hand from where that shard had cut her just above her wrist.

M4 assault rifle, check; 11-87 shotgun in its tactical sling, check. A shotgun had always been an old-fashioned town marshal's favorite weapon because it was deadly at close range, without requiring a rifle or pistol's pinpoint accuracy. SIG P229 pistol in its thigh holster, check. Four magazines each for the M4 and P229, plus an autoloader for the 11-87, so she should be set on ammo. Assorted other goodies, check.

She snorted at her own silliness. Who cared how many guns you had when you were about to face somebody who could order you to do anything—and you'd obey?

She needed an advantage, something to make that vampiro so eager he wouldn't bother to put a mind lock on her. So cocky he wouldn't think straight.

Yeah, right, like that was going to happen.

She shook her head and went back to basics.

Well, she was fairly sure the last bad guy wasn't lurking in the courthouse's ground floor. But that didn't tell her where to go.

One thing she did need to do was bandage her arm. It wasn't injured enough to slow her down. But her hand was getting a little slick, which could be a serious disadvantage. Body armor vests were exactly that—molded Kevlar which covered one's torso, nothing more. They didn't do a damn thing for one's extremities and her other portions had gotten rather bloody.

Bloody.

Weren't sharks attracted to the scent of blood?

She frowned, considering her palm. Could she use this? Did she have the nerve to do so?

She swallowed hard, remembering all the generations of her family who'd been lawmen in Texas. The ones who'd fought through prejudice and anger and despair to do what was right for their fellows, hoping one of their family could finally become a Texas Ranger again. She pulled her badge out and pinned it on her chest, flashing the star and the wheel for everyone to see.

Then she began to walk up Main Street toward the courthouse, laying a trail for her last prey to follow.

Ethan shook his head to clear his mouth of blood and fur and circled the courtroom, facing Devol. Ethan was limping but no worse than his enemy. He'd lost some teeth, too, and one of his ears was badly notched. But his nastiest injuries were the broken ribs from that last tumble across the room, making his breath burn his throat like napalm. As for healing any of them—hah! He had better things to do with his energy, like rip the bastard's lifeblood out.

Devol snarled at him, deep in his throat. Death glared out of the yellow eyes and would be eagerly dealt by the bared fangs. Only one of them would leave this room alive—and both were fiercely glad they were finally free to settle the old grudge.

Ethan growled back, squaring his shoulders, measuring his opponent and their setting. Lightning flashed outside, briefly flinging an unsparing golden eye into every corner. The old courtroom still faintly reeked of the combatants, despite how vampiro blood and flesh immediately disappeared when removed from its owner. The land outside smelled of mud and fresh-washed grass, the coming harvest—everything he'd dedicated his life to protecting.

He sniffed again, catching another scent. *Steve's* blood?

What in the name of everything holy was she doing on the courthouse's ground floor, especially if she was injured?

Coldness ran through him, and deadly earnest. The world narrowed to Devol—the hungry eyes, the dripping teeth, the furred throat.

No matter what it cost, he had to kill the brute *now* and get downstairs, before anything else happened to Stephanie Amanda.

Steve considered her hideout—or should she call it a nest? Considering she had four doors to watch, she didn't have much opportunity to build defensive walls against any of them. But she'd done her best, concealing herself on the ground floor behind the stairs leading to the second floor. She could see both entrances, which should allow her to control the situation, right?

Yeah, right—even with most of the windowpanes cracked.

She settled down, straining her ears to listen.

Suddenly a small object flew in through the entrance and rolled across the floor toward her. A grenade?

Without hesitating, Steve leapt through the closest shattered window, flinging up one arm to protect her face.

KABOOM!

She dived behind a pile of construction debris, her shotgun in her hand. She tucked her limbs closer and tighter, wondering where the hell the bastard was. Dammit, this stack of boards wasn't enough to completely hide her.

KABOOM!

Shattering agony punched into her, like being simultaneously hit by a dozen semis full of boiling magma. Her right arm was pure, undiluted pain, concentrated fury tearing through her veins. One leg screamed, warning her walking wasn't an option.

A chorus of shrieking furies swept through her ears, ringing bells loudly enough to drive out thought. Her sight began to fade, blackening at the edges like burning paper. She convulsed, the pain competing with her stomach's demand to empty itself, and her gun's hard shape cut into her so-called good side.

Lightning flashed again and a wolf bayed upstairs.

Ethan. Oh, dear Lord, Ethan.

Her shotgun had landed on the ground, its pistol grip next to her hand. She rolled herself onto her back, bringing it into the open, wrapped her fingers around it, and blinked away tears.

A blur resolved itself into boots and a man snickered overhead. "Pity you're not already dead. Worse, you're losing blood too fast to make a good meal."

Bastard.

Her index finger closed over the trigger. She squeezed twice, blasting thirty balls of double-ought buckshot into his black heart.

Devol's teeth slashed through Ethan's flank, almost hamstringing him. Ethan twisted back upon himself and bit deep into the other's shoulder, forcing him to flinch.

They broke away, covered in blood, their breath sobbing through the holes gaping in their windpipes—when two loud explosions sounded from below.

Gunfire. A shotgun, in fact—and more of Steve's blood scent poured into the air.

Like hell he'd allow her to be injured!

There was only one move left to try, which required perfect timing and the last of his energy. If he failed, he'd lose everything, including her.

He charged, pouring his energy into a burst of speed which would have rocketed him across a football field.

Devol's jaw dropped in pure astonishment. But he braced

himself, growling to show his teeth's readiness to destroy his foolhardy enemy.

At the last possible instant, Ethan shapeshifted into a wild boar, lowered his head, and tossed Devol high using his mighty tusks. The gray wolf spun, four paws scrabbling the air—and Ethan shifted again, back into a man. He caught Devol and hurled him out the broken window onto the Confederate veteran's bayonet, in the courthouse square below. Then he lunged for his own, more modern rifle.

Devol screamed, his body thrashing on the great bronze blade. Lightning streaked the sky and thunder drummed the earth.

The Louisiana alferez mayor rippled into dust and fell away from the Texas soldier's weapon. But who the hell had time to celebrate that?

Ethan raced downstairs to find his lady.

Steve blinked muzzily at the results of her first aid attempt and managed to chuckle. She didn't have a first aid kit on her, for starters. And the grenade had shredded her clothing too badly to use it for tourniquets. She'd put her belt on her right leg, the worst injured—but that still left her left leg, both arms . . .

At least it had been quiet upstairs for a few minutes and her radio still worked. God willing, the coded phrases wouldn't sound forced.

"Captain Howard? . . . Yes, I'm *praying* for that *Vegas* trip. A vacation looks real good right now . . . Thank you, sir. Reynolds out."

Her hand dropped and the now-unimportant bit of electronics rolled away. By the time anybody came hunting for her, Ethan would have figured out a good cover story.

Her eyes started to close and she tugged them open. She

wanted to talk to Ethan again. No, she needed to talk to Ethan again. But the square was so bright with all those lightning flashes.

She drifted somewhere soft and cold.

"Sweetheart? Stephanie Amanda?"

"Steve," she corrected Ethan.

He smiled but seemed a little rattled, which wasn't at all like him.

"How do you feel, sweetheart? I've called for an ambulance."

"Hazy," she answered honestly. "Bet they were fuzzy on when an ambulance would arrive."

His mouth tightened, his breath coming hard and fast through his gritted teeth.

Her fingers twitched, trying to reassure him. Then she fell back, exhausted. Poor darling was likely worried sick. Storm had probably washed out the only bridge and kept helicopters from flying.

The world blurred again.

"Steve, do you have a first aid kit in your truck?"

"Yup, just take my keys."

The world resolved itself into his face. He'd managed to bandage her and apply tourniquets. Then he'd tucked her into a nest of emergency blankets on the entrance portico, underneath some carved owls. But there was blood seeping through the bandages and she was so very, very cold in a world of ice-edged, gray fog.

She wasn't afraid, though, not of anything with him there.

"Steve." He kissed her hands. "You're bleeding to death and there isn't time to take you to a hospital. I might be able to save you by turning you into a vampira. But my master would probably kill both of us if I did."

"Probably? Might be able to save?" She blinked, struggling with his logic.

"He might not kill you because you're a woman."

Might not kill *me*? "What about you?"

"My life is forfeit if I do this."

"You're risking everything for me. Of course I say yes." Her tongue was growing clumsy. "And I won't let him kill you."

"Steve." Tears seeped from his green gold eyes. "Steve, my darling." He hid his face against her palms and she touched his golden hair, offering what comfort she could.

When he lifted his head, his expression was much more under control. "You must focus your mind on only one thought. Exactly one."

She nodded weakly, wishing she could pin down one of the myriad questions swimming through the fuzzy cavern she used to call a brain.

"You've lost enough blood that I don't need to drain you any further." He winced and his voice tightened for a moment. "When I offer you my throat, you must quickly drink as much as you can."

"Yes," she whispered. "Of course."

He wrapped his arms around her and rolled her close to him. She flowed against him, every bone and muscle knowing exactly where home and comfort could be found, despite the pain.

He kissed her mouth sweetly, a gentle kiss offering everything and demanding nothing. Tears welled in her eyes and she leaned closer. Her love, her heart's delight. No matter how small the chance, she'd take it to be close to him forever.

His hand came up, and he slashed his jugular open. He caressed the back of her head, gently turning her toward his throat. "Stephanie Amanda, darling."

Blood, his blood. She closed her eyes for a moment, then tasted it, her only hope of forever with him. Fiery sweet, running down her throat and into her belly like a ribbon of pure gold, spinning her world into a cascade of stars, every one of which carried his face.

NINETEEN

Even before the helicopter landed, Rafael had unbuckled his seat belt and was straining his eyes for a glimpse of his darling. His men yanked back the door and he sprang out, leaving his body-guards with their puny weapons far behind.

Dulce Grania ran to meet him, her red hair streaming down her back, and sprang into his arms. Their lips met and paradise was finally granted to him, as he'd never known before. Ah, such delight to fill his lungs with her intoxicating scent! The miracles of modern clothing, which allowed every inch of his body to quickly remember the curves of her sweet body, unlike the stiff formality of his old chain mail! For seven hundred years, he'd never dared to dream of such sweet ecstasy of homecoming, yet now he was enjoying it at last.

San Rafael Arcángel had been more generous to him than he'd ever dared pray for. He would have to make a very gener-ous offering of thanks, perhaps a chapel—after he'd thoroughly cherished his beloved cachorra, of course.

He kissed her with increased enthusiasm.

She shook her head teasingly at him and ran a finger over his lips when he finally lifted his head. "Do you mean to conduct our entire celebration here at the helipad, Rafael?"

"Of course not." He chuckled and offered her his arm. "We

have an hour yet before first light, more than enough time to see you safely indoors."

She drew herself close to him, snuggling together until they walked as one person along the pathway through the gardens. Fountains sang and the roses bloomed: green grass flowed amid gurgling waters to meet the panoramic vistas of the great Texas hills and valleys. His home and his esfera, safe now for his lady.

His people walked behind them, sharing their joy—Jean-Marie and his Hélène, Gray Wolf and Caleb, Luis, Emilio, Lars, Rough Bear, Hennessy, Peter, and more. All of his men had gathered here in April, wearing their finest garb. Now they were attired in warrior's garments, with wounds that must be tended and gear showing the signs of hard battle.

But they hadn't provided an accounting of their activities. He hadn't demanded one during the flight back from Gilbert's Crossing, given his Ranger audience—but now?

"How many of Devol's men did you kill tonight?" he asked idly, more concerned with the supple grace of Grania's fingers.

No answer came except splashing fountains.

He frowned. Ethan wasn't present, which was very odd—but perhaps he'd gone out to feed. Given the number of other senior commanders present who'd normally be equal, perhaps they were confused about who should answer.

"Rough Bear"—he enunciated the name with great clarity—"how many of the names on the list did you eliminate tonight?"

"All but seven, *mi Señor*—Devol and six others." A rusted watermill would have displayed more enthusiasm than Rough Bear.

Rafael whirled to face them. "All but Devol and six? With those, he could take Compostela, if he had a good enough plan, given the anchor watch we left here. *¡Mierda!* What happened?"

"Ethan and his Ranger killed them," Grania answered, moving to face him. "He went out alone to face them, refusing to weaken Compostela's defenses by taking even one compañero. But his Ranger learned of it and joined him."

"A vampiro and prosaica against seven vampiros?" Rafael whispered. A vehicle was working its way up the driveway, in the front of the house. "*Madre de Dios*, they were lucky."

"They were your best," she retorted, "and they served Texas well."

The noise resolved itself into Ethan's truck.

"Let us welcome him home to Compostela!" Rafael encouraged. "Such a feat of arms deserves the highest honors we can give."

Grania inclined her head formally and rested her fingers on his arm, her expression unreadable. She'd raised her mental shields against him, the adamantine ones which he could only bypass through their conyugal bond. He flicked a sideways glance at her but said nothing.

They met the big, black pickup in front of the main house, where the drive made a great circular sweep before a spectacular view of the eastern valleys. Gray Wolf and Rough Bear stood in the house's shadows with the rest of his vampiros. Compañero snipers lined the roofline in an honor guard for their leader, while prosaico warriors marked the driveway's edge.

The sky was dark and the evening star was fading. The house's front was in shadows. They were counting the minutes until the sun rose.

The last time he'd come here at dawn was when Lucien Saint-Gerard had brought Shelby Durant as a young cachorra, only to see her die. Here were the same men, in exactly the same formation, at the same time . . . Shadows whispered over his skin.

The muddy truck jerked to a stop on the macadam drive's east side. Rafael strode eagerly forward, leaving Grania and Jean-Marie behind on the steps.

Ethan flung open the door, his chambray shirt and jeans filthy beyond belief.

Rafael frowned. *Sí*, he could accept mud. But the blood wasn't Ethan's, nor did it belong to a vampiro.

Ethan's mouth tightened and he bowed awkwardly to Rafael, while remaining in the truck. "Master."

He hadn't publicly addressed Rafael as that in decades, not since before he became a vampiro.

Rafael's expression hardened into a wary watchfulness, while Ethan stepped out, flung his seat forward, and turned back to the pickup's shadowed interior.

But when Rafael's *dulce* Grania took his hand, he kissed her fingers and held on to them desperately. She was the *luz de su vida*, the light of his life. No matter if everything else turned strange and unpredictable, he could face anything with her at his side.

Ethan produced a silvery cocoon, a bundle wrapped in layers of survival blanket, out of the truck. His face was hard edged, engraved in exhaustion and bitter resolve. But his head came up, his green gold eyes steady. He held his burden close and carefully, as if it contained everything in the world to him.

Its scent was female, that of an incredibly young cachorra. She was alive.

Grania's breath hissed out.

Ethan dropped to his knees before Rafael and laid her at Rafael's feet. *¿Ay de mi*, what was he doing?

Terrified for a reason he wouldn't admit even to himself, Rafael's nostrils flared and he took a deeper sniff.

The vampiro's blood on the cachorra—the creador who'd sired her—was Ethan. How could he have betrayed him like this? Rafael had to have only his own hijos in Texas, so he could totally trust them lest he be destroyed, as he'd killed his own creador thanks to his creador's sloppiness in enforcing the bond.

That was the reason for the First Law. If he let Ethan give El Abrazo, where would it stop? Who could he trust? Would he ever believe Grania was truly safe in a world where brutality like Madame Celeste's was commonplace?

Rafael growled, baring his fangs completely. His men came to attention with a firm stomp but didn't draw their weapons.

Ethan lowered his head, baring his neck to his patrón and the laws he'd flouted.

"This is Ranger Stephanie Reynolds, who has worked with me, for our esfera, for many years," he said carefully. "She was mortally wounded in tonight's fight and I . . . I . . ." He stopped, his throat working. "I couldn't stand to see her hurting," he choked out.

He loves her, Grania whispered.

That is unimportant compared to the laws he has broken!

What would you have done to be with me, in Toledo?

Rafael's mouth abruptly closed on a sharp retort. How many times throughout those tortured centuries in that stinking cellar had he sworn he'd do anything for another hour with his lady? Risk any trial? Dare any haughty lord?

"Let me see your face," Rafael snapped, playing for time. "I must be sure I am speaking to an hijo of Texas, not an imposter."

Ethan sat up but didn't rise, choosing to settle on his heels. Rafael's army was motionless and silent, making the predawn breeze sound like a herd of stampeding longhorns.

"I know I don't have a place to bring her safely through La Lujuria or the strength, let alone the skill." Ethan's voice was hoarse but his words were clear. "Will you please give her a home, out of compassion for a good woman? She'd be an excellent addition to the mesnaderos."

Rafael barely caught his jaw before it gaped most unattractively. Ethan was asking him to raise his hija? To bring her through La Lujuria when the blood bond would be most firmly established? Reynolds would be loyal to him after that, not Ethan.

"And you?" he asked, as haughtily and noncommittally as possible.

"My life is forfeit by the laws of Texas." Ethan shrugged, the lines in his face deepening. "I will walk into the dawn or you may kill me in any way you wish. All I care about is Steve."

Rafael frowned and fought not to chew his lip. Lose Ethan, the hijo who'd shown him how to build an army of vampiros to hold Texas? Stalwart, aggravating, but ultimately reliable Ethan? Especially for something he'd have done himself, given the chance.

Plus, the lady was a personage he would have eagerly recruited if she'd only been a man.

Ethan was entirely correct in his estimation of his creador's softness toward ladies: He could not easily kill a woman and would therefore adopt Ethan's cachorra, bringing her into Compostela. However, the odds were miniscule that any female would survive La Lujuria, especially the first few hours. Her only slim chance was if her beloved was with her the entire time.

But that siege of the mind and body was far, far worse than what Blanche had faced at Toledo all those centuries ago. He would have hewn his way through armies to be with her, yet her death hadn't been guaranteed—as Ethan's Ranger's death was a near certainty now.

Yet the agonies he'd suffered of how he'd failed her because he hadn't stood beside her—still suffered, in fact!

Grania gently rubbed her thumb over his hand, a delicate reminder they were united at last, as they had not been seven centuries ago. He quickly twisted his hand, capturing her fingers. In a few centuries, he might not be as greedy for reassurance. Perhaps.

Could he deny Ethan the chance to stand beside his lady in her hour of need, the chance he and Blanche had never had?

Madre de Dios, if she died during La Lujuria, Ethan deserved to face that trial with her.

But how to present it to his other men without seeming a weak fool?

He spun to face them, standing between Grania and Ethan. A quick, brutal command brought his hijo to his feet, with the Ranger in his arms.

"¡Mis hijos y compañeros!"

Boots and guns clanked in acknowledgment when all his men came to full attention. Jean-Marie's and Luis's eyes scrutinized him particularly closely.

"I was previously introduced to the work Ranger Stephanie Reynolds of the Texas Rangers has done for Texas. Some of you have already had the honor to work with her and personally know her deeds."

The silence was intense, sharp enough he could hear every drop falling into the great fountain.

"Do you agree she is worthy to join us?"

"Yes!" shouted Rough Bear, echoed a second later by Hennessy and Jean-Marie. A roar of acclaim went up from the crowd.

Rafael inclined his head, a little surprised by the strength of their approval. But perhaps the lady's participation in tonight's combat explained it.

Grania's soft chuckle briefly touched his mind.

"After her injuries in tonight's great battle, my alferez mayor gave her El Abrazo and brought her home to us. I welcome her as a vampira of Texas"—Ethan gasped—"and hija of Ethan."

Ethan's head whipped around to stare at him, hazel eyes wide with incredulous joy.

"I add one condition to this," Rafael said sternly. "As you know, anyone who breaks the laws will be executed. In this case, should the lady break the law, her creador will also be killed."

"I swear to you, it will not be a problem," Ethan protested, bowing.

Rafael shot him a disbelieving glare. *So you would have said yesterday, idiot, about this situation!* he retorted.

Ethan gritted his teeth, while Rafael's army erupted in cheers.

"But we have less than an hour to protect your Doña Stephanie from the cruel dawn," Rafael said, pleased to be gracious now he'd reinforced his position as patrón. "Take her to the Rose Suite, where we have always housed our most honored guests. It is completely soundproofed and she should be entirely safe." *It also contains no memories of any cachorro's awakening,* he added, *to haunt your future.*

Ethan nodded thoughtfully and started to turn, shifting his darling closer to his heart.

"After you're finished, wash up and come find me. You will need to feed well and have much to learn if she is to have any hope of surviving. She will remember nothing of tonight, which may be a blessing."

Despite his best attempt at regal benevolence, Rafael's voice roughened slightly on the last word. Ethan flinched, his jaw tightening, but said nothing more before he left.

What are their chances, darling? Grania asked softly.

Hers? They are essentially nil, querida. *Worse than yours, since you'd already started to become my compañera when you were given El Abrazo.*

And his? Her blue eyes were fixed desperately on his. He hated to give her the only answer he knew.

I wish I thought he had much. But since he was willing to bring her back to me, to give her even a chance of surviving La Lujuria, while believing I'd kill him for breaking Texas's first law—he growled and slapped his thigh, taking out his anguish on a bit of dust—*well, he's bound up everything he has in her.*

We will pray for them tonight, Rafael. A single tear hung on Grania's eyelash before she blinked it fiercely away.

"Dismiss the men, Rough Bear," Rafael snapped with unnecessary force. Perhaps there was something more he could teach Ethan, which would give him a better chance.

Ethan slowly circled the great suite, ticking off its virtues on his fingers. The room was a magnificent example of the finest modern Scandinavian design—vast expanses of smoothly polished woods, with only brilliant rugs to break up the incredible perfection. Even the great bed was a pristine sweep of the smoothest silk, except for the raven-haired beauty sleeping in its center.

Once he'd seen this suite as a proffered guarantee of security—after all, who could possibly bug anything so immaculate?—but now he thanked God for its privacy. For the layers of sound-proofing hidden behind the paneled walls and steel shutters, plus their complete lack of distractions.

Any sound, however small, could destroy his darling now, or any bit of light. But Steve wouldn't start screaming here because a chandelier's pendants danced together, their crystal harmony becoming a cacophony of dragons' teeth tearing her apart.

She would awaken with a vampira's full sensitivity but, unlike a man, she would try to understand every sense all at once. Vampiros usually focused on a single thing, the goal they'd held when they'd received El Abrazo.

But he hadn't even been able to promise Steve whom she'd awaken with, when he gave her El Abrazo! How could she have kept a single image to guide and protect her now? Her chances were so damn small . . .

He snarled and thrust the thought away, clenching his fists. Any fear now would be a certain death sentence for her.

Her first meal was the most critical, since it taught her the emotions she'd need for the rest of her life. If she learned to hunger for terror—he shuddered, remembering the many ways Devol had invoked that feeling in his prey—then Don Rafael would have to kill Steve tomorrow. God help him, Ethan would understand, too—even if it sent him walking into the sun afterward.

No, he had to be confident tonight, certain she'd survive.

Above all else, she needed to recognize him and accept him as her creador—and perhaps one day her cónyuge, the greatest joy of all. They'd been lovers for fifteen years. She knew his body the way she knew no other man's. Surely she could come willingly to him now, as easily as she had at Calatrava when she'd walked away from those greedy idiots in the bar.

After all, she'd accepted El Abrazo despite her concerns over his undue familiarity with the darker side of the law.

He must remember the night at Calatrava and believe she'd come to him again the same way, as innocently as she slept now. If she had enough sanity to say his name, all would be well, even though she'd received El Abrazo in a hurry. He'd have time later to teach her how to shapeshift her teeth into fangs, like most young cachorros.

Her body had earlier cleansed itself of its prosaica aspects, violently but naturally. Ethan had masturbated a few minutes ago, inspired by memories of their first time together, to fill the room with lustful scents, as a lure to her most primal being.

Was there anything else he could do for her? He spun, calculating the room's potential, which sent his hair whispering against his nape. For a moment, he almost felt her fingers playing with it. He glanced over at her, smiling.

Dear God, she'd pushed back the sheet and a light sweat had formed on her skin. She was about to awaken.

For the first time since he'd stood at his nephew's grave and said good-bye to his last relative, he crossed himself and said a quick prayer.

He bit down hard on his lip, sending blood welling over his

chin. Something stirred in the darkest recesses of his mind, as if not even aware how to touch him.

Blood and lust, my darling—anytime and as much as you want, he silently promised her. *Come to me, my Stephanie Amanda, and drink your fill.*

Ethan crossed the room back to her in a few quick strides and slipped under the covers, gathering her to him. He twined their legs together, uniting them gently but intimately. He'd never dared dream of being one with her at Compostela Ranch.

But she was limp, doll-like in his arms, not at all the fierce cop he'd always known. He whispered into her hair, barely daring to croon her name. "Steve, darling."

She stirred—and whimpered, pushing awkwardly at him. But she hadn't screamed. There was hope.

Fill the room with the sound of your love, Jean-Marie had suggested. Even though he wasn't a smooth talker like the heraldo, Ethan needed to learn now.

"Steve, you are my life. Uh, the most beautiful, wonderful cop in the world." He nuzzled her cheek, making the words into a soft hum to sink into her bones. "The best shooter, the most fabulous partner."

He kissed the sweet spot behind her ear. "Darling, darling Stephanie Amanda."

She thrashed, shoving against him, and tried to roll away. Well, she'd never enjoyed being called Stephanie.

He gathered her into his arms and sat upright on the bed in the lotus position. Then he swept her legs around him and draped her arms over his shoulders. Her head lolled back and she swayed slightly, but she wasn't fighting.

Better. Maybe she recognized his scent, which he'd now rubbed so thoroughly across her skin. His blood was lightly smeared across her jawbone.

"Beloved Steve," he crooned again, strengthening his voice. "My darling lady of the star and wheel."

He kissed her throat, scraping his fangs gently down the long tendon. He repeated the caress, in memory of all the times she'd begged for more—and she moaned, arching up against him.

He stilled, hope running sweet and hot through his veins. She had enough sense to ask for more?

"Steve, honey," he purred, and happily cherished her again. But now her nipples rubbed his chest, as intrigued as her voice.

For the first time, his cock stirred, as if scenting the potential for pure pleasure instead of necessity.

He shifted his hands lower, to support her back, and happily nuzzled and licked and kissed his way over and along her shoulders and breast. Every inch, every curve, every vein, the sweet circles of her areolas, the hardening buds of her nipples . . .

Perhaps he was teaching her his scent, or learning the entirely different taste of her skin.

But the way she shivered and groaned and clutched at him, wordless in a way she'd never been, yet entirely clear about her needs—made his heart pound and his skin tighten with crackling heat. Her scent was sweet and rich, more fascinating than a small-batch bourbon.

Was she acting out of pure reflex? Were there any thoughts behind those tightly closed eyes? How could he know, when hunger was ravaging his own ability to ask?

He nipped at her collarbone, daring to push his tough cop a little further. A tiny drop of blood welled up, making him remember his hija's fragility. He jerked away, his heart pounding.

"More, Ethan!" she growled, and yanked him back to her.

Ethan? She'd already recognized him, despite La Lujuria's insanity.

"Steve, sweetheart!" He crushed her in his arms and kissed her, splitting his lip further and sending more blood into her mouth.

She moaned deep in her throat and clung closer, growing wilder and wilder for him, whether it was taste or touch or scent. Her hands roamed him ceaselessly, as if simply shaping his body could bring her satisfaction. She rubbed herself over him, shaping every plane and curve and line of her lithe body to match his and shuddering when she came into contact with his blood or sweat—or the pre-come seeping from his cock.

Bones weren't made to support hunger like his, nor nerves steady enough to keep thoughts flowing. Flames lashed through his skin wherever she touched. Lust sparked and danced, feeding the great wellspring of joy building at the base of his spine. It drummed through every bone, guided every touch, hummed in every pulse, rocked in his hips.

Steve, Steve, Steve . . .

He caught her closer and rolled them onto their sides, lifting her legs over his arms. For the first time he could see her eyes, in the room's very slight illumination.

She blinked up at him for an instant, caught in that helpless position. "Ethan, please." Her hands ran up his arms and pulled him down.

Trust, perfect trust. Thank God.

He shifted slightly, finding her with a creador's sure instinct, and entered. *Beloved Steve,* he crooned.

Oh yes, Ethan, she sighed.

Mind to mind at last—and control fled. He thrust hard, riding her like the madman she'd made him. She answered him eagerly, voraciously, locking her ankles behind his back, her nails drawing blood from his shoulders. Her cunt was hot and wet, sucking him in, perfect.

Passion hummed through his bones, while joy drummed at the base of his spine. Life was good, better than marvelous. It was time, while he could still control himself.

Ethan rolled her on top of him, then shaped a single claw and slashed his jugular deep for her. Fire ran through his veins, seeking to bind her. He immediately arched his throat, sending the crimson spray fountaining out.

"Ah, darling, my blood burns for you," she murmured—and bent, avidly seeking the flow.

A spasm rocked him, locking every bone and muscle. His eyes flew open and he gaped at her, shocked beyond words.

She was too young a cachorra to have any blood to spare in the bedroom. How could hers burn—or was she feeling his? Could she trust him enough to catch all of his emotions and sensations, like a cónyuge? Would anything make him happier?

She gripped his shoulders and held on hard, clinging to him like life itself. She drank him down eagerly—and she orgasmed, rippling around him like a Fourth of July fireworks display.

Joy, ah such joy, she cried, echoing his emotions.

The final proof she could become his cónyuge snapped his control. He climaxed, screaming his throat raw and uniting his mind voice with hers, their bodies utterly entwined amid the silk sheets.

AUSTIN COMMANDERY, THE NEXT NIGHT

"*Por Dios*, Emilio, cannot the news shows find anything else to talk about?" Rafael exclaimed. He and Grania had come to talk to the armorers about replenishing their supplies and stayed to spend the night relaxing with his vampiros. He'd not expected to find one of their favorite gathering places tuned to only one show, which had taken over the ten o'clock news.

The TV room was crowded with vampiros and compañeros, lounging on the many leather recliners and couches or seated on the floor. Every wall was covered with monitors, which could cumulatively cover dozens of different sports events. Yet every one was showing the same blue velvet curtain, set of flags, and batch of grinning politicians on a dais, no matter what language the unseen commentator was urgently hissing.

"¡*Maldita sea*, give me the remote and I'll look!" he growled.

Emilio flipped the plastic lump over his head without looking. Somebody gasped but Rafael simply caught it, still muttering. He began to rapidly scroll through channels, his thumb working the keys with the easy skill of long practice. The largest screen whirred and flickered desperately to keep up—but the same damn blue curtain kept showing up at the top.

Lars, Rafael's most trusted spy, drifted into the TV room from the billiards room, pool cue in hand. Several men silently made room for him against the wall, leaving him isolated as ever. Rafael frowned but said nothing for now.

Emilio tilted his head against his chair back to watch Rafael. "If you want to try the Brazilian channel, their camera is far off to the side, which gives them a different view," he offered, in an overly polite tone. "You can even see something other than politicians, such as a few lawmen. That Ranger captain is there, for example."

Who looked exhausted and grave, under that officially impassive demeanor. Pity they couldn't tell him yet Steve was well.

"In that case, we might as well watch it, too," Rafael acknowledged, and glanced around. The largest two recliners were immediately vacated but Grania waved off one offer, choosing instead to sit on Rafael's lap.

He contentedly wrapped his arm around her, wondering how soon he could find their quarters. Duty said he should be worrying about all those prosaico police who were still investigating Devol's bandolerismo and their killings. But surely cleaning up such items could wait until tomorrow.

"Texas governor hasn't been sleeping much," Rough Bear commented.

"But he does look happy to stand with the Louisiana governor," Emilio agreed. "Plus those U.S. district attorneys."

Two top federal prosecutors, plus the Texas and Louisiana executives? Rafael sat bolt upright, murmuring an apology to his darling.

"I now turn the mike over to the Texas governor." The eldest district attorney stepped back from the mike, immediately replaced by one of Rafael's old friends—who he hadn't spoken to lately. What the hell was going on?

"As you know, our great states have lately been troubled by some murders."

The commentators immediately became totally silent except for the text simultaneously scrolling along the bottom in a dozen languages.

"We have reason to believe El Gallinazo was responsible, thanks to the experimental date rape drug he was dumping in our states. Two days ago, the Rangers"—At least he didn't credit us!—"killed him along the border near Gilbert's Crossing."

The curtain was yanked back, revealing a stack of stained crates almost ten feet wide and almost as high. Beside it stood an easel, holding a poster of a once-well-dressed man, now bloated and ugly in death. El Gallinazo.

The room gasped—and exploded into an orgy of brilliant white light from flashbulbs.

"We captured these crates with his convoy," the Louisiana governor announced, her dulcet tones somehow managing to quickly reduce the room's clamor into schoolboy folly and ultimately silence. "A preliminary analysis has already confirmed this drug is capable of causing the deaths we sadly experienced."

"Our friends in Mexico raided and destroyed his factory yesterday, which was the only place in the world that could manufacture it." The district attorney had recovered the mike. "They have burned all the stockpiles there, and we will destroy these. El Gallinazo's chemist died in the convoy, ending any chance of re-creating this drug."

"We now invite you to return to your daily lives, to go out among your friends again." The Texas governor's voice was vibrant and confident. "We ask you to remember the little people whose businesses have been hurt in the past few weeks—the restaurants, the nightclubs . . ."

Mute buttons were punched around the room, silencing the platitudes.

"Well now, isn't that just too convenient for words," Grania drawled.

"They'll never prove they're wrong," Emilio pointed out.

"And they'll never prove they're right," retorted the scientist and veterinarian.

"We don't need them to have a perfect answer, *querida*," Rafael soothed her. "They only need enough to keep them quiet."

"And the people have been terrified so long they should be glad for an excuse to settle down." He could almost hear the cogs in her fine brain working, while she considered all aspects of the politicians' pablum.

His men began to shake themselves into action, preparatory to leaving the room. Emilio caught Lars just before he disappeared and the two left together, talking quietly about China.

"Did you have anything to do with this explanation, dearest?" she asked, turning to face him.

"*¡Por Dios, no!* Neither its creation nor its acceptance. But it will last longer because I didn't."

"Since it's more detailed and originated with more people, rather than being as a single vision into one person's mind."

"*Precisamente.*" He beamed at her. She would be a deadly warrior on Texas's behalf in the coming centuries, using her fine intelligence like a lance. "I doubt either O'Malley or Gorshkov did, either. Gorshkov loathes politicians; he took Trenton rather than Manhattan because there are fewer to be found there."

"And O'Malley's a California patrón so he has good ties to the media, giving him the ability to create the basic idea—but not the law enforcement connections to polish the story."

"*Sí.*" He kissed her hand. "Do you want to keep discussing political secrets in a room full of leather chairs, *mi corazón*? Or can we continue this privately, where I can also sing of how your beauty drives men wild, *mi vida?*"

She blushed adorably, the hot color mantling her cheek until it blended with her fiery hair's silk. *Dios me salve,* she'd always have the ability to do that.

TWENTY

Grania waved to the crowd again, her heart full. A year and a half ago, she'd been terrified to even appear in public with Rafael lest it get him killed. Now she was riding to her wedding and everyone in San Leandro had come to cheer.

She'd asked for an old-fashioned wedding, and Rafael had turned the world upside down to give her the ceremony she would have enjoyed seven centuries ago. It was midnight on the winter solstice, the longest night of the year. The sky was so clear she could count every star and almost kiss the Man in the Moon.

San Leandro's sturdy granite buildings were decked in wreaths and bows of evergreens, wrapped with red and gold ribbons. Brilliant white lights sparkled throughout the courthouse square and surrounding streets. Her darling autocrat had even managed to persuade the independent Texans to avoid colored lights just this once.

He'd covered the streets with dirt, too, returning the town's appearance to the frontier it had once been. The residents were so delighted they'd dressed in nineteenth-century fashions. Now cowboys and gunslingers, barely respectable ladies and schoolmarms with bright-eyed children at their knees, waved to her from the boardwalk or tossed roses and sweet-smelling herbs into the road to make a carpet. Afterward, they'd eat barbecue and a wedding cake from an old Toledo recipe at the concert hall, where San Leandro's First Saturday festivals were normally held.

She blew kisses to them from under her magnificent lace mantilla, her heart light enough to float her over the rooftops.

Ahead of her, old-fashioned carriages conveyed the most distinguished guests to the ceremony, which would be performed by the Archbishop of San Antonio. To her surprise, the governor of Texas had invited the U.S. president, who'd jumped at an early escape from DC's year-end squabbling. Of course, his presence meant the Secret Service as well—and an excellent excuse for metal detectors and the speedy confiscation of all recording devices. Even the locals hadn't seemed to mind that, given their own procession to church the night before, ostensibly as a dress rehearsal.

O'Malley and his cónyuge were here, too. Their mesnaderos stood watch, allowing her Texan mesnaderos the freedom to attend.

Most of the guests had chosen to walk to the ceremony, especially the men, following the old Castilian custom. Boots and horses' hooves released the flowers' and herbs' sweet scents into the air, providing a delicious accompaniment.

Emilio was on leave from the SEALs, avoiding the desk duty his rank and ribbons had earned him. She suspected he'd retire in another year—but maybe not, unless he had something lined up here she didn't know about. He'd never dated Brynda, for example, even though he always seemed to know where she was.

Gray Wolf and Caleb had spent time in New Orleans after Madame Celeste's death, making sure the town was quiet and going through her papers. They'd returned as quickly as possible, of course, since Gray Wolf would never be content away from Texas.

Hennessy, New Orleans's new patrón, had brought Eldridge,

his police chief, tonight. Rafael had allowed him to take almost nobody from the Dallas compañía to New Orleans; he'd be building up his esfera's vampiros and compañeros from scratch. But Rafael had claimed him as an ally, rather than the more rigid bonds of a vassal.

The rest of Madame Celeste's former domain—Atlanta, Miami, Memphis, Nashville, and so on—was still in chaos, almost a Wild West. Rafael had allowed some of his vampiros to travel there, though, and attempt to build their own esferas.

"¡Mira, mama, las estrellas!" a child called.

Grania swung around in her saddle and waved. To be singled out as a star was definitely worth a special acknowledgment. Hélène and Steve did the same beside her, their cloth of gold coats blazing in the light.

All three of them rode, signaling the bride's transition from maiden to wife. After all, a wife was important enough to enjoy a knight's protection, as symbolized by his most prized possession—his horse.

Grania was mounted on Atalanta, Rafael's beautiful white Andalusian mare, on the most important journey of her life. Atalanta's tack and harness were covered in silver until she seemed a dream. She held her head high, pacing as sweetly and smoothly as any fairy queen's mount. Her half sisters were equally lovely under Hélène and Steve.

Each of their cónyuges' most trusted subordinates led their steeds, guaranteeing their safety should the crowd frighten the animal. Lars led Hélène's horse, Rough Bear had Steve's, while Atalanta's bridle was in Luis's steady hand.

All three women rode sidesaddle, wearing dresses made by Carolina Herrera, the same brilliant Latina couturier who'd garbed Grania for the duel with Beau. They had matching cloth of gold coats, outwardly shining like stars but cunningly lined with the latest high-tech fibers for warmth. The coats' full skirts were smoothly draped over the saddles and horses for the maximum display of Rafael's wealth and ability to support his new bride. (How she'd teased him about his medieval thought processes! And how utterly unrepentant he'd been, of course.)

Hélène's and Steve's dresses were red velvet, blazing like rubies. Steve had been absolutely incoherent at the first fitting, apparently rendered almost speechless by having a bridesmaid's dress designed to make her look good.

Grania sniffed privately again and waved to another pair of little girls. She'd be very interested to watch Ethan coax more of a "Stephanie Amanda" out of his Steve. Or maybe not—they'd have time to build their own version of happiness.

Hélène, of course, simply focused on spending every waking minute with Jean-Marie. Being French, she never allowed herself to look abominable. Otherwise, she spent the minimum time necessary in the fitting rooms.

Grania's wedding dress was somewhere between Elizabethan splendor and modern comfort. Brilliant crystals honored Texas's star, while seed pearls outlined Blanche's fleur-de-lis across its silken skirts. The tightly boned bodice was so perfectly fitted it was extremely comfortable. Great belled sleeves concealed for now her beautiful betrothal ring, which would soon be completed. Rafael, ever the traditionalist, had chosen to follow the medieval pattern and make their betrothal rings into the centerpiece of three-band puzzle rings, which would be their weddings bands.

Hélène and Steve disappeared around the corner in front of her, triggering a roar of acclaim. They must have entered the courthouse square and be able to see the church, where Rafael waited on the steps.

Oh dear Lord, make me worthy of him and keep me strong for him. Help me make him happy and always give him the truth. He needs someone he can trust . . .

Atalanta's gait shifted and her ears pricked forward. Luis's head and shoulders stood a fraction taller. He gripped the lead rope a little tighter. They turned the corner and the world changed.

The square was crowded with people, all cheering and laughing. They'd hung so many garlands interlaced with white roses on the old Confederate veteran, he'd almost become an Elvis impersonator. Lights blazed and evergreens filled the air with sweet pungency.

But none of that mattered. Only a few feet away, she could see the church steps where Hélène and Steve were dismounting. Best of all, Rafael and the archbishop stood at the top, Rafael handsome beyond belief in his Charro suit, sparkling with silver embroidery and solid silver coins. Jean-Marie and Ethan stood a step lower in slightly more sober versions of the same attire, openly grinning.

She kicked Atalanta into a faster pace. She'd been good for far too long. Soon it would be her wedding night and she couldn't wait to hold her love, her cónyuge, her life.

Luis spluttered but jerked into a jog alongside Atalanta.

She slid down from the saddle barely a minute later in front of the church, ignoring the rush of men to assist her and help settle her skirts.

Querida, the wedding planner is fussing, Rafael observed from the top of the steps.

Her response wasn't truly printable. *And I'm ready for the lazo* now, she added, picking her skirts up.

It won't tie us together until after our vows are made.

Jean-Marie and Ethan stepped back on each side to give him space, their ladies on their arms. People started to clap in unison.

Exactly!

Luis barely managed to toss Atalanta's reins to a groom and leap to her side before Grania started to run.

Rafael leapt down the stairs to meet her, without a second glance at the archbishop, and held out his hands to her.

She gripped his, trembling with joy. Their eyes met and they smiled, too happy to need words.

The crowd cheered loudly, drowning out anything they might have said.

Luis bowed, his brown eyes dancing, acting in loco parentis to show she'd been formally presented to and accepted by her betrothed. Rafael returned the bow with a few formal words of thanks, before worshiping her once again with his eyes.

Mi corazón. He kissed her fingers, lingering over the ring. *La luz de mi vida.*

Mi cónyuge. She smiled at him, longing to smooth back his hair. But if she started touching him now, she wouldn't be able to stop.

Es verdad, he agreed.

They turned to face the archbishop, who lifted an indulgent eyebrow. "Are you finally ready to become husband and wife, my children?"

"Yes, father," they chorused. And added more privately, *Always.*

"May I have this dance, Stephanie Amanda?" Ethan held out his hand, looking handsome beyond belief in his black Charro suit. Texas was so peaceful now, he wasn't even wearing a revolver at the reception.

Steve frowned at him. They were at Calatrava Resort's largest ballroom, among prosaicos who knew nothing of vampiros. The U.S. president and the Texas governor sat a couple of tables away.

Posada and his wife were farther back, closer to the chocolate fountain, near Captain Howard and his wife. They were still good friends even now that Steve'd officially retired from the Rangers for medical reasons. Ethan had told them she'd been badly wounded during the last shoot-out and needed to recover in a private, out-of-state hospital. Given her rocky health until recently, it'd been easy for them to believe.

The room was superbly decorated in the same red and gold colors used throughout the wedding, with flowers, ribbons, balloons, plus dozens of different expensive trinkets. A lavish buffet was being served to all comers, allowing vampiros' nonparticipation to avoid notice. The quality of the liquid refreshments was equally stunning and enjoyed by all.

She'd been a bridesmaid before; she knew what to expect, the duties and the awkwardness. But this outing hadn't gone that way, starting with her dress. Ruby red velvet, high-waisted, and long-sleeved, it was simple and elegant, and made her feel like a princess. There was nothing to trip over or tear. Instead, men looked at her as if she'd become beautiful. Odd, very odd.

She'd had a hard time during La Lujuria, spending months in a frenzied search for blood and sex. Thank God she didn't remember the very beginning when the hunger had been worst; the later memories were humiliating enough. At least Ethan had been constantly with her—feeding her, cherishing her, giving her the blood and sex she lusted for. Where would she have been without him? If that was what a creador did for his hija, Ethan was a first-rate example. She never knew exactly what he was thinking, though, only what he chose to tell her through the mind-to-mind link.

Even so, she'd only lately stabilized enough to start learning the basics of her new life, like how to control running with vampira speed or shooting with vampira eyesight and strength. She'd visited the Austin Compañía's armorers about customizing her first pistol and she'd watched her first muster, while Ethan carefully explained its principles and how she could participate.

Tolerating the fittings for her dress had been more difficult and more recent, given the necessity to allow somebody other than Ethan close contact with her body. She certainly hadn't had time to think much about what she'd do in it—like dance.

Other couples were dancing, led by the bride and groom. Don Rafael and Doña Grania were twirling around the dance floor, her skirts celebrating their joy better than any scene from a Disney movie. Jean-Marie and Hélène were doing a simpler version of the same dance, her eyes half shut and her face tilted ecstatically back.

Could Steve waltz well enough to look that good? No, especially after her previous experiences at weddings, the only place anybody would ever do that kind of dancing. She'd always worn abominations which punished any attempt to draw a deep breath or move freely.

"Steve?" Ethan prompted.

I can't dance, she answered, choosing honesty and discretion. She'd already learned it was useless to even try lying to her *creador.*

We can do a box waltz, he answered, not backing off.

Is that supposed to make me feel better? she demanded.

Yes. His eyes flashed with something more than laughter. *You can learn the steps easily, especially if I hold you very close.*

She eyed him suspiciously before rising. At least she could perform that movement graciously in this dress, thanks to taking lessons from Hélène.

He found a quiet corner of the dance floor, currently unoccupied by either of the other two couples, and held out his hands—left hand high and right hand low.

She considered him, remembering a lot of old movies on the late, late show. "Did you seduce many women this way when you were growing up?"

"Not particularly, no. It was much too obvious a tactic. Why?"

"Just wondering." She stepped into his arms, dropping her right hand into his left and placing her left hand onto his shoulder. His right hand promptly clasped her waist and they were joined, slightly off center. She stiffened, all too aware of his boots' closeness to her ankles.

"Relax," he whispered into her ear. "How can I hurt you?"

"This feels more intimate than . . ." She turned her head to look at him.

"Sex? Sometimes it can be." He stood perfectly still, his muscles absolutely relaxed. "When we start dancing, our center of gravity will be through our solar plexus—not our shoulders and definitely *not* our lungs. Try to remember that."

"Not our lungs?" She tried to imagine it. "But at a rock concert—"

"We'll do something different. This is here and now." He was tracing delicate circles on the small of her back, while his breath warmed the top of her head. Her fingers eased into his hold, instead of squeezing them.

"The waltz has a three-four beat. Just hold yourself upright, while keeping your shoulders steady, and follow me." His voice was soft and gentle, totally believing in what he said.

"Ohkayyy." She could trust him; she knew it after going through La Lujuria under his guidance. This had to be easier than that.

"And—one." He stepped forward, the movement conveyed through their bodies more easily than through their hands, and she stepped back.

"Two." He drew his feet together, settling into place, and hers gratefully echoed his.

"Three." His foot, not the one he'd started with, slid to the side. Hers leapt to follow, sending her skirts flaring.

Good girl, he crooned.

She blinked, startled by how easily she'd accomplished the moves and how feminine she'd felt.

"Let's do that again," he announced.

She nodded, her head whirling, and followed him a little more easily the second time, ending up exactly where they started. Her skirts whispered around her ankles and his buttons rippled down the outside of his legs. His shoulder was strong under her hand, its shape warmly familiar—bone under the layers of muscle and tendon.

Her stiff spine relaxed, not needing to hold itself separate. His familiar scent seeped into her nostrils and she sighed, happy again. It had been too long since she'd been close to him.

His voice deepened and dropped, settling into a note barely discernible from the music. "One-two-three, one-two-three, one-two-three . . ."

She danced with him in their little square, one step on each side, humming the count. Her eyes closed and her spine loosened even more. Their breath seemed to pass in a continuous loop from his lungs to her lungs and back again. He sped up a bit but she didn't need to grip his shoulder harder, since she was perfectly poised between his hands. His legs brushed hers and she adjusted her movements accordingly, until their cores were once again balanced, allowing their feet to be only a few inches apart.

She was dancing a real dance, waltzing like a princess.

Their feet were moving easily together, her dark red pumps a delightful contrast to his shiny black boots. His hands were warm but no hotter than the steam bellows of their breath passing from their lungs through their mouths, back down again to leap between their ribs. Perfect, absolutely perfect.

She closed her eyes, humming a little, building the joyous bubble brighter and brighter insider her.

He extended his stride, moving out a little faster. They dipped and glided more, her skirts dancing with them like a third partner now . . .

Metal thudding down both legs with the music's beat.

They were flying across the floor like birds, laughing for the pure joy of it. The music repeated itself but who cared about that? She could have done this for days.

Ethan tightened his grip on her waist and they reversed direction, sending fabric into a dizzying swirl but changing his trousers' silver coins to a syncopated rhythm.

"Da-dum." She thumped his shoulder, marking the exact instant they settled into the older, more predictable beat.

Ethan broke stride for a moment and she stepped on his feet. His eyes flashed open, as vividly gold and possessive as any hunting cat's.

She shivered, but not from cold. She couldn't imagine what had triggered it but she was more than eager to satisfy her creador's hunger.

"Just a few minutes more, darling," he purred, his grip subtly tighter.

She leaned a little closer, her skin suddenly crackling with heat.

A few bars later, the orchestra swept to a triumphant close. Ethan twirled her out before him and she curtsied, while he bowed—and the room erupted in cheers. Only three couples had finished the dance—Don Rafael and Grania, Jean-Marie and Hélène, Ethan and herself. All the guests had unanimously withdrawn to sidelines to watch and now they heartily applauded the wedding party.

Steve blushed and moved closer to Ethan.

The throng advanced fast and hard on the bride and groom, giving her a chance to escape with Ethan. He cut his way out using more efficiency than politeness, never stopping to apologize for any feet he might have stepped on. Steve simply gripped his hand and stayed close.

He yanked open the door to a withdrawing room, Hélène's succinct description for a small chamber containing a chair, sofa, table, and vivid picture of the Calatrava golf course. It had probably been originally designed for assignations but was now used just as often for phone calls, hence its guarantee of privacy from all the security forces here.

He slammed the door shut behind them and stared at her. "When you hummed 'da-dum,' what were you listening to?" he asked very carefully. His face was almost terrifyingly calm.

She frowned. Why was he asking the obvious?

"The botonaduras, the coins along your legs, Ethan. When we changed direction, they sort of shimmied before they settled back down."

"You couldn't have felt that on your own, Steve, because your dress's fabric is so thick. Only I could." He was completely pale, his eyes brilliantly green. "But I could feel the velvet flirting with my ankles, which my wool trousers and boots should have prevented."

She gaped at him. "How could we feel each other's sensations? Isn't that only for cónyuges, something that takes years and years to create between two people?"

"It means we *are* cónyuges," he corrected. He caught her by the waist and drew her up to him.

She rested her hands on his biceps, uncertain how much she should agree with his explanation.

"What was I thinking on the dance floor, hmm?"

"You were happy," she stated with complete certainty.

"Why?"

She hesitated, unable to voice the only explanation which came to mind.

"Come on, darling, why?" He chucked her under the chin.

"Because I was so relaxed? But that's silly!" she wailed.

"Two people can't dance a fast waltz well together unless every muscle is completely relaxed—which means full trust, something cónyuges must also share. Could you have given me that before you went to Gilbert's Crossing four years ago?"

"No." She worried her lower lip, gaining his fixed attention. Heat hummed through her skin.

"We've had more than sixteen years together," he pointed out.

"True." She cocked her head to one side. "Tonight I could have counted all of your buttons with my eyes shut, which should mean something. But—*cónyuges*?"

The implications were dazzling and wonderful. Ethan as a part of her soul forever?

"Loving you forever has never seemed long enough to me. Even when you pulled me over for speeding, I knew you were special. I hated it when you said good-bye and went off to Gilbert's Crossing to find a husband."

"Fred was nothing," she protested, "and he's guarding Chihuahuas now."

"Fred could give you more than I ever could—children. I wanted to kill him."

Her heart turned over at his anguish, even though its source had been years ago. She kissed his chin. "I love you. I'll always love you."

He pulled back to meet her eyes. "You've never said that before."

He was right and she'd hurt him because of it. "I've thought about it," she offered, sliding her arms around his neck and openly yielding her heart to him for the first time.

"But we've never had the words before." He tilted her chin up with his finger. "I love you, Stephanie Amanda."

For the first time, she truly identified with that name.

"And I love you, Ethan."

Their lips met in a long, sweet kiss, sharing everything between them. Lip to lip, their arms locked their bodies together until their hearts beat. Everything that she was, everything she could be—would be better with him. They'd have forever to share, while working to make Texas better.

Grania wiggled again, probably seeking a position which didn't put any strain on her bruises. *El pobre pequeña*, Rafael had enjoyed her long and hard—although she'd enthusiastically participated and, in fact, encouraged him. Even so, she was barely

more than a cachorra and a vampira mayora could have claimed
fatigue after their wedding night.

Their bedroom had been spectacularly transformed into a
white and gold bower of roses and silk. He'd selfishly given her
little time to admire it before he pounced. Now it was closer to
sunset than to noon.

He lifted her up on top of him, offering his own body for her
comfort rather than the crushed sheets. She yawned and slithered over his chest, settling herself more comfortably. Even his
cock was so sated it barely twitched at the delectable caress of
her silken thighs.

She pillowed her head on his shoulder and he gently stroked
her back. He could do this for centuries and still enjoy naming
her every vertebra, every muscle, every ligament . . .

"Have I told you recently how much I love you?" she asked
sleepily.

"Not in the past"—he craned his neck to look at the clock—
"ten minutes, *sonrisa de mi corazón.*"

"Giving your vampiros a loophole is wonderful." She kissed
his shoulder. "You're a great man, Rafael."

"Loophole?" His wife's adoration was delicious but the
sound of this particular reason made him uneasy.

"Oh, you know, what you said when Ethan brought Steve
home. If a fellow's got an intended who's good for Texas, he can
introduce her to you and ask for your blessing."

Had he truly left that impression? A suitable *novia* plus his
blessing would allow one of his vampiros to give El Abrazo? Of
course, the creador would still pay with his own life for his hija's
misdeeds—but still!

"This will make your men so happy and help Texas, too."
Her breath was warm, barely stirring his skin. "You just keep
coming up with new ways to make me love you. *Amarte para
siempre no sería suficiente.*"

"Loving you forever doesn't seem like long enough," he agreed, and kissed the top of her head. Perhaps he could live with the loophole. After all, it wasn't likely to be tackled anytime soon. "*Te adoro*, Grania."

"And I adore you, my vampiro."

AUTHOR'S NOTE

My deepest thanks go to Darlene Dunn of the Travis County Medical Examiner's office for providing a detailed summary of their caseload. These statistics gave me a vivid picture of the Travis County ME's office and helped me "flesh out" my killers' modi operandi.

Like many books, *Bond of Darkness* needed many people's knowledge to come alive. Special thanks go to Camille Anthony, Raven McKnight, Susan Millard of the Dallas Police Department, Rae Monet (Federal Bureau of Investigation, retired), Margaret Riley, the fabulous experts on Yahoo!'s Weapons Info loop, Karen Woods, Lt. Michael Woodcock of the Spartanburg County Sheriff's Office, Viki, and Willy—the warrior from many millennia—who helped me in so many arenas.